OF SECRETS AND SERPENTS

BOOK TWO

GABRIELA LAVARELLO

For more information contact:

Gabriela Lavarello

http://www.gabrielalavarello.com

ISBN Paperback: 978-1-7361363-5-5

ISBN Hardcover: 978-1-7361363-6-2

ISBN eBook: 978-1-7361363-7-9

First edition: November 2022

Cover illustration by Damonza ©2022

Map illustration by Travis Hasenour © 2020

To coffee and my writing friends. Thank you for helping me find joy in making art every day.

A pronunciation guide is provided at the back of the book, after
the acknowledgments.

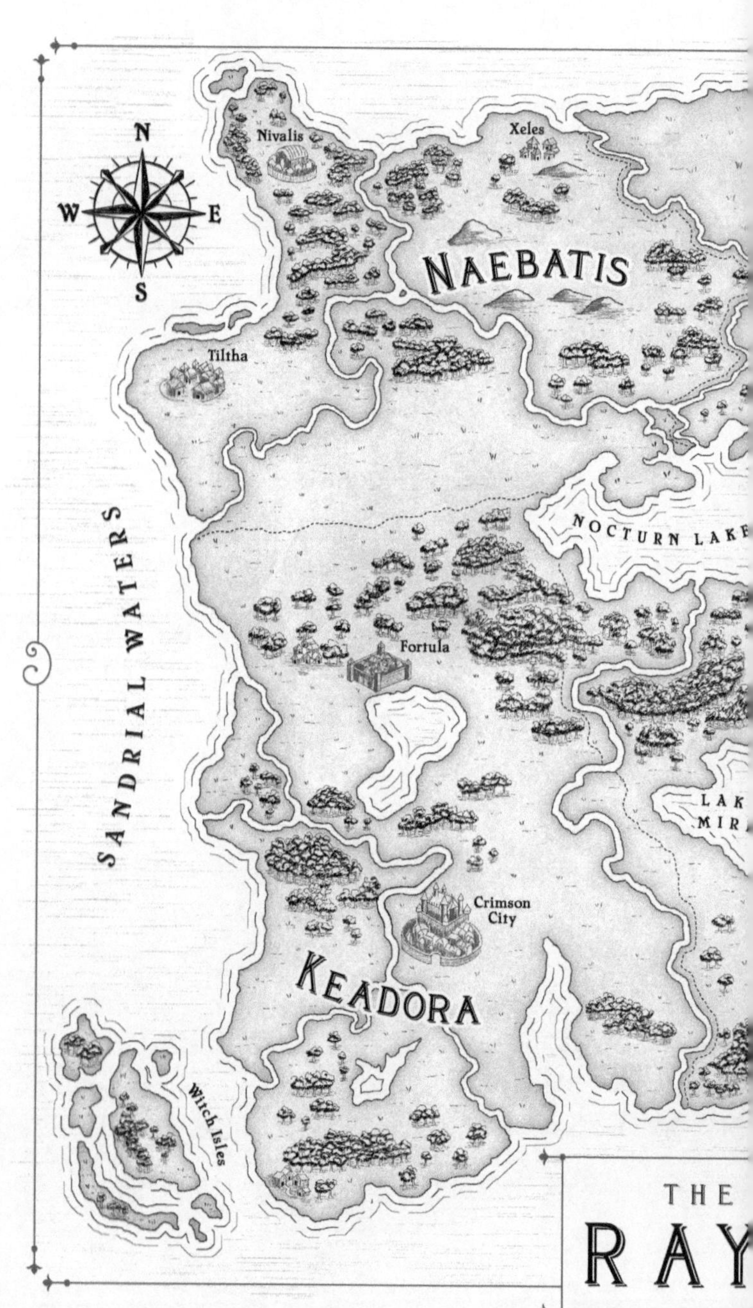

N
W E
S
Nivalis
Xeles
NAEBATIS
Tiltha
SANDRIAL WATERS
NOCTURN LAKE
Fortula
LAKE MIR
Crimson City
KEADORA
Witch Isles
THE
RAY

Dragonkeep
Clelac Crag
DROLATIS
Creonid
Mountain
EONID
LAKE
LAGDRANULE
Steel Mountains
The Keep
CRUBIA
Notharis
Citadel
RIA
Mitonir
Naldir
FARRADOR
OF
ARA

OF
SECRETS
AND
SERPENTS

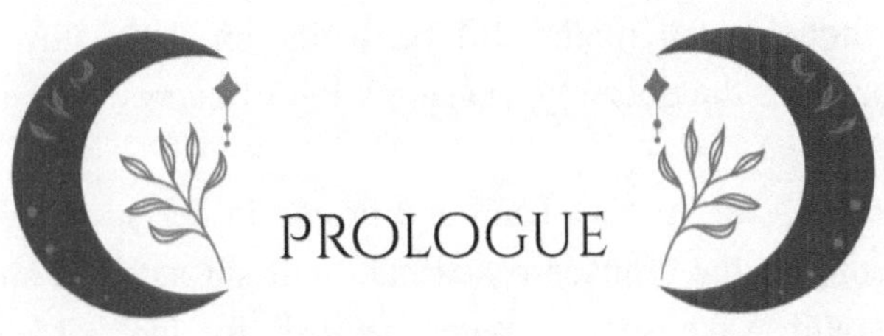

His hand was too cold.

It lay limply in hers as she watched his chest rise and fall slightly, the only sign that Tedric Drazak was still alive. She hadn't meant for things to go the way that they had, for the castle and life that she once knew to crumble around her in one fell swoop. Yet it had, and now Aeden Siltra was the queen of Proveria, and she was alone.

Again.

Aeden let her gaze drift from Tedric's blood-smeared tunic to his face, still beautiful, even though blood encrusted his smooth skin. She examined the dried smears of shimmering blood on his skin, obviously belonging to the countless fairy guards he had fought so many hours ago.

They were her guards now.

Weak winter sunlight bled through a window by the side of the small cot, though Aeden didn't care to look out at the forest beyond. The Clamidas festival would be over now, and the people would be returning to the cities and castle. *My people*, Aeden thought, and a wild bark of laughter escaped from her chapped lips. They *were* her people. After so long of hating her father and wishing him dead, Aeden had finally gotten her wish. But now that her wish had come true, she wasn't so sure she wanted it.

"I thought you might still be with him." The low voice sounded from the doorway, causing a jolt of energy to slam into Aeden's chest.

She dropped Tedric's hand and turned in her stool, nodding in greeting to the crimson-robed man half shrouded in shadow. "He should wake soon," Aeden replied, forcing her shaking nerves to calm.

"No, he won't," the Red King said. "It will take more than a few hours under your sleep enchantment to heal him from the injury he sustained. He must rest, though I'm still deciding if he deserves it."

Aeden bristled but forced a mask of calm to wash over her face before the Red King could take notice. She nodded again and stood to her feet, grimacing at the sight of shimmering dried blood staining her white jacket.

It was her father's blood.

Her blood.

"Will you be taking him back to Keadora?" Aeden asked, her voice sounding hollow in her ears as it rang through the crystal room.

The Red King smiled softly and inclined his head. "Well, of course. He is my most trusted commander. However, he must recover first. I don't believe he'd last on the road without passing to the Nether."

Aeden nodded, holding the Red King's black stare. The Red King smiled—a bone-chilling thing that made Aeden want to shrink away. But she did not and forced an easy smile onto her own face.

"You did well," the Red King mused. "You performed as perfectly as I trusted you would."

"And now I'm the queen of Proveria, all thanks to you," Aeden said.

The Red King's gaze sharpened, and he took a step closer. "It was part of our bargain, though I think you earned more than I offered you."

Aeden frowned. "I'm not sure what you mean."

"I think you do," the Red King said.

Aeden did not answer, finding that she was afraid of saying the wrong thing. She didn't believe she'd earned more than was offered. She had been offered revenge, a crown, and redemption. Instead, she'd received a broken castle and a crown she didn't know if she wanted anymore. And there was the strange surge of powers, but she didn't truly remember anything except burning-hot pain as the castle crumbled around her.

"You love him."

The words punched Aeden back into reality, and she swallowed a pained gasp as she focused on the Red King's face. "I—"

"Come now, child. I can smell it on you both, the same way your father could."

Aeden sighed. "It was not my intention."

The Red King laughed, a booming sound that made Aeden, again, want to shrink away from him. "It's never one's intention to fall in love and hardly in our control to stop it." The Red King narrowed his stare at her. "But it can be a great power if used to one's advantage."

Fear flopped like a frightened fish in Aeden's stomach. "How?"

"One loses their mind when newly in love. It is . . . distasteful," the Red King nearly snarled but quickly regained his composure. "However, the loss of one's rational mind can also be the greatest aid in altering their perception of reality—or even the side for which they fight."

"What are you saying?" Aeden asked, the fear hardening into unease.

The Red King merely looked at her with those piercing black eyes, and a faint smile danced upon his thin lips. "Bordin. Griffin."

Aeden barely had time to gasp before two of the Ten, the Red King's most trusted warriors, entered the room and closed in on her. Aeden took a step back, her legs knocking into the cot holding Tedric. The two men grabbed her arms, their blood-smeared faces impassive as their iron grips tightened around her.

"What are you doing? Unhand me! I am the queen of this kingdom!" Aeden struggled against them as they began to lead her toward the Red King, whose smile only grew.

"You are only the queen of this kingdom because I allow it," the Red King said calmly. "Just as you may be with Tedric only in the way that I allow it."

Fear melted into an icy rage as Bordin and Griffin forced her to stop mere inches from the Red King. The familiar power Aeden had felt when the castle crumbled around her began pumping through her veins in dizzying pulses, and the room brightened as her skin glowed softly.

"Not so fast." The Red King shook his head and grabbed her right forearm in a grip that sent a gasp of pain whooshing from Aeden's mouth as red hot pain scorched the place where his hand held her.

Aeden's skin stopped glowing at once, and she nearly sagged against Bordin and Griffin at the sudden wave of fatigue that settled over her. The Red King took the other hand and brought his pointer finger down upon her forearm, running a sharp fingernail over the length of her ruined jacket. The cloth sepa-rated where his finger moved, revealing milky white skin where the jacket was torn.

"What are you doing?" Aeden cried. "Tell your men to unhand me!"

"Don't you want to be with your precious Tedric?" The Red King sneered as he ran the finger over her forearm once more.

A whimper escaped from Aeden's quivering lips as faintly shimmering blood welled up from her arm and the Red King continued slicing into her flesh with his magic. Aeden truly did sag against the two men holding her as the Red King whispered two words, and more blood sprang from her arm.

"How are you doing this?" Aeden gasped. "You cannot do this!"

The Red King didn't look at her as he withdrew a small vial from his crimson robes and uncorked it. He brought the vial to her arm and pushed against the gushing blood with his finger, sending a small stream of her shimmering life force into it. It filled quickly, and Aeden blinked away dark splotches from her vision as the Red King corked the vial and tucked it back into his robes.

"You cannot be free to do as you wish with my commander, nor your kingdom. That would be quite inconvenient for me," the Red King said. "No, in order to be with him and be loved by your people, you must help me. You will become my very own serpent hiding in a garden of roses."

I

FINRIEL

"Stop it! You're going to fall off the boat again."

It was the second time Finriel Caligari had snapped those words at the man leaning precariously over the edge of the boat in which they traveled. The man only glanced at her from over his shoulder, his icy blue eyes flashing mischievously from beneath the hood of his cloak.

"That's why you're here to help me back on board, isn't it?" Lorian replied with a wink and settled back to peer down at the choppy gray depths of the Sandrial Waters.

Finriel rolled her eyes at the thief, her best friend, for what felt like the thousandth time that morning. She then glanced sidelong at the old fisherman standing with one gnarled hand on the helm near the back of the boat. His wind-weathered face was jovial as he watched Finriel and Lorian's bickering, though he remained silent.

They had met Gordon shortly after parting ways with Krete four days prior, and the man had kindly welcomed them onto his boat without much of a fuss after Lorian gave him a handsome purse of gold. Finriel was still in awe of the thief's quick thinking, telling Gordon that they needed to take supplies to the Witch

Isles and had missed their boat. Finriel doubted Gordon had heard or cared about their fabricated story after Lorian's payment had been placed in his hand, but she was grateful for his lack of questions or conversation. She still disliked speaking to and getting help from strangers, but Lorian's comfort about the matter had calmed her slightly.

The rising sun cast its glow upon the misty morning, marking their fourth day on the water. Gordon had told them the trip would take no longer than four days, and Finriel's eyes sharpened as she watched for signs of land.

A warm body brushed against her arm, and Finriel jumped as Lorian came to stand at her side. She gave him a sidelong look, and he gave her a crooked grin in return as he held up something wrapped in linen. "Breakfast."

Finriel took the bundle without a word and began to unfold the linen. Flaky crust and the smell of cinnamon burst through her nostrils, and Finriel jerked her head up to narrow her eyes at the thief.

"How did you get this?" she asked.

Lorian's grin only widened, and he lifted a finger against his lips with a shrug. She rolled her eyes and looked down at the pastry, hunger roiling inside her stomach. She didn't want to eat something that had potentially been stolen, but her hunger and desire to eat anything other than their meager rations was overwhelming. The pastry was slightly dry but still bursting with flavor as she bit into it. Finriel suppressed a satisfied groan.

"Don't eat it too fast, or else it'll just come right back out," Lorian said.

Finriel was about to snap at him through a full mouth when something caught her eye, and all thoughts about stolen pastries and aggravating men were whisked from her mind.

"There it is," Finriel breathed, a strange thrumming in her veins growing stronger with each lapping wave.

She jolted as Lorian's hand brushed against her own and the

misty shore came closer and closer, enormous cliffs made of black stone surrounding the island like a shell. A distant tree line fought through the mist, but not much else was visible. Wood thunked against sand, and Gordon leapt out of the boat, the old man's spritely movements surprising Finriel.

Lorian hopped out of the boat, offering a hand up to Finriel as she grabbed the large sack of their feigned supplies and glanced down at the shallow water below. Finriel plopped the sack into Lorian's outstretched hand and placed her own onto the weathered wood before vaulting over the ledge, landing in the shallow water with a splash. The water was frigid, and Finriel blinked away the flash of hands around her neck as she stepped onto the black sand beach, drawing her cloak closer around her body to fight against the biting cold.

"One last payment," Lorian said, and Finriel turned to watch Lorian hand Gordon the remainder of the gold he'd stolen from Naret during their mission.

Finriel couldn't see Lorian's face from this angle, but she could picture the easy smile that lit his face as Gordon grabbed the coins and nodded with a smile lacking several teeth.

"Good travels to ye," Gordon said in reply and leapt back into the boat.

Lorian came to stand at Finriel's side as they watched Gordon maneuver the small ship back into the deepening water, the surrounding cliffs making the boat appear minuscule. Soon, Gordon and the boat were swallowed by the mist, and Lorian flipped his hood down with a sigh.

"Thank the goddesses that's over. I was beginning to feel like my legs might never remember the feeling of solid land again."

Finriel flipped her hood back and nodded in agreement, taking in their surroundings as the strange feeling of energy swept over her once more. Black and red stone jutted out of the water like slumbering giants, surrounding the island in a rough shell. Finriel looked around the beach itself, though she found nothing but black sand and clear water caressing the shores. She angled her head back toward the distant stone tower near the middle of the island and the blanket of trees below it. The tree line ended in a patch of willows that danced in the slight breeze. It appeared to be completely deserted, though Finriel could only hope that it was far from the truth.

"Are you all right?" Lorian asked, and Finriel turned to face him.

Her heart constricted with an unfamiliar longing she still hadn't grown used to, even after having reconciled their friendship five days prior. Finriel took a tentative step toward the thief but stopped before they got too close. Dirt smeared against his angular cheekbones, and Finriel's hand itched to wipe it away.

"Do I have something on my face?" Lorian asked, a dark curl brushing across his eyes as the light breeze picked up into a steady wind.

She shook her head and looked away, wrapping her arms around herself with a shiver. They hadn't spoken about the night in Creonid, about the desire that had shrouded both Lorian's eyes, as well as Finriel's heart. She'd been too focused on the night of Clamidas, Aeden's betrayal, and the ardent desire to find her mother, to even think about what they were to each other. But now they were a team again and alone together until Krete hopefully found them again.

"I feel like we made a mistake." Finriel sighed, wrapping her cloak tighter around herself and drawing the conversation away from her troubled heart. "What if we can't find the witches?"

Lorian grabbed her elbow and spun her around so that she was at his side. His dagger was drawn, and his eyes were sharp as he surveyed the tree line. Finriel saw nothing, but she trusted Lorian's instincts, as well as his countless years of training as a thief, to know something was wrong. At that moment, her extended hearing picked up on something. A faint rustle in the trees and sliding of black sand under feet pricked her ears, and Finriel didn't hesitate to send a protective magic shield over them as ten black-robed figures stepped out onto the sand.

"I don't think you need to worry," Lorian muttered. "It seems that the witches have found us first."

2
TEDRIC

An abrupt thunk and the lurch of Tedric's body brought him into consciousness, a heavy pounding in his head sending a groan from his lips. He glanced around, finding himself in a box draped in red velvet.

Not a box, a carriage, Tedric thought as his body was jostled by a bump in the road. A small window gave him a view of leafless oak trees dispersed across a broad meadow of tall grasses. Tedric instantly knew he was back in Keadora, no doubt traveling back to Crimson City.

"Welcome back, Commander Drazak."

Tedric's body tensed at the familiar voice, and he slowly raised his head to find the Red King seated on the bench across from him. The clang of swords and a bright red moon flashed across Tedric's vision, and his body spasmed with an unfamiliar pain. Tedric attempted to lunge at the Red King, only to find his wrists and feet strapped to the bench and floor of the carriage by thick ropes.

"You," Tedric spat, and the Red King merely smiled.

"I'm sure you have quite a few questions," the Red King

said, and Tedric leaned back against the carriage and closed his eyes as a wave of staggering nausea rolled over him. "I would most appreciate it if you didn't get sick all over me. The robes are new."

Tedric's eyes flew open. "What happened that night?"

"You don't remember?" the Red King asked, his tone curious.

Tedric shook his head. "No—I mean, yes, I remember. I just don't understand *why.*"

"Ah," the Red King replied, "you are having a hard time accepting that you have been betrayed. I do not blame you for feeling the pain so freshly, as you've only just woken since that night."

"How long was I—"

"Nearly five days. And just long enough for me to clean up the mess you put me in with the new queen of Proveria."

"Aeden," Tedric whispered, and a new kind of pain lashed through him—this time in his heart.

"She performed as I had instructed her, but only just," the Red King continued. "I am disappointed in you, Tedric. You nearly ruined my plans by making her fall for you, though perhaps I might have to share that responsibility as well."

"I don't understand," Tedric grunted. "You were my king. I all but worshipped you."

"I still am your king," the Red King snapped, "and you will do well to remain on your knees like the good dog that you are."

Tedric's muscles strained against the ropes binding him in place, every fiber of his being yelling at him to end the man draped in red. "You seek to destroy Raymara," Tedric spat. "Why should I bow to you any longer?"

"I do not wish to destroy Raymara, only remold it."

"It sounds no better when you willingly break the peace law in order to gain whatever sick thing it is that you want," Tedric growled.

"Ah, but I am not the one now crippled by the consequences of the peace law." The Red King gave Tedric a steely smile. "You are."

Tedric's world skittered to a halt as the Red King spoke, and suddenly, the strange discomfort in his body made sense. And then he remembered.

"I killed the fairy," he said.

"And mortally wounded King Sorren, though I think Aeden is the one now cursed for his murder," the Red King finished for Tedric. "Though while we are on the subject of death, I must tell you that your father has passed to the Nether."

Tedric's body spasmed a second time, and dark splotches danced across his vision. Part of him wished he could fall back into the blissful oblivion of sleep again, if only to wake up and find out that this was some sort of nightmare.

"It was from his alcohol habit. He passed yesterday."

"How do you know this?" Tedric asked.

"I know all things that happen in my kingdom," the Red King replied simply.

Tedric did not answer. Instead, he looked out the window and watched the trees grow thicker as they drew closer to the city.

He was cursed. The one thing he had dreaded since he was a child had befallen him. And his father, gone. He hadn't even had the chance to say goodbye. At least Lorian and the others were safe. He hoped.

"What are you going to do with the pages?" Tedric asked, a strange corner of his heart tugging with worry for the nian.

"Don't you worry about that. They won't be used for a long while yet," the Red King replied with a smile.

Tedric rolled his eyes, though the king's words brought some relief.

"You did not fail entirely on your mission," the Red King said, and Tedric tore his gaze from the window to the king.

"What do you mean?" Tedric asked, his voice coming out as nothing but a hoarse whisper.

"You retrieved my storyteller, though three of the beasts still go unfound. No matter. I have men spread across the seven kingdoms in search of your other little companions. I have no doubt that they will be returned to me."

Tedric forced himself not to sigh in relief. His friends had not been found yet. At least it was some morsel of peace to which he could tie himself. "I'm glad I was able to serve you, Your Majesty," Tedric growled, and the Red King smiled.

"Yes, but I'm afraid your services are still needed."

No, Tedric wanted to spit, but he kept his mouth shut as the Red King began to speak again.

"While I cannot have you resume your position of commander, you will still have a position that is quite important. You will now be the personal guard of Egharis and ensure that he fulfills the duty of creating my army as I have employed him to do. It seems he is unable to carry out the job while able to roam the realm freely, so he will now do it in a cell, where you will watch him."

Tedric cursed, not caring about using foul language in front of the king. Tedric was nothing more than a slave now. Or maybe that's what he had been all along.

"You will also continue to bed Queen Siltra."

Tedric choked. "What?"

"If you do not love her, then you must simply bed her and act like you love her," the Red King said, and Tedric could barely register the stinging pain in his wrists as he fought against the restraints.

"I can never forgive her for what she did," Tedric growled. "I thought I loved her, but I'm not so sure that I can anymore."

It was a lie, and he knew it. His body ached with how much he loved her, but now it fought with the realization that she had betrayed him and his companions.

"Nonsense. Even if your heart can't, I'm sure that other... parts can," the Red King said, and Tedric grimaced.

"You want me to sell myself to her? For what reason?"

"She must stay obedient, and you seem to be the only thing I have over her at the moment," the Red King snapped, and Tedric stilled.

It was information. Very little, but at least it was something. "Why would I serve you?"

The Red King laughed. "Because I have something you want."

"And what would that be?"

The Red King smiled. It was a look of knowing that made Tedric's skin crawl and gave him an ardent desire to look away, but he forced himself to hold the king's obsidian stare. After an agonizing moment, the king's smile widened, and he opened his palms toward Tedric. "A medicine for the curse. Take it and the effects will not be felt, but not entirely gone."

"A drug, then," Tedric said.

"Not a drug. A temporary remedy until you need not take it anymore," the Red King said, and Tedric fought down another spasm.

"And if I don't take it?" Tedric asked, attempting to hide the nausea rising up his throat.

"You will have to carry out your duties in whatever miserable state you are cursed to now. You should be grateful that I am giving you a relief, Commander, instead of simply letting you decay."

Tedric mulled over the Red King's offer. He wanted to refuse, but he would be of no use to Finriel, Lorian, or Krete in this state. He would not be able to fight whatever sick plan the Red King was beginning to unfold. No, he would have to take it, and he would have to act grateful for it. Tedric grimaced against another wave of nausea and the offer he was about to accept, to whore himself and guard a man sentenced to destroy the realm, in exchange for a little bit of peace.

"Fine." Tedric sighed. "I'll take your damned potion."

A wicked smile bloomed across the Red King's lips once more, making Tedric regret his agreement almost immediately. "That is what I expected. You might just become my most precious asset yet."

3
LORIAN

"Hello, ladies."

Lorian tensed as Finriel's arm tightened beneath his grip, and he glanced down to find her glaring sidelong at him. The robed women stepped closer, and Lorian could barely make out their facial features as they neared.

The ten women were a mix of old and young, short and tall, though all were quite stunning in their own way, Lorian had to admit. They moved on silent feet, and Lorian and Finriel were surrounded in seconds.

"Who are you?" one of the women asked as she stepped closer, and Lorian gave her an easy grin.

She couldn't have been more than fifty, with olive skin much like Finriel's and striking hazel eyes. Her platinum-and-silver-streaked tresses were braided in a thick rope that hung over one shoulder and swayed as she shifted into a fighting stance.

"Lorian Grey, and this is—"

"Finriel Caligari," Finriel said, cutting off Lorian.

"You just interrupted my well-thought-out introduction." Lorian scoffed, and Finriel removed her arm from his grip and crossed her arms.

The women gave each other looks of surprise, and the light-haired woman spoke again.

"You must be the daughter of Yara Caligari."

Finriel tensed at Lorian's side, and he could almost feel the excitement radiating from her as she replied, "Is she here?"

The woman shook her head and turned, the other robed witches closing in and nudging Lorian and Finriel forward. "Come with us."

"Are you not going to ask why we have come or what's in this mysterious sack?" Lorian asked and grabbed the bag from the ground before he was nudged forward into a walk, Finriel at his side.

"The daughter of Yara is always welcome on our island," the woman replied. "And since she has brought you along, we cannot refuse you food and shelter."

Lorian raised his brow at the woman's back. "How very kind of you."

"It is not kindness," someone said at his side, and he looked over to find a young woman perhaps a few years younger than he was.

She was nearly as tall as Lorian, with thick dark curls that formed a halo around her head. Ebony skin contrasted with her light eyes, which were green, almost like Aeden's. Lorian shoved down the sharp stab of betrayal and blinked the image of the woman who he'd thought to be his friend from his mind.

"How is showing hospitality to a stranger not kindness?" Lorian asked, and the girl shrugged.

"We are bound by oath to welcome all witches that come to our island, even if they are not wanted. And you are no witch, but you are no man either, which makes me think that you are not one of the Red King's spies."

Surprise lurched through Lorian's gut, but he wiped any trace of shock from his face before she could notice. "The Red King has human spies?"

"Maescia, be quiet," a witch snapped from behind, and the girl at Lorian's side rolled her eyes.

"They demand that I watch my tongue, but what is the point of having one if I cannot use it?" Maescia sighed, and Lorian chuckled.

"I feel the exact same way."

"My mother isn't here," Finriel whispered, and Lorian remembered her silent figure at his side.

He squeezed her shoulder, hoping the small touch would give her any sort of comfort. "She may not be, but they know who she is," Lorian whispered. "Maybe they can tell us where she's gone off to."

The witches led Lorian and Finriel through a dense patch of bushes. The spiked brambles pricked at Lorian's legs as he moved behind the light-haired woman, Finriel and the other witches following close behind. They walked through the brambles and thick trees in silence, save for the occasional crack of a branch underfoot and the sounds of their breath. Cold mist rolled through the forest, and the scent of fresh pine needles and smoke drifted through Lorian's senses. He glanced at Finriel, who was going between inspecting their surroundings and the witches around them.

They soon broke out into a large meadow, and Lorian cursed in surprise. He wasn't sure what he'd been expecting to find, but a bustling village was not one of those things. Sturdy stone buildings were scattered around in an unordered maze, though they all surrounded one larger building with a dark tower that speared into the mist above. Large rolling hills spread out around them, herbs and swaying lavender smattering the brown grasses.

Hundreds of witches milled about, and some were gathered in small groups, either fighting or doing strange chanting exercises that sent a tingle of unease down Lorian's spine. Glittering dark water lapped at the edge of an inky-black pebbled beach, and the towering cliffs loomed some hundred feet across the water.

"Welcome to the Witch Isles," the older witch said as they stepped onto the dirt path that intertwined with others, something like a living artery through the entire village.

"Impressive," Lorian mused, and the girl called Maescia snorted, though Lorian chose not to ask why she had mimicked a pig.

"Come with me." The woman nodded to both of them, then pointed at the young witch. "Maescia, get their room ready."

Lorian felt Finriel tense at his side, likely at the sound of a singular room instead of two, which meant they would have to share it. He ignored the thrum that rushed through his veins and forced an ignorant smile onto his face.

The other witches dispersed, and Lorian and Finriel followed the older witch toward the main building at the center of the village. Witchlight illuminated the large room as they entered, and Lorian blinked away the colors that danced across his vision with the sudden dimness. The strong scent of cinnamon assaulted his nose, and he stifled a sneeze. Ten long tables were set in the center of the room, with bench seats tucked neatly underneath. Tall windows stretched along the wall to their right, letting weak gray daylight trickle inside. Lorian turned his head in the opposite direction to find a raised dais with a kitchen bustling with women fussing over large metal pots hanging over crackling fires. That explained the cinnamon, then.

The woman and Finriel continued straight ahead toward a darkened passage with a staircase faintly illuminated by witchlight. Lorian hurried after them, though not without offering a crooked smile to the curious cooks that watched them pass.

The steps were steep and slightly slippery, but he scaled them easily and soon found a warm inviting room at the top. Large windows surrounded the space, and Lorian inhaled sharply at the staggering view of forests and black cliffs jutting out of the

Sandrial Waters. He dragged his gaze away from the window and back into the room, where a large blue rug lay beneath two over-stuffed chairs and a desk littered with papers. A lit fireplace took up the only wall without windows, and two enormous book-shelves nearly overflowing with books flanked it on either side.

"So, what has brought you here after all this time?" the witch asked, glancing at Finriel curiously.

Finriel took a step toward the woman and squared her shoulders. "I've come to find my mother, as well as to learn."

The woman's brow arched upward. "I've told you before, girl. Your mother is not here. And I would ask for you to show me what powers you hold before I consider allowing you to learn our ways."

Finriel's jaw clenched, and her hands curled, but her voice was calm nonetheless. "Do you know where my mother is? Just telling me that she is not here doesn't help me know where to go next."

The woman sighed through her nose. "I do not know where she is. She was here briefly after your birth but disappeared again shortly after."

Finriel's face went blank, and Lorian felt a sudden ache to hold her. But he stayed put, and Finriel replied, "So she's dead, then."

The woman's stern expression faltered, and she shook her head. "It would be foolish to hope otherwise."

Lorian tensed, preparing for the worst. He knew the unfiltered power that raged beneath Finriel's skin, and this could very well be the thing to trigger an explosion of flame. The witch seemed to notice Finriel's sudden tension, and her eyes darted to the sparks that crackled from her fingertips. She straightened in her seat.

"My name is Lizabet Timore. I am the mother of witches here, which is the kinder way of saying that I run the way of the island and pass out orders given by the Red King."

Lorian glanced out the window once more before speaking. "It is curious to find you all so . . . free."

"The Red King put us here as a matter of disposal, and our bounty is just a mockery of the truth. We are stuck here, and if any of us were to try to leave, it is an instant ticket to Crubia."

Finriel hummed in annoyance, and Lorian crossed to one of the seats, plopping down with an unceremonious sigh. "Well, that does sound quite inconvenient," Lorian said, and Lizabet's brows nearly disappeared into her thick hairline.

"I still want to learn, at least until I have to leave again," Finriel said, changing the subject.

Lizabet regarded Finriel quietly, as if assessing her from the inside out. Lorian waited with bated breath, unsure as to why the silent exchange felt like it was charged with something more than it seemed.

"Show me what you can do," Lizabet said finally, the chair groaning under her leaning back.

Finriel did not answer. Instead, she lifted a steady hand, and flames erupted from her fingertips in sparks of blue and orange. Lizabet's unimpressed expression did not change as Finriel did this, but Lorian still felt the familiar surge of awe at her abilities. The flame coiled and swelled around her arm before sputtering and dying, and then a shard of ice exploded from her hand and embedded itself in the ceiling.

"Good, but messy," Lizabet said. "You may stay here for seven days, and I will teach you as much as I can. It is what your mother would have wanted, and I cannot refuse her wishes."

Finriel frowned. "Did you know my mother well?"

Lizabet let out a bark of laughter. "Know her well? We grew up together, child."

"You did?" Finriel breathed, and Lizabet nodded.

"I helped her escape on the night of your birth, which is why I am here."

"So you helped her escape, but you don't know where she

went?" Lorian asked, and both witches jumped, as if they had completely forgotten he was there.

Lizabet shrugged. "The plan was not for her to go to the Witch Isles at all. I must admit that she never told me exactly where she was planning to go."

"But *why* did she go?" Finriel asked with a note of desperation.

"I'm afraid that is not my tale to tell," Lizabet said with a sad smile. "There is much that you still do not know, but it is not my place to tell you something that must unfold in due course."

Finriel opened her mouth to say something likely insulting, and Lorian stood and quickly said, "Well then, I think that's our cue to leave."

Lizabet inclined her head, and Lorian moved toward Finriel, who, if looks could kill, would have broken the peace law and murdered him on the spot with her glare. He gave her an apologetic smile and turned to face Lizabet as she spoke.

"Maescia will be waiting for you at the bottom of the steps. She'll show you to your quarters and give you a tour of the village, but feel free to tell her to sod off and go to bed, if you wish. She's an unruly girl."

Lorian nodded and started toward the stairwell, not daring to touch Finriel and take her with him. He knew better than that. Finriel paused a moment longer before following him.

"How will I know where to go for training?"

"I will have Maescia fetch you," was all Lizabet said with her head already hunched over a paper.

"Poor girl," Lorian grumbled, but Lizabet did not reply and Finriel turned away.

They took the stairs in silence but were greeted by commotion when they reached the landing. The girl, Maescia, ran away from one of the cooks, who had a ladle in hand, looking quite ready to beat the young witch. Lorian spotted a bowl in Maescia's hand as she tossed her head back with laughter and easily sidestepped the cook's assault.

"Come back here, you insolent girl! Dinner is only fifteen minutes away, and you already took more than your share during breakfast!"

"There's plenty to go around." Maescia giggled and then waved them over from where she was already slipping out the door. "This way," she called, and the door shut behind her.

Lorian and Finriel exchanged a curious look before jogging after her, though not before Lorian offered a small bow to the cook, who still held the ladle like a sword.

"The tea smells delicious," he said, and Finriel took his hand and dragged him out the door.

A few witches stopped and eyed them curiously as Lorian and Finriel burst outside, only to find Maescia still cackling with the bowl in her hand. Finriel let go of Lorian's hand, leaving traces of her warm touch still tingling against his skin. Lorian clenched his hands into fists, trying to ignore the sudden rise of his heartbeat from the simple act of their skin touching.

"Oh good. I thought she had knocked you two out with her spoon," the girl said with a playful smile.

"It looks like she had good reason to be upset," Finriel replied coolly, nodding toward the bowl that Lorian could now tell was full of steaming golden liquid.

"Oh, please. She takes most of the tea for herself." Maescia scoffed. "I'm doing her a favor."

"I like the way that you think," Lorian said, and Maescia took a sip of the tea in turn.

"Come," she said with lips now gleaming with moisture. She turned on her heel and headed down a path that turned right, opposite of the leftward path from which they had come. Lorian glanced around at the stone buildings, finding himself surprised yet again by the simple splendor of the village.

"Lizabet told me to give you a tour, but there's not much to show you," the young witch said, throwing them a look from over her shoulder.

"How and when did she tell you to do that?" Finriel asked incredulously, and Maescia simply tapped a finger against her temple.

"Lizabet can communicate through the mind, though she has never done so without express permission, at least not to my knowledge."

"That could come in handy, especially if you're trying to escape from somewhere," Lorian mused.

"She's a very private person, so I wouldn't know if she has used it for unruly purposes, though the fact that she's stuck on this island gives me reason to think she might have," Maescia said.

Lorian thought of Lizabet's assistance in helping Finriel's mother escape, but kept his mouth shut. It seemed as though the mother of witches didn't tell her children everything.

The village thinned the farther along they went, giving way to smaller buildings interspersed among a large meadow with large mounds covered in herbs and flowers. Lorian narrowed his eyes at a small smudge of dark earth at the foot of one of the mounds. It appeared as though it had been tilled and then forgotten before anything had been planted. His interest was piqued, but he remained silent as he followed Maescia and Finriel to one of the last buildings in the row.

"You'll be staying here," Maescia said and then turned back toward the main village. "Dinner is in less time than the cook said, but there's a fresh set of clothes for each of you if you wish to change beforehand."

And then she was gone, headed back toward the main path, where a group of young witches had gathered to watch Lorian and Finriel. They tittered and moved away quickly when Lorian look at them, and he shook his head. It seemed that being a half-breed wasn't only looked down upon in Farrador.

Lorian glanced at Finriel with a smile, thinking back to Maescia. "She's lovely."

"She's a brat," Finriel shot back and pushed open the door.

The room was modestly furnished and clean. A green thread-bare rug covered most of the room, and a small water basin was set in the far right corner, nestled beneath a window that over-looked the village. Lorian's heart did a small skip when his eyes landed on their sleeping arrangements—or rather the singular arrangement that neither Finriel nor Lorian had brought up to the witches.

"You're sleeping on the floor," Finriel said matter-of-factly and moved to sit on the bed that could comfortably accommodate two people.

"You should at least give me the pillows," Lorian shot back, eyeing the very cold and very hard stone floor with lowered spirits.

"We'll see," was all she said in reply.

THEIR MEAL WAS UNEVENTFUL, if not a bit awkward. Lorian and Finriel had taken up seats at the far end of the table closest to the door. The witches didn't seem to mind them, though none of them approached Finriel and Lorian for the entire meal. Both Lizabet and Maescia were nowhere to be seen, and so Finriel and Lorian ate in silence, both lost in their own thoughts as they ate a motley array of stew, roasted root vegetables, fresh bread, and the same tea Maescia had stolen earlier. Lorian was surprised by the abundance they enjoyed on the island, though he wasn't quite sure what he had expected before they'd arrived.

Lorian gave Finriel a hopeful look as soon as both of their plates were empty and Finriel had finished the last dregs of her tea. "Shall we get a move on before the witches actually take an interest in us and kick us off their prison island?" he asked quietly, and Finriel nodded, ignoring his feeble attempt at making her smile.

Their room was dark yet warm against the winter frost when they entered, and Finriel conjured a small flame in her hand as they stepped inside and searched for light. Lorian glanced around and spotted candles scattered throughout the room, grabbing one that had been set upon the windowsill by the door.

"Here," he said and watched in mild fascination as Finriel closed her eyes and the flame glided from the palm of her hand to her index finger.

She dipped her finger down toward the wick, and it sputtered as it caught flame.

They lit only a few candles, enough for Lorian to attempt making himself something worthy of sleeping on for six nights. Finriel tossed him a pillow and a small blanket that was folded at the foot of the bed, and Lorian stifled a sigh as he arranged them on the scratchy rug and lay down, not bothering to remove the cotton tunic and trousers with which they had supplied him.

He listened to the soft sounds of cloth sliding against Finriel's skin and the rustle of blankets as she readied for the night. Lorian quickly turned on his other side so that he couldn't watch her movements. It's not that he hadn't thought of it before, but they were still on new ground with their friendship, and he wasn't sure if the *other* feelings he was experiencing were reciprocated. No, he would rather have Finriel as a friend rather than nothing at all.

Finriel's movements stopped after a few moments, and Lorian allowed himself to roll onto his back, the flickering candles making shadows dance across the ceiling above him. The blood moon entered his mind, and a sudden wave of sadness swept over his heart.

"What do you think happened to Tedric?" Lorian asked softly.

"I don't know," Finriel replied, and he noted the hint of suppressed anger and sadness that lingered there.

He hadn't allowed himself to think about Tedric or Aeden or even Krete. Not since their reality had been shattered four nights ago and he and Finriel were forced to flee. He wasn't sure if Tedric was even alive or if the falling crystal walls of the castle had crushed him and Aeden. Perhaps it would be better if he had fallen to his death, or if Aeden had. The mess they had escaped from seemed too great to clean up.

Finriel blew out the candles one by one, and they were soon bathed in darkness once again, save the waning moon that peaked through a window. The bed groaned as Finriel settled into it and sighed.

"It doesn't feel real," Finriel murmured. "I feel like it was all a bad dream, and I just haven't woken up from it yet."

Lorian gulped away the lump that formed in his throat and blinked back the burning behind his eyelids. "I wish it had been a dream," he replied gruffly. "Then we would all be safe."

And I wouldn't have had to abandon anyone else that I love. The thought went through his mind, but Lorian didn't say it out loud. That was his burden to bear, his darkness to trudge through. He knew Finriel had plenty of her own, and he was the reason for some of it. She didn't deserve the heavy weight of his demons.

"You can sleep on the bed," Finriel said, her voice coming out quiet and unsure.

Lorian blinked in surprise and silently cursed the sudden thrum of energy that shot through his body. "Are you sure?" he asked.

"Just do it before I change my mind," Finriel replied sharply, but Lorian still noted the slight shake in her voice, as if she were nervous about the sudden proclamation.

Lorian shot to his feet and grabbed his pillow before plopping it onto the bed and pulling back the thick covers. He repressed a groan as his body met a firm yet oh-so-soft mattress.

"I wonder how the witches can afford such luxuries this far away from anything." Lorian sighed. "Especially since this is a prison, technically speaking."

"I don't know," Finriel replied, and it was all Lorian could do to stop himself from gravitating toward the warmth radiating from her body.

The bed was large enough for them not to touch, but even from where he lay dangerously close to the edge, Lorian could feel the thin fabric of her nightgown against his wrist and smell her faint scent of honey and eucalyptus.

"Don't even think about stealing the blankets, or I will kick you off this bed," Finriel said, though sleep coated her words.

Lorian smiled and closed his eyes. "I wouldn't dream of it."

4
TEDRIC

Tedric slid into consciousness, finding himself strewn upon a small cot. Rays of sunlight streamed through thin cracks in the thatched roof, pooling on the rough linen blanket tangled around his legs.

Tedric glanced around, and sadness crushed him as he found himself in his father's cottage. He supposed it was his now. The cottage was small, but not uncomfortably so, as it had once accommodated him and both of his parents, along with the pigs during several harsh winters. His bed was pressed against the far end of the single room, and a large gray rug made of scratchy wool covered a portion of the stone floor. Two large windows mirrored each other on either side of the walls, and the door waited at the far end. A kitchen pressed against the right wall, with a small fireplace and countertop with various cups, bowls, and utensils orderly stacked along it. A few jars of dried fruit, nuts, oats, and flour sat in a cupboard above the counter. A wash-basin was set on the wall across, along with a chamber pot. A large plush chair and a stack of books sat near the foot of Tedric's bed, and his heart gave a painful squeeze. It was the chair he used to sit in and read to his father on the nights when he was much too sick from drinking and needed a distraction from the pain.

The cottage felt much bigger now that he was the only one left.

Tedric noticed a small stool next to his bed, which had once been the very stool upon which his father sat every day to drink himself into oblivion. Atop the stool lay a note tucked underneath a mug, which was filled with steaming liquid. Tedric glanced around the room, and when he found himself truly alone, he sat up with a small groan. He flung the blanket off to find himself starkly nude, and he cursed.

"What in the Nether?"

He wrapped the blanket around his midsection once more before leaning over and plucking the note from underneath the mysterious steaming mug. Tedric sniffed at the contents and wrinkled his nose at the bitter sweetness and cloves that rolled from what looked like nothing more than tea. With a sigh, Tedric unfolded the note and read, his tired muscles growing tenser with each word.

You wretched all over your clothes, so I had to remove them before putting you to bed. Couldn't find any clean ones. Your new armor is by the door. I'm afraid you have been stripped of your previous amenities.
Drink the tea. The king commanded it.
—Bordin

Tedric cursed again and crumpled the note in his fist, an unnaturally strong wave of frustration welling up in his sternum as he glanced at the tea. He knew it bore the contents of whatever magical drug the Red King had offered him, and he knew that he had accepted to take it. Yet, when Tedric stood, he ignored the steaming cup next to him as he moved toward a small wooden chest at the end of the cot. He opened it to find four bundles of clothing, and silently withdrew a pair of aged leather pants and a frayed cream-colored tunic.

Tedric pulled the trousers over his legs, dropping the blanket on the floor. Milky skin and green eyes flashed through his mind, and Tedric had to keep from shaking as he yanked the tunic roughly over his head. He had no desire to think of Aeden, not now. Not ever. She had ruined him completely and put him in this laughable new position. But he *had* to think about her, had to share her bed whenever it was that he would see her next.

A sudden wave of nausea rolled over Tedric, and he barely had time to run to the shoddy front door and throw it open before he was sent onto his hands and knees, heaving. After a few moments of being sick, Tedric wiped his mouth with a curse and scrambled to his feet. He shivered against the early winter breeze rustling through the tall grasses of the sprawling meadow beyond.

It was the one thing Tedric had loved about growing up in the small cottage with his father. Its secluded location near the outskirts of the city lent quiet and privacy, which were luxuries most citizens of Crimson City did not have. He glanced up to the sky, finding the sun had not made a very far ascent into the day. Perhaps he would still have time to catch Bordin and the other members of the Ten before they went off for midday training.

Tedric wiped a hand across his mouth with a grimace before turning back into the cottage and closing the door. He didn't look twice at the simple armor as he shrugged it on, the clasps and fastenings almost second nature as his mind drifted back to the terrible sensation roiling in his stomach.

He needed food, and he needed to stop thinking about Aeden. The ghost of her touch drifted down his arms, and Tedric growled, yanking the sheathed sword from his recent mission and strapping it to his waist.

Tedric glanced at the still steaming mug as he stood by the door, a strange curiosity tickling at the discomfort within. *Could it truly help?* Tedric wondered but shook his head and reached for the door handle. He would not bow down to the Red King's games if he could avoid it, even if it meant fighting against the curse every moment for the rest of his life.

Winter air brushed against Tedric's cheeks as he stepped outside and wrapped his cloak tightly around himself. It was a sunny day, and the grasses swayed and danced in the merry breeze. Tedric closed the cottage door and turned toward the city, being careful not to step in his vomit. Crimson City spread out at the bottom of the small hill, and Tedric turned to look at Crimson Castle, which loomed over the city like a marble beacon. His breath turned into a silver plume in the air with each exhale, and he clamped down on the pain of his hunger as he stepped into the bustling crowd.

Chatter and movement crowded Tedric's senses as he wound through the streets, and he kept his gaze down as vendors called out and noblemen and peasants alike went about their business. He let his eyes wander up from the cobbled street to the towering wooden and stone buildings, eyeing the vending carts lined on open stretches of walls and fences. His gaze caught on the sight of fresh sweet loaves, and drool welled in his mouth. He surged toward the cart, where a spindly man with salt-and-pepper hair smiled kindly at him.

"One of those, please," Tedric grunted, pointing at a loaf swirled with cinnamon and melted butter.

The man inclined his head and drew one out with wax paper, handing it to Tedric and offering the other hand out. Tedric withdrew a single coin from his pocket and dropped it into the man's hand.

"Enjoy," he said, and Tedric simply shoved the loaf into his mouth as he turned to walk away.

The taste of mold and bitterness assaulted his tongue as he bit into the loaf, and it was all he could do not to spit it out. He turned back to the man, who was already helping another customer but glanced sidelong at him.

"Is this bread old?" Tedric asked, trying his best not to wrinkle his nose with distaste at the stale bitterness in his mouth.

The man frowned and shook his head. "Baked only this morning."

Tedric clenched his jaw and nodded, then turned and started down the street once more, the cinnamon loaf now held limply in his hand. A young girl of no more than seven stood a few feet before him, her eyes set hungrily upon the loaf in his hand as her mother prattled about ribbons with another older woman. Tedric managed a smile and held the loaf out to the girl as he approached. She took it silently and gave him a shy smile before biting into it. He almost grimaced at the child's excited giggle as she took another bite, and then he continued to the training grounds.

A barking command rang out through the air, and Tedric picked up his pace as the wide dirt arena enclosed by wooden walls came into view. Tedric ducked under the low-hanging door and stepped into a corner as he watched the men jog in single file around the space. Sweat dripped down their bare chests and backs as a man ten years Tedric's senior yelled for them to begin a sprint across the perimeter of the enclosure. Bordin's muscles rippled under olive skin gleaming with sweat as he began the sprint, the others following close behind.

Tedric stood with his arms crossed, his mind blank as he watched the men he'd once commanded go through the first sprint, each cursing and panting. It did not take long for Bordin to notice him, and he barked a command for the men to begin the second sprint without him before jogging toward Tedric. He couldn't help but feel a jolt of bitterness toward the man after Tedric's life had been stripped from him, and Bordin had continued on as if he'd never been a part of it.

"Tedric, what are you doing here?" Bordin panted, coming to a stop in front of him.

"I wanted to see how you were managing without me." Tedric shrugged, and Bordin clapped him on the shoulder.

"We are managing just fine, though I must say I underestimated how difficult all of your obligations would be."

"You're commander now?" Tedric asked with raised brows, and Bordin nodded.

A moment of strained silence passed before Bordin sighed. "I'm sorry about all of this. Your father, your position—"

"It's not your fault," Tedric cut Bordin off, though it was partially because he wasn't quite sure he could stand hearing Bordin list off all the ways he had failed in the past three moons.

"I buried him by the flower field, in case you wanted to visit him," Bordin offered quietly, and Tedric nearly doubled over at the jolt in his gut, once again reminding him of his failures.

"Thank you, Bordin."

"It was the least I could do. Everything that's happened—it's a mess," Bordin said wearily.

"I don't even know what to think." Tedric sighed, and a flicker of anger welled up inside his already roiling core. "Did you know what the Red King had planned when you went to Proveria on the blood moon?" Tedric asked, his voice now cold.

Bordin's dark green eyes shrouded over with what looked like anger, and he shook his head. "I cannot speak of it. Even if I wanted to, I can't."

"Why?" Tedric growled. "I'm cursed because of that night. You at least owe me this."

Bordin clenched his fists and cursed under his breath, but Tedric paid his discomfort no mind. He deserved to know if they had been aware of the Red King's plans all along or knew something Tedric didn't. A young boy ran into the training grounds the moment Bordin opened his mouth to speak and stopped in front of the new commander, panting heavily.

"A letter of emergency for you, Commander Ildas," the boy said quickly, and Bordin took the folded letter from the boy's fingers.

Tedric watched Bordin's eyes flit across the page in tense silence, the only sound that of the eight men grunting behind them as they continued on with their grueling training regimen.

Could it be about Finriel and Lorian? Or maybe Krete? Tedric thought with a lurch of dread but quickly schooled any signs of panic from his face as Bordin let out a sharp breath through his nose and tucked the paper into his trousers.

"Tell the Red King that we will set out immediately." Bordin nodded to the boy, and the boy began to step away before looking at Tedric.

"The Red King told me to inform you that you must not be late to your post."

Tedric gave the boy a sharp nod, and the child turned away, starting his sprint toward the looming marble spires of the Crimson Castle.

"What was that about?" Tedric asked sharply.

Bordin looked at him hesitantly. "We're to go to the Witch Isles. There has been news of the two fugitives you traveled with landing there two days ago."

Tedric's heart leapt into his throat, but he still asked, "You're to bring them back to Keadora?"

Bordin nodded once, then turned and whistled at the other members of the Ten. They stopped sets of push-ups and sparring matches and moved for their belongings scattered along the railings.

"Were you told anything else? Of what their fates are meant to be?" Tedric asked.

He didn't care if Bordin thought him a madman for fearing for his companions so openly. His position had been forfeited the moment he'd embarked on the mission so long ago, and his old life along with it.

"I need to get my men to the Witch Isles," Bordin said finally. "Besides, you're over an hour late for your duties. I don't want to be responsible for your failures more than I already am."

Tedric sighed through his nose, giving Bordin a tight nod. "Right, then. I wouldn't want to put your honorable position at risk."

Bordin gave him a look that was on the border of pity, but that only fueled the anger and fear for his friends, making Tedric speak again in a tone that only Bordin could hear. "You are about to embark on a mission to hunt down my friends. They are good people and far better than the king you serve."

Bordin stiffened. "Be careful what you say, Tedric. The Red King has ears everywhere in this city."

"I don't care." Tedric laughed, receiving a few curious looks from the other men, which he paid no mind to as he continued. "The Red King knows which side I am on now. I'm only here because he holds my life in his hands, and I would rather like to live to see another day. I only ask that you do the right thing. Decide if you are still willing to fight for a monster."

Without another word, Tedric turned on his heel and stalked out of the training grounds, his insides roiling with both discomfort and anger. He supposed he couldn't blame Bordin for being afraid of saying too much, but he'd just spent the last three moons of his life traveling through the seven kingdoms to complete a quest that might have been completely pointless for all he knew. He deserved to know what the Red King was planning. He *needed* to know.

Tedric trudged up the steps to the Crimson Castle, not caring how loudly his boots scuffed against the marble, nor how little of an attentive guard he looked at the moment. He was miserable, and he was about to start guarding an innocent man for a king he was slowly beginning to hate.

The scent of roses drifted through his nose, and suddenly, the image of Lorian groaning about the terrible smell as they wound through the castle flashed through his mind. A sad smile tugged at his lips, and he rounded a corner and headed down another identical bright hallway as he remained deep in thought. Lorian was right about the smell; it was terrible. Downright sickening if Tedric were honest with himself.

Best not think about being sick, Tedric thought as his stomach gave a warning lurch, no doubt from hunger mixed with the constant discomfort with which he now had to live.

Unless he took the Red King's potion.

Tedric shook the idea away and clenched his fists as he continued down the hall, then stopped. He had no idea where the storyteller was being held or where he was meant to go, for that matter. Tedric whirled in a circle in an attempt to find anyone that might help him, when a serving girl came into view, carrying a stack of blood-red linens in her arms. Their eyes caught, and the girl stiffened visibly as she approached at a quicker pace than before. Tedric moved swiftly to intercept her when he realized that her change in pace was to avoid him.

"Excuse me," Tedric started, molding his voice into a honey-like tone as she stopped, her eyes wide with what he could only place as fear.

The girl was tall, the top of her head reaching the bottom of his nose. Flame-red hair was pulled into a knot behind her head, though a few strands had come loose from their binding and now framed her round face. Her eyes were a rich hazel color, almost on the verge of dark green. Aeden's eyes flashed through his mind, and Tedric had to keep himself from stumbling backward.

He forced an easy smile onto his face. "I'm meant to find the storyteller. Would you happen to know where he is being held?"

The girl bit her bottom lip and glanced from side to side as if someone would hear their conversation. Tedric placed a hand on her shoulder, and she tensed, but he continued. "You need not worry. You are in no danger."

The girl offered a small upturn of her lips before she spoke in a soft voice. "He is being held in the southern wing where the guest quarters are. They made him a room there."

Confusion made his lips tug downward, but he just squeezed her shoulder in thanks and inclined his head. "Thank you."

The girl gave a small curtsy before she scurried off down the hallway, and Tedric sighed. He didn't pass another living soul during his trip to the guest wing, and only his discomfort and the sickening scent of roses penetrated his reality.

The guest wing looked much the same as it had the last time he'd been there, with its thick stone walls and witchlight casting a warm glow upon the floor. He stiffened as his eye caught on two guards standing by a lone window at the end of the hall, along with a tall man in pale white robes. The Red King turned as Tedric neared, and a grim smile tore through his thin lips.

"Drazak, you're late to your post."

Tedric stopped a few feet away from the Red King and was just able to make out the storyteller's new quarters. It still resembled a guest chamber, aside from the fact that, where there was once a heavy door made of oak, now stood a door of cold metal bars. Tedric forced his attention back to the king and the two guards standing behind him, who looked at Tedric as though he were nothing more than a lowly peasant.

"Have you forgotten your manners?" the Red King asked, and Tedric gritted his teeth.

He would not bow to the Red King, not anymore. The Red King angled his head and scoffed.

"You will bow to me, soldier, or else you may find that you will lose more than you already have," the Red King said.

Tedric bit back a slew of curses as he bent at the waist, giving the slightest of bows to the king. The two guards sniggered but quickly quieted at the glare that promised violence Tedric shot at them when he straightened. He knew the two guards, though he had never bothered to find out their names, as they were two of the most insolent men he'd ever met in his life.

"You will stand guard and monitor Egharis's progress until sundown," the Red King said. "You will know you are free to go when the door turns into solid metal and Agonur comes to relieve you."

Tedric could do nothing other than give a curt nod, and the Red King leaned in and whispered in Tedric's ear.

"Do not try to run or contact your little friends. I have eyes everywhere, and I will know if you have taken even a single breath out of place." The Red King smiled humorlessly at Tedric before gliding away, the two guards close on his heel. Tedric waited until the king rounded out of sight before he let out a strangled curse and stomped in a circle.

"I would listen to him if I were you." The weak yet familiar voice sounded from behind the metal bars.

Tedric stilled, almost having forgotten that the storyteller was already inside the glorified cell. He looked through the bars and found Egharis seated at a desk situated on the crimson carpet before the bed, piles of parchment and inkwells scattered about.

The storyteller looked worn and older than he had the last time Tedric had seen him, though it had only been a few days. His white hair was clean but disheveled, and his silver eyes were dull as he met Tedric's gaze. His long ink-stained fingers rested limply upon the gleaming desk, and his thin body was wrapped in a dark blue dressing robe. Tedric looked away, embarrassment about the man's state of undress making his cheeks hot. He supposed he understood though, for there was no need for proper clothes if you were in prison.

"What do you mean?" Tedric asked.

The storyteller offered a sad smile. "You should not run, at least not yet."

Tedric tensed. "What makes you think that I would try to run? I'm not a coward."

"But you're miserable and don't know where your companions are," Egharis replied evenly. "Even so, you'd be putting them in more danger if you tried to find them."

Tedric frowned and was about to reply when a sudden wave of nausea rolled over him, making him stagger and lean against the wall for support.

"So it's true," Egharis whispered. "You and the fairy queen are both cursed."

Tedric swallowed against the bile that rose in his throat, and misery swirled in his heart. A few deep breaths forced the sickness down enough for Tedric to stagger away from the wall and face the storyteller, a sudden anger roaring through him at the sight of a half-finished drawing lying by the storyteller's left hand.

"You're making more of them." Tedric scowled. "Haven't you caused enough damage already?"

"I do not wish to make more beasts. Trust me on this." Egharis opened his arms to gesture around himself. "But look at me. It's not as though I have much of a choice in the matter."

Tedric clenched his hands into fists. "You started this whole mess with those beasts. This is your fault."

Egharis's smile vanished. "It is not my fault that you are cursed, Tedric. You made the choice to save the life of your friend in exchange for the life of another."

"That's not what I meant," Tedric ground out, and the fury rose higher. He wanted nothing more than to rip those bars apart and throttle the storyteller for all he had done. For making him lose everything.

Egharis sighed. "I know it isn't. And I know that I am the reason we are on the verge of another age of darkness."

"Then why did you do it?" Tedric asked.

"Because I had to," the storyteller replied, a new kind of pain now in his expression. "You still don't fully realize the depths of the Red King's cunning. It was not my choice, but I knew of the prophecy, and I knew that it would be I who set it in motion when the Red King took my family and cursed me."

Another wave of nausea rolled over Tedric, and he staggered until his back met solid wall, then sank to the floor. Despair and anger swept over him like a strangulating blanket, and he closed his eyes with a pained sigh.

"I'm nothing again," Tedric whispered under his breath.

"That's not true," Egharis replied, and Tedric opened his eyes in confusion.

"How could you hear me?" Tedric asked, and the storyteller shrugged.

"Magic."

Tedric rolled his eyes. "I'm getting tired of magic."

5

FINRIEL

F inriel woke to golden sunlight and a cold bed.

She turned over to find the covers on the bed flung to the side and vacant of Lorian. Her chest sank slightly, though she wasn't quite sure why. This had been their second night in the Witch Isles, and Finriel had yet to begin her training. She'd spent the entire day previous searching for Lizabet, but Maescia had simply told her there would be no lessons that day.

But her time was running out, and the goddesses would be damned before she allowed her time on the isle to be wasted.

Finriel flung the covers back and sprang to her feet, ignoring the cold floor that shot icy discomfort through her soles. She dressed quickly and was out of the door in a few short minutes, the frost-blanketed grass crunching under her boots as she headed toward the one place she was certain she would find the mother of witches.

The tower was empty as she strode into the grand room and crossed over to the steep stairwell beyond. Her breaths echoed within the narrow walls, and the anger swirled and welled in her abdomen as she neared the office above.

Finriel's mother was not here. She could be dead for all

Finriel knew, gone forever in a memory that would never be there. The terrible heaviness smothered her anger, and Finriel let out a choking sound as the weight traveled up into her throat.

But she would not give up. She couldn't after everything she'd gone through.

Enough, Finriel thought. *I am stronger than this.*

Deep breaths of frigid air forced down the heaviness, and Finriel blinked back the moisture from her eyes. She would be strong for her mother, for Lorian, and for Tedric. There had never been a choice to be weak, and Finriel would not give herself the luxury of giving up after so long of fighting for her freedom.

Finriel climbed up the last few steps and raised her hand to knock on the shoddy wooden door, but it creaked open on its own before her knuckles made contact. She bit the inside of her cheek as she crossed the threshold into Lizabet's office, finding the mother of witches seated at her desk, fingers steepled together as she watched Finriel's movements.

"Hello, Miss Caligari," Lizabet said without a smile. "Take a seat."

Finriel stalked over to stand before the desk, not bothering to sit down as she crossed her arms. "I didn't come here for a vacation."

"The Witch Isles is not a resort," Lizabet replied evenly. "But we've had students and work to do long before you and your little thief friend arrived. Forgive me if you felt ignored yesterday."

Finriel clamped down on a retort that would have surely gotten her and Lorian banished from the island and instead forced her lips to purse into a very forced smile. "I came here to train, and five days will already be barely enough to scratch the surface of what I want to learn."

"Oh?" Lizabet said, her brow raised. "And what exactly do you want to learn here?"

The answer died on Finriel's lips, and a terrible seed of

buried hopelessness returned. She didn't know what there was to learn; she'd never gotten the chance to find out.

Lizabet seemed to notice Finriel's pause and smiled. "Being a witch is more than using tangible magic. It's about how you treat the earth, communicate with the spirits, and honor Adustio. It's about how you treat yourself and others."

"I treat others fine," Finriel grumbled, but doubt still burned a hole through her chest.

"Knowing when you are wrong and taking criticism is also one of the pillars of wisdom by which I teach," Lizabet said. "You are scared of your own powers, Finriel, and that has forced you to become harsh to those who want to understand and help you."

"I—" Finriel started, but Lizabet raised a hand to cut her off.

"You are talented, far more talented than many of the witches on this island. I can feel your magic radiating off you like a beacon, but it would become even more dangerous if you were to hone your powers."

"So what are you saying?" Finriel snapped, a terrible mix of fear and frustration making her skin grow hot. "Are you saying you won't train me, then?"

Something dangerous glinted across Lizabet's hazel eyes, and the elder witch stood from her seat in a flash. "It would be a gift not to teach you. Your power is dangerous, and your mother would never forgive me if I became the cause of your own destruction."

"My mother is dead!" Finriel couldn't help her voice from rising, nor the hot tears from welling up behind her eyes. "You said it yourself—she's gone. I'm a grown woman, and I decide my future. If you won't teach me, then I'll find someone who will."

Finriel spun on her heel and started toward the door, but it slammed shut before she managed two steps. Anger licked and roared up, enveloping Finriel's body until she heard the familiar sparks of flame coiling around her fingers. She continued walking, determined to burn a hole through the damned door before Lizabet forced her to apologize.

But then a familiar pain crept up from the base of her neck, making her pause as it made its way up her skull.

Finriel blinked, shaking her head against the pain. It was familiar, all too familiar. A blood-smeared crystal floor and fallen bodies flashed through her mind, along with the pain and calm face of the Red King as he flung her and her magic aside like she was nothing but a speck of dust upon his robes.

A gasp flew from her lips as the pain clawed in deeper, and Finriel managed to turn and glare at Lizabet, though disbelief and that familiar fear clawed its way up to nestle with the pain.

"No," Finriel ground out, but Lizabet's stony expression did not change.

The world is a dangerous place. Lizabet's voice rang through Finriel's mind, the words clanging against her skull in a way that made her vision blur. *You are on the precipice of a world you do not want to enter. There are those who want to see you die, much like your mother.*

"You're like him!" Finriel cried out, and she faintly heard her own knees cracking against the stone floor.

I am nothing like the Red King, yet far too similar, Lizabet replied in her mind, and Finriel let out a cry of agony. *You are not yet strong enough to face the darkness. You would get squashed like a bug.*

The anger flared, transmuting into flame and enveloping Finriel's very bones. The pain stuttered, as though surprised by the sudden magic that met it. Finriel lifted her head to meet Lizabet's stare, and she could smell something burning as she let out a grunt of pain and forced herself to remain upright.

"Then. Teach. Me."

She would not let the pain take her, not again, not ever. Lizabet's expression faltered, but only just. A hard mask of nonchalance replaced the uncertainty in seconds, and Lizabet nodded. "If you can break out of the hold I have on your mind, then I will teach you."

Fine.

Finriel closed her eyes, allowing the flame to grow and swirl within her core before directing it upward, toward the pain. The heat licked at Lizabet's hold on her mind before the pain pulsed and Lizabet's magic turned to iron in her skull. Finriel felt her hands meet the ground, a cry of pain escaping her lips.

But she would not back down. She *had* to learn.

There had to be a place where the magic was weakest, a point that Lizabet could not quite reach. But where could that possibly be? She scoured everywhere—the anger, the pain of her mother, the incident with Lorian when they were children—but everywhere felt like it was coated in iron-clad pain.

"Fuck." Finriel groaned, her power stuttering slightly.

You would've been dead minutes ago if you were fighting a real opponent. Lizabet's voice slithered through her mind.

No. No. No. She would not die in this hypothetical fight.

And suddenly, she found it—a gear of forgotten power clicking into place. She had been forced to fight her entire life, and she wouldn't be able to stop now.

A sound more animalistic than human rose out of Finriel's throat, and with her remaining strength, she flung all of her power inward, toward the resolve that kept her going even on her darkest days. A gasp flew from her lips, and her own body bucked at the power that exploded within. It was like lighting oil aflame, instant and explosive. It leapt upward and attacked, eating hungrily at the foreign magic keeping her captive. Lizabet's magic faltered, and Finriel grunted as she pushed harder, allowing her magic to grow and swell around the pain, eating it entirely instead of simply banishing it.

Something wet and sticky pooled over Finriel's upper lip, but she ignored it as she willed her magic to keep eating, eating,

eating. It grew and rejoiced, like a beast finally set free after a lifetime in captivity.

And then the pain was gone.

The power snapped back, recoiling down into Finriel's core until she felt nothing again and collapsed onto her elbows as fatigue rolled over her like a tidal wave. Heaving breaths of air were the only thing that kept Finriel conscious—that and the soft rhythmic drip of something hitting the floor in front of her face. She opened her eyes and wiped at the stickiness above her lip, only to find it came away red with blood.

"Effective but messy, and potentially more dangerous to you than to me if you let your magic loose like that again," Lizabet said, now with her true voice instead of in Finriel's head.

Finriel let out a groan, but she was much too tired to come up with a retort. In truth, she had given everything she had to get out of Lizabet's grip, and she was exhausted.

Lizabet's footsteps rounded the desk and moved toward the door, but she paused before opening it. "Go get some rest. Maescia will collect you later for our evening practice."

And then the mother of witches was gone, and Finriel collapsed on the rug with a smile on her cracked lips.

6

AEDEN

"The repairs on the throne room are nearly complete, and from there, we will continue..."

Aeden stopped listening for what felt like the thousandth time since the dreadful council meeting had started, stuffed into a small chamber filled with the high fairy council from separate regions of Proveria.

This had been the second one in a week, and Aeden had listened to the first one just as little as she was listening to this one. She had no interest in listening to frivolities about reconstructing the castle. She knew it would be taken care of with or without her presence. Instead, she directed her focus on the ever-roiling discomfort in her abdomen and the image of her blood-soaked hands and the face of her father as the life drained from his eyes.

I'm cursed, she thought. Over and over again had she thought those words. It was like a song that was stuck in the crevices of her memory, unmoving no matter how hard she tried to ignore it. A burst of self-hatred radiated through Aeden's disquieted bones as she adjusted on the unbearably hard chair at the head of the council table, the cloth of her shimmering navy skirts rustling as she crossed one leg over the other.

The past week had gone by in a strange blur of meetings and long periods alone in which Aeden simply sat in her chambers and stared blankly out the window, as she did now. She had thrown herself into a game of secrets and lies and had betrayed everyone she'd grown to care for in the process. Aeden's chest clenched as the image of Tedric staring up at her from the bottom of the dais stamped itself behind her eyelids. The look of betrayal on his face had torn a hole straight through her heart at that moment, but she had been forced to behave like it had all been an act, even if it wasn't anymore. Aeden sighed and brought herself back to listen to the subject of who would be providing the flower arrangements for her coronation, which also caused a jolt of panic to surge through her. She would be the official queen of Proveria in one moon, and with that, she would have more power than she'd ever thought of having this early in her twenty years of life.

"We have gotten offers from—" One of the council members to her right broke off as the double doors burst open, and none other than Krete walked into the room.

Aeden's heart leapt with both delight and horror as her oldest friend met her stare. He looked tired, but well. He wore proper gnomish messenger garb, with brown trousers and tunic, as well as a dusk-colored cloak that brushed against his ankles. His trusty gray cap still covered mousy brown hair, and she could just barely see his many-pocketed vest beneath the cloak.

"Seize him!" A male guard standing near the door commanded, and the remaining two guards in the room swept toward Krete, who was already reaching into a pocket within his vest to withdraw either a weapon or a way out, Aeden was not sure.

"No, let go of him," Aeden commanded, and the two guards hesitantly let go of Krete's arms.

"Leave us. We can resume this meeting at a later time," Aeden said, and the council members quietly stood from their seats and shuffled out of the room without another glance toward Krete or Aeden.

Waves of panic swelled through Aeden's veins as they waited for the last of the council members to leave, and she jutted her chin toward the two guards stationed on either side of the doors. "You can go too," Aeden said, and the guard on her right, a short-haired woman, blinked.

"But, my lady—"

"Go," Aeden snapped. "I can protect myself. I will call upon you when you are needed again."

The guard simply closed her mouth and gave a short bow to Aeden before she and the male guard walked out of the door and shut it with a faint click.

Aeden whirled on Krete. "What are you doing here?"

Krete's jaw clenched, but he didn't back away from her stare. "I came to see if you were all right."

A bark of laughter escaped Aeden's lips. "You came to see if I was all right? Don't you and your little friends wish me dead now that I have betrayed you?"

Krete's face fell, but Aeden simply crossed her arms. She couldn't let her aching heart and regret show, not now.

"We scattered. Lorian and Finriel are gone, and Tedric—" Krete broke off, and Aeden realized that he likely didn't know what had become of the commander.

Aeden blinked back hot tears and dug her fingernails into her bare arms as a sudden wave of nausea rolled over her. "He's alive. Back with the Red King."

A sigh of relief whooshed from Krete's mouth, and he smiled, making Aeden press her lips into a thin line. She would not share his relief, for she could not. Not when the last time she'd seen the warrior, lying on that cot with fairy blood streaked across his body, was still imprinted in her mind like a brand. She was responsible for what had happened to him, his loss of honor, and her loss of his trust.

"Well, I am clearly all right." Aeden broke the silence. "You should leave before the knowledge of your presence here spreads."

"Am I not welcome in your kingdom anymore?" Krete asked, and Aeden could hear the test in his tone.

But she couldn't tell him anything, even if she wanted to. The thought brought a sharp pang of regret that she couldn't afford to feel right now. Krete likely hated her for all that she had done to betray him, and she deserved it.

"If you have come here simply to ridicule and taunt me, then I'm afraid you are not welcome," Aeden said, tilting her chin upward and looking down her nose at the gnome.

Krete frowned, that same sadness clouding his eyes. "I do not wish to ridicule you."

"Then why are you here?" Aeden asked again, the words constricting in her mouth.

A strange prickling sensation crept up her arms, and Aeden cursed as it drifted across her entire body. Krete noticed her sudden stiffening and took a step forward, but Aeden stepped back and put a hand out. "Don't."

"You're cursed, aren't you?" Krete said, his voice almost a whisper.

Aeden didn't respond. She only held his stare, willing him to back down. Krete didn't back down, however. The sadness in his eyes only strengthened, and the cord of pain snaking across Aeden's heart gave a terrible squeeze.

"You killed him, didn't you," Krete said, more of a statement than a question.

Aeden nodded, not having to ask Krete the name of whom he was referring. Krete knew of the pain and agony King Sorren, her now dead father, had caused her and how little he had cared.

"His reign of lies and deceit is over now," Aeden replied

simply, and Krete shook his head.

"You have gone too far. Was giving away all the good in your life truly worth a throne and the death of your father?"

Aeden laughed, a humorless sound that left her lips. "I do not mourn my father's death. You know all the things he did to me, to us."

Krete sighed. "But how do your new people react to this? Do they not question his passing?"

"They believe Sorren's prayers to Noctiluca were too strong on Clamidas and that the castle crumbled on top of him, ending his life so that he could be at our goddess's side. They suspect nothing."

Krete sighed, the sound something close to tired defeat. Aeden bit the inside of her lip, unsure of what else to say. She had been commanded to alert the Red King if any of her companions were seen in Proveria, and her hand drifted unconsciously toward her right forearm where a faint silver scar traced down her once flawless skin.

Krete tracked the movement with his eyes, concern flashing over his features as Aeden quickly dropped her hand and folded her arms behind her back, digging her fingernails into her wrist so hard that the stinging pain made her wince.

"My coronation is one moon from today," Aeden said, her voice thankfully having returned to the same haughty blandness she had mastered. "I am the new queen after all. I think I deserve a bit of a celebration in my name."

"Do you not see that your kingdom is falling apart around you?" Krete asked, his voice laced with worry. "Already the unrest about the storyteller's beasts is growing, and rumors of your father's untimely death are spreading. Not to mention whispers of strain in Keadora and even here. People are growing concerned, Aeden."

"There is nothing to be afraid of," Aeden spat. "We retrieved the beasts like we were told to do, and Egharis is back in the Red

King's control. Things can go back to the way that they used to be."

"Egharis being in the Red King's control is what concerns me the most," Krete muttered, then looked up at her. "Things will never go back to the way that they used to be. The Red King will start a war, Aeden. I simply hope that you will not let him step over you to get what he wants, whatever that may be."

A wave of skin-crawling discomfort rushed across Aeden's body, and she closed her eyes, pressing her nails in deeper, if only to feel something other than the terrible crawling.

"Aeden, are you all right?"

"I'm fine," Aeden sniped, opening her eyes once more to glare down at her oldest friend.

"What happened to you?" Krete asked. "You are not a monster."

Aeden swallowed and ignored the burning sensation that returned behind her eyelids as she replied, "Only a monster can defeat its kin."

A strange blankness washed over Krete's features—an expression Aeden had never seen from him before. It was almost as if he did not wish for her to know how he truly felt at that moment. Perhaps they had all changed a little, not only her.

Krete dipped into a short bow and gave her only a small smile as he said, "I hope for your sake that the monster can remember the kind woman it used to be."

Without another word, Krete withdrew what looked like a small pebble from his coat and drew a design on the polished quartz floor with a booted toe as he muttered words in gnomish. Aeden knew the glowing blue pebble in his hand to be a portal stone, and she knew she could be punished terribly for letting him go. Yet Aeden only watched as Krete stepped into the glowing circle without another word and vanished, leaving her alone with her thoughts and the faint sting of pain as blood dripped into her hand.

7

FINRIEL

"Where are you headed off to?'

Finriel's fingers slipped from the front door of the small cottage, the cool winter breeze kissing her cheeks as she stepped into the morning. A cough sounded from the path behind, and she whirled around to find Lorian standing not two feet away, his arms crossed and an all too aggravating smile dancing on his lips. She snapped her attention from that smile and glared up into Lorian's eyes, crossing her own arms as she stepped forward.

"I'm off to train with Lizabet and Maescia," Finriel said.

"Sounds like it will be painful," Lorian replied with raised brows. "I suppose I don't get to watch?"

Finriel rolled her eyes, her stomach coiling at the playful tone in his voice. She forced her breath to remain even, though her quickened heartbeat betrayed her. She allowed her gaze to travel down his body, and her brow raised in confusion at the sight of dirt caked along his cloak and pants.

"Did you roll in mud?" Finriel asked, looking back up to meet his stare.

His grin quirked to the side, and she bit down on the rush his gaze sent through her. "No, but close to it. I was looking for something I saw on the strange little mounds over there the other day, but I think I might have been imagining it."

Finriel frowned. "I didn't see anything."

"That's because you're not a thief," Lorian replied with a wink. "I can't help but notice potential danger everywhere I go."

"Thank the goddesses I'm not a trained idiot," Finriel said.

Lorian chuckled. "No, but you still somehow got it into your head to be reckless this morning."

Cold wind rustled through the trees and wrapped its chill around Finriel's bones, making the faint smile die on her lips. He had discovered her meeting with Lizabet that morning, even though she hadn't spoken to a single soul about it. "How did you find out?"

Lorian shrugged. "People talk."

Finriel sighed. "I have to learn, Lorian. It was clear Lizabet would have never agreed to teach me if I hadn't gone up there."

Something like worry clouded his eyes, and he took another step closer. Their cloaks rustled against each other, and Finriel could see the light freckles that speckled over Lorian's nose and high cheekbones.

"We don't know these people," Lorian said in a low voice. "I know they're your kind, but I don't trust them."

A humorless bark of laughter escaped Finriel's lips. "You don't trust anyone."

"I trust you," Lorian said darkly. "And I know you're more powerful than anyone on this damned island. I've seen it with my own eyes."

"What are you saying?" Finriel asked, not sure if it was the chill of morning or his nearness that made her feel short of breath.

Lorian's gaze dipped down before meeting her gaze again, and the corner of his mouth quirked upward. "I'm saying that I understand you want to learn, but you already know a lot more than you think."

His hand reached up to her wrist and squeezed gently, comfortingly. There were no words in Finriel's mind to reply, only shock and that terrible rush, making her feel dizzy.

And then he was gone, moving past her to slip through the door of their small cottage.

"Try not to kill Maescia today," he called out before the door clicked shut.

Finriel closed her eyes, the memory of his hand around her wrist like a brand that gave more pleasure than pain. She shook her head and flung her eyes open, beginning her walk to the forested area where Lizabet had told Finriel to find her for the lesson. There was no time to be thinking about rogue thieves or the fact that she was beginning to feel something that felt all too close to falling.

"Men," she grumbled and headed into the woods.

"You're late," Lizabet announced as Finriel entered the clearing.

Maescia was seated upon a log in the grand clearing, a space made of dark springy grass surrounded by thick pine trees. The young witch lifted a hand in welcome, and Finriel managed a wince in greeting before focusing on Lizabet, whose back was turned the other way.

"I was held up," Finriel replied, doing her best to sound kind, though her words came out more biting than she would've liked.

Lizabet turned on her heel, facing Finriel with a stare of cold calmness. "Very well, then. Let's begin." The mother of witches inclined her head toward Maescia. "Put her through the warm-up."

Maescia sprang to her feet and moved to stand in front of

Finriel. Her ebony ringlets were wrapped today, the plain faded gray fabric making her green eyes stand out further. She smiled at Finriel, but Finriel had had enough smiling for one day.

"Are you ready?" Maescia asked, and Finriel clenched her fists.

"Let's go."

The young witch nodded and began the warm-up, widening her stance to hip-width apart and arcing her arms toward the sky before sinking down into a deep squat, her fingers brushing against the soft grass before she straightened again. Finriel glanced at Lizabet, confusion making her frown. But Lizabet simply watched Maescia with the same expressionless face, not a peep of rebuke out of her mouth.

"It's to align and ground the energetic points of your body," Maescia explained, noting Finriel's apparent annoyance. "It looks stupid, but I've tried starting lessons without warming up, and it's not fun."

Finriel let out a huff to ease the tension in her chest and widened her stance, following Maescia's slow movements. It was harder than she'd expected, the deliberately slow bending and straightening of her legs in time with the arm movements making Finriel's muscles strain within the first few seconds.

"Damn the Nether, I'm weak," Finriel grumbled, and Maescia simply smiled.

"You aren't weak, and you don't need to be strong in order to do this. The strain is due to an uneven alignment of your energetic points, causing an imbalance in your overall power."

"That's enough," Lizabet called out, making Finriel jump. "Let's begin the lesson."

The muscles in Finriel's legs popped as she straightened, and she wiped away a bead of sweat from her brow. She hadn't expected a simple warm-up to get to her the way it had, and an unfamiliar sense of dread for what Lizabet had in store made her stiffen.

"We will stick with something simple today," Lizabet said as she walked over to stand by Maescia and Finriel.

Her slender hands came free from the folds of her heavy black cloak, and Finriel watched as she turned her palms toward the sky. Nothing happened for a few moments, and Finriel was beginning to wonder again what the point of this all was when a small stone appeared in Lizabet's right palm.

Another sphere of dark earth appeared in Lizabet's other hand, and the mother of witches looked at Maescia, nodding. Maescia held out her hands in the same fashion, and two swirling funnels of wind came to life. They were small yet spun with a force that caused a faint whistling sound to sing through the air, and Finriel watched in mild fascination as they spun in place, as though a tether held them securely so they did not float away.

"This is called Centering," Lizabet said. "It is the practice of absolute concentration of one's physical magic. The more concentrated and contained her magic, the more resilient a witch can become."

"But how would you get anything done with only a small amount of magic?" Finriel asked, still watching the swirling orbs of wind.

Maescia laughed, but one scathing look from Lizabet had her silent again.

"It is not a small amount of magic that I am showing," Lizabet replied. "This is arguably the strongest concentration of magic that a witch can wield. Forming big flashy rivers of destruction does not equal power. Focused and precise magic is the sign of a trained witch, not a weak one."

Before Finriel could open her mouth to reply, Lizabet turned on her heel and shot her hands outward. It happened so quickly that Finriel barely had time to blink, and a sound of harsh impact rang through her ears. Lizabet's hands lowered, and Finriel couldn't help the awe from making her frown as she stared at the two precise holes that ran straight through one of the surrounding trees. It was a straight shot through the middle, and weak daylight shone through the twin holes in the tree.

"A wildfire may burn a forest, but a single match can light even the darkest of nights," Lizabet said, facing Finriel. "Now you do it."

"But I don't have earth magic," Finriel protested.

"You don't need earth magic to do what I did," Lizabet said. "Maescia, please demonstrate your Centering to Finriel."

Finriel shoved down the rising fury and let out a shaking breath, pointing her glare toward Maescia. The witch was not paying attention to Finriel, however, and she nodded once before opening her arms wide and slicing them forward in a flash. The wind funnels joined midair and flattened, transforming into a nearly invisible blade that arced toward the tree Lizabet had attacked. What sounded like parchment being sliced filled the air, and then it was gone. Finriel frowned, glancing at Lizabet.

"Nothing happened," Finriel said, unable to help herself.

Lizabet's mouth quirked into a humorless smile. "Go to the tree."

Finriel moved toward the tree, rising laughter bubbling in her chest. Yet the laughter died and retreated deep down again when she reached the aged pine. A perfectly straight line made its way around the trunk, mere inches above the two holes Lizabet had created. It was a clean cut, so perfectly executed that the tree remained upright.

"If you were to push, the tree would break in two," Lizabet said. "Leave it, and the tree might be salvaged. This is the power of Centering."

Finriel whirled around to look at Maescia, only to find the witch watching her with a friendly smile. It bothered her that this girl had no ego attached to her skills; it would have made disliking her much easier. But Maescia showed no signs of gloating, only humble satisfaction at her impressive performance.

"Now you try, but only with the spheres at first," Lizabet said.

Finriel took in a deep breath and widened her stance, opening her palms the way Lizabet had done before. She felt the heat at once, curling and winding its way from her core up to her fingertips. Finriel bit her lip as the fire crackled to life in her palm, an orb the size of her head.

"It must be smaller," Lizabet reminded her, and Finriel noted a hint of tension in her voice.

Finriel stared at the flame, concentrating on syphoning some of the embers back into her core. The fire crackled and spat, tendrils of it snaking around itself to make the orb tighter, but not smaller. A bead of sweat slithered down Finriel's spine as the heat in her core swelled, like a hungry animal clawing its way toward its next meal. The flame craved to be free, to taste the air and consume Finriel entirely. She recognized this, and a grunt of fear escaped her lips.

"Concentrate on where your energy begins, Finriel." Lizabet's voice rang out. *Do not let your power consume you.*

The last words whispered through Finriel's mind, and it was a soothing sensation rather than the clanging pain she had experienced the day before. Finriel grunted again, and her fingers tightened around the orb, but the flames fought to grow even bigger still. Her arm began to shake, but she did not back down.

You are not my master, Finriel spoke to the beast inside. *You cannot consume me.*

The flame shrank, if ever so slightly. The orb was now the size of her fist, though it still spat and crackled as though frustrated that it was being contained in such a way.

"Better," Lizabet said. "But still too big."

Finriel lowered her hand with a gasp, and the flames sputtered before disappearing completely. She hadn't expected the seemingly simple exercise to be so difficult or so frustrating.

Finriel panted. "It won't get any smaller."

"The most powerful witch can make her element as small as a speck of dust. It is not the size that you cannot control, it is the amount of magic you allow to come forth at a time." Lizabet turned away from Finriel and stepped toward the edge of the clearing. "We are done for today. Maescia, have two garden witches come to heal Orris before nightfall."

"Of course," Maescia replied, but Finriel frowned.

"Who's Orris?"

"The tree," Maescia replied simply before turning away and following Lizabet toward the village.

Finriel glanced at the tree in question and shook her head before trudging after the other witches, frustration and exhaustion following her the entire way back. She could not allow a simple concentration practice to get the best of her. Shame made her cheeks hot, and Finriel clamped down on the heat that tickled behind her eyes. She was *not* a helpless little girl. She would find a way to master her flames, even if it meant she had to practice through the night.

Tomorrow, she would master Centering, and then the real training would begin.

8

KRETE

K rete's vision swirled from blue to dark stone as he arrived back in the portal room within Creonid Mountain. He trudged around the wide mouth of the swirling blue portal, which had not been used since Aeden's sudden departure eight days prior. Krete still couldn't believe Aeden had betrayed him, betrayed all of his companions that short of a time ago. It felt like an eternity had passed, yet no time at all.

Krete moved to a dark iron chest near the entrance of the room. He dropped the small portal stone onto the pile of glowing stones before slamming the iron lid shut and turning through the doorway, his mind numb and yet whirling from the conversation with Aeden.

The thick stone walls were illuminated by flickering torches, and Krete walked out onto one of the many walkways that were carved into the insides of the mountain in a dizzying labyrinth. Krete passed an outstretched tree branch with emerald leaves, but he paid no mind to the Viure that was planted hundreds of feet down at the bottom of the mountain. Chatter and laughter echoed from down by the tree, where the many gardens and lounge areas were being cared for and enjoyed.

But Krete could not enjoy those things—not anymore. He nodded numbly toward the few gnomes that passed him and turned into a narrow side passage. This tunnel was narrower than the one leading to the portal chamber, but the close walls felt comforting around him as he wound through the mountain.

Sunlight soon pooled against the stone, and Krete emerged into a large cave that opened up toward the meadows and a staggering drop below. An enormous black dragon was stretched out on the cave floor, its movements languid as it lifted its head to Krete's arrival.

"You look rather sad today." The dragon's low voice rumbled through the cave.

Krete sighed and crossed over to the dragon, the curving ivory horns on its head glinting in the winter light as it followed Krete's movements. Krete paid the hot breath that beat against his face no mind and skirted around the razor-sharp claws that were twice the size of his own body.

"It's Aeden." Krete huffed, plopping down against the dragon's side and relishing in the warmth that radiated from the dark scales.

"Did you finally see her, even though I've told you countless times that she's a crazy bat and got what she deserves?"

"Suzunne!" Krete exclaimed harshly but smiled sadly.

"I was just trying to make you feel better." The dragon sighed. "Did it work?"

"A little. Thank you," Krete replied truthfully.

"What happened? She clearly didn't arrest you," Suzunne said.

Krete rubbed a calloused hand against his tired eyes and shook his head. "We just talked, but she didn't say much."

Suzunne snorted. "That doesn't sound all too bad."

"It is when you've known someone as long as that," Krete replied bitterly. "It's as though someone else has taken over her skin and her voice."

"Sounds rather fishy to me," Suzunne agreed. "Perhaps that mean Red King did something to her."

"That's what I'm worried about," Krete said.

They sat in comfortable silence for some time, and Krete's head soon began to ache from the knots it was twisting into. Aeden's behavior was odd indeed, but she was not the only one to whom his mind strayed. He thought of Lorian, Finriel, and Tedric too. Tedric was alive. Aeden's vague explanation had revealed that much. Only that had given him a hint of relief, but still not enough. He needed to make sure that Tedric was all right and not under some sort of spell or worse. He had killed the fairy guard in order to save Krete's life, which could've only welcomed bad things.

"Where are your other little friends? I'm sure they could help with all that's ailing your thoughts," Suzunne said, breaking the silence.

"Last I heard, Finriel and Lorian were headed to the Witch Isles," Krete replied.

"That's only a three-day flight if I don't stop to rest," Suzunne said, but Krete shook his head.

"I don't want to put us both in danger without knowing if they are on the isle for sure. I'll have to speak to King Drohan to see if he's heard of any movements in Keadora."

"Well, I suggest you find them soon. I'm getting quite tired of you moping about at all hours."

Krete looked up, meeting the black dragon's amber eye with a scowl. Suzunne blinked and turned back to gaze at the meadow beyond.

"You are sad, Krete," Suzunne said slowly. "And I do not like to see my friends suffer."

A lance of pain sliced through Krete's heart, and he looked down at his lap as a tear slid down his cheek.

"She was like a little sister to me." Krete sniffled. "I just didn't expect to lose her in this way."

"She may not be lost, only trapped, as you say," Suzunne replied, and Krete let out another sniffle.

"It makes me feel worse thinking that it could be possible."

A growl rumbled against Krete's side as the dragon shook his head. "You are wise and have a solid head on your shoulders. Don't think for one moment that you cannot help her."

A squeeze of gratitude for the dragon wrapped around Krete's heart, and he lifted a hand to pat his smooth scales. "Thank you, Suzunne."

"You're welcome," Suzunne replied. "But you have to stop crying on the floor. I do sleep here."

"Sorry." Krete wiped his sleeve against his nose and blinked away the last few tears, one still clinging to his lashes.

"Will you go to Drohan now?" Suzunne asked, and Krete nodded.

"Yes, I think that's the most logical step to take now that I know I can't help Aeden alone."

"Wonderful," Suzunne murmured. "It will end well. I'm confident in that."

Krete sighed and closed his eyes, hoping to the goddesses and any shred of goodness left in the realm that Suzunne was right.

9

LORIAN

Utensils clinked against wooden bowls, and the scent of cinnamon tea wafted through Lorian's nose as he took a bite of porridge.

Finriel was seated across from him, shoveling spoonfuls of porridge and dried fruit into her mouth as though she hadn't eaten in days. Lorian was the first person to know what it was like to go hungry, but he'd never seen his best friend act so animatedly about anything other than telling people off.

"Are you preparing for a harsh winter?" Lorian asked.

Finriel glanced up at him through thick lashes before returning her caramel stare to her meal, shaking her head. "I have training in fifteen minutes."

"You may not even get there if you choke trying to eat like the wind," Lorian replied.

Finriel simply glowered at him and shoved the last mouthful of food into her mouth. She pushed the bowl away and grabbed the mug of tea, taking a healthy swig. "Are you going to keep playing in dirt today?"

Lorian shrugged. "Maybe. There's not much else for a half-breed to do around here."

It was a lie, but Finriel seemed too preoccupied for him to fill her in on what exactly he was trying to find. He'd felt a strange pull toward the mounds, as though there were something hidden beneath. He was curious, and that was a dangerous feeling for a thief.

"Just don't get too dirty again," Finriel said, setting her drained mug down with a thump. "I was forced to travel and sleep with your dirty body for three moons; I'd rather not have the bed full of your grime now."

"You're blushing," Lorian mused, noting her pink cheeks.

"I ate a hot meal, and it's cold outside," Finriel snapped, standing from the bench and whirling away far too quickly.

"We've been inside too long for that to happen!" Lorian called to her retreating form, and she raised her hand in a rude gesture before stalking outside and disappearing beyond the thick stone walls.

Lorian smirked, and he couldn't deny the surge of satisfaction that swelled through him at the sight of her reddened cheeks. Of course, his veins thrummed with excitement at her words, but he shoved them down. Finriel was still as closed-up as a tomb, and no matter how inviting or suggestive her words may be, he wouldn't believe that she was beginning to care for him in that way. She had barely forgiven him for their ten years of separation. It would be foolish to think she'd forgiven him *that* much.

Lorian sighed and finished the rest of his meal in silence. None of the other witches bothered him, though it seemed that was more out of wariness than being polite. He didn't mind though. Despite his enjoyment of meeting new people, he was determined to find the secret of the mounds, and he did not want to get distracted.

~

LORIAN'S BOOTS crunched against small stones that littered the dark path. An icy breeze slithered down his neck, and Lorian lifted the hood of his cloak over his head with a grimace. He might have grown up in an area where it snowed regularly during the winter moons, but he still hated wind.

The mounds rose up moments later, and Lorian wound between the few witches that crossed his path. None spoke to him, and he did his best to ignore their expressions of interest and mild alarm as they passed by. He understood they likely hadn't seen a man in months, if not years, but he wasn't sure if it was only his gender that made them look twice. Elves weren't the most liked race in the realm, and half-breeds weren't any better. But Lorian knew he was handsome, so he allowed himself that small comfort when deciphering their passing glances.

Finriel's face rose in his memory again, and Lorian clenched his fists. He was foolish for letting himself feel this much for her, but it had already started happening before she'd even forgiven him. She was like a mystery, but not to him. He knew why she did the things she did. He understood the way her mind worked. But it was maddening to know so much about her, yet not at all about what lingered in her heart.

"Shut up, Grey. You're going to turn into a ratty old scholar," Lorian grumbled under his breath as he stepped off the path and onto the first mound.

He scanned the area, and excitement sent his legs moving again once he spotted the patch of dark tilled earth only a few feet away. Lorian looked around, but there was no sign of life on the winding paths or in the stone cottages around the mounds.

Lorian knelt and sank his hands into the soft dark earth, the granules somehow warm against his skin. He began digging, and the soft earth gave way easily. Excitement coursed through his veins, and a strange prickling energy rose up to greet his fingers. The prickling energy continued as he dug his way through the dirt. Yet it didn't end, and minutes went by in this manner until sweat trickled down his temple and his fingernails were caked with soil. He'd dug for hours the day before, only to end up empty-handed, the way he did now. It was fruitless, but why did he feel like there was still something under the rich soil?

"Damned dirt," Lorian growled, falling onto his backside with a huff.

His hand pressed against something gnarled and firm, and Lorian blinked with swelling surprise as the dark soil gave way, falling into nothingness. He glanced back to find his hand pressed against a small root he hadn't seen upon his arrival, then pushed up on his hands and knees to look down at the gaping hole below.

It was a sloping tunnel with a pathway just barely visible below the shower of earth that had fallen upon it. Lorian scrambled to his feet and stepped toward the opening, a faint tickle of apprehension making him pause before heading into the tunnel beyond. Smooth rich earth clung to the walls, as did the scent of it to his nostrils. Even with the slightly keener eyesight from his elvish side, the dark was pure and blinding. He reached out his fingers to either side to brush along the narrow walls as the path descended downward and deeper into the ground.

"What in the Nether is this place?" Lorian grunted under his breath, and a sudden desire to turn back made him falter again. But there was a secret hidden just beyond, and Lorian would be damned if he didn't find out what it was. He knew there was something off with this island, though he wasn't quite sure how. Perhaps this was the missing piece.

Soft light spilled onto the ground, and Lorian blinked as he made out a bend in the tunnel that hid the source of light beyond. He pushed on, the light growing stronger with each step he took. And then he was around the bend, cursing in surprise at the source of such grand light.

They were witchlight crystals, uncut and magnificent from where they grew out of the earth itself. Lorian took a tentative step into the maze of golden crystal, peering at one whose jagged tip stretched out of the ground and reached toward the arched ceiling, which when Lorian looked up, was hundreds of feet above his head. Veins of green and blue pulsed through the crystal, sending small bursts of colored light to dance across the smooth floor.

Lorian picked his way through the raw witchlight, though confusion prickled his senses at the fact that the witchlight was brighter than any other source he had seen before. Perhaps it was simply because it was in the birthplace of all witches and magic was strongest here. Lorian shrugged and glanced around until he found an archway made of witchlight to his left. He moved toward it, careful not to touch or step on the crystals as he moved. He might be an idiot, but he didn't trust a rock that bright or big, especially not with a bunch of angry witches above that could rip his head off at first sight of him carrying a piece.

It is tempting though.

Lorian walked through the archway and nearly stumbled back a step.

"What in the Nether," he whispered, awe and disbelief making his knees weak.

A sand clearing that looked to be the size of the island itself stretched out beyond. Soft black sand much like that on the beach above spread out through the entire space. The arched cavern walls were littered with large witchlight crystals, though these emanated a dark blue light. A large pond took up the middle of the space, its lapping surface lit by a glowing sculpture nearly three times Lorian's height at the center of it. It depicted a beautiful woman in a flowing dress that covered her curvy strong body. Her hair flowed to her waist in thick waves, and her hands held a large orb that was likely supposed to be the sun. Her head tilted backward in ecstasy, as though the sun's warmth was the most delicious of embraces.

"The witches have a secret shrine for Adustio. How classy," Lorian muttered under his breath.

He couldn't deny his slight disappointment at the discovery, for he'd been expecting something much more exciting than a giant cave with the witches' goddess in the middle of it. It was better than nothing, however, and Lorian couldn't deny that his itch of curiosity had been thoroughly scratched.

"Lorian Grey, do not linger in the shadows," an old voice called out. "It is rude to hide from your elders."

Lorian froze, his hand reaching instinctively for the worn dagger at his belt. He tried to step farther back into the cave of witchlight, but an invisible hand bumped against his back.

"How do you know my name?" Lorian called out, then sent a silent curse to the Nether and beyond before stepping out onto the black sand to find himself face-to-face with a woman older than the isle itself.

Well, he didn't know that for sure, but her wrinkled skin was pale and saggy, and her likely once unnerving obsidian-black eyes were now pooled over with milky white splotches. She wore a robe of burnt orange, the vestment covering her from head to toe so that only her face remained visible.

"I know the name of everyone I am meant to come across in my life," the woman replied with a smile, showing a surprising amount of teeth.

"I wish I had that skill," Lorian replied with a returning smile.

The old woman turned without answering and walked toward the pond, waving a weathered hand behind her for him to follow.

Lorian sighed and started after her, blinking with a frown as two large red cushions popped into existence near the lapping pond edge and the old woman sat with surprising grace. Lorian sat on the cushion across from the old woman and gave her a small smile before looking around.

"What is this place?" Lorian asked.

"A temple of sorts," the old woman replied. "It is also a sanctuary for my sisters and me to work and communicate with Adustio."

Lorian suppressed a snort, for which the woman would've surely turned him into dust. He had long lost hope of the goddesses being alive, as there was no way they could still exist after the War of Seven Kingdoms. Even if they were still alive, they had disappeared, and Lorian didn't trust a god who placed a spell on their people and then left forever.

"Do you know why you are here, Mister Grey?" the old woman asked, and Lorian shrugged.

"Old habits and simple curiosity, I expect."

The old woman laughed. "You are a funny one."

Lorian gave her a confused smile. "I'm glad I could bring you some comedic relief."

"I called you here, Lorian Grey," the old woman said, her voice still dancing with laughter.

Lorian frowned. "How? I noticed the tilled earth on the mounds and grew curious on my own."

"Yes, but you remained curious even when you returned the next day and dug to no avail," the old woman replied. "Are you too proud to deny the strange pull of magic—or curiosity, as you put it—that you felt toward this place?"

Lorian opened his mouth and then closed it again, unable to argue against the strange elder. "I suppose you have a point."

The old woman smiled again briefly before her expression turned grim. "You must be wondering why I called you here, are you not?"

"It's my job to have a certain level of wonder at all times." Lorian shrugged. "Though I wouldn't be surprised if you'd simply grown tired of being alone in this big space."

"I am not alone in here," the old woman said with a dismissive wave of her hand. "But your coming here is still important, for I need you to bring me the fireling."

"Who?" Lorian asked, leaning forward.

"The witch to whom your heart belongs," the old woman said with a knowing glint in her eyes. "There was a greater reason for her coming here, and I must speak to her before it is too late."

"I—" Lorian paused, clearing his throat.

"You do not have to try telling me otherwise," the old woman said. "You are young, and forgiveness was only just given, but do not worry over the future of your heart, thief. It is all in good time."

"When do you want to see her?" Lorian asked, steering the subject away from his racing pulse.

"In the morning. It is late now, and I suspect she will be quite tired from her training."

Lorian nodded, then paused. "How are you able to see everything when you are so deep underground?"

The old woman smiled. "I am older than the thousand-year peace, boy. One learns not to only use their eyes and ears to see and listen."

"Do you have a name?" Lorian asked.

"Alima," the old woman said. "I am one of the oldest witches left in Raymara. I have seen darkness rise and fall, and I know the secrets of the future far better than most."

A shiver ran down Lorian's spine, and he couldn't stop the small inclination of his head in respect. This woman had called to him to do something important, something helpful even. He wasn't quite sure how Finriel tied into all of this, but a soft voice in the back of his head told him it was as important as Alima had said.

"I will bring Finriel in the morning," Lorian said and rose to his feet.

Alima nodded, though she did not stand. "Bring Maescia along as well. I have a feeling you will be wanting her company tomorrow."

IO

TEDRIC

Snow pelted against Tedric's cheeks, leaving tiny stinging kisses as it fell. He trudged down the vacant street, his weary bones and sick stomach strengthening his desire for the night to end. The sky swirled gray with snow and moonlight, and Tedric wished he could find the beauty like he once was able to do.

Now he simply felt nothing.

The scuff of a boot gave Tedric pause, and he angled his head to track movement in the shadows of a nearby building. His peripheral was enough to see two sets of boots, both worn and caked in mud.

He was being followed.

Tedric shrugged his cloak closer around his body and bent his head against the wind, forcing his tired legs to move faster. Keadora was a peaceful city, perhaps by law alone, but that didn't mean pickpockets and thieves didn't have their fair share of fun. Lorian's grinning face swam through Tedric's memory, and the pain in his gut twisted. He couldn't assume that these were bad men. It was going to be a cold winter after all, and Tedric's fine armor made him an obvious target.

Fool, you know better than to leave the castle after dark.

But the bars of Egharis's cell hadn't been replaced with solid metal until night had long since fallen and a chill swept over the stone floors. Egharis had still been hard at work when the magical door appeared and Agonur came to relieve Tedric of his duties. He hadn't had much of a choice but to wander back home in the darkness, unless he were to sleep on the floor beyond Egharis's cell.

Tedric placed a gloved hand on the pommel of his sword, sliding his fingers down to rest casually around the hilt. He would not kill again, not if he could avoid it, but he would not say no to a fight. The thought of using his muscles to the point of aching made his veins thrum with excitement, and a pang of shame washed through his gut. He had changed since the mission to retrieve the pages, from a peace-loving commander to a blood-thirsty fool.

Not bloodthirsty, Tedric reminded himself. He didn't have the desire to kill. In fact, the thought of watching the life drain from someone's life by his hand made the curse twist his muscles into knots. But he was a simple man, and he couldn't deny that he could use a bit of fighting.

The soft patter of footsteps quickened, and Tedric spun around, coming face-to-face with two ragged-looking men, who, to his own satisfaction, looked surprised that Tedric had even noticed them. One was tall and made of pure sinew, his face drawn and rodent-like. The other had a stockier build, but even so, neither of them had much meat on their bones. They both had dark hair, or perhaps it was simply the darkness and grime that coated their entire bodies that made it so.

"Evening, gentlemen," Tedric said darkly and realized with a pang that he was beginning to sound like Lorian.

"We'll be wanting whatever it is you've got on you," the taller one sneered.

Tedric sighed. "Well, at least you got straight to the point. Unfortunately, I'm not quite in the mood to walk home naked."

The shorter one spat at the ground, and Tedric grimaced as a few flecks landed on his boots. "You'll be doing as we say, soldier grunt. Unless you want us to cut off one of your pretty fingers."

"No," Tedric said, a terrible hot anger beginning to swell through his body and turn his vision red.

He would not be tossed around by two half-starved miscreants, let alone be told what to do. They were the grunts, not he. Tedric tightened his grip against his sword, though his muscles ached to draw the blade and show the thieves exactly to whom they were speaking.

The taller thief laughed, the sound nasally and ear-piercing through the calmness of the night. "Look at him, so cocky in his little uniform."

The shorter man grunted in agreement, then elbowed his friend in the side. "How 'bout we show him who he's saying no to?"

"Yeah," the taller one jeered. "Good idea."

"Do you know who I am?" Tedric asked, and the warning in his voice was enough to make the men pause. Tedric smiled. "I am Commander Drazak, and you would do well to leave me alone."

A moment of silence passed through them like suffocating cotton, until finally, the tall one's face changed from wariness to haughty defiance. "You're not the commander anymore."

"Yeah, you're the one who betrayed us all, coward," the short one spat. "Now we have an even better incentive to take your things."

Tedric's blood boiled, hot and maddening, until his very bones ached with anger. He was wasting breath trying to convince these men of his honor, though he wasn't sure if he had any to begin with.

"Fine," Tedric growled. "If you want my things, then you'll have to take them by force."

The thieves exchanged a glance before moving toward Tedric on surprisingly quick feet. The shorter one withdrew a metal rod from his coat, and Tedric eyed the rusted thing with a rush of adrenaline. It wouldn't kill him, but it would definitely hurt if the man wielding it hit hard enough.

The tall one struck first, aiming a fist at Tedric's face. It was sloppy, and Tedric dodged it easily with a simple duck. He lunged out a hand before his opponent could recover and struck, sending a punch into the man's side with a satisfying crunch of bone. The man wailed in pain, and Tedric stepped back, shaking his stinging hand. A grin rose to his lips, and a strange part of him reveled in the adrenaline.

"You bastard," the short one spat, and Tedric grunted as the short metal rod connected with his back.

Pain sliced through his skin, and an animalistic yell ripped from Tedric's throat as he whirled on the short man, whose arm was raised, ready to strike again.

But Tedric was too fast.

He shot a hand out and jabbed, his fist aiming true into a debilitating pressure point on the man's shoulder. The man cried out, and the weapon fell from his now limp grip, clattering on the cobbled street. Tedric attacked again, striking out with his foot to slam into the man's gut. He went stumbling back, falling against the wall of a nearby building and grunting as his head cracked against stone.

Something sliced against Tedric's cheek, and he whirled around to find the taller thief had recuperated and now held a short knife. The edge of it was dark with blood, but Tedric only smiled wickedly at the man.

"You chose a bad day to pick on me."

His hand found the hilt of his blade almost on instinct, and he withdrew it in a smooth motion. The thief simply gulped, his eyes widening at the expertly crafted sword. Tedric swung it in his hand, testing the grip and feel of his trusted friend. He readied himself in a fighting position, though he didn't care to raise his sword. Besides, he wasn't going to kill the man, only scare him.

Goddesses above, he'd had enough of killing.

The thief only continued to balk, the knife shaking visibly in his hand. The man turned on his heel and was gone within seconds, his booted feet slamming hard against the cobblestones as he retreated into the shadows. Tedric sighed and straightened, sheathing his blade. He crossed over to the shorter man, who was still seated, his eyes closed and head bowed. Worry lanced through Tedric's heart, and he crouched down to press a finger against the grubby man's neck. A steady pulse pressed against his fingers, and Tedric stood up with a sigh of relief. The thief's eyes fluttered, and Tedric smirked.

"You're a good actor. Perhaps you should try a life in that instead of ruining the nights of good people."

Tedric turned and stalked off, not caring to hear the short man's grumbled reply. The wind had picked up in earnest now, and snow swirled through the air like dancing ghosts. Tedric bent his head and flipped the hood of his cloak over, feeling nothing other than the stinging pain of his cheek and aching back as he made his way home.

HE STUMBLED through the front door, breath ragged and cheek burning from the slice the thief had given him. Tedric grunted as he slammed the door behind him and trudged over to the hearth, groaning in relief at the faint embers that still glowed from the fire he'd made that morning. He made quick work of rekindling the flame, and soon, a merry fire crackled and gave the small cottage enough light for Tedric to stumble toward the cushioned chair near the corner and plop down with a sigh.

The fight had drained him far more than he would've expected, and a small tingle in his gut told him it was the curse's fault. Tedric lifted a hand to wipe at the cut, only to find that it had frozen over with the freezing wind outside. He grimaced at the stinging sensation and let his hand drop back down to his lap.

This couldn't be the way life was now. He wouldn't stand for it.

"Nether damn me," Tedric cursed, and a terrible resolve made him stand and begin working at the clasps of his armor.

He was no use in this state, not to his friends or to himself. There was only one way out of this mess, and Tedric would have to take it, no matter the taste of bile that rose to his tongue at the thought of it.

Changing and wiping his face off with a damp cloth took only a few minutes, and soon, a good amount of warmth from the fireplace radiated through the stone walls, though he still felt cold. Tedric took in a shaky breath, his eyes traveling slowly to the counter where a small clay jar sat, waiting for him.

Despair, deep and unyielding, crawled its way through his bones, seeping into the very crevices of his soul. He couldn't go on like this, not if he wanted to be any help against the Red King.

But his father was dead, and Aeden was a monster.

He was cursed.

A sob rose up from deep within, and Tedric allowed himself to crumble to the floor, his hands grasping the edges of the counter as if it were a life raft. *What is the point of all of this?* he thought. *I never got to say goodbye.*

His memories brought him back to the first day of his mission three moons ago, when he'd been ready to go to his father and ensure that he would be all right while Tedric was away. But instead, he had let Bordin do that simple task, and Tedric hadn't even said goodbye.

His cheek stung where tears met the open gash, and he cursed loudly through the pain. It wasn't that he'd been especially close to his father as of late. In fact, his duties as commander had lessened his ability to see his father at all.

But that didn't make the pain go away.

"Get up, Drazak," Tedric ground out between clenched teeth.

He would be no good like this, not to anyone. Not to himself. He was good at being strong, and right now, he would have to move through the pain or simply continue living with it until he died. He had a realm to save and friends to find.

"Get up!" he shouted and forced his leaden muscles to work as he hauled himself to his feet.

Anger flickered behind the pain, and Tedric anchored himself to it as he blinked away the tears and snatched up the jar of shimmering brown powder and opened it. He didn't allow himself to question it or even think as he grabbed a mug and set it next to the jar. The old rusted kettle was still full and set over the fire, and Tedric grabbed it, ignoring the searing heat as he moved to the counter and poured steaming water into the mug.

This is for Raymara, Tedric thought as he grabbed a healthy pinch of the powder and dropped it into the mug. *This is for my friends.*

The faintly bitter-sweet scent wafted through the air as the powder settled into the hot water, and Tedric didn't allow himself to hesitate as he grabbed the mug and brought it to his lips.

This is for my father.

 II
FINRIEL 

F inriel's breath came out in a plume of silvery mist as she exhaled, and a shiver ran down her spine.

She and Maescia waited in the clearing in silence, as it seemed they were both too cold to pretend that they cared to speak to each other. A thin coating of frost turned the lush grass white, and it crunched under Finriel's feet as she walked in a tight circle in an attempt to keep herself warm.

"Can't you warm yourself from the inside out?" Maescia asked.

Finriel glanced up at the witch to find her watching her progress with a frown. She scowled, but a faint curiosity made her pause. "I've never tried. Battle magic is banned everywhere but here, if you haven't forgotten."

"No one would see that you're wielding your magic." Maescia snorted. "It wouldn't even be visible to you."

"Learning how to use my magic without letting it get out of control is why I'm here in the first place," Finriel snapped. "I doubt my magic would be invisible if I tried it right now."

"Ladies, stop bickering." Lizabet's calm voice rang through the clearing.

Finriel tensed and turned in the direction of Lizabet's voice, only to find that the witch was already stepping into the clearing. She was dressed in her usual dark robes, the hood folded back to reveal her braided platinum tresses. Lizabet surveyed Finriel and Maescia with a neutral stare before glancing at the edge of the clearing.

"Did you send for Orris's healing?" Lizabet asked.

Maescia dipped her head. "Yes, it was done before nightfall as you instructed."

"Good."

Finriel glanced toward the tree, blinking in surprise to find that it was indeed lacking any holes or lacerations. She shook her head and put her attention back on Lizabet.

"Begin with your warm-up and then move on to Centering," Lizabet began. "Concentrate on building up the energy in your core as you warm up. The exercise might feel foolish, but it's more important than any other technique I might show you."

Finriel nodded and stepped forward to face Maescia, who had already settled into a wide stance. She settled into the stance and followed Maescia's movements, bending her knees and sweeping her fingers against the ground before arcing them up toward the sky, exhaling as her core began to burn. They moved in silence, and after a moment, a strange tingling sensation crawled at the bottoms of Finriel's feet, making its way up her ankles and through her legs.

"Relax into the sensation," Lizabet said, seeming to notice Finriel's tension. "Allow it to flow through you."

Finriel exhaled and closed her eyes, forcing her muscles to relax against the tickling sensation that rose through her limbs and stomach. It curled and spread, and Finriel held back a curse as it rose up toward her neck and head.

"Don't fight it," Lizabet ordered. "Relax into the sensation of releasing control."

"Easier said than done," Finriel ground out but forced the muscles in her body to ease further into the sensation.

And then something snapped.

Finriel gasped as the tickling sensation solidified, snapping into what felt like one solid cord throughout her body. She blinked, everything around her suddenly sharper and closer than she remembered. A strange sense of calm radiated through her body, and Finriel almost wanted to smile.

Almost.

"Good," Lizabet said. "Now you may begin with Centering. Maescia, you go first to refresh Finriel's memory."

Maescia nodded, stepping into a more comfortable stance before flipping her palms up toward the sky and closing her eyes. The funnels of twisting wind appeared within seconds, and Maescia opened her eyes to give Lizabet a questioning look.

"Aim for Sonya this time," Lizabet said, and Maescia nodded.

"Sorry, but why do the trees have names?" Finriel asked.

Lizabet turned to her and shrugged. "Why not?"

Finriel closed her mouth, unsure of what to say. She instead focused on Maescia, who was gazing at a tree next to Orris. She moved quickly again, yet this time she did not join the scythes of wind into one. Her arms shot out in a flash, and this time, two nearly invisible blades connected with the trunk. The sound of slicing parchment echoed through the clearing once again, and Finriel scowled as two perfect slices marked the tree named Sonya.

"A bit flashy, but effective." Lizabet nodded.

Finriel began gathering her magic as Lizabet gave Maescia feedback, not caring to listen to their exchange. She would master Centering today. She had to. The new surge from her warm-up still made her body feel strange and stiff, as though the cord connecting her energy had tightened. She shook out her hands and was about to lift them when Lizabet shot out a hand for her to stop.

"Wait," Lizabet said. "I will create a better target for you."

Finriel's jaw tightened, but she forced the already coiling flame in her core to stand down as Lizabet opened her hand and shot it forward. A wall of hardened clay rose through the ground and formed into a circular plate, almost like a shield. It remained frozen in the air, as though it had always been there.

"I want you to approach it in the way Maescia did yesterday. Only one solid slice through the center," Lizabet commanded.

Finriel nodded and stared at the clay disk, the prickle of nerves making her breath feel short and strained. But there was no time to be nervous, and Finriel forced down a lungful of freezing air before opening her palms up to the sky.

The flame coiled and licked at the cord of energy connecting her inner body, and Finriel willed it to enter and travel down the cord. A spark erupted from her palms, and two orbs of flame followed suit. They were smaller than her attempts yesterday, yet still far too large for Lizabet's taste.

"Smaller," Lizabet said. "Imagine your energy points syphoning back any extra magic that may attempt to escape. The connection you feel is a way of controlling the output of magic, and you must put it to great use for this exercise."

"Why didn't you tell me that yesterday?" Finriel asked through gritted teeth as she focused on the cord of energy, willing it to eat away at the flames in her hands.

She watched Lizabet shrug out of the corner of her eye. "I wanted to see where you stood in your knowledge of basic practice."

Finriel chose not to respond to the flippant comment. Instead, she directed the flare of anger toward her core, transmuting and molding it into the tickling energy at her feet. The flames shrank in her hands, and Finriel exhaled as her palms tingled and the orbs began to swirl, both shrinking down to the size of a baby's fist.

"Good," Lizabet said. "Now slice the disk."

The orbs danced on her skin, as though in anticipation of what was to come. Finriel nodded and narrowed her gaze on the disk, willing her sharpened vision to single it out and forget everything else around her. She allowed the heat in her stomach to anchor her, to keep her tethered to and focused on the task at hand. Her vision was set only on the disk, and she was ready.

Her hands shot out in a flash, and she willed the orbs to join and mold into one before shooting toward the disk. The blade was slightly larger than Maescia's, but Finriel watched as a sizzling sound bounced through the trees and the flames disappeared through the disk, leaving a scorched line through the center of it. Finriel panted as the disk wobbled, and then the top half slid forward and tumbled to the ground in a crash of broken clay.

Triumph sent a smile onto Finriel's lips, and she didn't care to suppress it as she lowered her hands and looked at Lizabet. The witch's face was impassive, but Finriel noted a hint of surprise in the set of her mouth and curve of her eyebrows.

The mother of witches was impressed.

"You are a fast learner," Lizabet said with a nod.

"What are we working on next?" Finriel asked.

Lizabet chuckled through closed lips and shook her head. "We will be practicing this for the next hour, and then you will rest tomorrow."

"But I learned the exercise," Finriel said. "I only have three days left on the island. There's no way I'll be able to learn enough by simply doing this exercise and then resting tomorrow."

"You will do as I say," Lizabet replied evenly. "More is learned in the foundation of any skill than is learned in fancy tricks. A fool with many skills is still a fool."

Finriel opened her mouth and then closed it, heat rushing to her face at Lizabet's jab. The mother of witches gave her a nod and twitched her fingers toward Maescia. "Girl, go to my tower and retrieve the Book of Shadows. I will give you a private lesson later in the evening."

Maescia nodded. "Do I need to fetch the garden witches for Sonya?"

"Yes," Lizabet replied, and Maescia set off for the village without another word.

"I don't understand," Finriel said. "Why can't you teach me more? I clearly learned this exercise, and the magic I used against you in the tower was far greater than what we're doing now."

Lizabet's gaze narrowed on Finriel, and Finriel had a sudden urge to look away. She forced herself to hold the witch's gaze, however, and Lizabet's mouth quirked in a half smile. "You are very similar to your mother. Stubborn, talented, and blind to the truth."

The words were like a blow, and Finriel blinked against the pain that lashed at her heart. But Lizabet continued, ignoring Finriel's visible discomfort. "You are even stronger than your mother, however, and that's why I am making you learn only the basics while you're under my tutelage. Great power is nothing without mastery, and mastery is only found when you learn to do nothing in order to allow great results. When you learn how to release control, it becomes the thing that finds you."

Confusion made Finriel shake her head. "I don't understand."

"Which is precisely why you will continue practicing Centering until it feels like second nature," Lizabet replied. "You learn quickly, Finriel. Your ability to learn new skills is almost alarming, and I will not allow myself to be the reason for your destruction."

Finriel nodded, unsure whether to take her words as a compliment or an insult. And so she settled into position again, forcing the flames that fed her frustration to back down and transmute into something softer, something kinder. A small part of her understood Lizabet's reasoning, as well as her warning. Oftentimes, Finriel felt as though her flame would consume her entirely, and it scared her. It was why she wanted to learn so much, why she wanted to have control over her magic. It felt like something separate from her, like a living beast that simply slumbered until prodded.

And so she would learn the basics, if only to become one with the beast within.

THE CANDLES on Finriel's nightstand flickered as the door opened, and Lorian slipped into their quarters, silent as a cat. The door shut with a faint click, and Finriel looked up at the thief as he plopped unceremoniously onto their bed, gaining a hiss of annoyance from her as pages were sent floating into the air from his sudden movement.

She had arrived at the cottage hours before to find a black leather-bound book lying on the bed. A note from Lizabet had been placed atop it, saying that she was free to keep it and learn, so long as she did not perform any of the spells or teachings. Finriel had opened the book and immediately immersed herself in the aged parchment, ignoring the fatigue that rolled off her body in waves. They had continued training for hours, and Finriel was certain she had performed Centering over one hundred times. But she felt good. Each time, the clay disk was cut with more precision than before.

Finriel had almost forgotten her lesson at the sight of the book waiting for her, and though she understood little of the text, she could feel the magic that it held. It was an aged tomb, with every other page either loose in its binding or completely detached from the rest of the book, and Finriel had carefully stacked them on the bed as she went, marking the spot where each one belonged.

"Careful, you'll ruin them," she said and quickly gathered some of the loose pages before leaning over the large book in her lap.

"Lovely to see you too," Lorian replied.

Finriel rolled her eyes and glanced down to find him looking up at her, and a faint smile sprang to her lips as her heart constricted at the sight of him. A cheeky grin lit his striking face, and Finriel sighed, shaking her head.

"You want to tell me something, don't you?" she said as she returned to stare at one of the intricate spells on the page before her, her mind slowly becoming a puddle of confusion at the foreign words.

"Why in the world would you think that?" Lorian asked casually, and Finriel did not respond. "Fine, if you must know, I found an elder on the island who had some information you might find interesting."

"What?" Finriel blurted. She gathered the pages into the book before slamming it shut and facing Lorian. "What did she say?"

"Not as much as I would've liked. But she did invite me to go back and speak with her tomorrow." Lorian leaned against the pillows, his left arm bent to rest behind his head. She glanced down, feeling the tips of his fingers brush against her tunic. His hand went limp instantly, and she suppressed a shiver at his faint touch. "I figured I would ask if you'd like to join the conversation."

"Of course I would." Finriel nodded. "Lizabet gave me the day off of training anyway, so I wouldn't be doing much of anything."

Lorian met her gaze and smiled. "Wonderful. I get to have you all to myself again."

"What do you mean?" Finriel asked. "We haven't been apart for more than a few hours in over three moons."

"I know." Lorian looked down almost shyly. "But those moons have also been filled with the company of others."

"Well, we're alone right now, aren't we?" Finriel replied flippantly, and her breath caught in her throat as Lorian's ice-blue gaze met hers again.

There was a storm in those eyes now, and pricks of electricity shot through Finriel's arms and stomach as a languid smile graced his lips. "That is true, isn't it?"

Finriel didn't speak, didn't dare answer as her body stilled, and Lorian stood to pace the length of the bed, his gaze set hard against the floor, the smile gone from his lips.

"Lorian," Finriel said, though it came out far softer than the warning tone she'd hoped for.

He paused, turning to her. "Finriel."

He took a step toward her, and Finriel's back straightened as she looked up at him. Energy thrummed through her veins in dizzying doses, and she bit the inside of her cheek to keep from letting out a shaky breath.

"What are you thinking?" Finriel asked, unsure of what to say as she watched him, her stomach feeling like it was lodged in her throat.

"I'm thinking that I want to kiss you, but I'm afraid you'll turn me into a pile of ash if I were to try," Lorian murmured.

Finriel swallowed, unable to stop herself from glancing down at his lips. She *did* want to kiss him, but she would never admit it. How could she, when they had only just repaired their friendship a few weeks ago? But she had wanted to kiss him for far longer than that; she couldn't deny it.

She straightened enough so that their faces were close enough to touch, lips only a hairsbreadth apart. "I thought thieves were fearless."

His lips were against hers in a flash, soft and dizzying as he kissed her. She leaned into his touch, her hands reaching up to grab the front of his shirt to anchor herself. They drank each other in, and Finriel was sure that time had stopped altogether as his fingers wound through the hair at the nape of her neck. He was everything she had imagined and more, soft and yet slightly rough, gentle with an underlying promise of something more.

And then the cold came.

Rough hands around her neck and the ice-blue gaze of the boy she loved running away from her. A gasp tore from her lungs, desperate and hungry to escape. Her hands pushed against his chest, and he was all too willing to let go as they broke apart. Lorian's chest rose and fell quickly, and Finriel couldn't deny her own racing heartbeat. But the hands around her throat were only just fading, and the pain in her heart gave a feeble kick.

Finriel panted. "That was incredibly stupid."

Lorian ran a hand through his raven black waves, nodding in agreement, though his gaze dropped to the floor. "I know."

He turned his back to her, and Finriel felt her heart crack open just a bit more. She *had* wanted to kiss him, and she couldn't deny that her body craved to be close to him again, but her desires were different from what was true and right.

"Let's forget it ever happened," Lorian said, his voice rough and deep.

Her gut twisted, and her voice caught in her throat, desperate to be set free and scream that she wanted him, that she didn't care about the consequences. But she only bit the inside of her cheek and nodded when he turned to face her again.

"It never happened," she replied, though her voice cracked slightly.

Lorian closed his eyes and let out a sigh, and Finriel only watched as he turned and grabbed his cloak from the floor, sweeping it over his shoulders before slipping out the door with a soft click.

12

AEDEN

Golden light pooled onto thick crystal walls, sending fractals of green and gold across silver floors. But Aeden didn't pay the beauty of her home any mind, only the tightening grip around her heart. It was ever binding, fastening her being to nothing other than pain.

It was her own special prison, only second to her mind.

Yet she supposed she deserved this small suffering. She had betrayed her friends and the one she loved for a throne, and thus a curse was brought along with it.

An ache crept into her bones, slowly at first, but with a strength that made a groan escape her lips. She wasn't sure if the curse affected everyone the same way, but if it did, she knew Tedric was feeling something similar. The aching spread, coiling around her organs and caressing her veins until it was the only thing that existed. Aeden wrapped her hands around herself, sinking deep into the silk chaise she'd ordered to be set in front of the window a few days before.

"Your Majesty, are you all right?"

The low voice came from the corner, and Aeden squeezed her eyes shut at the nausea the sound of her guard had caused.

She shook her head, sucking in a mouthful of air before forcing herself to speak. "Find someone to fetch my tea, now."

The guard's footsteps disappeared through the gilded door behind, but Aeden still heard his near-silent retreat seconds after he had gone. It had been one of her favorite games to play as a child, and she'd called it "spy ears." She had honed her elevated hearing with that game and was certain that, because of it, her hearing was better than most fairies.

But now the sound only made her feel sick.

"Nether damn me," Aeden whimpered and spurned all pretenses of manners as she curled into a tight ball, the soft silk chair caressing her aching body as she held herself and hot tears fell down her cheeks.

She was exhausted and heartbroken, and yet a small voice in her head told her she should be happy. She'd gotten everything she wanted: glory, revenge, a crown, and above all, respect. It was a small gift to see her council and guards regard her with expressions of awe whenever she passed by or entered a room. It was all she'd ever wanted, even above revenge. She'd simply wanted her opinion to matter to others, for her voice to be heard.

But she wasn't sure if it was even her voice anymore.

"Your tea, my queen," a high-pitched female voice squeaked, and Aeden cracked her eyes open to find a small maid with silver hair holding a tray with both a steaming chalice, as well as a folded piece of parchment.

Aeden pushed herself into a seated position, ignoring the lurch of her stomach. She took the chalice with trembling fingers and brought it to her lips. The tea was slightly bitter and sickly sweet, but she paid it no mind, as the instant relief was above any taste. She finished the drink in three large gulps. Then, not caring about propriety or manners, she set it back down on the tray and wiped her mouth with the back of her hand.

The Red King had been generous to offer her a relief from the curse, and a small flicker of gratitude swelled through

Aeden's now painless heart. She knew he was simply looking out for her, and the scar on her arm was a distant memory. There was no reason for her not to trust him, as he had never given her a reason to think poorly of him.

She was his serpent, and she finally belonged somewhere.

The maid watched Aeden warily, and Aeden smiled at the girl. "Please excuse my rudeness. Simply some general aches from the cold."

The maid gave her a small smile in return and curtsied. "A letter also arrived for you a few minutes ago, my queen."

Aeden glanced down at the folded parchment and reached out to take it from the maid. The familiar seal of a sun surrounded by roses sent a lurch through Aeden's throat, and she quickly opened the letter, scanning the words with rising nerves.

Queen Aeden Siltra,
I invite you to Crimson Castle for a brief stay. You are expected in two days' time. I will have my private guard at your gates by nightfall, and they will escort you to Keadora at dawn.
Please do enjoy your trip. I look forward to your company.
Regards,
RK

Tedric's face swelled through Aeden's vision, and excitement sent an involuntary grin to her lips. She would be leaving her crystal prison for some fresh air and politics, and perhaps she would see Tedric. The thought made her fingers tremble, and she tucked the letter into her lap before looking at the maid, who still stood, waiting for further orders.

"Thank you," Aeden said with a smile. "There will be guards from the Red King's court arriving in a few hours. Please ensure that they are properly dined and roomed."

"Yes, Your Majesty." The maid curtsied.

"Come to my rooms in one hour," Aeden added. "I will have

a note for you to leave with the council. I'm going on a brief trip and will need them to continue organizing the coronation without me."

The maid curtsied again. "Of course, my queen."

Aeden gave the girl another smile and watched as she scurried out of the room, the tray and chalice still balanced in her delicate grip. Aeden leaned back against her seat and gazed out the window, the swaying trees and setting sun suddenly looking a bit more inviting than before.

13
LORIAN

Lorian blinked to consciousness, groaning as he stretched. Sunlight filtered through the singular dirty window, bathing the room in weak winter light. Finriel was still sleeping at his side, her chest rising and falling slowly as she dreamt on. She was on her side facing him, and Lorian watched her usually scowling face now soft and almost ethereal in the morning hours. His eyes glanced down at her lips, and his heart clenched dangerously.

Their kiss had been everything he'd imagined and more, but it had been foolish. They had only just found even ground in their friendship, and he wasn't ready to lose her altogether simply because his heart wanted more. He couldn't risk wanting more than she did and ruining things all over again. But her lips on his had been hungry and willing, and he couldn't deny that he wanted her more than he could ever say.

He reached out and brushed a finger along her cheek, the soft tanned skin warm under his fingers before he let them fall to the mattress once more. Finriel's eyes fluttered open, and she let out a loud yawn as she stretched her arms outward, her fingers brushing against his chest. Lorian laughed as her eyes opened wide and their gazes met, though his heart constricted again as she looked at him.

"Sorry," Finriel grumbled and quickly retracted her hand. "I forgot that I was forced to share a bed with you."

"You hurt my feelings," Lorian retorted but kept the easy smile on his face as she turned onto her back to gaze out the window and groaned.

"What is it?" Lorian swung his legs over the bed, cold from the stone floor shooting up the soles of his feet as he stood.

"I didn't think I could be sore from magic." Finriel huffed.

"Training in anything will make you sore if you do it right," Lorian said and threw her a wink before shrugging a fresh tunic over his head.

"You're disgusting." Finriel rolled her eyes and slid out of their bed with another pained groan.

"Simply telling the truth." Lorian shrugged.

Finriel paused but kept her back to him as she asked, "Where did you go last night?"

"I went on a walk and wrote a letter," Lorian replied calmly, but tension still wavered near the surface of his emotions.

It was the truth. He had made himself walk until the electricity in his veins and ache in his heart eased, if ever so slightly. The letter had been hastily done, but it'd helped take his mind off what had happened between him and the witch. He hadn't returned until Finriel was already asleep, and a small part of him had been grateful for it.

"A letter?" Finriel asked. "To whom?"

Lorian waved a dismissive hand and leaned down to pull thick woolen socks over his feet. "Hopefully no one."

"Lorian—"

"It's all right," Lorian cut Finriel off, and she turned to meet his stare. "We don't have to talk about it again."

A shadow passed over Finriel's eyes, but she nodded and turned away again, letting out an almost silent sigh.

"Do you still want to meet the elder with me today?" Lorian asked, blinking quickly against the tears threatening to fall.

Finriel nodded again and stooped to pick up the folded dark green dress on the floor. She began shrugging off her nightgown when she found him watching, and Lorian chuckled as she stuck her tongue out at him and lifted her hand in a shooing motion. "Don't look."

Lorian shook his head but obeyed, turning on his heel to stare out the window and the day beyond them. Witches milled about, some in groups doing breath work or lessons and others simply walking from place to place. The magic surrounding them was nearly palpable, even in this room and even for Lorian, who had as much magic as a mealworm.

"How does it feel to be in a place where magic is used so freely?" Lorian asked, and he heard Finriel pause her dressing for a moment before replying.

"It's intimidating if I'm being truthful. I'm not used to being surrounded by witches who know more about magic than I do—or at least about battle magic."

Lorian nodded thoughtfully, thinking back to the few days before he had been sent to retrieve the bloodstone for the lord of bandits four moons before. He remembered the strange discomfort of being surrounded by so many seasoned thieves and bandits, some that knew of him even when he had never even heard their names before. "It's as if you should feel at home, but you feel more on the outside than ever."

"And how would you know of that feeling?" Finriel asked quizzically.

"You still know very little about how I spent my time after we parted ways as children," Lorian replied smoothly.

It was true. There were so many things she still did not know about him, things he had done just to keep the shirt on his back and the curse from his soul.

"Do you feel like an outsider because you know less than

them, or is it because you are more powerful and could smite them with a single thought?" Lorian asked, changing the subject back to the previous topic.

Finriel snorted and came into view as she strapped the belt holding her sheathed dagger around her waist—a habit Lorian guessed she would not give up anytime soon.

"I don't know," she replied. "But I deserve to find out more about my powers. I don't care if I have to feel a little bit out of place in order to do so."

Lorian grinned. "Spoken like a true madwoman. I like it."

"Come on," Finriel replied. "We'll be late for breakfast."

Lorian and Finriel had a quick meal in the main hall and were mostly ignored by everyone, save by Lizabet, who nodded grimly at them from across a separate table, and a few other witches who were not entirely put off by their presence.

LORIAN'S BOOTS crunched over a bundle of discarded lavender as he followed Maescia and Finriel to the large mound he had explored the day before. An icy wind wound through the village, though none of the witches seemed deterred as they went about their business and the many groups had their morning training.

"I'm surprised the elders didn't turn you into a vegetable or animal after you trespassed at the temple," Maescia commented as they neared the area of tilled earth by the base of the mound.

Lorian smiled and watched her push on the gnarled root that stuck up from the ground, the dark earth falling away into a steep tunnel leading into the darkness. "If I'm known for nothing else, it is my charm," Lorian said and followed Maescia through the passageway.

Maescia and Finriel snorted in unison, and Lorian shot them both an incredulous look, though it was unseen in the swallowing blackness.

"Have you two become best friends in this short amount of time?" Lorian whispered to Finriel, who walked close to his side.

"No," she replied quietly. "It just seems witches are all able to smell bullshit when it's thick in the air."

Maescia snorted again, and Lorian only shook his head, unable to help the grin that played at his lips. He was glad Finriel had come to like his quips and even reply with her own witty remarks from time to time. It had been the way they interacted as children, but after what had happened in the river, he wasn't sure that their relationship would ever return to that place, even after she had forgiven him.

Even after more than forgiveness was given.

"The elders don't typically allow for new people to visit them," Maescia said as she led them deeper into the small hillside.

The smooth walls reminded Lorian of when they had entered Dragonstone and found their final beast, the black dragon, Suzunne. Lorian smiled at the thought of the strange dragon as he followed behind Finriel and Maescia.

"How did you come to find the elders in the first place?" Finriel asked.

"I'm almost offended that you're surprised I found them," Lorian replied with a smirk but didn't say anything further. He doubted she truly cared to hear about his endless scouring and eventual stumble onto the root that had revealed the tunnel.

"Almost there," Maescia announced, and indeed, Lorian blinked against the sudden lightening of their dim surroundings as the raw witchlight crystals came into view.

Finriel inhaled sharply behind Lorian, and he turned to find her shaking her head at the enormous golden crystals that protruded from the widening tunnel walls.

"They grow through the entire hillside, but most of us believe that the witchlight is more plentiful because of the presence of the elders," Maescia said, the enormous crystals looming above and around as they passed through.

The glowing tunnel soon opened into a large labyrinth of crystals and various tunnels that Lorian hadn't noticed before, and Maescia gestured for them to follow her toward the archway to the left. They walked through it, coming to find the shallow pool of crystal clear water and enormous sculpture standing in the middle of the depths. The witchlight crystal had been shaped by expert hands, and Lorian was impressed yet again by the detailed textures and curves of the sculpted witch goddess.

"Who dares enter the temple?"

Finriel jumped next to Lorian as a warbling woman's voice sliced through the silence. Lorian angled his head toward a sitting area of pillows near the edge of the softly lapping water, only to find the same old woman he had encountered the day before. Her black eyes watched them curiously, though not in an unwelcoming way. Blue witch light reflected off her wrinkled skin, and her white hair was braided in thick coils around her head today. A burnt orange robe swathed her body and pooled on the ground around her.

Maescia bowed deeply, and both Lorian and Finriel hastily followed suit.

"Elder Alima," Maescia greeted, her lively spirit seemingly snuffed out by the old woman's presence.

"Maescia, I appreciate that you decided to join the thief today," Alima said by way of reply. "And I was hoping to meet you, fireling."

Lorian met Finriel's wide-eyed look before she took a tentative step toward the old woman.

Alima laughed and waved them over with both of her hands. "Please, I am far too old to bite. Sit, sit."

They gathered around and sat upon the remaining pillows, Lorian offering the elder a friendly smile. She returned it and spoke. "You were right. She did come."

Lorian focused hard on the elder and not Finriel, whom he could practically feel glaring a hole into the side of his face. The elder seemed to notice the witch's surprise, for she laughed once again.

"Please, girl. Do not be angry with your man friend for bringing you here. He was simply doing as he was told."

"Why did you want to meet me?" Finriel asked, and Alima waggled her brows.

"Because you are the last of the firelings, my dear girl."

"What does that mean?" Maescia cut in, her expression blank, yet Lorian noted a tinge of curiosity and perhaps jealousy there.

The elder met the girl's stare, and her ancient face turned serious. "Look at our goddess," she said, gesturing toward Adustio's enormous statue in the pool before them. "What do you see?"

Maescia remained quiet, but Lorian spoke up. "It depends on whether you want us to observe the outward appearance or the meaning behind the pose in which she was built."

Alima nodded, though her eyes remained on Maescia. "The thief has more qualities of a witch than I have seen in you, dear girl. Though you have power, there is still much for you to learn."

Maescia scowled but remained quiet as Alima continued.

"It is both the statue itself and the way she is standing that matters. The sun is held in her hands, which signifies the birth of our kind and her love for her children. Yet it is the *sun*, and instead of cowering from the heat and power, she revels in it."

"What does that have to do with me?" Finriel asked.

"Have you seen any of the witches on this isle wield flame?" Alima asked.

Lorian watched Finriel's expression change from anger to confusion and then curiosity. He had to admit he was equally curious, as Alima had told him nothing more than to bring Finriel down to the temple.

"I've seen a few wield flame," Finriel began, her voice quiet.

"But you have not seen them dance with it or allow for it to be nurtured and expressed with such a capacity as you possess," Alima finished for her.

Finriel blinked and nodded.

Alima gestured to Adustio's statue once more. "It is because you carry ancient blood in your veins, girl. And it is up to you to either use it for the healing of our poisoned earth or the furthering of its destruction."

Lorian frowned, something tickling the back of his memory at the elder's words.

"The prophecy," Finriel breathed, and Lorian remembered.

"Yes, though you are not the only one who can change the nature of the future. There are five keys, and they all must survive if there is to be any hope."

"How did you know about the prophecy?" Lorian cut in. "We were told by a group of frolicking fairies all the way in Proveria."

Alima's ancient gaze swept to him, and Lorian stifled a shiver at the sheer power that radiated there. "The Sythril are not the only creatures who can see the future. We all have a mother goddess, and it was theirs that communicated the prophecy to them through their art of scrying. Here, in the womb of the earth, my sisters and I have trained to listen to the messages of Adustio. I have not been the only one to hear the prophecy, and you would do well to know that the dark force aiming to sweep over the land knows well of the keys."

"The Red King," Finriel whispered, but Alima's expression gave nothing away.

"You must find each other again. You *must* reunite with the other keys," Alima insisted. "War is coming, and unless you learn the truth, we have no hope against the coming age of darkness."

"What truth?" It was now Maescia's voice that echoed softly among the glowing crystal walls.

But Alima did not answer. Her eyes were closed, and her shoulders were tense, as though she were preparing to jump to her feet. Lorian and Finriel exchanged a glance and then looked to Maescia, though she seemed more concerned than confused. Alima's eyes flew open a split second later, and only urgency remained.

"Soldiers have set foot on our shores," she said. "They are looking for the two of you."

"He found us," Finriel said, and cold dread seeped through Lorian's bones.

Maescia scrambled to stand up. "What do we do?"

"You must give them the boat," Alima said.

Maescia groaned. "It's our last one."

"Do as I say, child," Alima snapped, and both Finriel and Lorian sprang to their feet.

"Can we not just stay down here?" Finriel asked, but Alima shook her head.

"Even this place is known to the soldiers that have come."

"What will you do if they come down here?" Lorian asked, confident that the old woman wasn't as spry as she might think.

"Don't think about my pains, young man. Go now! Maescia will guide you to the boat," Alima hissed, shooing them away with a gnarled hand.

Maescia gestured for them to follow and turned on her heel. Lorian grabbed Finriel's hand and dragged her behind him as they sprinted behind the young witch. Lorian blinked away gray light as they emerged back into the open, where the sounds of the Ten yelling orders to find Lorian and Finriel echoed through the winter air.

"Come quickly." Maescia motioned for Lorian and Finriel to

follow, and Lorian crept behind Maescia as she led them through a thicket of brambles that spread underneath the tall trees.

"Over there! They're escaping through the trees!" A male voice rang out through the air, and Finriel cursed under her breath.

Lorian looked over his shoulder to find the figures of three men sprinting after them, one holding a bow aimed at their backs.

"Shit," Lorian muttered, dread making his hands turn clammy as Maescia led them through the thinning brambles and onto the black sand of the island shore.

"Our cloaks," Lorian said, and Finriel cursed again.

"The pages!"

"No time to go back now. You must hurry!" Maescia pressed, and Lorian lifted his eyes to where she was leading them.

A small boat was washed up on the shore, tethered to the inky black sand with a rope and wooden stake. Lorian forced his muscles onward even though they protested to turn back and get the pages before the Ten found them first.

"Lorian..." Finriel panted. "What if it's Tedric?"

Lorian slowed his pace and looked over his shoulder again at the three soldiers closing in, now flanked by three more men.

"I doubt your friend is with them. Go—" Maescia gasped in pain as an arrow hit her in the shoulder, sending her sprawling upon the sand.

"Maescia!" Lorian lunged toward her, but the witch was already standing.

"It's nothing. Those buffoons can't stop me with a single arrow," Maescia growled and yanked the weapon straight from her shoulder with a gasp of pain.

The girl wrenched the stake from the ground with her unin-jured side and gestured for them to get into the boat. Lorian glanced back at the men to find them rushing onto the dark shore, the same archer already knocking another arrow and readying to fire.

Before he could think, he reached into the single pocket of his pants and yanked out a folded piece of parchment, shoving it toward Maescia. "Take this," Lorian said. "A friend might come looking for us here. Give it to him if he does."

Maescia took the parchment without any questions, shoving it into her cloak pocket as she continued moving. "Go now!"

Lorian jumped into the boat without a second thought, and Finriel quickly followed suit. Lorian kept his eyes trained on the approaching men, fear for Maescia flooding through his bones as the archer released another arrow and it sailed through the sky, this time directed toward Finriel. The arrow dissolved in a spatter of ash and sparks as Finriel sent a ball of fire to meet it mere feet before her chest.

"Good one," Lorian said, but Finriel ignored him as she caught the rope Maescia flung toward them. The young witch whispered a short spell with her uninjured arm outstretched.

The boat was pushed backward into the choppy dark waters by a phantom wind, and soon, Finriel was sitting down to find her balance in the small wooden boat.

"How did you manage to keep this boat hidden from the Red King's men for so long?" Lorian asked in amazement, knowing very well that the witches were not supposed to have any way of getting off the isle.

Maescia simply whispered another spell, and a dark bundle, along with a cloth sack that bulged strangely, materialized in her hands. The witch waded into the water and held the bundle out to them. "You'll be needing this," she said through gasps, and Lorian leaned forward and gathered the bundle from her outstretched hands.

"Maescia, the men—"

"Will be more of your concern than mine," Maescia said before Finriel could finish her sentence, then flung out her hand again to send another blast of phantom wind against the small boat.

"I will rally my sisters to help you in this fight," Maescia called, a stark image against the black waters that lapped around her thighs. "Send a letter and we will meet again."

"She's going to be taken captive," Finriel hissed as she and Lorian watched the six members of the Ten finally reach the beach's edge.

But they did not wade into the water, nor did they call for Maescia to return to land. They simply turned on their heels and ran along the edge of the beach, likely to whatever ship had transported them to the island. Finriel shot her hands out toward the dark waters, and the boat shot forward again, knocking Lorian onto his backside with a grunt.

"Careful," he winced, but Finriel ignored him.

"We need to get out into open sea as quickly as possible," was all she said, and Lorian glanced around the small boat in hopes of finding an oar. But there was nothing.

"You'll deplete your magic if you try getting us all the way to the mainland like this," Lorian said as he untied the bundle Maescia had provided. He let out a whoop of relief as both navy and black cloth unraveled before him. Their cloaks. Lorian handed Finriel's to her, and she took it silently, though Lorian swore there was a trace of relief on her face as she wrapped it around her shoulders and fixed the clasp around her neck.

"The pages?" she asked and reached into her inner pockets.

Lorian dipped his hand into the inner pocket of his cloak, and another sigh of relief escaped his lips as his fingers brushed against rough parchment.

"I could kiss that girl." He sighed, and Finriel shot him a wary glance.

"It's a figure of speech," Lorian said quickly, but Finriel did not answer as her gaze drifted to something behind him and horror flooded her beautiful face. Lorian swiveled around to see what she had spotted, only to blanch and bite the inside of his lip. "That is not good."

A large ship emerged behind them like a beast through the thickening mist. It appeared that the soldiers had reached the boat, and Lorian spotted the faint outlines of nine men dashing upon the enormous wooden beast that sliced through the choppy waters, which gained on their meager boat much too quickly for Lorian's comfort.

"What in the Nether do we do about that?" Finriel asked through gritted teeth as she urged their small boat on.

Mist shrouded them in a thick blanket, the cliffs surrounding the isle like dark monsters hibernating in the gloom. Lorian narrowed his eyes, now unable to see the men on the ship that was gaining on them. The mist was becoming much too thick to see details, but Lorian hoped he could perhaps catch a glint of Tedric's fair hair, if the commander was even aboard the ship. An arrow sliced through the air, whistling before it thunked loudly into the side of their boat.

"I don't think Tedric is on that ship," Finriel said, a hint of worry lacing her voice.

Lorian's spirits dropped, the same thought flashing through his mind. He met Finriel's caramel-and-flame stare and shook his head. "No, I don't think he is either."

"I say we destroy it," Finriel said stonily, and Lorian blinked.

"And how exactly do you suggest we do that? It's massive."

Finriel simply lifted a hand, and blue flame shot from her fingertips. Lorian shook his head.

"We can't give them more of a reason to hunt us than they've already got," Lorian said, and Finriel's face returned to its stony glare as she watched the ship, the flame sputtering into nothingness before she let her hand drop. A frown soon lined her face, and Lorian faced the ship.

"It's slowing down," she muttered.

Indeed, the ship had faded slightly into the distance, and Lorian's brow raised in confusion.

"I wonder why that could be," he replied, and Finriel shrugged.

"We're on open sea now," was all Finriel said, and the familiar look of slight sickness washed over the witch's features.

She had hated their long journey with Gordon to reach the Witch Isles, and Lorian was sorry her time on solid ground had been cut short. But they had to get as far away from the Ten as they could, as well as from Keadora. A grim idea entered Lorian's mind, and he opened his mouth to speak. "We—"

An ear-splitting explosion erupted through the air, and Lorian threw himself over Finriel as splinters of wood rained over their heads, a large wave sending their small boat lurching deeper into the dark sea.

"What in the goddesses' names was that?" Lorian exclaimed as soon as debris had stopped falling from the sky and he righted himself.

The smell of smoke burned Lorian's nostrils, and he gaped in surprise to find flames dancing through the mist where the Ten's ship had once been sailing. Shouts coming from the sea rang out, and Lorian was barely able to spot a small boat only slighter larger than the one he and Finriel were in sailing away from the destroyed ship.

"It seems as though one of the witches had the same thought as you," Lorian said and watched as the small rowboat containing the members of the Ten veered to the left and disappeared into the mist away from them.

"It doesn't make sense. I'm the only one in that entire group of witches that could have done something to that degree," Finriel replied, shaking her head.

Lorian shrugged. "There is such a thing called teamwork. I do believe you were forced to partake in that practice for three moons."

Finriel ignored him, and he watched as her gaze drifted from the ghostlike flames of the blasted ship to the direction of the mist where the Ten had gone.

"They're leaving us alone," she said.

"You almost sound disappointed," Lorian replied, but he couldn't help his own feeling of confusion at the realization. "They're going back toward Keadora, no doubt."

Finriel shivered. "I don't know which direction we're going in anymore. But it seems like they gave up on the chase much too quickly."

"Or perhaps they weren't truly chasing us at all," Lorian offered. "Maybe Tedric was in their company after all and just saved our necks."

"I don't think so," Finriel said. "I only counted nine men."

Lorian sighed. "I suppose that's a question for another time. I'm just glad their boat was blasted to bits before they reached us."

Finriel's expression turned grim. "Now we just need to find out where we're going."

14

TEDRIC

"You took the Red King's potion, didn't you?"

Egharis's voice echoed within the lavish walls of his cell, and Tedric glanced at the man hunched over his small table, creating another asset to Raymara's demise.

Tedric looked down at his hands and nodded, but found he didn't feel a single morsel of remorse about the action. It was the first time in nearly two weeks that he did not feel the constant desire to empty his guts, and the terrible thirst and hunger had therefore subsided following the large feast he'd consumed after discovering the tea had worked.

"I do not judge you for taking it, you know," Egharis said, his voice laced with something almost like amusement.

Tedric raised his brows, and Egharis looked up, charcoal smeared across his fair skin. The storyteller's disheveled state had grown worse in the time since Tedric had first guarded him. The man's stark white hair drooped sadly over his forehead, the strands greasy from lack of hygiene.

"I'm not surprised to hear that, coming from a man who's building an army of beasts for a monster."

A shadow of anger fell over Egharis's face, and he quickly turned back to shading in whatever terrifying beast he had decided to create this morning. The parchment glowed under the storyteller's hand as charcoal bit angrily into paper, and Egharis whispered something in a language Tedric could not understand.

"I do not wish to serve the Red King. Why else would I be locked up in this room with you watching over me like a hawk?" Egharis said quietly but laced with enough anger to send a flicker of shame through Tedric.

"I shouldn't have said that. I'm sorry. I still don't know what you're hoping to get back in return, aside from your family."

"Is getting my family back not a good enough reason for you?" Egharis spat. "They are the only things I have left in this life. My Akiva and darling Persela."

Tedric pushed from where he leaned against the wall and looked inside Egharis's glorified cell, finding the man staring out of the wide windows, clearly lost in thought. "Your wife and child?"

Egharis jumped, seemingly shaken from deep within his mind. "Yes." He nodded. "My wife and son."

"How old is your son?" Tedric asked.

"He's on the cusp of sixteen."

Tedric smiled. "He must be a proper nightmare, then."

Egharis laughed—a strange thing Tedric had never heard from the storyteller. It was low and seemed to carry the knowledge of something deeper in the world.

"He is the wisest boy I have ever known. There have been times when he seemed to have a calmer head on his shoulders than either me or his mother. He is measured and confident in the way that he speaks and has taught me more than I care to admit."

"I think I would like him," Tedric replied, and Egharis smiled.

"Yes, I think you would."

Tedric returned Egharis's smile, contentment settling in his being for the first time since before the Clamidas festival. He knew things were not right, but he couldn't help but enjoy the feeling of momentary bliss, even if the Red King had been the one to give him this small window of relief.

He needed to get more information about the king and what exactly he was planning to do with this army of beasts being created before him and why. But Tedric couldn't seem to care about that right now. He wanted to enjoy this moment of painless contentment and simply exist, no matter how selfish it was.

"What of you?" Egharis asked.

"What of me?" Tedric replied, slightly confused by the story-teller's question.

"Do you have family? I did notice a spark between you and the new queen of Proveria," Egharis said, and Tedric forced himself to remain casual, even though his heart tightened painfully.

Tedric shook his head. "The queen and I have no relationship outside of the mission we carried out together. She betrayed me that night, and I cannot accept her good graces."

The storyteller nodded thoughtfully. "And no other relatives? A sibling, perhaps?"

"No. I am the only child my parents bore." Tedric shook his head again, and Egharis pressed his lips together, inclining his head as he noticed the pain that must have been obvious on Tedric's face.

His father's death was still too fresh to speak about, even if his father's spirit and will to live had already left many years ago. There was an ardent desire to crumble to the floor at the mere thought of his father, but now was not the time to do such a thing. Tedric sighed and shivered against a sudden cold draft in the hallway, his cloak doing little against the winter air. Footsteps echoed in the distance, and Tedric straightened, warily directing his attention toward the incomer.

Tedric raised his gaze in surprise to find Griffin and another unfamiliar dark-haired guard approaching, Griffin's dirt-smeared face showing no signs of emotion as he approached. Tedric glanced at Egharis, who had started on a new beast, apparently unaware of their visitor.

"Griffin." Tedric nodded in greeting. "You've returned from the Witch Isles so soon."

Griffin nodded and shrugged. "Your two little friends snuck off before we could get to them."

Tedric suppressed a sigh of relief at the news, then asked, "Only two? The gnome was not with them?"

Griffin shook his head and then gestured toward Egharis. "I've been directed to have Sam here take up your post for the remainder of the day."

Tedric frowned, briefly forgetting about Lorian and Finriel's escape from the Witch Isles. "Why? Am I in some sort of trouble again?"

Griffin jerked his chin at the guard, Sam, who moved to the wall as Tedric stood at Griffin's side. "I've been sent to take you to the queen of Proveria. She wishes to have an audience with you."

Surprise jolted through Tedric's body, followed by a wave of dread that he couldn't shake away. Why was Aeden here? And why did she want to see him?

"The Red King approved of me leaving my post for this?" Tedric asked, anger flaring through his body.

Griffin gave Sam his orders before turning and gesturing for Tedric to follow him down the hallway. Tedric glanced back at Egharis one last time, finding the storyteller's silver eyes directed at him. Egharis gave him a sympathetic nod, and Tedric quickly followed after Griffin, not daring to nod back.

Tedric came to walk at Griffin's side, his mind whirling. Lorian and Finriel were safe, but what had become of Krete? Perhaps he had escaped back to Creonid with Suzunne. Tedric hadn't heard any news involving the gnome kingdom, likely because they were a greatly overlooked sector of the realm.

"What happened on the isle?" Tedric broke the silence after a few moments.

Griffin glanced at Tedric before looking back at the marble portrait-lined hallway. "It was an unsuccessful mission. It seems as though Bordin had some nerves on his first serious assignment as commander. Lost aim with his bow."

Tedric's heart leapt into his throat. Perhaps his harsh words to the archer had sunk in. Perhaps there was hope yet.

"You didn't go after them?" Tedric asked, attempting to keep his voice as even as possible.

"We did," Griffin growled. "But we weren't properly equipped. The ship was blown to bits and we had to pile onto the life raft just to get out alive."

Tedric looked away from Griffin as he smiled, though he was able to suppress the laugh of relief and joy that threatened to escape his lips. It seemed Finriel had fully recovered from the Red King's hold on her mind. Tedric was not surprised though. Finriel was one of the most powerful witches he had ever met in his life.

"Bordin told me about what you said," Griffin said in a low voice, and Tedric jerked his head toward the second-in-command, his smile dying. Griffin noticed his stare and continued gruffly. "Do you really think the Red King wishes to destroy the realm?"

Tedric sighed. "That's what I'm trying to find out."

"You'd best be careful with that. It would be a shame to see you end up in the dungeons for the rest of your days—or worse."

"He can certainly try sending me down there," Tedric growled, then changed the subject. "Why is Aeden—Queen Siltra—here?"

Griffin shrugged. "I know nothing about it. I arrived with Bordin and the others to inform the Red King of what happened, and the queen was already present. The Red King told me to retrieve you on her orders directly afterward."

Tedric swallowed, not daring to betray what he was feeling beneath the cool exterior he was showing the Ten's second-in-command. He knew Griffin the least out of the men he used to call his brothers, and he had to be careful with what information he shared. Even if it did seem as though Griffin wasn't too distraught about the fact that they had just failed a mission—one the Red King was particularly passionate about being seen through.

Griffin stopped in front of an unfamiliar closed door, backing away as he gestured to the grand oak threshold. Tedric nodded at the scout and reached for the brass door handle. Griffin paused, seemingly deciding whether or not he should speak. Tedric faced the man as he finally did.

"You know, I believe what you told Bordin," Griffin said. "They're good people. I'm not sure they're the ones we should be hunting."

Griffin turned away without another word, leaving Tedric stunned at the doorway and whatever doom he was meant to face. Had Griffin just given the reason behind their failed mission away? Had Finriel even destroyed their ship, or had that simply been a guise to keep up appearances? Tedric shook his head and replaced his surprise with a mask of calm as he knocked once against the heavy wood. On the other side was the prison of his heart, and he was about to willingly enter its clutches again after vowing not to.

He stepped into the room, the dread that was becoming a familiar friend seeping back into his bones, his eyes locking on the woman he had never wished to see again.

Aeden was still as beautiful as he remembered, her rich violet locks braided and wrapped around her head in a crown. Golden leaves and flowers were laced through her hair, framing her face in a golden halo. His eyes drifted from her eyes to her full red-tinted lips that were parted in a silent gasp. His eyes drifted lower to her thin but powerful body, draped in a dress of gold that matched the flowers and leaves on her crown. The bodice wrapped around her frame tightly, accentuating her midriff and chest. The gown drifted around her like liquid gold, pooling to the marble floor in waves.

Tedric wasn't sure if he wanted to smile or empty his guts at the sight of her, the internal fight almost unbearable. But he couldn't look away, no matter how hard he tried.

"Tedric, how good of you to join us." The deep voice rang through the room, and Tedric nearly jumped, glancing over to where the Red King was seated in a chair near a large window.

Tedric hadn't realized the king was in the room at all. The Red King smiled knowingly, and Tedric suddenly felt more sick than anything else. He gritted his teeth together as he gave a shallow bow to the king, then turned to Aeden. "I suppose I am meant to bow to you as well now," Tedric said, surprised at how calm his voice sounded in his ears.

Aeden blinked, as if she only now remembered that she was a queen. A queen who had lied and hurt him. A queen who had blood on her hands and therefore was just as cursed as he was.

"I suppose you are," Aeden replied, her voice calm, though Tedric noted the ghost of a quiver in her tone.

Tedric bowed, though he didn't remove his gaze from hers. He wasn't quite sure if he *could* look away, no matter how much he hated himself for it.

"Lovely," the Red King said and stood smoothly from the chair. "I simply wanted to be present to make sure you had received my message of the queen's request."

Tedric did not smile at these words, nor did he deign to respond as Aeden smiled and inclined her head toward the Red King. Disgust at her kindness toward the man made Tedric's gut clench, but he remained impassive as the Red King drifted toward him, the scent of roses nearly choking the air as the king paused by Tedric's ear and whispered so that only the fallen commander could hear.

"Remember what you could lose."

Tedric fought down a shiver as the Red King glided past and left through the door, leaving Tedric and Aeden standing before each other like two lost puppies. Aeden bit her lip and glanced at the floor, her discomfort nearly palpable as it filled the room.

"You must be angry with me," she said finally, and Tedric pressed his lips together.

"You lied to me." Tedric shrugged. "You lied during the entire mission."

"I know," Aeden said slowly. "And I don't expect you to ever forgive me for it."

Remember what you could lose. The Red King's whispered warning echoed through Tedric's mind, and he bit against the angry retort that formed on his tongue.

"I don't understand why you betrayed me, or your friends and entire court."

Aeden stiffened at his words. "I didn't betray my court. You have no idea how terrible my father was."

"You didn't have to murder him in cold blood for it!" Tedric roared, then took a steadying breath as Aeden's soft features hardened into a defensive mask. "I'm sorry," he murmured. "I simply don't understand why you did it. Did Krete know of what you were going to do?"

"No," Aeden said. "He knew nothing of what I was planning."

Tedric scowled. "But he knew that you were the princess of Proveria."

"Yes, and I asked him and all of the courts to keep my identity a secret so that we could complete the mission without complications on my part," Aeden replied evenly. "I also ordered him to send another message to King Drohan, ensuring Creonid's silence about my status if we were to enter the mountain during the mission as well."

"And for what? For a poisoned crown?" Tedric spat, pain of betrayal lashing through his heart.

Aeden's expression darkened at Tedric's words, and he suddenly wished more than anything to leave the room and head back to Egharis's cell. Aeden sighed and rubbed at her temple, and a flicker of curiosity went through Tedric as his eyes landed on a thin raised scar running along her inner arm. Aeden put her hand down and drifted toward the lavish bed, sitting on the edge of the silken sheets.

"You wouldn't understand why I did it, even if I tried to explain it," Aeden said finally, and Tedric snorted.

"You believe me that narrow-minded?"

Aeden shrugged. "You don't seem too pleased about my actions as of late."

Tedric clenched his fists and looked out the snow-flecked window, taking a moment to mull over his next words. "Aeden, you lied during the entire mission. You killed your father and used your friends to gain a throne. You betrayed us and nearly got us killed in the process, and worked with the Red King toward something we spent three moons trying to stop, so forgive me if I'm a bit slow to understand your actions."

Aeden's face fell, and she whispered, "I'm sorry."

"You're sorry?" Tedric bellowed. "I'm cursed for the rest of my life because of you! I can't eat or drink without being sick, unless I take whatever poison the Red King shoves down my throat so that I remain his faithful dog."

The room was bathed in silence for a moment that felt like an eternity. Then Tedric growled as another thought flitted through his mind, and his heart constricted. "I loved you, Aeden."

Tedric barely even noticed the words flying from his mouth, but Aeden's sharp intake of breath made him lift his gaze to meet hers. She stood, green eyes wide as she took a tentative step toward him. "Tedric—"

"Don't." Tedric threw a hand up, and she stilled. "I don't need to know why you did it. I only need to know what sick game you've entangled yourself in with the Red King."

"I can't tell you that," Aeden replied softly.

"He's building an army of beasts. I can only guess what he wishes to do with it," Tedric said. "Has he ordered you to rally forces?"

Aeden shook her head. "I can't tell you. The Red King has his reasons for the things he does. It will all be revealed in due time, and he will rely on your services to help him in the future."

Tedric swallowed the curse before it fell from his lips, terrible resolve settling over him as she spoke. She would not yield, would not tell him a shred of information in this state. Their trust had been broken too badly for her to tell him anything.

Remember what you could lose.

Tedric bit down on his lower lip as a tumult of feelings wrestled inside him. He couldn't help the Red King—not until he knew for sure that he meant no harm to the seven kingdoms and that he wouldn't sacrifice the lives of others to get whatever it was that he wanted. But he also wouldn't get any information unless he acted the role he'd been assigned. Tedric swallowed his self-disgust as he looked at Aeden, who watched him with that same unyielding iciness. At that moment, she looked the role of a queen—cold and emotionless.

"Why did you send for me?" Tedric asked finally.

That cool mask slipped slightly as Aeden returned to her perch upon the edge of the bed. "Is it so bad that I simply wanted to see you? You were nearly dead when the Red King took you from Proveria."

Tedric forced a lazy grin to form on his mouth as he gestured down at himself. "I am as good as ever. Demoted to a simple guard who is cursed for the rest of his days."

"But you're alive," Aeden said, and there was something in the tone of her voice that made Tedric's heart clench.

"I am, and you look well."

Aeden's eyes narrowed at him. "I look well? That's a terribly basic compliment to give a queen."

Tedric laughed, ignoring the sick feeling that grew in his stomach. *She betrayed you.* "I would give you a witty reply in return, but I'm afraid that I haven't been in the proper company to do so."

Aeden smiled, though not as widely as he had hoped. He knew they both thought of Lorian at that moment, as the thief was nothing but witty remarks for the duration of their mission.

"I've missed you," Tedric said and found that it felt too much like the truth.

Even though she had killed his trust and ruined the lives of innocents in order to become queen, he *had* missed her. Perhaps it was his fault for falling in love with a monster. Aeden stilled and watched him like a bird of prey as he took two steps toward her.

Remember what you could lose.

"I thought my betrayal would have ended any feelings you may have felt for me."

Tedric shook his head. "I can't stop feeling something that quickly. And seeing you now... It's difficult not to feel something."

Perhaps he could do this. Perhaps he could hang on to whatever shred of hope he had that she and the Red King were not planning on destroying the realm and use it to his advantage.

She betrayed you.

Aeden took in a deep breath and watched Tedric's movements as he took another slow step toward her, his muscles growing tense with both the desire to run away and to wrap her in his arms. It was a disgusting feeling, he finally decided, but relented as he stopped before her, their knees brushing against each other.

"And what is it that you feel?" Tedric asked, lowering his voice to a near growl.

I hate myself for this. I cannot hurt her this way, no matter how badly she hurt me.

But still, he watched her, ignoring the voice screaming inside his head to run. Aeden looked at him through her thick dark lashes, sending a terrible sensation of excitement coursing through Tedric's veins that made the self-loathing rear its ugly head.

"I've missed you too," Aeden replied. "More than I'll ever care to admit."

I cannot do this. I cannot.

Remember what you could lose.

Tedric cursed under his breath as his inner voice fought with that of the Red King's, and Aeden stiffened. Tedric shook his head, forcing a faint smile to cover up the agony he felt inside.

This is your only way of getting more information about what the Red King might be planning to do with the army and what his relationship with Aeden's court might mean.

"It's difficult, knowing what's right when it conflicts with what you feel inside," Tedric murmured and lifted a hand to brush his fingers across Aeden's warm cheek.

He could have sworn she shivered at his touch, and he ignored the lurch of dread as he focused instead on the butterflies that flitted feebly in his stomach.

This isn't right. You cannot do this.

"I don't think I've heard you say something more true since I've known you," Aeden replied with a sad smile.

Tedric let his hand drift down her shoulder, his fingers brushing the hard plating of her gold dress. "How in the world did you get into this thing?" Tedric asked, half to himself.

Aeden laughed. "You don't want to know. It would be quite a bit easier to take off, I think."

She killed her father, and she lied to you.

"Is that so?" Tedric raised his brow, focusing only on the terrible excitement beginning to course through his veins.

This was wrong. This was so terribly wrong. He couldn't do this. He wouldn't do it.

Remember what you could lose.

Tedric took a step back, common sense flooding his senses. He wouldn't stoop to her level to get what he wanted. It would make him no less of a monster than she was. But at that moment, something strange filtered through him, almost like the sensation of just realizing one is intoxicated. Tedric sighed and shook his head, and Aeden frowned.

"What's wrong?"

Tedric shook his head again. "The curse. It's still something to get used to, even with the potion."

Aeden chewed on her bottom lip as she nodded. "Indeed it is. Though the potion helps take the edge off a bit."

So she was being given the same potion, then. That was one bit of information that could be useful. Perhaps the Red King was using it as an advantage over her, or perhaps she was working with him on whatever secret plan he had of her own accord. Tedric stepped toward her again and reached a hand out to touch Aeden's cheek once more.

Remember what you could lose.

Goddesses be damned.

"Perhaps you and I aren't so different after all," Tedric whispered, and Aeden's eyes fluttered closed as he leaned down and brushed a kiss against her lips.

Aeden answered the kiss with enthusiasm and brought her hand around the back of his neck to pull him closer. Tedric couldn't stand the longing that filled him, could not stand that what he was about to do went against everything he had ever believed to be right. But Tedric only deepened the kiss, letting his hands brush along her bodice as he shoved down the nearly sickening guilt. Tedric could not win this fight the valiant way, the right way. No. In order to find the serpent's lair, he had to become one and make himself a home within the darkness.

15

FINRIEL

Finriel kept her gaze trained ahead as she and Lorian made their way through the slowly thinning mist, her stomach churning wildly as she caught a glimpse of something sleek glide through the water beneath the small boat.

"We're going to be stuck here forever, aren't we," Finriel grumbled, more of a statement than a question.

Lorian was huddled in his cloak near the front of the boat, his eyes watching the strange shapes of water creatures below them glide in and out of sight. The thief shrugged and glanced up at her. "I doubt it will be forever. I can assure you that whatever odd beasts are lurking down there would be glad to make our time on the boat quite short."

Finriel gulped and injected a bit more of her weakening power into the phantom wind, which she was manipulating to move their boat through the Sandrial Waters. She had never felt so lost in her life, and that was saying a lot.

"Screw us to the Nether." Lorian groaned. "We are so incredibly stupid."

"Speak for yourself," Finriel retorted, her wearing nerves not helping much in keeping a good mood toward her companion.

"The map. Maescia had to have remembered to stick it into one of our cloaks," Lorian said, completely ignoring her comment.

Finriel groaned, cursing herself for her narrow-sightedness in their hurry to leave. She ignored the faint splash of something to the left of the boat as she momentarily released her magic from moving them forward and ruffled through her pockets. Worry flopped in her stomach when she found only the page of the rakshasa in the folds of her inner pockets.

"I don't have it," Finriel said, but Lorian pulled out a folded piece of yellowing parchment Finriel instantly recognized as the map the Red King had given the companions for their mission to find the storyteller's beasts.

"Good thing I do," Lorian replied with a smile, and Finriel released a sigh of relief.

"Where are we?" she asked and reached her hand out to send them forward once more.

The mist continued to lift, revealing a weak sunset bathing the dark waters in a fiery glow. Lorian gazed down at the map and chewed his lip, clearly mulling something over in his mind. Finriel glanced down at his full lips, and her heart gave a sickening lurch. That night still played on repeat in her mind, but they had both stopped it, and Lorian had seemed all too eager to make the kiss end. There was no time to think about it now anyway. They were lost at sea, and Finriel wasn't sure the creatures below were harmless.

"What is it? Where are we?" Finriel asked again, and Lorian seemed to shake out of his reverie as he looked up at her, then back down at the map.

"We're nearing the gulf that divides the southern regions of Keadora and Proveria."

"We should find a place to hide in Proveria and send a message for Krete to take us back to Creonid," Finriel said, the thought of being back within the enormous mountain more alluring than their current situation.

Lorian shook his head. "Aeden and the Red King will be expecting that of us. We can't go anywhere they would expect."

Finriel bit her lip in growing frustration. "And where exactly would they not expect us to go?"

"Farrador," Lorian said quickly, and Finriel almost laughed.

"Are you serious? You and I both know Farrador is not a welcoming kingdom, especially not to you."

Lorian grimaced, and she was sure he was thinking about his family, his mother stripped of her title and wealth for falling in love with a human, and Lorian's own difficult childhood, all for being a half-breed.

"They won't look for us there," Lorian said in a clipped tone. "We'll be safer there than in any of the other kingdoms. Unless you'd like to try your hand at stepping into Crubia?"

Finriel rolled her eyes. "You're not being funny right now."

"I'm not trying to be funny. Going into the death kingdom and shriveling up is likely the safest that we'll ever be at this point."

Finriel sighed, mulling over Lorian's words. He had a point. They were wanted by the Red King and still in possession of two pages they had been hired to find and give back to him.

"You want to see Nora, don't you?" Lorian said softly, and Finriel snapped her attention back to the thief, nodding once in reply.

It was true. She missed the enormous feline greatly. The mogwa had been her only friend for the past ten years. Finriel hoped Krete was taking good care of Nora, if he wasn't currently on the run from the Red King or Aeden himself.

"We can send him a message to bring her back to you once we reach dry land again," Lorian said, his hard expression softening slightly as their gazes met.

Finriel nodded again, but her mood didn't lift. It wasn't only

Nora's absence that caused the ever-present roiling in her stomach. It was everything and nothing all at once. Her thoughts and feelings were muddled, and every time she grasped for a strand of logic to her emotions, it would slip away like an eel in water.

"I hardly learned anything from Lizabet," Finriel said, and a fresh wave of frustration rolled over her frazzled senses.

Lorian's gaze softened, and Finriel dropped her gaze to the wooden planks of their small boat.

"But you did learn something," Lorian offered. "It's not every day that someone learns how to slice a tree in half."

"What good will that do me when we're fighting the Red King?" Finriel let out a huff of indignation. "I feel like an idiot. I should have pushed Lizabet to teach me more."

Warm comforting skin slid over her knee, but Finriel tensed nonetheless as Lorian took her hand that had been resting on her leg. Electric pinpricks everywhere their skin touched made her pulse lurch, but Finriel didn't pull away. Instead, she looked up at him and was again struck by the beauty of him, and also the wonder of how her best friend had grown to become a good man, despite the fact that he was a wanted criminal. He smiled faintly, but there was still that pain in his eyes that made her bite the inside of her cheek.

"You are more powerful than you think, Finriel. Remember what Alima said. You're a fireling or whatever nonsense she called you. Lizabet could have taught you countless things, yes, but she would have never truly been able to teach you how to use your true powers."

Deep down she knew he was right, but it didn't stop the frustration.

"I just wish there was someone else out there who had my magic," Finriel said. "It would be a lot less—"

"Lonely?" Lorian offered, and Finriel nodded.

"It's terrifying if I'm honest," she admitted. "I only follow what feels right when I use my fire. Everything I did was pure luck on our mission, not real skill."

Lorian's smile grew into a grin, and he squeezed her hand again. "Well, it takes real skill to pretend to know what you're doing, and you fooled all of us wonderfully."

Finriel rolled her eyes, but a small smile made its way onto her mouth as he let go of her hand.

"I know someone in Farrador that can keep us undercover, maybe even help us if we ask nice enough," Lorian said. "Maybe with some cover, you can keep practicing what Lizabet taught you and explore whatever else you can do."

"I wasn't aware that you had any friends in Farrador anymore," Finriel said, furrowing her brow in confusion, and Lorian clenched his jaw.

"I'm not sure I would consider him a friend." Lorian shook his head. "But he's the only chance we've got."

"So what, then? We just sit in this boat and skirt along the continent until we reach Farrador?" Finriel asked, trepidation making her bite her cheek again at the thought of having to ride in the boat through the night, especially with the strange water creatures following them.

"I think it's our safest option," Lorian said and tilted the map so that she could see the intricate lines of the realm in the quickly dimming light.

"How long will it take?"

"Seven or eight days, if we stop on the western border by Proveria's eastern border." Lorian pointed at the small outcropping of land by Proveria's eastern border.

"Where is this mysterious friend of yours located?" Finriel asked, and Lorian's face darkened slightly when he replied.

"Mitonir."

"Mitonir?" Finriel echoed.

"I am wanted there for aiding in the kidnap of the queen's

lover, but I think they should have forgotten by now," Lorian said.

"That was you?" Finriel gaped. "The news was in every last corner of Keadora when that happened."

Lorian gave her a sheepish look. "They said I could pick anything I wanted in exchange for being a distraction."

"What did you take?" Finriel asked with narrowed eyes.

Lorian looked away toward the water. "I don't remember. It's been three years."

"You don't want to tell me," Finriel countered.

"You wouldn't want to know," Lorian replied, his tone harsh and nicking pain into her heart.

She clenched her jaw, hating that he affected her as much as he did. He looked at her, and his expression softened at the look on her face.

"I'm sorry," he murmured. "It wasn't one of the best jobs in my career. I don't really like thinking about it."

Finriel shook her head and shrugged, hoping that it was enough for him to know she wasn't angry. She would have wanted to blow his head off just a few months ago, but now she only wanted to take his hand, to hold his pain. Finriel gulped and ushered the boat forward a bit faster as her thoughts began to race. She was still getting used to the unfamiliar sensation that swept over her every time she looked at him, but she still worried that their kiss in the cottage had been a mistake, that it had been a passing moment of heightened emotions and he didn't feel that way anymore. She shook her head as if the thoughts would fly out of her mind that way and looked out at the misty expanse before them.

"Traveling through Farrador might prove to be a bit more dangerous than it was during our mission," Finriel warned, and Lorian smiled.

"I'm a thief, and we'll be traveling through my home kingdom. I'm quite confident we will be perfectly safe."

16

AEDEN

Aeden's footsteps were almost silent as she strode down the marble hallways of the Crimson Castle, the scent of roses thick in her nostrils as she approached the Red King's council chamber. She followed closely behind a stiff-backed guard, the short man walking quickly in front of her.

Part of her wondered if his quick pace and shallow breathing were because of Aeden herself. It wasn't very often that a fairy visited Keadora, and a queen no less. Aeden didn't pay the guard any mind as they made their way through the castle, however. Her mind was too focused on the night before.

She hadn't expected Tedric to even agree to see her, much less sleep with her. But he had, and Aeden could not keep herself from shivering at the memory of his hands upon her skin. The night had been passionate, though Aeden had felt a deep anger within the commander-turned-guard as they'd held each other. He hadn't said a word about forgiving her either, but Aeden hadn't cared while he kissed her, nor did she find herself caring right now. For a part of Aeden knew that he would never forgive her. It was the same part of her that hated herself. If she could not have all of Tedric, then this small bit of his forgiveness would be enough.

Aeden's attention was brought back to the castle as she and the guard approached two large double doors flanked by guards on either side. They pulled the door open without a word, and the guard leading Aeden ushered her in before hurriedly bowing toward the room itself and scurrying out before the doors closed behind him.

"Good morning," Aeden said, bowing to the Red King, who sat upon his iron throne, looking at her with a glint in his eyes that made an uncomfortable shiver run down her spine.

"It has been a good morning, at least for you," the Red King replied, and it took all Aeden could muster not to screw her face up in disgust at the king's implication.

"I am a queen, you know. You ought to treat me with more respect," Aeden said, doing her best to keep her voice even beneath a sudden strangling rage inside.

The Red King tilted his head to the side and considered her for a moment before snapping his fingers. A small door to Aeden's left opened, and the gnarled figure of the Red King's faithful gargoyle emerged from the darkness.

"Agonur, find the queen a seat," the Red King said. "And her morning tea, please."

Agonur bowed low before turning and hobbling back through the same door from which he had come.

"I do think a bit of tea will set your mind at ease," the Red King said with a smile. "I've been told that the curse is a pestering thing."

Aeden clasped her hands behind her back, flinching at the raw spots in her palms where she had accidentally cut herself with her own nails during the meeting with Krete.

"Why have you called me here?" Aeden asked, changing the subject from the gnawing discomfort that was beginning to settle throughout her body.

"I need to speak to you about a few political matters. Quite boring, I know, but I thought it would be better to speak about this in person rather than over letters."

The small door opened, and Agonur shuffled through once more, this time holding a steaming chalice. A wooden chair with a satin seat upholstered onto it floated through the air, trailing after the gargoyle almost lazily as the strange creature approached.

"Your Highness," he rasped, bowing as he held out the chalice toward her.

Aeden took the tea with an inclination of her head, her hands nearly shaking as she reached for the steaming contents that would help ease the growing tremors of the curse within. Agonur flicked a gnarled long-taloned hand toward the chair, and it settled onto the floor with a soft thud.

"Anything else for you, my lord?" Agonur asked, and the Red King shook his head.

"That is all, Agonur. Leave us now."

The gargoyle bowed once more and shuffled out of sight, the door clicking shut behind him. Aeden sat on the chair, the hard wood more uncomfortable than she knew it truly ought to be. She tried not to squirm with the desire to stand as she rearranged her gown of periwinkle and lace around herself in a more becoming manner—a habit she had formed since her formal schooling at a young age.

Aeden lifted the goblet to her lips, taking in a mouthful of the hot bittersweet tea. She fought off a gag as it coated her tongue, knowing perfectly well that all she had to do was take a few more sips for it to begin taking effect. She then would enjoy the notes of sweetness that blended with whatever unsavory herb had been used to make the concoction. Aeden took another mouthful of the tea and swallowed it quickly before looking back up at the Red King, who was watching her intently.

"What political matters do you wish to speak of? I've been

feeding you information about everything that goes on in my meetings. I have nothing to hide," Aeden said, and the Red King steepled his long fingers together in front of him.

"It is nothing about what has been already happening in your kingdom. This is more on the subject of a new development I wish to incur upon both of our lands," the Red King replied, and confusion nipped at Aeden.

What more could he possibly want, short of taking over her kingdom? She was already as much of a puppet for his doings as a queen could be. Aeden lifted the chalice to her lips once more and took a larger gulp of the substance, and the familiar tingling sensation she had grown to crave made its way through her body, sending a wave of relief through her as the tea began to take effect.

"And what would that be, exactly?" Aeden asked, trying to keep her voice calm, though she truly wanted to gasp with relief at the feeling of complete peace and hint of ecstasy that washed over her.

The trace of a smile played at the Red King's lips, and Aeden wondered if he had noted her relief. "I wish to place soldiers along the outer and inner bands of our kingdom borders."

Aeden nearly spit out her tea as she finished up the final dregs of it, almost sad to see it gone. "Why in the Nether would you want to do that?" she asked, and the Red King's eyes darkened.

"You know what I am planning, Aeden Siltra. Do not play a fool," the Red King said with a slight warning in his tone.

Aeden shook her head. "I just don't understand why you want men at the ready so soon. You don't even have a finished army yet."

"The storyteller has made nearly one hundred new beasts, and he makes more each day."

Aeden scoffed. "That is not very many."

Something dangerous glinted in the Red King's eyes then,

and Aeden set the empty chalice on the marble floor, if only to do something other than look into those obsidian eyes.

"Do not underestimate me, girl. I have more forces, more plans that not even you know about," the Red King said in almost a growl. "But having men lining both of our kingdom borders is more of a precaution anyway."

"A precaution against what?" Aeden asked, and then it hit her. "You wish to find Lorian Grey and Finriel Caligari."

The Red King made a shooing motion with one hand before clasping them together. "I care little about the thief half-breed, though I do think finding and sending him to the Nether would be useful, if only to finally have him away from the witch. No, it's Finriel that I am more interested in catching alive."

"Why?" Aeden asked, ignoring the faint pang that hit her every time she thought of her companions and their days together as they searched for and retrieved the five beasts. It felt like a distant memory now, and it was becoming easier to ignore the guilt that shot through her every time she was reminded of the pain she had caused her friends.

"Finriel Caligari possesses battle magic that can go unnoticed by the peace law's spell, and it would be useful to me," the Red King replied, and this time, Aeden did laugh.

"By the way she spat at you and threw a ball of fire at you on Clamidas, it seems a rather slim chance that she would help you of her own free will."

"That's why I will take that pesky little thing you call *free will* away from her," the Red King almost spat, and Aeden recoiled.

She had never seen him so tense before, and it struck her as odd that a girl such as Finriel would cause him to act so untethered. Perhaps it was simply because he desired to find her so badly, or perhaps . . . Was he afraid of the witch? Aeden didn't voice that thought though, and instead put the subject back on course.

"How many men are you putting inside my borders?" Aeden asked, and the Red King's face was once again a mask of pure calm.

"Fifty inside and fifty outside each main entry point of the kingdom borders, though I expect for you to make an order to begin the makings of your own army," the Red King said.

"Why so many?" Aeden asked. "If it's just to catch Lorian and Finriel, I doubt we will need that many soldiers."

"You know nothing of war." The Red King chuckled. "You have never known a battle, nor do you know the signs of how it starts. The soldiers on the borders are not only for finding the two miscreants, but also to ensure that our borders are contained and all who enter and exit between our kingdoms are monitored. Reports on all who leave or enter your border from my kingdom must be sent back to me."

"And what of the so-called army that you wish for me to build? Isn't having a force of that size unnecessary? No creature in the entire realm has fought in over one thousand years," Aeden said, a strange sense of foreboding washing through her at the idea of commanding a legion of trained fighters for a battle she knew very little about.

The Red King laughed. "I wish for an army of this size so that I can wipe out any in the realm who oppose my rule, my dear. Aside from your court, of course."

Aeden shivered. It would be a slaughter, a complete decimation of thousands of lives, all for his fist over the entire realm. And for what reason was she helping him anymore? To maintain a hold over her crown? To attempt to set the wrongdoings of her father's rule right? She might not even have a chance at maintaining order in Proveria if the Red King decided to wipe it out anytime soon.

"You are questioning your role in all of this, aren't you?" the Red King asked, and Aeden fought the urge to look away as she met his black stare.

"It's still just slightly unclear to me as to what exactly I am getting out of this agreement, aside from my head remaining on my shoulders."

"You are wise to question it." The Red King inclined his head. "A good ruler always second-guesses any agreement. You want to make sure you end up on the victorious side, not the losing one."

Aeden waited for the Red King as he considered his next words, doing her best to maintain calm even though a strange excitement coursed through her veins at what he could possibly offer her. She blinked, frowning internally at the strange greed that had crept its way into her desires. She should not feel excited about the death of thousands, perhaps even her friends, just in exchange for whatever it was the Red King might give her.

"You will get anything it is that you desire. I can order Tedric's relocation to Proveria so that he can be your personal guard or whatever it is you might desire of him."

Aeden blinked. "Why would you take him from Keadora? This is his home. What of his position as commander of the Ten?"

"You surprise me. I thought you would be excited about the offer for Tedric to become a part of your court," the Red King said, and Aeden shook her head.

"I wish for Tedric to be where he pleases because he wants it, not simply because I want it," Aeden said, and she found that she truly did mean it. No matter how much she would enjoy for Tedric to be in her company every day, she could not expect that of him, especially not when their relationship was still tense and uncertain. She didn't know if he truly forgave her for everything she had done or if their night together had simply been due to residual desires and passion that they'd only been able to express once before.

"Very well, then. We leave the decision to Tedric," the Red

King said. "But you will be free to make whatever laws you please. You could even rule the realm at my side if you continue proving yourself a worthy queen."

Rule the entire realm at his side? The Red King laughed at the obvious worry that appeared on Aeden's face.

"Don't worry. I do not wish to wed you. You may do that with whomever you please. No, we would rule together in name only, not by being bound to each other."

Aeden nodded. "That is a lot of responsibility."

"And a lot of power," the Red King reminded her. "You would have no one to answer to, no one to tell you to keep your mouth shut or that you are wrong. Imagine how free you would feel, knowing that you could rule half of an entire realm that way, doing with it as you see fit."

A shiver ran down Aeden's spine at this. She wanted more than anything to be above the words of anyone else. She had spent too much of her life being shut down and told she was wrong, too many years being forced to stand in a corner while everything she loved fell apart before her eyes. But would the Red King hold true to his word? Especially when he had already bound her to his cause and forced her to serve him through the terrible spell that was woven into the realm itself? She wished she had more of the tea left when her stomach gave an uncomfortable flop at the thought. But no, the Red King had been kind to her after that day—even welcoming, now that she thought of it. He had listened to everything she had said and given her counsel, even supported her desires.

"I simply don't understand why you wish for a war of this magnitude. It won't even be a fair fight," Aeden said almost to herself.

The Red King leaned against his throne, black eyes blazing with an expression Aeden could not quite glean. "This war will not be one-sided; I can assure you that much. My performance in Proveria during Clamidas, as well as your father's death, has caused alarm in Creonid and Farrador. Relations between Keadora and Farrador have never been very friendly, and I am certain that your little friends have already informed King Drohan of what occurred in Proveria."

Aeden thought of Krete coming to see her only four days ago, and she swallowed, knowing the Red King was right in thinking that Krete had likely informed the king of Creonid of that night's events. She attempted an easy smile and swept her violet waves behind her shoulder with a hand. "But what could King Drohan and Queen Arbane possibly be alarmed about? Your actions didn't reveal anything about wanting to take their thrones."

"Don't play the fool with me, Aeden. The storyteller let his tongue slip to your companions about my desires, and it was made quite clear that I am his employer. They do not know the full capacity of what I'm planning, but I am sure they are already doing what they can to find out," the Red King replied with a vehemence that surprised Aeden.

But he was right. Egharis had spoken to her and her companions in the dungeons of Creonid, and he'd told them that his employer wanted to virtually destroy the realm. She would not put it past Finriel and especially Lorian to put the pieces together from the Clamidas festival and the Red King's actions to know who exactly the storyteller's employer was. Aeden sighed and bit her lip.

"How can I ensure that I would get the rewards you promised?" Aeden asked.

"With my word, of course," the Red King replied. "But if you desire more, then I can let you be a part of war meetings and give you some of my own men to help train your legions. I do wish for us to have a successful victory, and I feel for you, Aeden. I know what it is to crave freedom from the rule of others and complete control over your life and the lives of others around you."

Aeden loosed another breath and nodded, meeting the Red King's gaze with a sudden jolt of excitement. She would be truly free from the threat of anyone wanting her throne. She would be able to live her life as she pleased, to remedy all of the wrongs she found in the laws her father had made, as well as the laws she found distasteful in other parts of the realm. The prospect made her heart sing, and Aeden straightened her back and lifted her chin as she spoke. "How do we stop Finriel and Lorian from rallying forces against us?"

A smile bloomed on the Red King's lips. "We throw them a party and lure them straight into our traps."

17

LORIAN

Hunger gnawed at Lorian's stomach as they continued their trek through endless miles of water, though it had thankfully been smooth sailing for the near five days since they had escaped from the Witch Isles.

Water lapped against the boat as it swayed in the water, and Finriel's chest rose and fell evenly as she slept on. Directing the boat and moving them through the unfamiliar ocean had all but drained the witch since they had started their strange journey to Farrador, and it had taken Lorian nearly halfway into their first night to convince her to rest. Lorian looked away from her and back down at the map in his hands, determining their position relative to Farrador's shores. They were getting closer. Perhaps only two more days and they would finally be able to get off this damned boat.

Lorian rolled up the map and wiped at his face, fatigue rippling through every part of his being. Sleep had been difficult for him and Finriel to muster these past five days, what with the constant swaying of the water and strange creatures that swam underneath their boat on occasion. His desire to look down into the undulating waves had subsided, and Lorian now made more of an effort to keep his gaze locked upon the endless sea beyond instead of below, if only to avoid tipping over the edge and into the mysterious depths.

Lorian's thoughts drifted from their boat to the past, to the very land they were hoping to reach before long. He wanted nothing else other than to never return to Farrador, to forget about the wretched lands and all the memories that came along with it. But he could not, and it was now his and Finriel's only chance at safety, at figuring out what their next move would be.

Finriel groaned and eased her way from the bottom of the boat, rubbing her eyes as she settled herself into a slumped seated position. Lorian watched her and smiled as their eyes met. Finriel looked around the endless ocean and faint mist, huffing with annoyance.

"What, wished you would wake up to find us magically on Farrador's shores?" Lorian said, breaking the silence.

"I'm hungry," Finriel grumbled.

"I am too," Lorian agreed. "I couldn't eat anything during your long nap, however. You were using the food stash as a pillow."

"Oh," Finriel said with the same groggy tone as she looked down and reached for the now very light sack of food that Maescia had mysteriously gotten for them.

Finriel opened the sack and looked inside, face falling as she took in the contents—or lack thereof. She pulled out a single apple that was beginning to brown in some places, along with a chunk of bread that was stale when Lorian bit into it. He grunted with disappointment but was grateful nonetheless for any food at all.

"This reminds me of our mission a bit," Lorian mused, nodding at the apple Finriel was now slicing with her dagger.

She raised a brow. "Except with slightly worse food and a lot more water."

Lorian snorted and took the half of apple Finriel handed him. It was grainy but still quite flavorful as he bit into it, and the two of them ate in calm silence with nothing more than the soft lapping of the ocean and the faint call of a bird as it flew overhead. Silence stretched over the water. Lorian had never traveled this far into the Sandrial Waters before, and a shiver ran down his spine at the possibilities of what lurked beneath the waves. They had only seen glimpses of scaly creatures drifting and gliding beneath their small boat on their first day of escape, but Lorian could only imagine what other undiscovered creatures might be watching them from below.

"Finriel," Lorian began, his heartbeat quickening as his mouth moved before his brain could prevent it.

"Yes?" Finriel replied, her brows raising.

The terrible feeling of not knowing what he wanted to say made him pause. There were too many things he wanted to say to her, but he didn't want to make things worse.

You damned fool, you know exactly what you want to say.

Lorian huffed and looked down at his hands before speaking. "About the—"

He didn't get to finish his sentence as the boat lurched to the side, like it had bumped against a rock.

"What was that?" Finriel asked, her eyes widening as she retracted the uneaten apple from her open mouth.

Lorian shrugged and attempted a smile, ignoring the sickening flop that his stomach gave as he peered over the edge of their small boat and searched the endless darkness below. The water was calm, but as he leaned back into his seat, Lorian swore his eye caught the flash of something long and scaly.

"I think we have a friend joining us," Lorian said, attempting to keep his voice as calm as possible, even as the vessel lurched again.

"Shut up," Finriel spat, her hands now braced on either side of the boat.

"I'm just trying to ease the tension before we're eaten," Lorian said, but Finriel's look of horror only grew at his words.

"We are not going to get eaten, not if we can't help it," Finriel said, but the boat lurched again, and it was now Lorian's turn to grab the sides to steady himself.

Another flash of emerald scales swam past, followed by a guttural moan that echoed across their calm surroundings. Lorian's stomach felt as though it was about to drop out of his pants at the eerie sound, and too soon, it echoed across the water once more.

"What. Is. That?" Finriel said, but Lorian could only shake his head.

"I'm afraid I don't know this time."

The still water shivered with the eerie cry of whatever lurked beneath the waves, and Lorian's stomach threatened to empty the small amount of food he'd eaten. But then the air became silent once more, and Lorian could no longer spot the flash of scales, and their boat carried on steadily.

"I am *not* okay with dying in the middle of the ocean," Finriel announced and stood to her feet with fire flickering in her palm.

But it was too late. An ear-splitting crash broke through the air, and a creature like none other shot from the water. If Suzunne had been large, this thing was enormous. Glittering green and effervescent silver scales coated a long neck and eyeless face like armor, and large gnashing teeth emerged from its mouth like an army of swords.

"I don't think your flame will do much against that thing," Lorian said, feeling quite sure that he was going to be sick.

A scream tore from the creature's maw, and Lorian clapped his hands against his ears as the boat shook and water sloshed inside. The world set into slow motion as the creature arced and dove toward them, and Finriel stretched her hands out to conjure a force field moments before teeth met flesh. The monster bounced off the force field, but Finriel let out a cry of pain as the shimmering air cracked and dissipated.

"Think of something, quick!" Finriel yelled, and Lorian scanned the boat furiously.

"Like what?" Lorian shot back, but Finriel was already struggling to produce another force field.

His mind was blank. There was nothing—

The small gray sack of food caught Lorian's eye, and he lunged for it before he could think twice. "Light this on fire as I throw it!" he yelled and dared not look straight at the enormous monster that was about to rear down on them once more.

He wasn't sure if Finriel was simply in a panic, but she didn't even balk at his command and shot a ball of flame as Lorian hurled the sack into the air. It grazed against the beast's scaled neck. The last loaf of bread and two apples flew from the sack just as it was engulfed in flame, and it fluttered toward the water. It was a good throw, and Lorian cursed in relief.

It was enough. The monster angled its head to the side and dove toward the sack and scattered food.

"Go now!" Lorian hissed, and Finriel sent a blast of wind behind them that made Lorian fly back onto his backside with a hard thud.

They sped forward, and Lorian watched as smaller creatures sped toward the floating food. Soon, the sounds of fighting and crunching bones filled the water, and Lorian thought he'd be sick for the tenth time just that morning.

"Don't stop," Lorian commanded, and a pang went through his chest at the sight of Finriel's sweat-coated skin and shaking hands.

But she did not stop, and soon, the sounds of fighting faded away as they were engulfed in the mist.

"What was that thing?" Finriel gasped, taking a short break. The wind had thankfully picked up and pushed their boat along at a slow but steady pace.

Lorian shook his head. "I don't know. I've never heard or read about it in my life."

"Me neither." Finriel shuddered. "It's as if it's been a secret until now."

"Must have been," Lorian said. "Or maybe whoever has come across it just hasn't lived to tell the tale."

"Don't say that," Finriel snapped, but by the slight fall in her expression, Lorian could guess she'd had the same thought.

"Let's just pray to the goddesses, and even Nex, that it doesn't find us again."

18

TEDRIC

Cold wind nipped at Tedric's face as he stood in a field that was once covered in vibrant flowers of varying colors but was now blanketed by a fresh layer of snow. The gravestone was a spire of darkness within the sea of white, and Tedric stared at it numbly. His whole being was numb, from the tips of his fingers to the shattered remains of his heart. There was nothing written on the gravestone, and the tilled earth Bordin had strewn over his father's dead body was now covered in snow. Tedric was almost glad not to see the evidence, to only be able to see the dark stone as an indication of where his father now lay.

Memories flashed through his mind in quick succession. His father, smiling at Tedric after teaching him how to ride a horse and laughing the first time he fell off of one. His father, showing Tedric how to use a sword, as well as how to chop firewood and gather wild mushrooms from the small forest near the coast. His father, heaving and sick from drinking too much. His father, yelling at him for bringing up his mother's name.

His father, dead.

Footsteps sounded from behind, and Tedric quickly turned, reaching for the empty scabbard at his side as he beheld his visitor. But it was only Bordin coming up to stand next to him, wrapped up in a thick black woolen coat and black pants to match. Tedric's shoulders relaxed, and he looked back down at his father's tombstone, saying nothing as Bordin came to stand at his side.

"Thoris was a good man, aside from any of his wrongdoings," Bordin said through the whistle of the wind.

"I did my best to keep him alive, to help him feel like there was more life worth living," Tedric muttered, shaking his head.

"He did the best he could," Bordin replied. "And so did you, lad."

"My best clearly wasn't good enough, or else my father wouldn't be buried at my feet," Tedric said, blinking quickly against threatening tears.

"It's not your responsibility to make someone else happy with their life. It's up to that person to wake up every day and decide if they want to live it or not."

Tedric looked to his old friend, at the flecks of snow that flurried around his brown hair now streaked with a few gray strands. Bordin was growing older, and Tedric only now noticed that the man was clearly ten years his elder.

Bordin met Tedric's gaze with a sad smile and reached up, giving him a hard clap on the shoulder. "Come, let's get you somewhere warm. A good drink will settle the spirits."

Tedric snorted. "Drinking to ease the pain of my dead alcoholic father, how fitting."

Bordin gave him an apologetic smile as he led Tedric away from the grave and toward Crimson City, the arches of Crimson Castle now nothing more than a faint outline in the thickening snowstorm. They trudged through the blizzard in silence, and Tedric was grateful that Bordin let him be with his thoughts as they made their way past the city walls and down a large street, now empty of vending carts and citizens. The shutters of homes and shops had been shut in preparation for the storm, and Tedric wrapped his heavy woolen cloak tightly around himself as they wound through Crimson City and found glowing witchlight near the entrance of a nameless pub, the door still open and welcoming even though the wind had picked up and snow was beginning to pelt against Tedric's and Bordin's backs.

The warmth of the pub stung against Tedric's frozen face as he followed Bordin into the building lined in witchlight, a roaring fire crackling merrily at the far end of the room. Laughter and loud conversation crashed into Tedric's senses, and he blinked in surprise to find such a large amount of people inside, sitting in booths and tables, as well as on seats along the bar that was a near-perfect circle in the center of the large room. Witches and men alike were gathered around, enjoying drinks and hearty vegetable stew as they watched the strengthening storm outside from the comfort of the large pub.

"Come, there's an empty booth by the fire," Bordin said, gesturing toward a small round table flanked by two empty seats right next to the fire.

Tedric followed, grateful he had taken the potion again that morning, for the strong smell of ale and cooked vegetables would have surely made him sick instead of tempted if he had let the curse take its toll that day. Tedric took a seat next to Bordin and settled in comfortably with his back now warmed by the delicious fire. Finriel's fierce scowl drifted into his mind at the thought of the flames, but Tedric was quickly torn from his reverie when a plump woman wearing a simple blue dress and a head of wild strawberry blonde curls ambled toward them, a friendly smile on her young face.

"Two hot ciders, and a stew for this one," Bordin said, pointing a thumb toward Tedric as he spoke.

"Coming right out for you, Commanders," the woman said with a smile, then curtsied before heading toward the large bar, where a large balding man worked, making intricate drinks and pouring ale from a large tankard.

"She called us both Commander," Tedric said with a hint of confusion, and Bordin chuckled.

"They're all unused to the sudden change in position, and none of the members of the Ten have had the heart to tell anyone of your change of position," Bordin replied. "I think everyone here just thinks you've been injured and are recovering before you can take back your position."

Tedric blinked as the woman returned with two steaming mugs and a large bowl of thick stew, setting them down on the table with another smile.

"Anything else for you two?" the woman asked.

"Maybe later. Thank you, Meredith." Bordin winked, and Tedric thought he saw a blush reach the woman's cheeks as she curtsied again and drifted off to tend to other customers. "She's a pretty one," Bordin said with a nod toward Meredith, and Tedric nodded, though rather halfheartedly.

Bordin seemed to notice this, and he raised his brow. "What's wrong with you? You used to always have an eye out for the ladies."

Tedric shrugged and lifted the cider to his lips. "I suppose I haven't been in the mood recently." Tedric took a large swig of his drink, the warm liquid burning slightly as he swallowed.

Bordin nudged the bowl of stew toward him and nodded. "You're beginning to look like a little boy again. Eat."

Tedric gave his friend a sidelong look but obliged, grabbing the spoon Meredith had set on the aged wooden table and dipping it into the thick soup. Flavors burst through his senses, and Tedric found that his stomach didn't give its usual lurch of sickness at the entrance of food.

"Tell me," the commander began. "What happened on that mission? I've only heard rumors and whispers of some valiant quest on which you fought dangerous beasts and wooed pretty women."

Tedric snorted as he shoveled another mouthful of stew into his mouth, deciding his next words carefully as he chewed. "I fought one beast and tried, then promptly failed at wooing a singular woman," he replied, his heart giving a painful squeeze at the mention of Aeden and the bed they'd shared only the night before.

Bordin remained silent for a moment as he drained the remains of his ale, then yelled at Meredith over the din for another pint. "It's that new queen of Proveria, isn't it?" he asked, and Tedric had to keep himself from cringing in surprise at Bordin's proclamation, even if it was correct.

Bordin laughed. "Come on. I know she joined you on the mission. It was clear something had happened between you when we met on Clamidas. The tension between you two was palpable."

"You don't even know the beginning of it," Tedric grumbled and reached to drain the rest of his cider as well, the burn of alcohol now welcoming inside his once roiling stomach.

Meredith sidled over to them, two even larger mugs held in her hands. Bordin smiled as she set their drinks on the table and winked before she turned and sashayed away.

"Come on, Tedric. I've known you since you were a young boy and I was nothing more than a stupid young lad," Bordin said, but Tedric did not answer.

He hadn't spoken of the mission to anyone, hadn't even allowed himself to think of the memories, good or bad. But perhaps it was time to share the memories and unravel the mystery of how he never noticed Aeden's deceit throughout the entirety of their mission. Tedric released a sigh, and a pleasant lightness washed over him as the cider began to take its effect.

"All right, I'll tell you, but brace yourself. It's a long story, and I have to admit that I made very stupid decisions on quite a few occasions," Tedric said, his head feeling less filled with worries than it had in quite some time.

Bordin leaned in closer and nodded, excitement flickering in his dark green eyes, and Tedric began to tell the story.

~

"And then the black dragon offered to take us to Creonid Mountain, saying that he needed to sun his wings or something of the sort," Tedric slurred some hours later.

It was the peak of the night, and the pub roared with such laughter and yelling conversation that Bordin and Tedric were ignored in their small corner of the room. Meredith had returned with drinks throughout the night while Tedric told the story of how he, Lorian, and Finriel had started their journey before meeting Aeden and Krete in Millris Forest.

Bordin had listened to Tedric's tale with rapt attention, only speaking when asking a question or giving an exclamation of surprise. Tedric's mind was positively blurred now, but the memories of his mission were still crystal clear as he neared the end of his story.

"He offered you—but he was one of the storyteller's creations. A beast of nightmare!" Bordin exclaimed, and Tedric laughed.

"No, no. Suzunne was the kindest beast of them all, actually. Said he could see my aura among other odd things," Tedric replied and gave a rather girlish giggle at Bordin's expression of confused amazement.

"He gave himself a name? A black dragon?"

Tedric nodded enthusiastically. "Yes, and he was created for Krete no less, the small little fellow."

"What happened then? Did you arrive at Creonid Mountain?"

Tedric nodded again. "Yes, we spent two nights there. It was where we met Egharis—I mean, the storyteller."

Tedric delved into the story once more, recounting their meal with the gnome king and meeting with Egharis. Tedric told only a few details about what the storyteller had told them, though he was not drunk enough to tell Bordin absolutely everything. Confusion and something else flashed across Bordin's eyes when Tedric mentioned the curse binding Egharis to secrecy and their forced ignorance of who had employed the unfortunate storyteller.

"And then..." Tedric trailed off, his heart becoming heavy even though alcohol roared through his veins.

"And then what? You drank weird gnomish ale and partied till dawn?" Bordin joked, but Tedric shook his head.

"No... Then there was the girl."

"Ah," Bordin said, leaning back in his seat with a knowing glint in his eye. "You professed your love for her."

"What? No, I—" Tedric spluttered, but Bordin only laughed.

"Please, it's been clear throughout your entire story that you've fallen madly in love."

"I am not madly in love," Tedric countered.

Bordin raised a brow. "I'm not an idiot, Tedric. She cleaned your wounds, saved you from swallowing sand, laid her heart out to you in that mountain pass—what else could that lead to?"

Tedric glowered and took another large swig of his fifth drink, ale dribbling down the sides of his mouth as he swallowed. "Look," he said after wiping the droplets of ale from his chin. "I might have told her I loved her, and she might have said something about a mating bond before we shared the night together, but it means nothing."

Bordin frowned, lowering his mug. "A mating bond? I thought that was just old fairy lore."

"It is. It was part of her plan," Tedric almost spat, then sighed. "It was a wonderful night. She was beautiful, strong, and smart. A perfect woman."

"You're speaking of her as though she has died," Bordin mused, and Tedric swung his head toward his friend.

"She is dead, or at least the version of her I knew," Tedric replied darkly.

"What happened for you to hate her so much?" Bordin asked, his words slurring slightly.

"You were there," Tedric replied with a casual wave of his hand. "She used the portal in Creonid to take her and the story-teller back to Proveria without telling us, so we followed her and discovered who she truly was."

Shadows flickered over Bordin's eyes, and he nodded, clearly remembering the very night Tedric spoke of. "I'm surprised I didn't kill a man that night," Bordin said. "Though it was close."

Tedric smacked his lips and opened his arms, as if welcoming Bordin for an embrace. "I did kill a man to protect that damned gnome. Now I'm cursed."

"I didn't know who to fight for, if I should be with or against you," Bordin admitted, sounding far more sober than he had in the last few hours.

Tedric shook his head. "I didn't know either. That's why I tried to avoid you and the others as best as I could. But I cannot fight for the Red King anymore, not with everything I know and am continuing to find out."

Bordin's face hardened, and he lifted his mug to hover at his lips before muttering, "I'm not sure it's safe to speak of this here. I heard he has spies nowadays, watching all of us."

Anger flared in Tedric's stomach, but he forced down the bitter words that tasted foul on his tongue. He lifted his ale and washed it down, hot alcohol burning his throat and making him wince.

"And what of the queen? She's staying in the castle for the next two days, is she not?" Bordin asked, and Tedric's gave the commander a guilty look.

Bordin opened his mouth with a look of complete surprise. "You didn't sleep with her again, right?"

Tedric did not answer, and Bordin cursed.

"You did, didn't you?"

Tedric shrugged sheepishly. "It was an accident."

"An accident?" Bordin blurted. "You just saw her and stumbled into her bed and on top of her somehow? Come now, Tedric. I'm not that stupid."

"I didn't want to do it!" Tedric exclaimed. "I didn't even want to see her."

Bordin frowned. "So then why did you do it?"

"I don't know," Tedric mumbled. "Part of it was duty, and the other part..."

They fell silent for a moment, and Tedric sorted through his jumbled intoxicated thoughts.

"Duty?" Bordin screwed up his face with either confusion or disgust, Tedric was not sure. "Duty to whom?"

"You wouldn't believe me even if I told you," Tedric bit out, anger flaring in his stomach.

The anger quickly died though, and Bordin seemed to notice his pain, his sadness. The commander clapped a hand on his shoulder, causing Tedric to sway dangerously in his seat. Tedric looked up at his friend and smiled, even though his thoughts were still on Aeden and the pain that held tight over his heart.

"Is it bad that part of me still loves her, even if she is a monster?" Tedric asked, his voice almost a whisper.

Bordin sighed. "The matters of the heart have never been something I've excelled at, which is why I stick to the bow."

Tedric shrugged and ran a hand through his likely wild-looking hair.

Bordin blew out a breath at his side. "I don't think it's bad, son. I think you are still in love with the fairy girl you stumbled upon in the forest, not the queen we all see today."

"It doesn't help that they share the same skin," Tedric grumbled.

"They are the same girl, but she chose to let the wounded side of her win, not the caring and courageous one that was so alluring," Bordin said. "So, you've got to decide. Do you want to lose the woman you fell in love with, or leave the queen and keep the memories of the one you did love inside of your heart?"

Tears threatened for the second time that day, and he scrubbed at his face, willing his sadness not to fall. "I'm much too drunk to have a conversation like this, Bordin. Let's have another ale and forget about her completely, shall we?"

Bordin gave Tedric a knowing look, but he nodded anyway and smiled. "Yes, I think that's a brilliant idea."

TEDRIC STUMBLED out of the pub with Bordin's arm slung over his shoulder some hours later, the cold bite of snow flecking across their faces as they swayed and shuffled down the road. The wind had died down now, and some part of Tedric's brain that was not completely intoxicated sent a word of gratitude to the goddesses for the storm's end.

"I can't remember the last time I was this blasted," Bordin slurred at Tedric's side, and Tedric lifted a pointed finger into the air.

"I remember the last time I was."

Bordin gasped. "When was it?"

"Never," Tedric said with a belch, and they both broke out into a fit of laughter. "Urgh, I don't think my legs can walk anymore." Tedric groaned and looked down at his legs, which looked oddly like four instead of two at the moment.

Bordin shook his head. "I think I could fall right about now. Let's just sleep at my house tonight. It's very much closer."

Tedric nodded purposefully, even though he had never been to Bordin's house in his life. "Very much closer."

They continued their wobbly journey through the snow-covered streets, and soon enough, they found themselves rounding a corner and entering the gates of a neighborhood of well-maintained stone houses. Bordin pulled Tedric toward a large two-story house with wrought iron gates and snow-flecked ivy that ran up the dark walls.

"Why are we going in there? It's much too fancy," Tedric said and began to resist slightly against Bordin's pull.

"This is my house, you idiot." Bordin hauled Tedric toward the stairs.

"Oh." Tedric giggled as Bordin opened the sturdy arched door and let him inside.

It was positively pitch black in the space, and Tedric had to fight to stay on his feet in the disorienting darkness as Bordin cursed and fumbled with something. Flame burst to life in a large fireplace a few feet away, and Bordin sat on his backside as he prodded and coaxed the fire to catch on the logs, flint and steel discarded on the stone floor beside him. Tedric lifted his head and looked around at the grand space, his jaw dropping. They stood in a large sitting room, where a grand staircase led up to the second floor. Tall windows were encrusted with snow, the darkness of the night held off by the gray flecks. A hallway beneath the stairs led likely to the kitchen and whatever other rooms existed in the grand house.

"Oh dear. I think I've lost my legs," Bordin said as he attempted to push himself up to his feet and promptly failed.

"They're right there." Tedric pointed at the commander's legs which were folded neatly underneath him.

Bordin was so silly at times.

"You're right. I've just spotted them," Bordin said with a sigh of relief and tried to push himself up to his feet again to no avail. "Don't think they work anymore." Bordin shook his head.

"Ah, well. They served you well." Tedric shrugged and stumbled toward a plush sofa across the room.

Tedric let himself plop down into the seat, the soft cushions welcoming him in a hug as he settled upon it. He let out a satisfied sigh and closed his eyes against the spinning room. His worries and pains now felt so far away, and he wondered why he had let them affect him so badly before. "I think I know why my father took up drinking. It makes all the pain inside much easier to forget."

"I might be absolutely out of my mind right now, but I don't believe that I'd want to feel like this all the time," Bordin replied, and Tedric cracked open an eye to find his friend now lying spread eagle on the floor, the fire crackling steadily in front of him.

Tedric sighed. "You're right, as always. I wonder if I will ever be as smart and lucky as you, Bordin."

Bordin snorted and shook his head against the floor. "I'm not that smart, but maybe a little bit lucky."

Silence stretched between them in a comfortable lull, and Tedric found himself drifting off to sleep with the warmth of the fire and the soft cushions holding him so tenderly. Bordin let out a long sigh.

"I might not be so lucky after all," Bordin said groggily.

"No?" Tedric forced himself to ask, though sleep still beckoned to him sweetly.

"Not at all." Bordin sighed. "I've been lucky with my safety and a good home, but I have no family and have been serving a king that I now don't know if I like all that much."

"He's a terrible red man." Tedric huffed.

"He's not—actually, I don't mind calling him that when I think about it," Bordin said. "From all the things you've said in your thrilling stories and the things he ordered me and Griffin to do..."

Bordin trailed off, but Tedric's attention perked up at this, and he suddenly felt slightly clearer in his mind. "What did he have you two do?"

"Oh, you know, just specialty things that the Ten are supposed to do," Bordin drawled. "He had us hold your fairy queen while he put some sort of binding thing on her. She smells quite lovely."

Tedric straightened as best he could even though the room spun dangerously at the sudden movement. "He put a binding spell on Aeden?"

Bordin tilted his head downward in what looked to be an attempt at a nod. "Cut her arm and everything. She put up quite a fight as we held her."

"Do you know what the binding was for?" Tedric asked, worry and something else—perhaps hope—welling in his chest.

"Not a clue," Bordin replied, his speech slurring as his eyes began to droop closed. "He only took her blood, said she couldn't be free to do something..." Bordin's eyes shut completely, and an even long breath escaped from the commander's open mouth as sleep enveloped him.

Tedric's exhausted mind began to tangle as he tried to make sense of Bordin's piece of information, but only another giggle escaped his mouth as he thought of how pretty Aeden was. And at that moment, Tedric couldn't quite remember why he'd felt so worried just a second ago, and he leaned back in his seat and closed his eyes, letting sleep finish sweeping over his tired body.

19

KRETE

"Krete, you are making my elbow numb."

Suzunne's low rumbling voice tossed Krete from his snooze, and the gnome jolted upright. "Sorry, Suzunne. I dozed off for a bit."

"I noticed," the black dragon replied. "It seems that my stories about how it feels to be in that wretched page aren't compelling enough."

Krete sighed. "Suzunne, it's the same story each time. It's black all around, yet you can move around and bump against the confines of the page."

The black dragon let out a growling sigh, and hot air billowed throughout the open cave. Krete had stopped cringing at the trembling walls that accompanied each of Suzunne's sighs or laughs some time ago, though most of the gnomes still kept far away from this sector of Creonid Mountain. Krete found it comforting, knowing that any darkness they might face, he would have Suzunne at his side.

"You make it sound far duller than it actually is." Suzunne huffed. "This is why if you listened to my stories—"

The dragon paused, his golden eyes pulsing as he focused on

something beyond the cave walls that Krete could not sense. The muscles in Krete's body tensed, and fear crawled its way into his gut.

They couldn't be in danger, could they?

"What is it?" Krete whispered, and brilliant black scales glinted in the sunlight as Suzunne shook his head.

"It's your sister."

Krete scrambled to his feet, straightening out his vest as his sister stepped through the tunnel entrance that led into the cave. She looked well, though her long mouse-brown hair looked duller, and there was a shadow of sadness across her hazel eyes.

"Brinna," Krete began. "Is everything all right?"

His sister approached Suzunne, offering him a tentative curtsy. The dragon's eyes blinked, and he said, "Hello, Queen of the Small People."

Brinna smiled. "Hello, Suzunne."

She turned to face Krete and let out a sigh, the corners of her mouth working in a way Krete knew meant she didn't know how to begin an important conversation.

"What is it?" Krete asked, nerves and fear beginning to make his skin itch.

"You're sweating a bit," Suzunne commented.

"Shut up." Krete shot a glare at the dragon before turning to his sister. "Has something happened?"

Brinna shook her head. "Not quite. It's only that Drohan and I have been discussing the events from the past few moons..."

"And?" Krete encouraged.

"And we think you need to leave Creonid for a short while," Brinna said finally, guilt making her suddenly look like a young girl again, not the queen of Creonid.

Krete took a step back, hurt and shock knocking into his chest like a physical blow. "Have I done something wrong?"

"No!" Brinna exclaimed. "No, you haven't. But you haven't

been acting like yourself since the winter solstice. We are worried about you, Krete."

Krete frowned. "I have been acting exactly like myself."

His sister rolled her eyes. "You barely sleep, you mumble to yourself constantly about your companions, and you spend most of your time in this cave with Suzunne."

"It *has* gotten on my nerves," Suzunne said. "He takes up far more space than a man of his size ought to."

Krete shot another glare toward Suzunne, but the dragon paid him no mind as he examined one of his gleaming talons.

"I'm worried is all." Krete sighed, his eyes drifting to the floor. "I was part of this whole mess. I feel responsible for it, as well as my companions."

Brinna placed a comforting hand on his shoulder and gave a squeeze, and Krete smiled weakly at her. He was grateful to have a family like Brinna and Mott, as most of his friends didn't have any family at all. His thoughts drifted to Aeden, and with a jolt of pain, he shook his head.

"The king and I are formally commanding you to find Lorian Grey and Finriel Caligari," Brinna said.

The floor nearly fell from Krete's feet.

"You want me to do *what*?" he asked, and Brinna smiled.

"We are grateful you told us everything that happened in Proveria on Clamidas, and we think it imperative that you find your friends, if only for your own sanity."

"But what does this have to do with you and the king?" Krete asked.

"It has nothing to do with us," Brinna admitted. "Though perhaps, if you find them, we can keep you all safe here in Creonid until we know what has become of the storyteller and his employer."

Anger flared in Krete's stomach. "You mean what has become of the Red King."

Fear flashed across Brinna's eyes, and she shook her head.

"We still cannot know that for sure, and I don't wish to argue with you about this again, brother. I want you to find your friends so that you may feel hope again. That, and you can give the mogwa back to the witch. The gardeners are complaining about her using the Viure as a scratching post."

Krete cringed and nodded. It was true that Nora had spent most of her time lounging on the Viure or wandering through the halls meowing so loudly that it grated everyone's ears. He was sure that she missed Finriel, and Finriel likely missed Nora just as much.

"All right." Krete sighed. "Suzunne and I will begin the search for them at dawn."

"You will have to fly above the clouds," Brinna said. "You are still wanted, if you haven't forgotten. You are only safe in Creonid because Drohan has given you legal safe haven."

"And you still question if the Red King is truly behind this madness." Krete rolled his eyes. "But you are right. I will be as safe as I can."

"Good," Brinna said, smiling again. "I will have servants prepare you food and proper attire for your journey."

Krete nodded and stepped forward to envelop Brinna in a tight hug. Since they were children, she had always known his emotions better than he did. He was grateful for it, even if it sometimes drove him mad.

"This is all very touching," Suzunne said, and Krete stepped away from Brinna.

"Thank you for taking care of him," Brinna said, looking up at Suzunne.

The dragon inclined his head. "I am bound to him through the magic of my creation. And besides, I think I'm ready for another adventure."

20

AEDEN

Excitement tickled at Aeden's stomach as a soft knock sounded on the door to her chambers. It was her last day in Keadora before she and her few guards returned to Proveria, and Aeden had every intent on making the most out of her spare time. She had sent a servant to run a note to wherever it was that Tedric lived or was stationed and made a point for the servant to find him as soon as possible.

Aeden jumped from the plush seat where she had been spending her last moments of freedom reading before a meeting with the Red King, which she was told could last many hours. She snapped the old leather cover shut and set the book on the dresser next to the seat, then crossed to a large mirror that hung on the opposite wall. Her reflection looked far better than it had in months or at least since Aeden had gotten access to a mirror again since the mission. Her violet hair was separated into two sections, the top half having been braided and situated in an intricate style that made it look similar to a crown. The bottom half settled around her shoulders in thick waves, brushing against her bare back. Her dress was an image of the night sky, with folds of midnight blue satin draped in a daring cut over her bosom and pulling in tight around her waist, puffing out ever so slightly around her hips and giving her figure more shape than the thin muscle with which she had been born. Aeden pressed down a wrinkle in her dress and pinched her cheeks to bring some color to her pale skin.

"Come in," Aeden called, and the door opened as she turned from the mirror to watch Tedric enter the room.

Aeden's spirits dropped at the sight of him. He looked positively terrible, with dark circles beneath his eyes and golden hair sticking up at all angles. The warrior looked like he had crossed into the Nether for a quick visit before returning to Raymara as an undead. Aeden forced a smile to her lips, trying to ignore Tedric's terrible state and welcome back any feelings of excitement she had felt seconds before.

"Good morning," Aeden offered, and Tedric only grimaced.

"Is it only the morning?" Tedric winced and rubbed at his head with a groan.

"You look terrible," Aeden said and found her voice layered with worry.

"I feel terrible," Tedric muttered. "Drank too much."

Aeden frowned. "And why did you drink so much?"

Tedric tensed and met her stare with a hard look. "I don't need to explain my actions to you."

Aeden only blinked, surprised at the harshness in Tedric's tone.

"Why have you called me here?" Tedric asked. "I received your note."

Aeden conjured a playful smile to her lips and took a step toward him. "Well, it is my last day here before I go back to Proveria to prepare for the coronation in two weeks' time."

Tedric only looked at her with that same tired and slightly sick expression, clearly not understanding what she was implying. Aeden bit her lip with rising frustration and took another step toward him. "I thought we might be able to spend some of that time together before we must be apart again."

Tedric's eyes widened, and Aeden guessed that he finally understood what exactly it was she was implying. He took a step back and dropped his gaze to the floor, and Aeden frowned.

"You don't want to?"

Tedric looked back up at her and sighed, taking two long strides toward her until the gap between them was completely closed. His hand was against her cheek, and his lips pressed against hers before she could think, and Aeden returned the kiss without a second thought. His tongue tasted of alcohol and apples as it swept over hers, and Aeden pressed herself into the hard planes of his body as she brought her hands into his hair. His hand traveled lazily down from her cheek to her neck, sending a trail of shivers as it brushed down her arm.

His hand clasped around her wrist, and he broke away suddenly, turning her arm over and looking down upon the long silver scar running along her milky skin. Aeden froze, panting as he inspected the scar before meeting her mortified stare.

"How did you get this?" His voice was ragged and gruff, but Aeden only shook her head.

"I've had it for years."

"You're lying," Tedric growled. "I hadn't noticed this scar until a few days ago."

"It's nothing," Aeden said, her tone hardening into a solid wall.

"The Red King did this to you," Tedric said blandly, as if what he had just said was no different than talking about the weather.

Aeden pulled her wrist from his grip and crossed her arms over her chest, both fear and anger rising within her at an alarming speed. She inspected Tedric's face and kicked herself internally as her gaze paused at his lips for a moment too long. Her skin still tingled from his touch mere moments ago, but the excitement of the kiss had worn away much too soon. Now she only wanted him to explain himself and then leave her chambers. She opened her mouth to speak, but Tedric held a hand up.

"Don't try to say otherwise. I know that he did it. I only want to know *why* he did it."

"I don't have to tell you that," Aeden replied haughtily, her arms tightening around herself.

"Aeden, how can you trust the Red King?" Tedric challenged. "He hurt you. I don't know why, but I can guess."

Aeden swallowed down her rising nerves, forcing her face to remain calm. "I couldn't even tell you if I wanted to. The Red King's motives are not mine to say."

Tedric sighed and took a step back. "I can't do this anymore, Aeden. You've completely lost your mind."

Anger flared, and before she could think, Aeden's hand flew through the air and collided with Tedric's cheek. He staggered back a step and cursed. Aeden looked at her stinging hand in shock before regaining her composure and glaring up at him.

"You will *not* insult me," Aeden spat, and Tedric only looked at her with something close to sadness, her handprint an angry red splotch against his beautiful face.

"You've gone too far," Tedric said. "And I am much too hungover for this conversation."

Tedric rubbed at his temples, and Aeden couldn't help but feel sorry for the man, even if he had just insulted and completely mortified her within thirty seconds.

"You don't want to see me any longer?" Aeden asked, her tone strong despite the current pain beginning to overwhelm her heart.

Tedric took a steadying breath, the sadness in his brown eyes an arrow through the heart as he looked down at her. "I can't see you, not if you choose to continue down whatever path of death and destruction the Red King is planning."

Aeden bit her lip, and anger flared up inside her at his words once again. "I would watch what you say. You have not even the faintest clue of what the Red King wants, or what I want, for that matter."

"Do you really want to work with him? He's treating you more like a pet than a queen," Tedric shot back.

"How dare you," Aeden spat. "I am no pet, nor would I ever let the Red King treat me as one."

Tedric clenched his jaw. "Are you sure about that? I know that the Red King put a binding spell on you with that scar, and you did nothing to stop him."

Aeden blinked and opened her mouth but closed it again when words did not form.

Tedric took a step toward her. "Aeden, what did he bind you to?"

Aeden shook her head and took a step back, her hand drifting toward the scar on her right forearm.

Tedric followed her movements with a knowing gaze and let out a tired sigh. "You are under his rule, whether you like it or not. Now, I don't know what he's planning, but I know that I won't stand for it, and I won't sleep with a woman who has betrayed and hurt me beyond my greatest imagination."

"I've told you how sorry I am," Aeden croaked and didn't fight the tear that slid down her cheek. "It was just to get my father off the throne. Tedric, please."

"It doesn't matter, Aeden," Tedric said gruffly. "You used me for your own gain the entire time and never told me, not even when I told you that I had fallen for you. You lied about who you were, and you even made up the entire mating bond foolishness just to make me feel more inclined to chase you when you left Creonid with the storyteller."

"I had to," Aeden said quietly. "It was the agreement. I couldn't go against the plan even when I wanted to so badly."

"Why not?" Tedric spat.

Aeden could almost see the pain swirling in his dark eyes as he took a step closer and put a hand around her wrist. She swallowed, and another wave of tears cascaded down her cheeks as her heart broke at the pain written so clearly across the warrior's face. Pain that she had caused.

"What is it that the Red King has over you that has turned you into such a monster?" Tedric whispered.

Aeden gasped and yanked her wrist from his grip, the skin tingling in the spots he'd touched. "You should leave," Aeden said, and Tedric's eyes widened at her dismissal.

His expression quickly molded into a hard mask, and Aeden swore she almost heard her heart crack a little bit at the sudden coldness that replaced his pain. The man that had held her, kissed her, and spent the night with her only the night before, was gone. Perhaps she would never see that man again, not after today.

Tedric nodded curtly. "Very well. I hope you know that I will not stand for whatever it is you and the Red King are brewing. I care for my people, and war would only hurt them."

"You don't know what you're talking about," Aeden snapped.

"Maybe I don't yet, but I will soon enough." Tedric promptly turned on his heel.

And then he was gone. The man that her heart had given itself to, even against her better judgment, was gone. He was gone and hated her for all that she had done to save herself and her kingdom.

A sob tore out of Aeden's chest, and she sagged to the ground, her midnight blue skirts pooling around her like a starless night sky. Her breath came out in heaving gasps as her vision blurred and tears streamed freely down her face. She was broken, her heart a shattered mess laying in her chest. Tedric's love had been one of the only things that had kept her going these past few weeks, even if it had been mostly broken on Clamidas. But now it was truly over. His cold gaze flashed through Aeden's memory, and another sob cracked her open, pain of the worst kind enveloping her entirely. A soft knock followed by the scrape of the door jolted Aeden, and a young girl walked in. She was tall, and her thick red hair was fashioned into a braid down her back.

"Hello—oh, my apologies, my lady. I did not know you were still in here," the girl said softly, curtsying as she spoke.

"No, no. It's all right." Aeden sniffed and wiped the tears away from her face with haste as she stood to her feet and brushed a hand across the crinkles in her dress.

The serving girl paused for a moment and considered Aeden, her expression changing from fear to wary kindness. She took a step forward, a wicker basket propped against her hip. "Is everything all right, my lady?" she asked, and Aeden's muscles tensed in defense.

"Yes, everything is just fine. I was just leaving."

Aeden started toward the door with as much haste she could manage without running, and the girl had to step sideways in order for Aeden not to knock into her. Aeden yanked the door open with more strength than she had anticipated, which caused it to fly open and crash against the wall.

"Make sure to change the sheets. They're dirty," Aeden called over her shoulder and promptly shut the door, muffling the girl's reply.

Aeden started blindly down the hall, not quite sure where she was headed. Her mind was too wrapped in Tedric, his decision to break away from her, and his ridiculous proclamations. She had no intent on ruining the realm. She was going to make it better, fairer. And the Red King had promised to help her do just that, as long as he got what he wanted. Maybe it was for the better. Maybe their breaking was just the thing she needed to have the room to focus on her plans and her coronation.

21

FINRIEL

F inriel's body jolted as their boat connected with solid ground, and a groan of relief escaped her mouth at the lack of swaying and bobbing from the water. Lorian threw a leg over the edge of the boat and rose onto wobbly legs, bracing a hand against the rim as he offered a hand to Finriel.

On any other occasion, she would have ignored his hand and gotten off the damn boat on her own, but right now, Finriel wasn't sure if her legs would even hold her up if she stood. Eight days on the water without standing, aside from their encounter with the sea monster, had left Finriel's legs aching with stagnation. Finriel grabbed Lorian's hands and allowed him to help her onto her wobbling legs, a strange feeling of vertigo making her vision blur as her legs still carried the sensation of being on water, even though they were on a sandy beach.

"Up and over, let's go," Lorian grunted as he half hauled, half directed Finriel's swaying body onto the beach.

"You seem a lot less affected from being on a boat for eight days than I am." Finriel groaned and braced herself against Lorian, who then staggered as they both swayed dangerously.

"Well, I've surprised myself as much as I've surprised you

with this impressive feat," Lorian replied, then snorted and pointed toward the ground. "Or should I say *feet*."

Finriel rolled her eyes and attempted to hold her own body up without Lorian's aid. After a moment, she caught her balance and managed to shuffle back toward the boat and grab their meager belongings. "Map?"

Lorian patted his cloak. "Safe and sound."

Finriel nodded and turned to look at the looming Farridian trees ahead, the sand of the beach quickly changing into hard red clay as it neared the forest border. The calm air was still bitingly cold against their faces, and Finriel tucked her chin into the warmth of her cloak as best she could. "Where are we?" she asked, and Lorian took the map from his cloak pocket.

He pointed to the illustration of a village not too far from where their small dot on the Farridian coast was placed. "We should be able to make it to that village before sundown. Maybe we can find horses there and get to Mitonir with a day of hard riding after that."

Finriel gulped at the thought of going from ocean legs to horse legs not two days apart from each other. She nodded anyway and took a deep breath. "I just need a moment for my legs to adjust to solid land before we start walking."

"ARE you sure this place is safe?" Finriel asked, eyeing the dingy inn.

They had reached the small village in a few short hours, but the shortened days of winter meant that the sun had already set by the time they reached the dark cobbled streets and buildings with smoke trailing out of their chimneys. Not a soul wandered the streets, but a merry glow pooled from the dirty windows of the unnamed inn before them.

"As safe as any other place in this village." Lorian shrugged. "Besides, a lot of bandits and men on the run stay here."

Finriel paused, her foot hovering inches above the rickety steps leading up to the dust-smeared establishment. "That makes me want to stay here even less."

Lorian sighed from behind, and Finriel turned to look at him.

"I've stayed here loads of times," Lorian said.

"Your point being?"

"A lot of half-breeds and other races stay here. This place is safer for us than any other inn in Farrador. They won't question a witch within their walls, just as they won't question me in there. There's also the fact that we're wanted criminals, and almost half of the people in there likely are as well."

Finriel opened her mouth, then promptly closed it. He had a point, and by the tired droop of his shoulders and her own over-whelming fatigue, they had no other choice.

"Fine," Finriel said, and Lorian gave her a tired smile before leading the way.

An uproar of music and hearty conversation assaulted Finriel's senses as Lorian opened the door, revealing a large room nearly filled to the seams with people. Mingled smells of ale, fire, and sweat made Finriel's nose crinkle, but she shoved away the discomfort and schooled her face into neutrality, just in case someone were to look in their direction. She let Lorian take her hand and lead them through the masses, who thankfully paid them no mind as they made their way to the front counter.

"A room for the night, as well as some food if you have any left," Lorian said to the elderly elf woman, who despite her years, looked regal and not at all like the owner of this place.

She nodded, not looking up from the stack of papers strewn before her. "Two shillings," she said in a low voice, and Lorian placed two dull silver coins on the table without a word.

The elf woman took the money, and Finriel glanced at him sidelong. She had no money to her name and was certain he'd used the rest of his stolen money from Naret for their fare to the Witch Isles. Apparently, she was wrong.

"Stew is about to be served to those who paid, and your room is the first one on the right," the woman said, pointing toward a corridor behind the throng of tables before slapping a worn iron key on the counter.

"Thank you," Lorian said with a smile, though the woman still hadn't looked up and paid him no mind. He grabbed the key and folded it into Finriel's hand, moving them to the side of the bar. "I'm going to find us horses. Get some food and then go straight to the room. Don't let anyone talk to you."

Finriel opened her mouth to reply, but he had already turned away, the warmth of his hand fading from her skin as he wove through the crowd of people and disappeared into the night.

A huff pushed past her lips, and a sudden feeling of unease swept over her. The urge to run into their rented room and lock the door until Lorian returned was almost overwhelming, but the pain in her stomach made her feet stay rooted to the floor. Food first, then she would escape to the safety of solitude.

She eyed the crowd, fully taking in the array of frayed cloaks and weary faces. There was an even mix of men and women, though they all looked equally haggard. A single man played a lute, his fingers weaving expertly over the instrument as he sang a merry tune. A few people sat at their tables, perfectly content watching the musician, while others clustered in groups and spoke in hushed voices, and others roared with boisterous laughter.

"Stew and bread." The voice cut through Finriel's observations, and she spun around to find a steaming bowl of stew and a chunk of thick white bread next to it.

Finriel looked up to see a hunched figure shuffle toward the back of the bar, where a shoddy kitchen made up of a large fire and iron cauldron took up half the wall. She took the wooden bowl and bread before turning into the throng. A single table by the wall caught Finriel's eye, and she moved for it, making sure to keep her head down and her breath even. She was never one for crowds, and now being alone in one after a week on open water made her dizzy.

The table was thankfully vacant when Finriel reached it, and she pulled out one of the chairs before sitting down and hunching over her meal. The stew was surprisingly good, though slightly over-salted. The bread was buttery and light, and Finriel sent a silent prayer to the goddesses that it wasn't like the dark bread she'd been forced to eat every day for three moons.

"An ale for you, miss."

The unfamiliar voice made Finriel jump, and she looked up at her visitor. Shock made her freeze at the sight of long limbs and tresses of long golden hair. A round face framed golden eyes and a kind mouth, which tilted up in a smile.

Finriel quickly schooled her expression, shaking her head. "I didn't ask for ale."

The Sythril's smile didn't waver, and they simply sat across from Finriel, placing a clay cup in front of her bowl. The hairs on Finriel's arms raised in alarm as she eyed the fairy, remembering Lorian's advice not to speak to anyone. But she couldn't help the curiosity that nagged at her stomach, and the question bubbled over before she could stop it.

"Where is the rest of your group?" she asked, glancing at the crowd for any signs of more Sythril.

The one before her shook their head, their smile waning slightly. "I come here alone."

"Why?" Finriel asked. "I thought your kind stayed in groups."

"We do, but we can be cast away if the collective thinks us unworthy," the Sythril replied, their calm tone unwavering.

Finriel suppressed a shudder at the Sythril's words. "You were banished?"

"Matters of mine are of no importance," the Sythril said. "I have come to you with a warning."

Finriel's heart leapt into her throat, but she forced a half-hearted chuckle and shook her head. "Not another prophecy. The last one didn't even come to pass."

"Didn't it?" they replied, and Finriel paused.

"Think of everything that has happened of late," the Sythril continued. "You were sent on a mission of great importance and discovered the beasts you once thought to be dangerous—"

"Were actually kind to us," Finriel finished for them.

Each key will play their part in the game, but not until they are reunited with their locks.

They nodded. "One of your companions has proven to be a liar, a snake in the rose garden, so to speak."

Some players of this game are not who they seem, and you will all feel the sharp pain of betrayal when the serpent is revealed.

Tension clawed its way into Finriel's body, landing like a block of iron in her stomach. The prophecy was real, and things had already come to pass. Aeden's betrayal, the Red King's mysterious plans, the beasts.

"The storyteller told us he created the beasts for us," Finriel said, remembering their conversation with the strange man in Creonid. "He said that he knew of the prophecy."

The Sythril nodded grimly. "He was the catalyst of the prophecy's beginning, though also a reason for us to feel hope."

"And the war..." Finriel said, her mind grasping to remember the prophecy's entirety.

Blood is coming. The age of peace has come to an end, and the time of war has begun.

"It is nearly upon us," the Sythril said, "which is why I must warn you not to let your beasts out of their pages."

Confusion made Finriel set down her bowl and stare at the

Sythril. "I thought we needed to be reunited with our locks, so to speak. How can we do any good if they're locked away?"

"You and your friends are in great peril, and your beasts even more so. Though they were made to serve you, they are still beasts. It will be difficult to form a connection strong enough to have them under your command or as equals."

Finriel thought of Suzunne and shook her head. The dragon was kind and seemed to enjoy working with her companions. His bond with Krete seemed strong enough, but then again, he hadn't tried to kill them upon their first meeting, where the chimera and Rey had.

"I don't understand." Finriel shook her head. "We are going to be in danger until this mess blows over. I can't see how waiting now will give us any other chance to let them out in the future."

Something close to sorrow crossed the Sythril's golden eyes at this, and they placed a delicate hand on the grimy table. "I have seen a vision of a witch and a man in a place of sand and stone. Only when you have reached this place can you free your beast from its page and learn its ways."

A place of sand and stone. Finriel mulled over those words, but her confusion only grew. There was no such place in Raymara that she knew of, though perhaps there was some hidden valley in Creonid or Drolatis that they would find.

"Do you know when we will come across this place?" Finriel asked, and the Sythril's expression hardened.

"Sooner than you deserve."

"What does that mean?" Finriel asked, but they only shook their head.

"I have already said more than I should've. It is why my cluster banished me, but I found no other option than to find you and warn you of the danger that will come if you let your beasts out now."

"One beast is already free," Finriel said, thinking of Suzunne again.

"Yes, but he was always meant to be free. The smallest key is one of the strongest parts of the game, but he would have not gotten a chance to do his part if his lock remained out of reach."

"Nether, you all speak in riddles," Finriel mumbled, both fatigue and confusion making her head swim.

"I shall take no more of your time," the Sythril said, gliding to stand. "I have tested the fates enough by telling you this."

"What do you mean?" Finriel asked.

The Sythril turned to face her one last time. "Prophecies are meant to unfold naturally, both the path of success and destruction of equal balance until the end is seen through. My cluster warned me that my vision was an illusion of fear, but I could not take that chance. Heed my warning, daughter of flame. I fear that if you do not, the darkness will find you before you can prepare to fight back."

And with that, the fairy turned and disappeared into the crowd, leaving Finriel alone with her uneaten meal and a mouth full of questions.

FINRIEL COLLAPSED into the small cot, her body still swaying slightly on a fantom wave. Three bowls of stew and nearly half a loaf of bread later, she was sliding into unconsciousness with utter exhaustion.

The Sythril's warning still clanged in her mind, as it had during the rest of her silent meal. Exhaustion made their conversation melt and mold into half-spoken sentences and mixed-up words, and Finriel clamped down on her thoughts with a groan. She would have to speak to Lorian about it in the morning once they were both rested and far away from the inn. It had been some time since Lorian had left on his mission to find horses, but

Finriel found that she was simply too tired to feel worried for a man who thrived in danger.

As if she had performed a summoning spell with her thoughts, a soft knock sounded on the door, making Finriel jump back into consciousness. She cursed and hauled herself out of the small bed, trudging over to the door and pulling it open to find Lorian looking half-asleep on his feet, blinking back at her.

"Horses?" Finriel mumbled in question as she turned and promptly flopped back onto the bed.

"Found two of them," Lorian confirmed with a yawn, and moments later, she felt the brush of his arm against hers as he, too, plopped unceremoniously onto the bed.

"Good job, thief," Finriel smiled, and with that, she closed her eyes and swirled into sleep, the Sythril's warning following her into strange dreams.

22

KRETE

Frigid winter air beat against Krete's stinging face, and he leaned closer into the milky spike before him as Suzunne banked to the left.

The choppy blue waves of the Sandrial Waters beat down below them, like a hungry beast waiting to strike. A shiver ran down Krete's spine at the sight of open water, hiding whatever creatures lurked beneath.

"Have you ever thought of what lies beyond the ocean?" Suzunne asked as his wings opened wide and they coasted along the graceful winds.

Krete hugged the spike tighter and shook his head. "There is nothing beyond the Sandrial Waters. The realm simply ends."

Krete jolted at the vibration of Suzunne's chuckle. "That is highly unlikely."

"No one has disproven the theory otherwise," Krete replied. "Raymara is all that exists. There would have been visitors by now if there were anything beyond."

"Only one continent?" Suzunne asked, and Krete lifted a brow.

"Suzunne, you were born from a drawing. How do you seem to know more about this than me?"

Suzunne sighed. "I'm claiming no such thing. I simply find it odd that we live on such a tiny rock."

Krete smiled and shook his head, ignoring the small flutter of curiosity that Suzunne's comments had stirred in him. There was not even the most remote possibility of there being a world beyond Raymara; Krete knew any thoughts to the contrary were foolish.

"There it is," Suzunne said.

Krete peered over the dragon's shoulder as far as he dared, and his stomach lurched into his throat at the sight of the dark cliffs surrounding a deep river and the Witch Isles below. A loud meow from behind made Krete jump in his seat, and he twisted around to find an enormous feline harnessed between two of Suzunne's larger spikes. He gave Nora an apologetic smile, but the mogwa simply glared at him with intelligent amber eyes.

"We're almost there," Krete said, and Nora merely hissed.

"Thank the goddesses for it too. That cat has been digging into my back for the past two days," Suzunne grumbled and angled his wings closer to his sides as they began their descent into witch territory.

Any excitement that Krete might have felt at the sight of the Witch Isles quickly dissipated as they neared land. He leaned over Suzunne's back as much as he dared as he peered at the silent village. "It shouldn't be this quiet," Krete said, eyeing the countless buildings and main stone keep at the center of the isle.

A thin stream of smoke rose from the chimney of the main keep, and Krete clenched his jaw as he tore his gaze away and continued his search for any witches milling about. There were none.

"Do you think something is wrong?" Suzunne asked, and Krete clutched at the spike before him as Suzunne stretched out his powerful legs and landed on the grass with a loud thump.

"I'm not sure," Krete admitted as he made his way down Suzunne's leg and landed on solid ground with a grunt of relief.

Nora let out a piercing yowl from her spot atop Suzunne, and Krete gave her an apologetic look. "You're staying there until I know Finriel and Lorian are here."

Suzunne huffed. "I suppose I'm required to wait here as well?"

Krete shifted his gaze to Suzunne and nodded. "The witches here are lenient, but—"

Something crashed from behind, and Krete spun around to find that a few doors of the stone homes had been thrown open, including the grand doors of the main keep. Women in dark robes filed out and strode toward Krete, their hands raised and different kinds of magic swirling and crackling around their fingertips.

Krete scrambled backward until his back was pressed against Suzunne's side. The dragon remained still except to move his head slightly to observe their attackers.

A familiar woman with white-blonde hair strode through the mass of witches and approached Krete, her usually serious face a mask of neutrality as she stopped and met his gaze. "This is the second time in two weeks that our isle has received unwelcome visitors," Lizabet Timore said, though her eyes glittered with recognition. "What are you doing here, Krete of Creonid Mountain?"

Krete waited to respond until the countless witches extinguished their magic, though their expressions of mingled distaste and fear at the sight of a dragon remained.

"I've come looking for my friends, Finriel Caligari and Lorian Grey," Krete said. "The last time that I saw them, they said they were headed for these parts."

"Your friends did indeed come here," Lizabet replied.

Excitement and relief made Krete smile and take a step toward the mother of witches.

"However," Lizabet continued, "they fled nine days ago."

Fear landed like a ball of stone in Krete's stomach. "They fled? Why? To where?"

Lizabet shook her head. "I do not know where they went, but the Ten came looking for them and followed them on a boat into the Sandrial Waters."

The ball hardened in Krete's stomach, and something like anger inflamed his already frazzled emotions. The Red King was ruthless and had already endangered, if not captured, his friends far too soon after Clamidas.

"So they're gone," Krete said, mostly to himself. "The Red King likely has them in his hold already."

"Wait!"

Krete looked up, frowning as a halo of lavish curls moved through the sea of witches and a girl no more than eighteen years old broke to the front of the line. She was dressed plainly, though a thick bandage covered her right shoulder and chest. Lizabet rolled her eyes at the young witch before giving Krete an apologetic look.

"Maescia here helped them escape the isle," Lizabet explained, gesturing toward the girl, who nodded at Krete. "Though she was—"

"Lorian told me to give this to a friend that would come to the isle," Maescia said, cutting off the mother of witches and thrusting a folded piece of parchment into Krete's face.

Krete took the parchment from Maescia with slightly trembling fingers, giving the witch a grateful smile. "Thank you." He unfolded the parchment, and hope bloomed in his chest at the simple message written within.

Krete,

If you're reading this, things have likely gone badly for Finriel and me. If we are not in the Witch Isles when you arrive, we have gone to Farrador. We will be with an old friend of mine near the outskirts of Mitonir. Ask Suzunne to track the scent of this parchment. We will be waiting for you if we haven't died already.

Don't get too worried,

L.

A smile broke out on Krete's face, and he looked up at Maescia and Lizabet. "I think I know where to find them."

Lizabet inclined her head, and Maescia took a step forward. "Are you one of the companions who collected the five beasts?"

Krete nodded. "Krete of Creonid Mountain, and this is Suzunne, one of the storyteller's creations." He gestured toward Suzunne as he spoke, and the black dragon inclined his head, though the movement provoked a growl from a very upset Nora.

"Pleased to meet you lovely ladies," Suzunne said, and Maescia gave him a curious smile.

"I didn't know dragons could be nice."

"They aren't nice." Suzunne sighed. "Which is why I'm here with the little man instead of communing with my kind in Drolatis."

Maescia snorted, and Krete spoke before the conversation got too carried away. "Did the Ten target any of you?"

Lizabet shook her head. "Maescia was injured in the crossfire, but they all but ignored the rest of our witches."

Krete nodded slowly, trepidation rising in his gut. The Red King truly did have eyes everywhere, it seemed. The bounty on their heads was no lie, and Krete had just willingly left the security of his home in order to find his friends.

Raymara wasn't safe anymore.

"Thank you for your help," Krete said, bowing deeply.

"You will find them, won't you?" Maescia asked. "You're going to fight against whatever is going on out there?" The girl pointed at the misty shores as she spoke, and Krete clenched his jaw.

They couldn't fight against the Red King, not without knowing what they were up against. Besides, their team was scattered, and Aeden was now a puppet for the dark side, along with the entirety of Proveria because of it. He hated the lack of hope inside himself, but their mission had changed him, and now he only cared to make sure that Lorian and Finriel were safe and out of trouble. Perhaps in time, if they found Tedric and truly discovered what the Red King was planning, Krete would feel more hopeful.

But right now, all he felt was tired.

"We will do our best," Krete replied finally, offering a weak smile.

"We stand with you," Maescia said, and Lizabet shot her a warning look that the girl didn't see. "Or at least I will, if I figure out how to get off this dreaded island."

His smile turned genuine, and Krete bowed again before taking a step closer to Suzunne. He was running out of time, and he hated feeling anxious.

"Be well, Krete," Lizabet said with a nod. "And take care of that girl. She is far more dangerous than we know."

Krete frowned. "Finriel? She's not dangerous—perhaps a bit reckless, but I've never felt afraid of her."

Lizabet's frown deepened, and she grabbed Maescia's uninjured shoulder, leading the girl back to her side. "She could become powerful, more than all of us put together. And the last powerful witch we saw before her wants to destroy the realm."

A shiver ran down Krete's spine at her implication, but he shook his head nonetheless. Finriel would never become as corrupt as the Red King. She cared too much about everyone, even if she constantly tried to act otherwise.

"I must get going," Krete said finally, turning to Suzunne with the note outstretched. "Can you track Lorian with this?"

Suzunne's hot breath blasted against Krete's hand as the dragon sniffed the note, and after a moment, he gave his best nod. "It's faint, but I think I can manage."

"That's good enough for me." Krete clambered onto his customary spot atop the dragon's back.

Lizabet and the other witches were still watching when he looked down again, and discomfort tingled at Krete's senses as the words of the mother of witches ran through his mind again.

"She's good, you know," Krete said.

Lizabet gave him a sad smile. "No one born from a union of flames and ice can be innately good. She will have to learn it if that's what she wants."

And with that, Lizabet turned away, dragging a stubborn Maescia in tow. The rest of the witches turned their backs as well, though they simply spread about the village instead of entering the countless homes from which they came.

Krete sighed and turned to look at Nora, who was still crouched low, but her eyes were now closed. Mogwas were very neutral creatures, but Nora's moral compass always seemed more sensitive to him. He simply couldn't believe that she would choose to follow Finriel across the entire realm if the witch had sinister desires.

"Don't worry too much," Suzunne said, seeming to know what Krete was thinking about. "Let's simply focus on finding them for now. Then you can ask Finriel if she plans on taking over Raymara."

Krete smiled, giving Suzunne a grateful pat on one of his enormous scales. "Thank you, my friend. That sounds like a wonderful idea."

"Good," Suzunne said. "I really wouldn't be able to handle you in a sour mood for two more days."

"Do you think it will take that long to reach Farrador?" Krete asked, worry making his stomach knot again.

Suzunne tensed before taking a few steps and launching into the air. Wind streaked against Krete's face, and he grasped the spike tightly as Suzunne found higher elevation and glided above the water that lay between the dark stone cliffs and the isle beyond.

"The scent is faint, so I will have to be more careful with how quickly I move," Suzunne answered finally.

Krete nodded in understanding. "Take the time you need. The most important thing is that we find them."

23

FINRIEL

"Wake up. It's time to get going." Lorian's voice cut through Finriel's slumber, and she blinked her eyes open to find them in the cramped room in the small Farridian village.

She sat up, rubbing the sleep from her eyes with the heels of her palms.

"The horses are outside, and I've already got us some breakfast and provisions for the journey," Lorian said as he turned toward the door.

"Don't sound too chipper. You'll make me want to burn you," Finriel growled as her sleep-muddled brain slowly gave way to full consciousness, and she followed Lorian out of the door.

The tavern was nearly empty at this early hour, with no more than five people seated by the window with steaming mugs and bowls before them as they watched the sunrise. Finriel scanned the faces of the people hunched over their breakfasts, but none bore the familiar elegant stature of the Sythril. Concern prickled at her insides, remembering her conversation with the fairy the night before.

Lorian wove through tables, silently leading them to the threshold and stepping outside into the chill morning with a soft thud of the inn door. Finriel stepped onto the cobbled street to find their horses tethered to a wooden post, and her knowledge of riding and proper horse care made a jolt of agitation bite into her already dull spirits at the sight of the two fluffy animals tied by their bits.

"The gray one is yours. I'll take the roan," Lorian said in a lighthearted tone and walked down the wooden steps and onto the street.

Finriel approached the gray horse Lorian indicated for her and held out her hand for the gelding to sniff. The horse was tall and well built, its long legs strong and powerful even though they were covered in a thick winter coat. The horse's warm breath shot across the top of her hand as it sniffed her, and she untied the reins from the post as soon as it licked its lips and nudged her gently, as if in acceptance of her presence.

"Do you need help getting on?" Lorian asked, and Finriel shot a glare to where the thief had already mounted the even larger strawberry roan mare that now pawed at the cobbled street in anticipation.

"I'm tired, not incompetent," Finriel snapped and quickly gathered the reins as she put a booted foot into the metal stirrup and hauled herself into the saddle, her still sore legs protesting at the sudden movement.

Her horse stood patiently as Finriel arranged her cloak in a way that wouldn't flap too cumbersomely as they cantered and wouldn't choke her either. Once she was ready, she took up a light feel to the reins and nudged the horse forward. Lorian's mare began to prance in place with anticipation as he met Finriel's gaze and nodded. "Ready?"

Finriel patted her horse on the neck and took up the reins even more. "Ready."

Without a warning, Lorian clicked to his horse and gave her a nudge. The mare jolted forward into a canter without a second thought. Finriel's horse lurched forward, and she scrambled to grab its long mane with a curse as it sped after the galloping mare.

MILES OF TREES and frost-coated meadows stretched past them as Finriel and Lorian rode through the morning and into the middle of the day, taking only a few short rests to drink water and let the horses regain their energy. Breakfast at the beginning of the day had been meager, with only a bit of dried fruit and bread to fill her stomach. Finriel's face felt as if it had been pressed against an ice cube for hours, her lips now chapped and her eyes watering as they came down from a canter and into a brisk trot. The forest that surrounded Mitonir stretched out ahead, and the dark gray spires of Queen Arbane's castle peaked through the endless sea of leafless trees.

"I spoke to a Sythril last night," Finriel said.

Lorian turned in his saddle and gave her a molten stare. "I told you not to speak to anyone while I was gone."

A hot wall reared up in her chest, and Finriel snapped, "I'm not an insolent child, Lorian. I can handle myself."

The thief let out a sigh and shook his head. "This is different. The people in that inn—"

"Ignored me completely, save for the Sythril," Finriel said. "And with good reason too."

"What did the Sythril say?" Lorian asked, an apologetic smile making his eyes twinkle.

She knew he was only worried about her, and after everything that had happened between them, she couldn't blame him for his fear of losing her again. But Finriel was still a witch with fire roaring through her veins and a tongue sharper than most blades.

"They came to me with a warning," Finriel said. "That we shouldn't let the chimera or Rey out of their pages until we reach a place of sand and stone."

Lorian's mouth slid into a grin. "Maybe it was another riddle, and they were saying we should let them out as soon as possible."

Finriel rolled her eyes. "I don't think so. They mentioned the prophecy and said they were cast out of their cluster for wanting to tell me what they'd seen."

Lorian's smile faded, and he shrugged. "Well, I'm not too keen on getting thrown against a tree again, so I wouldn't complain if we left Rey where she is a little while longer."

She shot him a scowl, but he only grinned. He was right, however, and so was the Sythril. Their current state of being wanted and on the run didn't warrant a safe atmosphere to unleash a demon and an extinct monster into the realm.

"I thought the entire point of this was for us to reunite with our locks and stop the Red King." Finriel sighed, allowing for the sour pit in her stomach to rear its head.

"We don't have to figure everything out right away," Lorian reminded her. "As I like to say, strive low and then you will always be impressed by the results."

"How does that have anything to do with letting out the beasts?" Finriel asked, though she couldn't help a faint smile.

Lorian shrugged again and gave his mare a pat on the neck. "We will get through this no matter what. Beasts or no beasts, I know that we will win this war together."

His gaze slid up to hers as he spoke, and a shiver trickled down her spine as they locked eyes. There was no joking thief playing at the corners of his mouth now, no sign of laughter or dishonesty. He was a book that had finally opened, and what lay within was more beautiful than she could bare.

Finriel looked away first, biting the inside of her cheek to keep from cursing. Lorian didn't hold back, however, and her extended hearing picked up a hushed slew of curses under the thief's breath.

"The journey went a lot faster than I thought it would," Finriel said, grasping for something to steer them back to safer waters.

The sun was still quite high in the sky for this time of year, and Finriel guessed there were still at least a few hours of daylight left for them to enter the city before the gates closed. Finriel brought her horse down to a relaxed walk beside Lorian's mare as they entered the forest, the horses' hooves crunching over the large dead tree leaves that scattered the earth.

"I made sure to find the fastest horses possible," Lorian replied with a pat against the roan's neck. "I seem to have done a better job than I thought."

"We should try to keep these horses," Finriel said and looked down at the gelding's fluffy gray ears as they twitched and listened to distant creatures or perhaps simply imaginary things.

Lorian raised his brow. "Nora is nearly the size of a pony. Why don't you attempt to ride her when Krete brings her back?"

Finriel shot him a withering look and reached out to play with her horse's long white tresses. "Nora would likely kill me if I tried to do that. And besides, our journey today has made it clear that we cover a lot more ground this way."

"All right, consider these our shared animals." Lorian nodded.

It was now Finriel's turn to raise a brow. "And who said I was sharing? You have enough on your hands with that horse."

Lorian's mare suddenly jolted to the side, clearly having just scared herself by brushing too close against one of the enormous gnarled trees. Lorian took up the reins again and brought the mare down to a walk with a shake of his head. "I think you're right. I think she can keep her name though, if they're staying with us."

"And what exactly is her name?" Finriel asked.

"Ed," Lorian replied with a shrug, as if naming a hot-tempered mare Ed was one of the most normal things a person could do.

"That's a terrible name!" Finriel exclaimed, and Lorian waggled his brows at her.

"That one's name is Oats. The old man who sold him to me said the damned thing got into their feed room and nearly stuffed himself on oats to the point of bursting."

Finriel gave Lorian an unimpressed look and shook her head, but faint sounds cut through to her extended hearing, making her forget all about the unfortunate names of their horses. "We're almost at the gates of Mitonir," she said, and Lorian nodded.

"We'll have to make a stop there to find that friend of mine before we go to Notharis."

Finriel looked at the thief with muddled confusion and frustration. He had never divulged any friends in Farrador during their mission to recover the beasts, nor had he said anything before they'd almost been caught by the Ten. But as Finriel looked at Lorian's tense figure and serious face, she wasn't sure if she should ask who this person was, at least not until they met.

"Do you know where in the city we'll find this friend of yours?" Finriel asked instead.

Lorian took a deep breath and sighed, the tension in his shoulders visibly relaxing as he turned in his saddle and gave her a carefree smile. "Don't worry about that bit. I'm quite sure he'll be the one finding us."

"What exactly do you mean by that?" Finriel asked in alarm, and Lorian only gave her a wink before turning forward once more, clucking and nudging the mare into a canter.

"Come on, Ed. We've got a city to infiltrate."

Finriel huffed and urged her gelding, Oats, into a canter after Lorian, who was now goading Ed into a flat-out gallop. Finriel's mood soured with every hoofbeat, and soon, the tall city walls of Mitonir loomed ahead as they reached the city. She had only traveled to the capital once in her life when she and her ward had first traveled to Farrador, and Finriel had only known discomfort and fear as they'd walked through the streets and gathered supplies. Witches were not a very common sight in Farrador, no less in the capital, where most of the citizens despised and mistreated anyone belonging under the Red King's rule as far as the peace law would allow them. She only hoped that Lorian knew the streets enough to keep them safe or at least moderately hidden.

It took all of ten steps past Mitonir's gates to confirm that they were not going unnoticed, nor were they very welcome. The white stone city rose up around them in a bustle of elves, shops, and busy streets, yet Finriel swore the noise dimmed slightly as soon as they stepped foot through the city walls. Angular faces and broad shoulders blurred into one as the tall beings paused and watched their descent deeper into the city.

"I don't think people are exactly giddy to have us here," Finriel muttered.

"Pay them no mind," Lorian said, throwing a wink toward an older elf woman, who had stopped to sneer at them.

Finriel *did* pay them mind, her knuckles turning white against her grip on the reins as she followed Lorian toward an extravagant barn made of white wood that was placed alarmingly close to the castle, the home of Queen Arbane. Finriel's gaze traveled up the castle walls, which were made of thick gray stone. It was quite at odds with the elegant light stone that made the rest of the city and looked like a sore standing out upon smooth skin. She tried to ignore the elf scouts that were lined up on walls and visible through arched windows as she and Lorian rode into the dim barn. It was surprisingly empty, save for a few horses and two stable hands that buzzed about, completing their duties.

"Good morning, gentlemen," Lorian announced as he swung off Ed and led her toward one of the boys.

The elf boy was young, perhaps thirteen, with shaggy red

hair and wide brown eyes. Lorian tossed Ed's reins at him, and the boy scrambled to catch them, the roan mare's head bopping up at the sudden movement.

"Please water and feed our horses. We shouldn't be too long," Lorian said, and Finriel swung off Oats with a glower toward the thief's cockiness.

"Sir, this is the private stable for the elf scouts and royal household," the boy said with some uncertainty, looking at Lorian with as much belief that he was royalty or a scout as Finriel was certain that she was a male.

Lorian scoffed. "Please, I am a close friend to the queen. She'll pay no mind that I've used her facilities. As you were."

The boy bit his lip, and Finriel quickly gave him Oats's reins before she could think better of it and allowed Lorian to lead her back out into the street.

"What in the Nether are you doing?" Finriel hissed as she was led toward a pastry shop full of elves.

Lorian shot her a grin and moved into the bustling crowd. "I'm getting us seen."

Finriel opened her mouth and then promptly closed it again, at a complete loss for words. Lorian had either lost the rest of his mind, or this was one of his dangerous thieving tricks. Both options made a lump of trepidation rise in Finriel's throat, and she glanced around at the curious onlookers.

They sat at a small metal table that looked out onto the well-groomed street. A cacophony of scents wafted through Finriel's nose, both herbal and dirty, from the few citizens that did not seem to have such a comfortable life. Noise filled her ears, and the towering buildings and quaint shops were almost dizzying after so many days on the water and in a quiet forest.

Lorian returned to their table with two small bundles wrapped in thin brown paper. Finriel took one of the bundles from his outstretched hand and unwrapped it, her mouth instantly watering at the sight of a gleaming flaky pastry with small seeds on it, and what smelled like saffron.

"What is this?" Finriel asked, and Lorian simply unwrapped his and took a bite.

"Sartol," he mumbled through a full mouth, and Finriel frowned. "Just try it."

Finriel paused before biting into her pastry. It was like nothing she had ever tasted. Buttery pastry melted in her mouth, and the burst of saffron and—

"Is that chocolate?" Finriel exclaimed and looked down at the pastry.

Indeed, a well of warm chocolate pooled within the pastry and coated her tongue. It was the oddest combination of flavors she'd ever tried, and yet she found herself bringing the decadent treat up to her mouth once more.

"It used to be my favorite treat as a child," Lorian said before taking another bite. "I actually used to steal these, even after we had already met."

"Why didn't you ever steal one for me?" Finriel grumbled, licking stray chocolate that had dripped onto her fingers.

Lorian grinned. "I had a hard enough time stealing one. I wouldn't have wanted to try stealing two. Besides, I would gobble it down before my mother could take notice of what I'd done."

Finriel looked out upon the street once more, watching the many courtiers and common folk milling about. Mitonir was beautiful—she could not deny that—but the knowledge of their unwanted presence was beginning to override her enjoyment.

"Who is this friend of yours, anyway?" Finriel asked, Lorian's insistence on mystery driving her mad.

Lorian shrugged. "I'm not sure he'll come, so I'm not quite sure there's any point in telling you."

Finriel huffed and shook her head but remained silent as they watched the city and bustling crowd.

But it happened too soon.

"Oy! It's that boy who tried to kidnap the queen!"

Finriel jerked her head toward the voice that rang out to find a small group already congregating around a wiry old man with wild eyes and hooked nose. The group came closer, and their hushed voices and excited whispers made the ever-present flame in Finriel's abdomen come to attention. She shoved it down quickly and looked at Lorian, who was already rising smoothly to his feet.

"What marbles are left of your brain, boy? You'll be thrown into Crubia for your treachery!" the old man yelled with a shaking fist.

The group cheered, and the man spoke again with raging confidence. "Why'd you try to steal the queen, boy? I can tell from them pointed ears of yers that ye must be one of us, or are you a blasted half-breed?"

The flame coiled in her stomach, poised to strike, but Finriel shoved it down with a shaking breath. Lorian wore a smile in place of her furious frown, and Finriel blinked in surprise as he lifted a hand in greeting, completely ignoring the fact that the growing group was about to ruin their lives—potentially forever.

"While I'm humbled by the fact that you still remember me after all this time, I will take the liberty of setting a few key points straight before we depart."

The elves looked at each other in confusion, and Lorian continued, "First and foremost, I certainly did *not* try to kidnap the queen. It was her lover."

"The one with the large boil?" a noble elven man asked from the back, his face twisted in disgust.

"Exactly the one." Lorian nodded jovially. "Second, I am a half-breed and wear the dirty badge with honor. However, no one could have marbles in their brains and get out of this city unscathed after what I did—boils or not. And lastly, you are more likely to be thrown into Crubia for your terrible nose than I would for being a terrible thief."

They stood in stunned silence, and Finriel glanced between Lorian and the group. *The audacity.* After a moment of glancing and muttering with one another, the elves seemed to unravel the slew of moderate insults and decided their fate. The man with the hooked nose stepped forward and spat on the ground. "Yer just cocky half-breed shit. Call the scouts!"

Lorian met Finriel's gaze and tilted his head to the side. "That's our cue. Follow me."

Finriel barely had time to think before Lorian pivoted and sprinted away from the group, and she pushed after him. Elves stopped and watched their quick sprint through the city, but Finriel paid the blur of bright colors and rich clothes no mind as she ran as fast as she could. Whistles and yells of men calling to each other caught Finriel's attention, and she nearly stumbled at the sight of five elf scouts sprinting toward them. She glanced at the castle to find a lone scout running along one of the high walls, his steps sure and quick as he sprinted along the precarious ledge.

A hand grabbed her wrist, and Finriel cursed, trying to fight her way out of the grip until she looked down and found Lorian's skin on hers. She caught a flash of ice-blue eyes and a grin before he looked forward again and veered them both to the side, into a dim overhang near an alley. Finriel skidded into the overhang, nearly slamming into Lorian. His chest rose and fell quickly, but she was sure it was more from adrenaline than exertion. Her own chest was heaving, and she met his glimmering eyes with a scowl.

"Are you trying to send us to the Nether?" Finriel hissed, but at that moment, Lorian's gaze slid to the street, and he froze, throwing a hand over her mouth.

Finriel ripped his hand away and turned to sit next to Lorian as six scouts approached the overhang. Finriel held her breath, her heart feeling like it might burst from beating so fast. The footsteps slowed but veered toward the alley and past the over-hang—all but one pair of boots, which headed straight for them.

The flame was burning on Finriel's hands before she could think. She clenched her jaw with the effort of snuffing out the heat as the boots stopped and the scout crouched before them. Finriel stifled a gasp.

Brown hair curled at the nape of his neck, his skin only slightly tanner than Lorian's. Dark blue eyes framed by thick lashes stared between Finriel and Lorian, and his angular jaw was clenched, pressing his lips into a grim line. He looked terribly familiar, and it took all of Finriel's will not to light him on fire.

"Aren't you going to arrest us?" Finriel demanded.

To her dismay, the scout only leaned lower and dipped into the overhang, crouching before Lorian. It was harder for his tall and muscled frame to fit, but he seemed to make do with surprising ease.

This was decidedly worse than being arrested. Much worse.

"Lorian, what in the Nether are you doing here?" the man hissed, and Finriel looked between the two with rising confusion as Lorian grinned at the elf.

"Hello again, brother. It seems as though I owe you for saving our lives yet again."

"What?" Finriel hissed, trying to keep her voice quiet, even though she wished very much to yell at the thief. "You didn't tell me you had a brother!"

Lorian shrugged. "I never had the chance."

"I think you've had quite enough time to tell me you have a brother!" Finriel exclaimed, and the elf scout and Lorian both cringed at her raised voice.

"It's not safe here. We need to move before someone finds you," the scout said and quickly darted from the overhang.

"Well, come on now. Don't want to keep our host waiting, do we?" Lorian said with a wink before darting out after the elf.

"I should have killed him when I had the chance," Finriel growled and took a deep breath before rallying her courage and darting out of the safety of the overhang.

She spotted Lorian sprinting across the main street toward the barn where they had left the horses. A shout from the elven scouts cracked through her eardrums, and Finriel cursed as she watched Lorian disappear into the shelter of the barn. She stomped in moments later, her lungs burning as she sucked in the frigid air.

"Get on Oats as fast as you can and follow me," Lorian called, and Finriel barely had time to think before reins were thrown into her hands and Oats's nose nudged against her arm. Finriel glanced over her shoulder, scanning around for the elf scout, but he was nowhere to be found.

"Where's that scout?" Finriel asked, but Lorian shook his head as he swung up onto the saddle and wrangled Ed down from a rear.

"He'll be with us in a moment," Lorian said, and Finriel hauled herself into the saddle without a second thought.

"Ready?" the thief asked, and Finriel nodded.

Finriel burst out of the barn hard on Lorian's tail, their horses' hooves sounding like a shower of stones against the street as they veered to the right and raced down a narrow alley. The citizens on the street were a blur of bright colors and shouts as they whipped by, and Finriel did her best to maneuver Oats past any unfortunate souls that could not get out of their path in time.

More raised shouts from the elf scouts sounded behind them, and Finriel dared a glance behind her shoulder to find a man atop a large cream-colored stallion galloping behind them. A high-pitched whistle echoed through the air, and Finriel barely had time to duck before a flurry of arrows shot past her head and thunked into surrounding trees.

Pounding hoofbeats sounded from behind, and the enormous stallion came speeding beside her, the elf scout astride it. He glanced at her and nodded before urging his horse faster. It soon caught up with Ed, and Finriel pushed Oats on as they moved deeper into the Farridian Forest.

Finriel and Lorian wove between the gnarled trees as they followed the nameless man, their destination quite unclear. Her only indication that the man was leading them to safety and not into another trap was that he and Lorian were apparently brothers, though she wasn't sure if that fact made her feel any better about following him blindly through Farrador. Oats's breath came out in loud puffing snorts, and Finriel ached to let him stop and catch his breath after an entire day of quick travel. Her thoughts were thankfully heard, and the man slowed his gleaming stallion to a walk as the faint outline of a small village appeared ahead.

"My home is there. Follow me." The man pointed to a place to the left of the village, and Finriel had to squint in order to spot the small cottage and barn situated in a way that camouflaged it against the cluster of dried bushes and tall trees surrounding it.

Their horses were unsaddled and placed in surprisingly large stalls within minutes, and Finriel soon found herself walking behind Lorian toward a home made of thick gray stone.

The scout opened the dark wood door to reveal a spacious and clean interior. A long dining table was placed by a window to Finriel's left, with two large wooden chairs at either end and a bench along either long side. The kitchen lay to the right of her, with long countertops and ample space for cooking. A passageway led straight ahead. Finriel could make out a sort of foyer and the landing of a wooden staircase.

The elf sat in the chair at the head of the table with a loud sigh, looking between Lorian and Finriel with a piercing dark blue stare. Finriel crossed her arms where she stood by the door, returning the elf's stare with her most withering glare. She didn't trust him for one second and wanted an explanation before she told him anything.

"Who are you?" Finriel asked coolly.

"My name is Odonir Grey, and I am unfortunately Lorian's brother," the scout said, ruffling his dark brown hair with a dirt-splattered hand.

"Half brother, if the details of our shared blood make you feel any better," Lorian offered with a confident smile from where he now sat in the chair at the opposite end of the table.

Finriel opened her mouth to speak but found the new information was still too shocking to bear. She closed it again and shook her head, disbelief making her almost dizzy.

"Why are you here, Lorian?" Odonir asked, looking at him with a slight scowl. "You are both wanted by the Red King, and Queen Arbane has already sent out extra patrols, which you two have experienced firsthand with your unceremonious arrival."

"Ah, well, that is part of the reason why we are here," Lorian replied easily. "We were hoping you might let us stay with you. Perhaps our dead mother's house in Notharis would be accommodating if you still have it."

Odonir blinked. "You are as terrible as the day that I last spoke to you, brother. Maybe even worse if that's possible."

"Can you both stop your banter for one moment and tell me how in the Nether you've hidden the fact that you've had a brother since I've known you?" Finriel asked Lorian, still finding that her brain was having difficulty computing what had been revealed.

Lorian sighed. "I'm sorry, but I really have to secure our heads on our shoulders before I can tell you stories about my enthralling family history."

"But—"

"How long would you need to stay here?" Odonir asked, cutting Finriel off before she could properly yell at Lorian.

"At least a few weeks or until we can rest and gather more

information about what exactly is going on," Lorian replied. "I'll need to send another letter, now that I'm thinking of it."

"Fine, just go ahead and tell him everything," Finriel growled. "It's not as if he can turn us in to the elf queen."

Odonir gave her a strange look. "Actually, I can."

Anger fired through Finriel's brain. "It was a sarcastic comment."

"I have no patience for sarcasm." Odonir shrugged before replying to Lorian. "I can let you stay here on a few conditions."

Lorian leaned back in his chair and raised his brow. "I'm listening, brother."

Odonir scowled. "First of all, do *not* treat me as if I'm an insolent child. I am your elder, if you haven't forgotten."

"How could I ever forget that my brother is an old man? Will you need help getting out of bed in the morning?" Lorian's grin only widened at Odonir's look of fury, but the elf ignored Lorian's insult and continued.

"You will honor the rules of this house. You will not break anything, and you will not, under any circumstances, steal from either the village or Mitonir. If I still had mother's house in Notharis, I would send you two there without a second thought, but unfortunately, I had to sell it in order to purchase all of this." Odonir waved a hand, gesturing around the space, but Finriel was barely listening as he rattled off the rules they'd have to live by if they indeed stayed with him. She instead wracked her brain on how this man was familiar.

She took in his tall frame, which shared the same lean build as Lorian. A lean build was one of the trademarks of being an elf, though they were still typically bigger than fairies' petite frames. Her gaze traveled from his dark buckskin breeches and brown leather jacket to his face, which was slightly tanner than Lorian's, but the shape was nearly the same. The same high angular cheekbones and full lips, the intense almond-shaped eyes, though his were like the sky before nightfall, not Lorian's eyes of ice blue. It was the elf's more elongated ears and shortly cropped brown hair that differentiated them the most and what kept throwing Finriel for a loop.

And then it hit her.

Their mission, when Finriel and her companions had climbed up the tree to hide from the elf scouts. The man who had thrown Tedric's fallen satchel back up to where Lorian and Finriel peered over the edge of the tree.

The same blue eyes, the serious face.

"You saved our necks in the Farridian Forest," Finriel blurted, cutting off Lorian and Odonir in the middle of an argument.

They paused, and Odonir met her gaze, but Finriel only continued as a strange sort of excitement and confusion muddled up her thoughts. "You saw us in the tree and kept us safe from the other elf scouts."

Odonir nodded. "It was the first time I'd seen Lorian in six years. I thought he was dead before that day. I was shocked enough to see him alive, no less with you."

Finriel frowned. "With me? How did you know about me?"

"I might have told him about you the last time we crossed paths. A pretty girl with caramel eyes who I failed to save from a ten-year-old boy."

Finriel's body tensed at Lorian's words, but it was easier now to let the memories of that day drift in and out of her mind.

"It was a shock, and I didn't know enough about your mission to alert the others about you," Odonir explained. "I didn't want my brother to fail, especially when this was his first mission doing something that wasn't only for his own gain."

"It was mainly for my own gain at first," Lorian pointed out. "Then I got distracted by a beautiful woman and a sudden desire to keep the realm from being destroyed."

"We haven't kept it from being destroyed quite yet," Finriel replied with a sudden pang of nerves that she tried her best to hide.

She knew it wasn't the time to pause on Lorian's comment about her being beautiful, but goddesses be damned if her heart didn't stutter. The echo of his lips on hers made her jolt, and she shook her head as she refocused on the conversation.

". . . which is why we need your help," Lorian continued. "The Red King wants our necks because we know more than we should, and we kept the pages."

Odonir blanched. "You have the storyteller's beasts with you? In here?"

"Only two," Lorian said quickly. "A chimera and a rakshasa."

"What in the world is a rakshasa? And how are you not terrified about having a chimera in your cloak pocket?"

"They were actually quite friendly once they got past the point of mortally injuring us," Lorian said, and Odonir scoffed.

"And now they're in danger, which is also why we need somewhere safe and hidden," Finriel cut in. "The beasts seemed to know something we didn't—or at the least the ones who could speak."

"They can speak?" Odonir croaked, and Lorian nodded.

"One of them is quite pretty too, at least when she's not a leathery demon."

"Will you help us?" Finriel asked, ignoring Lorian's last remark about the rakshasa.

Odonir sighed through his nose, bringing up a hand to run through his hair as he mulled over their words. Finriel knew it was a lot to ask for, especially when he and the other elf scouts had been ordered to arrest them if they ever came into contact.

"You say you know what the Red King is planning? And this information is all viable?" Odonir asked, and Finriel glanced down at Lorian, who replied.

"We only know that he seems to be making some sort of army with the help of the storyteller."

"An army of those beasts?" Odonir asked, and both Finriel and Lorian nodded in confirmation. "That's not good."

"Which is why we need somewhere to hide the beasts we do have in order to keep them from falling into the wrong hands," Finriel said. "Or at least have a safe place to train and return to as we try to figure out exactly what it is the Red King is planning to do with that army."

Odonir nodded after a moment, resigned resolution set on his face. "Very well. But I expect to be informed and part of your discoveries from now on."

"We wouldn't dream of keeping you in the dark." Lorian winked, and Odonir huffed before standing from his seat.

"I need to return to Mitonir and tell the scouts to stop searching for you." He moved for the door. "You two are safe here, as long as you don't leave this house and property."

"Thank you," Finriel said, and he only gave her an unimpressed look in return.

Finriel stepped away as he came closer, and he barely glanced in her direction as he opened the door and stepped outside, mumbling, "Don't thank me until the realm is safe again."

24

TEDRIC

I t was the first time in two weeks that Tedric's body felt better than his mind.

Memories of his night with Bordin swirled through his thoughts on repeat, even if they were disoriented and blurry from the amount of alcohol he'd consumed. There was one thing for certain, however, and it was that Aeden was not acting completely of her own volition.

The realization made the ache in his chest lessen, if only a little. Maybe she wasn't completely gone, and his decision to end things with her had been foolish. He'd been massively hungover when she'd called him to her rooms the day before she left, and the pounding in his head had kept him from thinking clearly.

Regret seeped into his bones, but pain met it in the middle, making a sigh escape from his lips. Maybe ending things had been for the best; he wasn't sure how much more emotional distress he could take.

The image of her anger-stricken face swirled through his mind, and Tedric shook his head. Everything was far too complicated, and the Red King would be furious if he found out that Tedric had decided to act against his wishes. He simply could not continue things with Aeden, not without knowing exactly what had happened to her.

Another betrayal would make him break completely.

Approaching footsteps echoed down the hall, bringing Tedric out of his racing thoughts and into reality.

The methodical scratch of charcoal against parchment was the only sound that came from Egharis's cell, and Tedric sighed as he turned to look at the hunched man.

"You should stand at attention. The Red King is coming for you," Egharis said calmly without lifting his head.

The distasteful emotions already roiling inside of Tedric lashed out, and he bit his tongue to keep from snapping at the storyteller before he turned and straightened, calming his features as two figures emerged from around the corner.

It was indeed the Red King, with Agonur at his heels. Tedric blinked in surprise as they approached and stopped in front of him.

"Good morning, Drazak," the Red King said without smiling, and Tedric forced a bow.

"My lord."

The Red King peered into Egharis's cell. The man still scribbled at his drawings, yet perhaps now with a bit more fervor than he had before the king's arrival. Tedric kept his gaze forward, forcing himself not to glare at the Red King as he inspected the storyteller and the slow progress he made toward building the army of beasts. The Red King turned and faced Tedric, and Tedric could almost feel his eyes burning two small holes into the side of his skull.

"Drazak, you are to accompany me to Proveria in three days' time," the Red King announced, and apprehension lurched into Tedric's throat.

He turned to face the Red King, trying his hardest to keep his expression neutral as he replied, "Yes, my lord."

"Good. I will expect you on your horse and by my carriage

on the third dawn." The Red King nodded and turned on his heel, he and Agonur promptly retreating the way they had come.

Tedric released a breath and hunched, his heart beating rather uncomfortably in his chest. He was to go to Proveria. To see Aeden likely, or to carry out whatever other plan the Red King had in mind.

"He's testing your allegiance," Egharis said, and Tedric nearly jumped. He had forgotten the storyteller was there for a moment, his thoughts too wrapped up in the brief interaction with the Red King.

"Why do you say that?" Tedric asked and turned to face him.

Tedric found Egharis's silver gaze already set upon him, the look he gave something close to that of a father forced to explain something difficult to their child.

"He knows that you do not trust him, and he knows you and Aeden are not on good terms, that you vowed never to touch nor to speak to her unless forced, ever again."

Tedric blanched. "How do you know that?"

Egharis gave him a weary smile. "I've come to know you very well over these few weeks, Commander. I can read your body language, the tension in your shoulders, and the grinding of your jaw. You are upset about something, and I know of the job the Red King charged you with, of giving yourself to her."

"How could you possibly know that I ended things?" Tedric asked through gritted teeth.

The storyteller wiped at his face, a streak of charcoal smudging across his pale skin as he did so. "Your tension has subsided slightly. But I also feel a great sadness coming from you as well. There is only one clear answer to why that might be."

"And the Red King has likely found that out by now." Tedric huffed, his anger shriveling at the truth in Egharis's observations.

"He's going to make you revoke what you said to her. You know this, don't you?" Egharis said, and Tedric nodded sharply.

"I will simply refuse," he said with icy resolve. "I'm not his pet. I don't need to sell myself for his cause when I have no desire in supporting it. I'm a slave here, unable to leave for risk of losing my life, but with no desire to stay and serve him either."

"You cannot refuse," Egharis said with a sudden demand that made Tedric's eyes widen in surprise.

"What did you say?"

"Listen to me. You *cannot* refuse," Egharis said again, his voice almost a hiss as he beckoned Tedric closer and walked to the bars of his cell. "You are one of the most important assets to fighting this war, Commander. The king thinks you are a broken man, weak and angry. He does not suspect that you will act against him, not now and not even after he has shredded the world we know to pieces."

Egharis paused and glanced toward the hallway, as if to make sure they would not be overheard before he continued. "You must continue acting as if you are broken, even though I see the wounds you bear inside are beginning to mend. You must continue taking the potion, even if it is slowly making you addicted. You must continue to sleep with Aeden, and you must *not* let the king know you are strong enough to act against him."

"But why? It's only hurting me more if I do this," Tedric replied hotly.

"You are strong, Tedric. Your wounds will heal fully over time, but this realm will not if you turn your back on it. You must gather more information, make the king grow to trust you again and become sloppy with the amount of information he gives you."

Tedric's mind began to spin, but understanding was now blossoming as well. If he could get into the Red King's good graces, it could help him learn more about his plans. He shook his head. "The Red King is smarter than I think even you know.

He will never fully trust me again—if he ever did in the first place."

"Then you must make the queen trust you," the storyteller replied, giving Tedric an apologetic look at the pain that clearly flashed across his eyes. "Show her that you can be trusted, can be told whatever information the Red King has given her. She is alone now in these times, having betrayed you and your companions and being a newly appointed queen."

Tedric's heart cracked at the storyteller's words, knowing that what was being asked of him was to become like Aeden. To gain trust before breaking it for his own gain.

"I don't know if I can." Tedric sighed. "I would have to become like the very people I am trying to fight against."

Egharis shook his head. "We will all be forced to become people we don't entirely like in order to achieve the greater good. I am caught in a game of blackmail, charged with creating an army for the Red King, but you, you are free to maneuver through your part of the game in whichever way you please."

Tedric paused for a moment, mulling over Egharis's words. Perhaps if he were to ask for Aeden's forgiveness and make her trust him again, he could rally her against the Red King. But he had to first find out exactly what it was the Red King wanted, as well as what he'd done to her with that scar.

"So you're saying that I would become an entirely different person—a spy almost?"

Egharis nodded as Tedric spoke, a smile blooming across his cracked lips. "The Red King sees you as a wounded soldier with nothing left to give. He does not think you have the ability or desire to move against him, not fully. He sees you growing comfortable with your position as my guard, taking your potion and drinking with your friends. It was only your sudden break from Aeden that has caused him to question you again. You must douse his concerns and make him believe that you have fallen to his cause completely, that your addiction to the potion and your love for Aeden is more important to you than stopping him."

Tedric blew out a long breath, nodding slowly. His concern for the realm and his friends was far greater than he'd ever expected. But he had been raised to live a life of honor and righteousness, to fight for the cause he believed in, no matter the cost.

"You are far stronger than you think you are," Egharis said, and Tedric looked back into that silver gaze. "You can find new information and begin to move against whatever is brewing out there and in here." Egharis hitched his thumb over his shoulder, toward the pile of half-finished drawings on the desk behind him.

"Thank you," Tedric said and found that he was truly grateful for the man standing across from him. "I will help find your family too, or at least find out where they might be held."

Something close to hope bloomed across the storyteller's haggard face, and he nodded. "Now get back to your post. Your new mission begins soon."

Tedric gave Egharis another grateful smile, then turned to stand against the wall next to his cell once more, a new and greater purpose washing over him as he glanced out the window toward the setting winter sun.

25
LORIAN

Sunlight dappled merrily across the bed, and Lorian blinked his eyes open as a ray of bright light flashed across his face. He groaned and sat up from the comfortable bed. Finriel was no longer in the room, the heavy gray quilt thrown back halfway over him.

It had been a few minutes of arguing and Finriel threatening to set him on fire before they'd finally concluded to share a bed once again, mainly because the modest house only had two bedrooms. Lorian had suggested that she sleep in the barn with Oats, which had nearly landed him with a head of charred hair in return. Their evening had gone by uneventfully after such argument, yet there was still a suffocating tension between him and Finriel in moments of silence, and he wasn't sure if he could take it for much longer.

He would have to muster the courage to speak to her about the kiss again, as his first attempt had been rudely interrupted by a sea monster.

Lorian stretched his arms overhead and yawned, his body finally feeling rested after over a week of constant tension and fatigue. The stone floor was cool under his bare feet as he padded to his clothes and shrugged on his tunic, followed by his trousers and boots.

"Good goddesses, I smell terrible." Lorian cringed at the stench of sweat and dirty horses that clung to his clothes.

A bath and taking some of Odonir's clothes would certainly be in order, Lorian thought as he crossed the room and opened the door, finding Odonir and Finriel sitting across from each other with a respectable spread of food on the table between them. Lorian blinked in surprise, not at the fact that Finriel was actually being respectful to his brother, but that she was talking to him and even smiling. Lorian hung back to watch their interaction, and Finriel's smile broke out into laughter at something Odonir said. Two steaming mugs of tea sat before them, and Lorian rolled his eyes at the familiar sight.

"Good morning," Lorian said with a smile as he entered the front room, and Finriel glanced up at him with a smile still on her face. "I thought you would have dropped that silly herbal nonsense by now, Odonir."

His brother only shot him a tired look before grabbing the mug and taking a sip. The tea was supposed to help with his nerves or something of the sort. Lorian had tried it once and never felt a thing, which gave him something else to annoy his brother about.

"You seem to have slept well," Finriel said.

Lorian nodded and sat down on the bench by the window. "Yes, but unfortunately your boisterous conversation woke me up."

"We were talking about you, actually," Odonir said, speaking for the first time since Lorian's arrival.

"Ah, my favorite subject," Lorian replied with a cheeky grin as he plucked an orange from the table and began to peel it.

Finriel looked between Lorian and Odonir, and Lorian chuckled.

"Are you worried that I'm jealous of the two of you getting cozy with one another?"

Finriel scowled. "No, I'm not. It might be a surprise to you, but I don't spend every minute pining for your approval."

Odonir's cheeks went slightly pink at this, and Lorian snorted. "It's no matter because I have no reason to be jealous."

Finriel's brows inched toward her hairline, and Lorian met her gaze with a satisfied smile. Before, he would have been wary of getting a rise out of the witch, but now he simply loved it. Likely because he loved getting a rise out of anyone he interacted with.

"You don't need to keep talking," Finriel replied, and Lorian's smile only widened.

"Well, of course I do. I mean, you are friends with one of the most handsome and respectable men in the realm." Lorian winked. "But I am also quite unconcerned with you and my brother doing anything... foolish."

"I'm sitting right here, you know," Odonir growled through clenched teeth, but both Finriel and Lorian ignored him.

"And why would that be?" Finriel asked with narrowed eyes.

"Because my brother prefers men warming his bed, and the last time I checked, you are most certainly a woman."

Odonir choked on the tea he'd brought to his lips, and it was now Finriel's turn to blush a deep red. She glanced up at Odonir and then back down at her hands, which were now clasped in her lap. "I'm sorry. I didn't mean anything by pushing the subject."

Odonir seemed to have recovered from his near-death experience and offered her a faint smile. "Don't apologize. I don't blame you for trying to get anything other than that annoying grin out of my brother."

"Half brother," Lorian chided as he popped a slice of orange into his mouth, the fruit exploding with juicy citrus as he bit down on it.

Both Finriel and Odonir ignored him.

"Are you with anyone at the moment?" Finriel asked, and Odonir shook his head.

"I have never been with anyone, at least not seriously. The life that comes along with being a scout does not make it easy to maintain relationships of any kind."

"I'm sorry," Finriel said again, and Odonir took another sip of his tea before standing from his chair.

"It's nothing to worry about. I've given up on matters of love." Odonir shrugged on his leather jacket that had been slung across his chair. "I'd much rather focus on my duties to the queen."

"You sound like Tedric," Lorian muttered under his breath, but Odonir ignored him as he crossed to the door and said a brief goodbye before exiting the house.

Lorian was still surprised they'd been able to convince Odonir to let them stay, if even for a short while. After some deliberation, Lorian had told Odonir about their mission and what had happened in Anemoi Citadel. Odonir had remained silent the entire time, his face paling when Lorian told him of Aeden murdering King Sorren, as well as the Red King's hand in it all. He'd agreed to the importance of Lorian and Finriel's safety almost immediately, explaining that their information could prove helpful in protecting Queen Arbane if anything were to happen against the elves. His agreement to Lorian's extended company had surprised him, but he couldn't help feeling slightly happy about his brother's reluctant warmth.

"You shouldn't have embarrassed him like that," Finriel said pointedly as she brought a dark clay mug to her lips. "It's clearly not something he's comfortable speaking about."

"You shouldn't have asked if I was jealous." Lorian shrugged. "I was only being honest. Odonir is not ashamed of who he is either. It's actually quite common in Farrador for people of the same sex to be together and have a family."

"First off, you were the one who brought up jealousy, not

me," Finriel said. "Secondly, how can you have families of the same sex, but you can't have a family with a different race?"

"They don't care who you're with as long as they are still an elf," Lorian said. "I don't understand it either."

"I guess it makes more sense as to why you're so confusing," Finriel grumbled, and Lorian's heart stuttered as they both froze.

Lorian pasted an easy smile on his face, trying to shrug off the way her words made his pulse race. "Women are statistically more confusing than men." He lifted a finger. "We are simple creatures and only need three things."

"I highly doubt that," Finriel replied.

"I can confirm it." Lorian grinned and lifted his other hand to tick off his fingers as he spoke. "One, food. Two, the company of beautiful people." Finriel's brow raised, and Lorian's grin widened as he continued. "And three, a bed to sleep in, preferably with another person. Oh, and money is nice too."

"That's four things."

Lorian sighed. "Finriel, I'm a thief, not a mathematician."

Finriel opened her mouth, only for her reply to be drowned out by a yell and loud crashing sound outside. Lorian and Finriel were on their feet and racing through the door within seconds, adrenaline pumping madly through Lorian's veins as he looked around at the mess before them.

The small shed where Odonir kept his firewood had been reduced to nothing more than a pile of boards and dust, and Odonir himself was sprawled on the ground, trying to both regain his footing and hold his horse as the large stallion reared and snorted in fear. It was not difficult to find the reason for the sudden disruption. In fact, Lorian guessed that even a blind man would be able to spot the enormous black dragon standing in the clearing, now folding its large membranous wings against its scaled sides.

"I didn't think Krete would be the extravagant entrance type, but I guess I was wrong." Lorian grinned, and Finriel gasped, then ran toward the beast.

"What in the Nether are you doing?" Odonir yelled at the witch. "It's a black dragon! It will kill you!"

"Don't worry yourself, Odonir. We know this one," Lorian called to his brother, who had thankfully calmed his stallion enough so that the horse was not trying to escape.

"Krete!" Finriel called up to the small man beginning to crawl his way down the dragon's gleaming side.

An ear-splitting howl ran through the clearing, and a large gray blur sprang down from the dragon, landing on the ground before Finriel. A sob tore from the witch's throat as she lunged forward and wrapped her arms around the enormous feline, who began purring and rubbing against her.

"Nora, I thought I'd never see you again." Finriel sniffled.

Lorian passed them and approached the black dragon, who regarded them him large amber eyes. "Hello, Suzunne."

"Little thief, you look dashing today. Though perhaps a bath should be in your future," Suzunne replied in that strange guttural voice that most dragons possessed.

Lorian beamed. "I hope so. Perhaps you can convince my brother here to tell me where his bath is."

Lorian glanced to where Odonir was still standing frozen with his horse a few meters away. His blue eyes were wide as saucers as he took in the dragon, mogwa, and gnome, who was now making the final descent from Suzunne's leg to the ground.

"You're all mad." Odonir blanched, but Lorian ignored him as he turned back to face the gnome.

"Krete! I'm surprised you found us here so soon."

Krete beamed up at Lorian, and they joined in a hug, the gnome's head just barely reaching Lorian's chest. Krete looked nearly the same as the last time they'd seen each other in Fortula after the blood moon, but new lines had formed on the man's face, and his gray cap was slightly skewed on his head.

"Suzunne is surprisingly good at tracking," Krete replied with a smile, and Suzunne angled his head as though in thanks. "He's the one who found you through your letter. I don't think I could have done it without him."

"Perhaps it'll convince you not to shove me into that stuffy page this time," Suzunne said, and Lorian could have sworn it sounded like the dragon was upset.

Krete simply waved a dismissive hand at Suzunne, who let out an annoyed puff of hot hair, making Odonir jump back in alarm.

"Well, it's good to see you again." Lorian beamed. "I'm glad Maescia was able to give you the letter."

"Is she all right?" Finriel asked, coming to stand next to Lorian. "She had an arrow through her shoulder the last time we saw her."

Krete smiled. "She was the young one who kept interrupting Lizabet. Yes, she seemed healthy, though still bandaged."

Finriel didn't respond, but Lorian could see her shoulders relax from the corner of his vision. He instead glanced toward his brother, who was still standing frozen at the edge of the clearing.

"Krete, this is Odonir. He's letting us stay in his home for the time being."

Krete nodded kindly toward Odonir, who simply stared with that same expression of mingled surprise and horror. Krete's eyes narrowed, and then his smile widened as he spoke.

"You're the scout who let us go unnoticed in the forest when we had to climb the tree," Krete exclaimed, patting Suzunne's clawed paw that was nearly three times bigger than him.

"Krete caught on much quicker than you," Lorian said to Finriel with a grin, and Nora padded over to rub against his leg. Lorian scratched the mogwa behind the ear before looking up at Odonir. "Well, don't just stand there like a lost puppy. Come meet my friends."

"I really must be going. My duties begin shortly," Odonir

said as he hauled himself onto the snorting stallion. "I will return after sunset."

"I'm sorry about your shed," Krete said. "I'll fix it right away."

Odonir glanced between the gnome and the black dragon before he nudged his horse onward, and they were soon gone with nothing but a trail of dust left behind galloping hooves.

"He's a bit prickly," Krete mused, and Lorian snorted.

"Hard to believe that we're related."

Krete gaped at Lorian, but Finriel was the one to speak this time. "Don't worry, he didn't tell me either, until we were running for our lives."

"Brother?" Krete asked, and Lorian nodded.

"We only share a mother, thank the goddesses. But yes."

Krete nodded and turned back to Suzunne, who sighed hotly through his large nostrils. "I know, I know. It's time for me to go into the page so that we're not discovered."

"It will only be for a short while. You'll barely notice," Krete replied apologetically as he withdrew a sheath of rolled-up parchment from one of the compartments in his many-pocketed vest.

"You said that last time," Suzunne grumbled. "I was in there for an entire week."

"I promise it won't be that long this time." Krete smiled, and the dejected black dragon reached forward to touch his nose against the parchment, his body shimmering before it disappeared into the page.

The clearing felt much bigger now that there wasn't a ship-sized beast in the middle of it, and Lorian was able to spot the few trees that had fallen under Suzunne's sudden landing.

"Well, he's got more firewood now," Lorian said, nodding toward the unfortunate trees.

Krete shook his head. "I'll use those to rebuild the shed."

"You don't have to rebuild it for him. It looked rather shoddy anyway," Lorian replied, but Krete only smiled at him.

"I broke it; I'll repair it. Besides, I'm a very good builder."

"You can build later. We need to talk now," Finriel said and gestured for the two to follow her back inside Odonir's home.

Warmth enveloped Lorian's cold skin as they entered through the door, and he promptly returned to his seat, picking up the orange he had discarded upon hearing Krete's arrival.

"This is a lovely home," Krete said appreciatively as he looked around the stone walls. "Sturdy."

"I'm sure my brother built it himself, knowing the bastard," Lorian said, ignoring the slight twinge of jealousy in his abdomen at the comment. It wasn't that he was jealous of Odonir himself, only that his brother had managed to do some things Lorian was sure he would never achieve in his long life.

He had a home, a good living, and comfort.

Lorian shook his head and took a bite of orange, letting the joy of seeing Krete again paste a genuine grin on his face. "So, how have you been since we ran away from the Red King?"

Krete's face fell, and he shook his head. "Not all too well, if I'm being honest. Suzunne grew tired of my moping, which is partially why I've come to find you two. But I also told Drohan what happened during Clamidas, and he fears the Red King could be planning a war."

"War?" Finriel cut in with a raised brow. "But there's the peace law. How can there be war unless everyone curses themselves in the process?"

Krete shrugged. "I don't know. He talked about the chances being slim, but our forces are being trained and preparing for it anyway."

"What about Aeden?" Finriel asked, and hurt lashed through Lorian's chest.

Krete's face fell again, and he blinked quickly before replying. "I only saw her a short while ago, but it's not a very good situation."

"But she's the queen now?" Lorian asked, and Krete took in a shaky breath.

"She will be soon. But I'm worried about her."

"I'm more worried about her sending her shiny fairy guards to find us," Lorian replied.

"She's still a girl," Krete snapped, and Lorian sank in his chair. "And there's something off with her. I've known her since she was only six, and she's different."

"Power can change people," Finriel murmured, and Lorian nodded.

Krete shook his head. "It's not only that. There's a darkness around her, something that doesn't belong there."

A shiver ran down Lorian's spine, and he and Finriel exchanged a worried glance. Had the Red King done something to her that they hadn't known about?

"Was it a spell?" Finriel asked.

"I don't know," Krete replied. "But it felt like she was trapped somehow and forced into this mess."

"There's only one way we can find out," Lorian said, and Finriel shot him a glare.

"Whatever you're thinking, don't."

"What?" Lorian said. "We all have more questions than answers, and Krete thinks there could be another reason behind Aeden's sudden insanity. If we can find that out, then maybe we can figure out what exactly it is the Red King is planning on doing, as well as how he plans to involve Aeden."

"He has a point." Krete nodded.

"That's a death wish!" Finriel snapped. "Weren't we trying to stay as far away from the Red King and Aeden as possible?"

"Yes, but you have to taste a little bit of danger in order to know how to stop it," Lorian replied. "We would need some sort of way to get into Proveria unnoticed."

Krete and Finriel gave him looks of equal disbelief, and he looked between them with a shrug.

"It only makes sense. It would be smart to find out if Aeden and the Red King are truly planning something that could hurt the entire realm. If you are worried that she might be being used against her will, having the fairy court on our side when the Red King inevitably strikes is a smart move."

"Since when are you actually good at strategy?" Finriel asked, and Lorian winked.

"I only do it when direly necessary."

"We're going to get ourselves killed if we do this," Finriel muttered, ignoring his comment.

"You are more than welcome to stay behind," Lorian replied, but Finriel shook her head.

"No. I'm helping, even if it's just to save your asses when they inevitably need rescuing."

"Wonderful." Lorian smiled and looked at Krete.

The gnome was deep in contemplation but met Lorian's gaze with a ready answer. "My duty is to Creonid and Aeden. I will do whatever it takes to make sure the queen and the people are safe."

"That solves it, then." Lorian clapped his hands together. "Where do we start?"

"We could first figure out what Aeden is planning or being forced to do," Finriel said, with a hint of resignation in her voice. "Krete, why did you say she's *almost* queen?"

"Rulers need to be coronated before they're allowed to officially rule," Lorian replied, and Krete nodded.

"The coronation is in ten days." Krete sighed.

Lorian glanced between him and Finriel, who was chewing on the inside of her cheek. "That could give us enough time to plan a way to get in and find out more about what she's planning," he pointed out. "And maybe we can try to find Tedric, or at least find out if he's still alive."

"Are you mad?" Finriel exclaimed. "We'd be walking straight into a trap."

Krete cocked his head to the side with raised brows, and Lorian returned the expression.

"Is there something you know that we don't?" Lorian asked.

"Not necessarily, and Finriel is right. All three of us are wanted in Proveria and Keadora especially," Krete replied. "And the Red King will be in attendance."

"But?"

"But," Krete continued, "I think we might be able to figure out a way to get inside unnoticed. Or at least the two of us who are not trained thieves."

"How?" Finriel asked.

Krete rubbed his face with a hand, his gray cap falling slightly askew on his mouse-brown hair again. "It's customary for fairies to wear a special headpiece called a suphiera during large events, such as balls or coronations. It's very similar to a mask, but instead of human faces, they depict those of animals."

"Sounds perfectly simple to me," Lorian said.

Finriel huffed. "What exactly would be the purpose of going though, if only to risk our necks just to see if Tedric still has his? I doubt we will be able to gather information from Aeden or even get close to her, for that matter."

"People spill secrets when they're intoxicated, and I would wager a pretty large sum of gold that there will be both council members and alcohol on the premises," Lorian explained. "We can speak to them, see what they know. And if Tedric is still alive, then I would assume he could tell us something of Keadora's motives."

"I doubt the Red King will have told him anything at this point," Krete said doubtfully.

"But maybe he has spoken to people who have been told," Lorian said. "And perhaps Aeden has seen him. Do you think it would be safe to send her a letter?"

Krete looked down at his boots. "I'm not sure. She didn't seem quite in her right mind the last time I spoke to her, but she didn't call the guards on me, which I suppose is a step in our favor."

"Do you think it's worth potentially exposing our motives just for a silly letter?" Finriel asked. "It could be a bad idea, especially if we are planning on crashing her special night."

"It's worth a try," Lorian said. "I think I would sleep better knowing that our friend is alive. Perhaps we could somehow learn if he's going to attend the coronation, and if not, perhaps Krete can convince her to send him an invitation."

"I can certainly try," Krete offered, and Lorian smiled.

"Good man. I've always loved crashing large events."

"What will we wear though?" Finriel asked. "There's no way we will be able to find special fairy masks in Farrador."

"I think I might be able to take care of that," Lorian said as an idea popped into his head.

Finriel's eyes narrowed as she considered him. "What do you mean?"

Lorian shrugged. "Queen Arbane and her subjects will have to somehow receive the sapphires—or whatever it is Krete says they are."

Both Krete and Finriel gaped at him, and Lorian leaned into the tension with a confident smile.

"It's called a suphiera," Krete said.

"You mean to steal from the queen? Have you hit your head and forgotten what happened the last time you attempted to steal from a kingdom ruler?" Finriel asked.

Lorian waved his hand dismissively. "Don't worry. I don't think I'll forget being thrown into the dungeons of Crimson Castle anytime soon."

Finriel threw her hands up in the air, but Krete now only looked at him doubtfully. "How do you think the same thing won't happen to you this time? You were wanted in Farrador even before our mission."

"I know the same thing won't happen this time," Lorian said pointedly, "because last time, I didn't have a brother who worked for the Red King, and this time, I conveniently *do* have one that works for Queen Arbane."

"First of all," Finriel said, "you will likely get caught before you step foot through the city gates, and second, I doubt Odonir would ever help you."

"I wouldn't be so sure about that."

"And why is that?" Finriel crossed her arms.

"Because he's coming with us to the coronation, obviously," Lorian said, marveling at how slow his companions could be at times.

"He's right," Krete agreed. "If Odonir is a scout in Queen Arbane's inner circle, then he will likely have to help keep an eye on her during the coronation."

"So what, then? You and Odonir are just going to sneak into the castle, steal the suphieras of Queen Arbane's court, and we're going to sneak into Aeden's coronation?"

A grin spread onto Lorian's mouth as excitement bloomed inside him. Finally, they would be doing something interesting instead of just running. "That's exactly what we're going to do."

26

FINRIEL

"Absolutely not."

Odonir's face was flushed with anger. He sat in his usual seat at the table, cutting furiously into an apple. Finriel's already tense nerves rattled, and she turned on Lorian, who was seated next to her, his boots propped upon the corner of the table.

"I told you he would say no," Finriel shot at the thief, but Lorian did not seem surprised in the least by Odonir's refusal.

"It wouldn't be that large of a crime," Lorian explained. "We would be in and out of the castle before anyone noticed."

Odonir's scowl deepened. "It would not be that large of a crime for *you*, but you are already a criminal. I would be betraying my queen and going against every rule I have been trained to follow as a scout."

Lorian made a face and waved his hand. "Rules are just silly suggestions to keep people compliant. Besides, what is a small crime in exchange for potentially saving the entire realm?"

Finriel nodded. "He's right, Odonir. I like it as little as you do, but it could be our only chance."

Odonir's jaw worked as he digested their proposition. The door opened with a burst of frigid air, and Krete stomped through the threshold with pink cheeks and a satisfied expression. He closed the door and plopped onto the long side bench, small bits of wood tinkling to the floor as he did so.

"It's fixed," Krete said with a friendly smile, but Odonir only looked at him warily.

"What do you think, Krete?" Finriel asked quickly, as to keep Odonir from having to answer in his current state. "Is it worth stealing the suphieras from the queen?"

Krete wiped his brow and considered for a moment before answering. "Yes, I do. Aeden's state is far more concerning than I had anticipated, and I think this is our best opportunity to go straight into the thick of it and find out what's going on."

Odonir sighed. "I just don't understand why you wish to steal from Queen Arbane. She has done nothing to spite any of you. In fact, she hates the Red King as much as any of us."

"Which is why she is the one most likely to forgive us for doing what we must to learn more about his motives," Lorian said pointedly.

"I don't like it." Odonir shook his head and put down both the knife and apple on the table. "I'll think on it for a moment. Forgive me." The elf stood from the table and exited through a doorway leading to a room full of books, and Finriel sighed. Convincing him was not going as well as she would've liked, but there was at least a little bit of hope of him not immediately squashing the idea.

"He'll come around. Just give him a few minutes," Lorian said as he reached forward and took a slice of Odonir's discarded apple.

Krete and Finriel exchanged a glance, and Finriel was sure that Krete was thinking the same thing. Lorian was overconfident about his brother's desire to help their cause.

"What if he says no?" Finriel asked, and Lorian said the exact words she'd been dreading.

"I'll just retrieve the costumes myself."

"That would be suicide," Finriel said. "The bounty on your head is more than this entire house is worth."

"It's worth the risk." Lorian shrugged.

Footsteps approached, and the companions quickly silenced and watched as Odonir reentered the room. He wore a look of dejection that Finriel knew only meant one thing.

He was going to help them.

"There is a parade in three days' time, and Queen Arbane will be holding a speech. We can sneak into the castle and do it then, depending on if the garments have been delivered by that time."

Lorian beamed at his brother, but Finriel frowned. It was true—they had no way of finding out when the garments would arrive to the queen or if they would arrive no more than a day before the coronation.

"You can find out when the suphieras arrive, can't you?" Krete asked Odonir.

"Yes, just ask one of the queen's servants if they know anything about an arriving package from Proveria," Lorian said.

Odonir sighed and sank into his chair, pausing as he noticed a missing slice of apple. He looked up at Lorian with narrowed eyes before shaking his head and taking a slice for himself. "You are all asking a lot, and it will be dangerous," he said gruffly.

"It's the only chance we have," Finriel replied. "I know what the Red King is capable of. Our conversation with the storyteller was enough to prove there's something deeper at play that none of us know of."

"It's just hard to imagine what they could be planning," Odonir said. "Raymara has been under a peace law for over one thousand years. No one can break a magical law put in place by the goddesses."

"Not that we know of at least," Lorian pointed out. "And the Red King was alive when the law was created. Who knows what secrets or loopholes he learned of that day?"

"Why would he wait until now?" Odonir puzzled.

"Because everyone else who was alive and well during that time is long since dead," Krete said. "And we have all grown comfortable with the peace law. No one in the realm fears for their lives, and no one would ever guess that someone might be planning to destroy their safety."

Odonir considered Krete's words as he chewed another slice of apple, and Finriel leaned back into her chair as she thought over the gnome's words as well. He was right. Other than fearing things being broken into or perhaps being robbed and mildly scraped up, Finriel had never feared for her life. Not counting the day the elf boy had nearly drowned her. Barrin had truly been dangerous, but not like most people in the realm. If the Red King was planning an actual war with those beasts, they needed to know, for they were all severely unprepared.

"It's settled, then. You'll help retrieve the garments?" Finriel asked, and Odonir nodded.

"It's the only way."

"Good," Krete said and stood from the bench. "I think King Drohan will allow for me to attend the coronation as an escort for my sister. No harm will be able to come to me if I am under the king's protection."

"How is that possible?" Finriel asked. "You're wanted just like the rest of us."

Krete shook his head. "Any formal gatherings of royalty force a truce between all races, even if there are disagreements between one or more courts. If a large event occurs that involves multiple kingdoms, they are required to stay civil and pause all legal matters until the event is over."

Lorian snorted. "Well, that's convenient for you, being the queen's brother and all."

Krete gave him a kind smile. "Yes, and I will attempt to send a letter to Aeden or perhaps even sneak in a visit if I can. I have to depart in a few moments, but Suzunne and I will return in six days with more information. Maybe then I can stay until the coronation, if that is all right with you, Odonir."

The elf inclined his head. "Of course."

Krete's smile widened. "Wonderful. We can use those remaining days to come up with a solid plan, though I assume you three will already be scheming before I return."

"Why are you leaving now?" Finriel asked. "It's so late."

"It's safer for Suzunne to fly under the cover of night, especially so far from Drolatis," Krete explained. "Plus, most people are asleep by now, so it's unlikely we will be spotted."

Finriel, Lorian, and Odonir stood and followed Krete out the door into the dark winter night. Finriel shivered against the cold, wishing she had thought of putting on her cloak before stepping out. Krete was nearly invisible in the darkness, but the rustle of parchment followed by a blinding yellow light made it clear that Suzunne had just been released.

"Ah, much better." Suzunne's voice echoed through the darkness. "Are we leaving now?"

"Yes," Krete replied, and Finriel saw nothing but Suzunne's glowing amber eyes.

With a few grunts, it seemed as if Krete had managed to get safely atop Suzunne, and his voice called out to them. "I will be back in six days, at dusk."

"Be safe, and please don't do anything too stupid," Finriel called up to him.

"I don't agree with the second thing she said," Lorian said from beside her, and Finriel rolled her eyes, not the least bit surprised by what he said.

"I will follow Finriel's advice," Krete replied with a laugh. "Suzunne, are you ready?"

"Quite," Suzunne confirmed. "Be well, little people."

And with that, they were off, the mighty gust from Suzunne's wings blowing icy air against Finriel's face. She turned and headed inside, with Lorian and Odonir following closely behind. Finriel walked into the room full of books, hoping that the fire in there would do something to warm her bones. A smile lit her face as she entered the room and found Nora sprawled out before the fire, her side rising and falling evenly as she snoozed, though an amber eye cracked open to watch Finriel, Lorian, and Odonir enter.

Finriel crouched on the floor next to her mogwa and placed a hand on her side, the soft fur hot to the touch from the merry fire. Nora let out a croaking sound that Finriel guessed was as close to a meow as the dozing cat could manage at the moment.

Lorian and Odonir sat in the two plush seats a few feet away, and Lorian opened his mouth to speak. "So, how exactly are you planning on being my aid to steal the suphieras? Won't you be busy guarding the queen for the Festival of Ashes?"

"I can duck out for a few moments. She'll be too busy speaking to notice I'm gone," Odonir replied easily, and Finriel looked between the two of them with curiosity.

"What is the Festival of Ashes?"

"The Festival of Ashes pays tribute to Farrador's rebirth after the War of Seven Kingdoms. Since most of the ancient forests were burned down by the Red King's mighty flame, the festival honors the fields of small saplings that are now growing, as well as a more theoretical approach toward the actual residents honoring our beginning as a race," Odonir explained.

"The Red King burned down Farrador's forests?" Finriel asked, her memory flashing to an enormous field of ashes and small trees growing through it. She and her ward had skirted the area during their journey to Farrador, though her ward kept their mouth tightly shut when Finriel had asked about the cause of the carnage.

Odonir nodded with the flash of a frown. "You didn't know this?" Finriel shook her head, and Odonir sighed. "Of course not. The Red King chooses to keep any incriminating information about his wrongdoings from Keadorans."

"But it would have been in history textbooks and stories, wouldn't it?" Finriel pushed, and Odonir shrugged.

"Every kingdom has their own history books, and if you read them all, you'll find that they each say something different, and there is often a clashing of facts. It's up to the individual to decide what they believe, though the burning of Farrador is not something I could ever mark as a hoax."

"While this dive into our troubled realm's past is riveting, I do think we need to stay on topic," Lorian interjected, clearing his throat.

Odonir shot Lorian a narrow look but carried on. "The festival is celebrated with dances, face painting, and giving offerings to Anima."

"Don't forget the fertility gatherings," Lorian said with a grin.

Finriel frowned, unsure if she liked the sound of that.

Odonir rolled his eyes and leaned back in his seat. "It's not what you think. It's just a special party for men and women of age to mingle and dance, as well as for some to propose and marry."

Finriel nodded, shooting Lorian a sidelong look. He was such a boy.

"So you're planning on sneaking into the very castle you were almost arrested in to steal the suphieras?" Finriel asked after a moment of silence, and Lorian nodded.

"You will be able to slip in and out easily, as long as we're smart with time," Odonir said and then gave a mighty yawn. "It's been a long day. I will be gone before you two rise, and I will try to find out whatever I can about the delivery."

"Thank you," Finriel said, and Lorian gave her a look of surprise but didn't say anything.

Odonir nodded and walked out of the room, leaving Finriel and Lorian alone with Nora.

"You said thank you of your own free will?" Lorian said. "You surprise me every day."

Finriel's lips tilted upward. "I'm not the only surprising one. I didn't really think Odonir was going to help us at first, but he seems overly eager to help our cause even though he knows barely anything of it."

Lorian leaned back in his chair, and his eyes drifted shut. "Odonir has always been a man of order and peace, much unlike me. He feels a great duty for the safety of his queen, which I suppose has grown into caring for the entire realm."

"But why?" Finriel asked. "And how do you know so much about him when you never even mentioned him during our childhood?"

Lorian opened his eyes to gaze down at Finriel, and prickles of energy rushed down her arms and stomach at the look. "Do you remember when my mother and I would leave for a week every new moon?"

Finriel looked back on her memory and nodded. "I would always complain about being bored without you and ask to join on your adventure."

"We would sneak into Mitonir to see Odonir," Lorian explained. "He eventually told us to stop visiting him, that it was too dangerous with my mother being banned and all. But I still went to him after . . ."

"After that day," Finriel finished for him with a lurch of tightness in her stomach, and Lorian nodded.

They didn't talk about the day Finriel had almost been drowned and Lorian had run off to get help, which only resulted in his capture by a group of bandits. It was no longer a painful memory for Finriel, at least not the part when Lorian had left her. She knew now why he had done it and knew that Nora's rescue had been his doing. The flashbacks had not left though, and Finriel doubted they would anytime soon.

No, she still woke most nights in a cold sweat with the ghost of hands clasped around her neck. Bathing in a cold body of water still made her body rigid after the panic settled into her bones. But she had forgiven Lorian, and that was all that mattered for now.

"Odonir was furious that I had abandoned our mother like that and told me to get out of the city immediately. He was already a scout by then, and I can only assume he would sneak off to see her and make sure she was all right after I left."

"How did you know that your mother had died?" Finriel asked, almost afraid to ask such a personal question.

"Odonir sent me a letter when it happened five years ago, only one year after I'd last seen him," Lorian said almost wistfully. "I was in Fortula finishing a mission for some wealthy duke when I received it."

Finriel remained silent, and Lorian continued after a moment, his pale eyes clouded over in thought or memory, she wasn't sure.

"It was the last thing I heard from him before that day in the forest when he saved us." Lorian's gaze slid back to hers. "He's a good brother, even though I'd like it if you never told him I said that."

Finriel snorted and stood, her legs groaning from the sudden movement after sitting for so long. Nora stretched her legs out and gave a mighty yawn, her two rows of teeth just barely visible in the dimness of the room. Finriel waited for the mogwa to stand and follow after her, but Nora only curled her long tail around herself and closed her eyes once more. *A giant house cat indeed*, Finriel thought.

"We should go to bed. I'd like to practice some magic and maybe even have you show me a few fighting moves in the morning," Finriel said and started toward the door.

"Finriel, wait."

Finriel paused, turning around to face the thief again. Lorian was standing, his attention caught on her like she was the only thing in the world. She hated the way he looked at her. She hated the way it made her feel something new, something unfamiliar.

The thief took a step closer, and Finriel dropped her hand from the door handle.

"I wanted to talk to you about that kiss," Lorian said. "I was going to bring it up on the boat, but there was the sea monster and all."

Finriel's heartbeat stuttered, and she bit the inside of her cheek to keep from saying anything regrettable. Lorian only watched her, as if waiting for her to accept his desire to speak and continue the conversation. Her mind was screaming at her to stop, but her heart said otherwise.

"It was just a kiss, Lorian," Finriel replied finally.

"You know that's not true," Lorian said.

The room suddenly felt much too hot, and Finriel dropped her gaze to the rug with a shrug. "You agreed that it was a foolish idea."

"Because I was terrified of losing you again."

Finriel looked up at this, and her heart cracked at the anguish in her friend's eyes. His shoulders were tense, and the muscles of his crossed arms pushed against the fabric of his tunic. It was as though he were as ready to flee this conversation as she was—or maybe to flee from his own honesty, she wasn't sure.

"You won't lose me again," Finriel said and was surprised by the sincerity in her voice. "I forgive you, and even a silly kiss couldn't make me hate you again."

"But was it silly to you?" Lorian asked, and Finriel's pulse lurched.

No, it hadn't been silly for her. It had made her stop thinking completely and helped her feel more awake and present than she'd ever felt in her life.

"I don't know if you want me to answer that." Finriel hated how much her voice quavered.

"I wouldn't have asked if I didn't want to know," Lorian murmured, then ran a hand through his dark curls.

Finriel huffed, wishing her heart would simply stop racing. Perhaps her thoughts would clear, instead of only focusing on the memory of their kiss.

"Fine," she said after a moment. "I didn't think it was silly, not for a second. It scared me more than anything, but it wasn't a joke for me."

Silence enveloped the room, and the stone walls seemed to close in around her as she fought to breathe. She stared at him, and he stared at the floor as his jaw worked. He wasn't pacing, which was a surprise, but Finriel wasn't so sure he wouldn't start.

"What about you?" Finriel asked. "Did you get a good laugh out of it after you left that night?"

Lorian's gaze lifted from the rug, and Finriel had to bite the inside of her cheek again at the fire blazing in his eyes. "Kissing you was no laughing matter to me, nor will it ever be."

And then he was walking toward her, any glimmer of the joking thief now gone from the man's powerful strides and serious stare. He stopped barely a foot before her, and the scent of lavender and pine made her spine tingle. He had cleaned up sometime during the day and wore a black tunic and buckskin breeches that Finriel had never seen before.

He looked like a dream bathed in midnight, and she was terrified by how it made her feel.

"Where do we go from here?" Finriel asked.

Lorian uncrossed his arms and reached one out to her. Finriel looked down at his long fingers laced with silver-white scars, pausing for a moment before she finally took it. His skin was calloused but warm, and she let him pull her closer as she tilted her head up to meet his stare.

"How do you feel about me, truly?" Lorian asked. "No games, no lies. Simply honesty."

Finriel couldn't help but laugh at his question, shaking her head. "The king of games asks me to be serious for once."

The corner of Lorian's lips twitched upward. "There's a first time for everything."

The smile died on Finriel's lips, and she sighed. "I feel a lot of things, Lorian. You're my best friend, and I want to kill you sometimes. But I can't deny this . . . way that I feel whenever I look at you. I don't know what it is. But in the back of my mind, I'm still afraid that you don't care enough to stay, and that frightens me."

His hand slipped from hers and moved up to cup her cheek, sending warmth blooming through her skin. His gaze was molten ice as he looked at her, and Finriel was sure the world was spinning a bit too fast as he drank in her features and shook his head.

"Listen to me. I will *never* leave you again. It would kill me, and you know how much I hate feeling like I belong to something."

Finriel gulped and nodded.

"I can't fight this, no matter how much I want to," Lorian said. "I'm so good at running away—it is my job after all—but every time I've run away from you it's only been because fate made me. You're the only thing I've never wanted to run from."

"But what do you *feel*?" Finriel said, her voice no more than a whisper.

Lorian silenced at this, shaking his head. Finriel's heart sank like the Ten's ship in the Sandrial Waters. It had been no more than a moment of fleeting passion for him. Perhaps the lighting of the witches' cottage had made her look more alluring and less like his best friend. With a chest-squeezing sigh, Finriel gave him a knowing bob of her head and began to step away from him.

"Finriel," Lorian murmured, his fingers tightening around her hand, the other tilting her chin up to meet his gaze.

"What, Lorian?" Finriel huffed, though the pressure of his

fingers on her skin made electric shocks shoot through her stomach. "Just say it. I won't break."

Not a second went by before his lips were pressed against hers, hot and hungry to tell her what words could not. She found herself leaning into his touch, allowing their mouths and hands to explore each other in a way she had never allowed herself to experience before.

He broke away, leaving them both panting and staring at each other. There were no words in Finriel's mind, only a buzzing sense of *rightness* that left her terrified yet yearning for more.

"Did that answer your question?" Lorian asked huskily, and Finriel rolled her eyes. "I'll take that as a no."

His chuckle vibrated against her hands, which were now pressed against his chest.

"I feel so much for you that I honestly don't know how to say it," Lorian admitted. "You frustrate me beyond belief, and you scare me."

Finriel narrowed her eyes, confusion and the high from kissing him melding together. "I scare you?"

Lorian nodded. "Yes. I've seen what you can do when someone gets on your bad side."

"Those were two very negative things you named," Finriel said, looking down at her hands still resting on his chest.

"Yes," Lorian said. "But I also love the way you bite the inside of your cheek when you think. I love the way we work well together without having to say much of anything at all. I love how determined you are—"

"So what are you saying?" Finriel asked cautiously, trying to calm her racing heartbeat into a more rhythmic pulse.

But how could she calm down when his thumb was tracing idle circles on her jaw? Or when his other hand was now caressing her waist, and his eyes bored straight into her soul? He didn't have to say how he felt; his eyes said it all.

But she had been hurt far too many times in the past, and she was beginning to lose trust in herself.

"I feel the same way you feel about me," Lorian said finally. "And likely more."

"I doubt that." Finriel snorted, and her cheeks warmed at the accidental admittance.

Lorian's lips quirked upward, and his eyes softened as he looked at her. "There's only ever been one woman in my life, and I intend for it to stay that way."

Past Finriel would have scoffed in his face—or worse, told him to shove the proclamation up his ass. But she knew what he said about his feelings was true, and for once, she let herself believe him.

"I . . . I don't know what to say," Finriel admitted, and Lorian smirked.

"For once, I have left the witch speechless."

Finriel rolled her eyes again, and Lorian only chuckled. "You should get some rest. I can stay the night in here with Nora."

Finriel frowned. "Why?"

She had grown so used to sleeping in the same bed as him, and the thought of having all of that space to herself and no one else warming the sheets made her feel strange. Goddesses above, she was growing weak.

"Because I fear what could happen if I'm near you for one more second," Lorian said, his voice suddenly low and full of dangerously sweet promises.

Warmth flooded every part of her body, and even the flame coiled around her core reared its head in response. Finriel bit the inside of her cheek and nodded, not daring to let her desire show. There was only so much she could give in one night.

"Right." She made herself speak, then turned on her heel and left before her heart made her stay, damning any consequences.

27
DESPAIR

Magic leaked from his fingers and dripped from the very walls caging him in.

There was no emotion behind the dull repetitive motion of creation. For was it truly creation if the beasts within were designed to do nothing but destroy?

Scratch.

Sigh.

Rub.

Curse.

They were the only sounds to have filled his mind for weeks, save for the moments when he was joined by the key. The darkness that dwelled in his heart had eased slightly, knowing that his pain was shared by the soul of another. Different pain of course, but pain nonetheless.

He dropped the charcoal, flexing his sore fingers and staring blankly at the creation of talons and teeth growling up at him. He was creating the end of it all, though he wished for his own end now.

The goddesses had spoken, however, and he would not know oblivion until it swallowed the entire world.

28
FINRIEL

Sunlight coaxed Finriel to consciousness. She rolled over with a sigh, relishing in the warmth of morning pooling onto the bed. When her hand found its way to the side typically occupied by a rogue thief, it landed on nothing but smooth linen sheets. She frowned, cracking an eye open to find that she was very much alone. Then last evening rushed back into her memory, and Finriel lurched into a seated position. She'd slept so deeply that she'd forgotten his decision to sleep in the study, as well as his lips on hers.

Enough of that, Finriel thought, shaking her head.

After rolling out of bed and finding a pair of plain black pants and a white tunic, both purchased by Odonir, Finriel braided her hair before padding to the kitchen. It, too, was empty, and a tinge of worry made her stomach tighten. She moved toward the door, but it opened before her fingers grasped the handle.

A curse slipped past her lips as she stepped back, suddenly very aware of Lorian standing in front of her. His hair was tousled, and his cheeks were flushed. He gave her a grin as he slipped to the side and closed the door.

"Morning," Lorian said.

"What were you doing?" Finriel asked, and Lorian's grin only widened.

"Preparing for our first lesson."

"What?" Finriel frowned, rooted to the spot even though her stomach growled with hunger.

Lorian shrugged. "You said you wanted to learn the art of violence last night, and I've never turned down the opportunity for a good fistfight."

Finriel opened and then promptly closed her mouth, unsure of how to respond. Her desire to fight had been the last thing on her mind after everything that had happened between them. The taste of his lips and his proclamation of wanting her had made even their mission fade away, if only for a moment.

"I'll need breakfast before any fistfights happen." Finriel made her way to the pantry, where Odonir kept his provisions.

ONE HEARTY MEAL of porridge and a mug of Odonir's calming tea later, Finriel found herself in the clearing in front of the house, face-to-face with a bale of hay from the horse barn and two long staffs made of light-colored wood. Trepidation and excitement mingled together in her gut, and Finriel took a step toward the staffs with curiosity.

"We'll begin with basic technique." Lorian's voice rang out from behind, and Finriel jumped, whirling to face him.

He was standing not one foot behind her, his head tilted down to watch her. Her gaze caught on the curve of his lips, and that annoying warmth spread through her stomach. She looked away before he noticed, though by the intent look in his eyes, he was likely thinking the same thing.

"Your silent tricks aren't funny," Finriel said, shaking her head as he smirked and walked past her.

"They serve me well, and you'd be smart to learn how to move silently too," he replied. "But we'll do that another time."

"So what is basic technique?"

Lorian's expression molded into one of purpose, and he took a step back from her. "We warm up."

Disbelief flooded through Finriel, rooting her feet to the ground as she stared at him. "You warm up? I thought thieves fought dirty." Finriel balked, winning a laugh from Lorian in turn.

"Of course I fight dirty, but that's because I know what I'm doing." His smile widened. "If I were to begin fighting with you the way I would another skilled fighter, you would be on the ground in less than a second."

A thick feeling seeped into her chest, like tar wrapping around her good spirits. "I know how to hold my own in a fight," she grumbled, crossing her arms.

Lorian arched an eyebrow. "You're telling me that you'd be able to stand your ground if I came at you this very moment?"

She wasn't sure of it at all, but there was one thing she hated more than anything: being underestimated.

"We can find out." Finriel shrugged.

"Fine."

One moment, he was standing before her. The next, he was gone. Something flashed in the corner of her left eye, and she acted on instinct, though not before tamping down the fire that swelled in her core. Finriel widened her stance before turning, but she was too late. Lorian had slipped behind her and locked an arm around her neck. Without thinking, she shot her right leg out to disarm his balance. He grunted, but his grip held fast. Finriel grasped his forearm, the thick muscle rippling beneath her touch. Heat soared through her veins, but with a groan, Finriel halted the magic before it reached her fingers. She didn't want to use magic to win this fight, and she especially didn't want to burn the poor man.

"See? Not even one second," Lorian whispered in her ear, and thick fury melted any thoughts of sparing Lorian's pride.

"So quick to claim victory." With a grunt, Finriel used all her strength to bend and yank Lorian off her, sending him flying over her back and landing on the ground with a groan.

Lorian coughed, then began to laugh. Finriel frowned, crossing her arms again as she watched the thief shake his head and climb to his feet.

"Not bad," he said with a grin.

"I just knocked you onto your backside with no training." Finriel glared. "How in the Nether are you going to teach me anything?"

He returned her stare, and she repressed a shiver at the intensity of his gaze.

"I was just testing you." He shrugged. "You definitely have the quick thinking needed to fight the way I do, so this should be fun."

"I'm not sure that I'd consider being thrown to the ground fun."

"You'd be surprised how exhilarating a good fight can be," Lorian replied. "Now, let's get started."

He ushered her closer with a hand, and she took a few steps so that they were close enough to touch. Lorian bent his knees slightly, planting his feet hip-width apart.

"First, I'm going to teach you how to punch someone without breaking your hand," he said, raising his fists as an example. "Never tuck your thumb into your palm. That will break it if you hit someone like that."

He extended his fist, showing how he wrapped his thumb on the outside of his other fingers. Finriel nodded, raising her own hands in the same way. Lorian straightened and took a step closer. He tentatively took her wrist, and she ignored the electricity that shot through her skin at the contact.

"Always keep a straight line between your fist and elbow.

Don't let your wrist bend one way or the other, unless you want to break that too."

Finriel frowned, looking up at him. "I'm not sure I like how often you've mentioned the potential of breaking bones."

Lorian shrugged, letting go of her wrist. "It's the nature of fighting. Someone will always break in the end."

She didn't respond, only adjusted her stance and silently tweaked the position of her arms when he told her to. She wasn't sure how she felt about being taught how to fight by Lorian and was sure she would have preferred Tedric's more formal methods. But there was a life-altering prophecy looming over them, and Finriel didn't have the time to fight clean.

Once he was happy with her position, Lorian nodded and stepped away. "Good. Now you're going to throw a few punches, slowly at first so you can get the feel for it."

"Is there a proper way to do that too?" Finriel asked.

"Of course, but remember that I'm teaching you." Lorian winked.

"What does that mean?" Finriel frowned, and Lorian only shrugged.

"Just punch."

Goddesses above, she was going to kill him.

Without thinking twice, Finriel drove her fist forward, straight at Lorian's face. He was gone before it made contact, however, and a gasp flew from her lips as fingers wrapped around her wrist. Her feet were forced to turn as Lorian pinned her arm behind her back.

"You're going to have to be faster than that," Lorian murmured in her ear.

Frustration swelled in Finriel's abdomen, and the flames within swelled too.

She panted, hating how out of breath she was already. "It seems like your only move is getting behind someone."

The thief's low chuckle made her toes curl in both annoyance and desire, and she spun away as his grip on her wrist loosened.

"If you want to kill someone you love, do it from behind. If you hate them, kill them from the front," Lorian said, his expression hardening slightly.

Finriel paused. "Why?"

Lorian bent down to grab a staff from the frostbitten ground. "I think it would be rather satisfying to watch the person I loathe most realize that I took their life away from them."

He was insane.

Finriel shook her head, taking the staff he held out to her. It was light and easy to wield, and she wondered what exactly he was going to teach her with a stick and straw.

"We're going to move on to swordplay," Lorian said. "I would be reprimanded for bouncing amongst so many types of fighting, but I think it's more entertaining this way."

Finriel shrugged, not daring to admit that she didn't enjoy the close proximity of fists. The staff in her hand felt safer, and she had a feeling this type of fighting would be much more to her liking.

"What's that for?" Finriel asked, gesturing toward the hay bales with the butt-end of her staff.

"That," Lorian said, "is the person you will be fighting today." He stepped toward the stack of straw, drawing his staff up like a blade. An upward arc and then quick slash down brought the staff bouncing lightly off the dummy. "That's the head," he said, then drew a swift blow to the side. "Neck, heart, and gut." He performed a different movement for each body part that rolled from his lips, and Finriel watched him repeat the movement two more times, each occasion faster than the last. Finally, he stepped to the side, giving her a dashing smile. "Your turn."

Finriel took a tentative step forward, switching her grip to the same fashion with which Lorian held his staff.

"Slowly first, then quickly once you get a feel for it," Lorian said. "These are the easiest points to incapacitate someone without killing them."

"Not fatal?" Finriel gaped. "I am a healer, you know. Each of these points are very much fatal."

Lorian shrugged. "Not if you hit them light enough."

It took all of her strength not to roll her eyes, and she lifted the staff. The motions came much easier this time, and Finriel had no issue rotating her body and maneuvering the staff to her will. It felt much closer to using her magic, as she could remain a healthy distance away from the target while manipulating an object separate from herself.

"Not bad. Now faster," Lorian said.

Finriel nodded and rose the staff again. The shock reverberating through her muscles with each blow was equally as painful as it was exhilarating, and she couldn't stop the determined smile from growing on her face. Why hadn't Lizabet jumped straight into her magic lessons the way Lorian had with this? She would have learned so much more in the few days she'd gotten with the elder witch.

Frustration grew in her stomach, and Finriel began the rotation again without Lorian's command. Heat burned through her muscles, but she relished the stinging pain as she continued to stab, swipe, and slash.

Her mind drifted to Tedric, and the scent of copper clung to her nose. He, too, had slashed and parried the way she did now, but his fate was now nothing but uncertainty. She paused and shook her head, the sensation of her boots sticky with shimmering blood suddenly palpable. A shiver whispered down Finriel's spine, and the staff fell from her fingers. She didn't think she'd ever have the gall to kill someone, curse or no.

He's alive. He's alive. He's alive.

"Are you all right?" Lorian asked, cutting through her thoughts.

Finriel blinked, nodding quickly. "What if the curse is as bad as they say?" she asked, unable to stop the question.

"Is this about Tedric?" he said instead of answering, and Finriel nodded.

Lorian took two long strides closer, his hands whispering against the cloth of her tunic before resting on her shoulder. "Tedric is one of the strongest people I've ever met. I'll eat my brother before believing him unwell."

It was enough to bring about a weak bloom of hope in Finriel's chest, and she nodded. It was true; Tedric was stubborn and foolish when it came to things such as duty, but he was relentless in his perseverance.

"Besides, he'd probably claim that the curse has helped him realize how little he knew about suffering," Lorian said with a smirk.

Finriel sighed. "I just wish we could have done more to help. And Aeden—"

"She's the worst of it all," Lorian agreed, hurt dancing across his features.

Finriel hadn't allowed herself to think of their friend and the pain she'd caused the entire realm. It simply didn't feel right, the weight of it all. Tears prickled the backs of her eyes, and Finriel blinked quickly.

"This has all turned into so much more than a silly quest." Finriel sighed, looking down at Lorian's chest.

His hand traveled from her shoulder to her hand, and she let him squeeze her fingers reassuringly. The simple contact was enough to ground her, if ever so slightly. At least all of this madness had brought him back to her, as little as she'd wanted it before.

Lorian tugged on her hand, and her eyes traveled up to meet his. He was watching her with an expression of sadness and something else she couldn't place, though it made her shiver. "Come on. I think we've had enough training for the day."

29

TEDRIC

"Keep up, Drazak."

Griffin's rough voice whispered through the entourage of common guards and select members of the Ten that surrounded the Red King's carriage. Tedric sat astride Dario, his gray stallion that had been a friend for many years. They had started the journey to Proveria at dawn, and the Red King had ordered a group of guards and Griffin to ride around him, should he try to escape or otherwise. Tedric hadn't cared in the moment, as he'd barely slept before setting out. His stomach was in knots, and it wasn't because of the curse.

The thought of having to face Aeden again after what he said to her was sickening, and Tedric would have to act like he hadn't meant a word. Perhaps by getting close to her again, he would be able to figure out what that scar on her arm meant and how the Red King was controlling her with it. It was an internal battle, trying to decide between what was right and what was honorable. At one point in Tedric's life, he would have thought the two words interchangeable in meaning. Now he wasn't so sure.

"What in the Nether?" one of the Red King's sour-faced guards cursed by Tedric's side.

Tedric snapped to focus and scanned their surroundings. They were reaching the familiar kingdom border between Keadora and Proveria, the shimmering blue wall ever present. But it wasn't the border or the familiar smattering of dark stones he, Finriel, and Lorian had camped by a few moons ago that made Tedric's pulse stutter.

It was the small army standing guard at the kingdom border.

At least fifty men in gleaming armor were lined up at the edge of the shimmering border, and Tedric squinted to see the faint shapes of guards lining the Proverian border as well.

"What is this?" Tedric ground out.

"The Red King and Queen Siltra put their men out here as a matter of safety—whatever that means," Griffin replied quietly.

"But why so many men?" Tedric asked. "We're still a peaceful realm, and he has the storyteller. No more beasts have been let out to put anyone in danger."

"We don't know that for sure." Griffin glanced sidelong at Tedric. "Your friends are still wanted."

The realization hit Tedric in the chest. These men were stationed to stop Lorian and Finriel. He suppressed a snort, knowing very well that his companions were likely as far from Proveria and Keadora as possible. Or at least he hoped they weren't foolish enough to come back.

A familiar tickling sensation made Tedric shudder as he and the large succession followed the king's carriage through the Proverian border. His mind still whirled at the many soldiers lined up on the Proverian and Keadoran borders, with humans and fairies alike standing guard on either side. He noticed that they all wore the same dark gold armor when he passed by, which made Tedric more uncomfortable than he dared let show.

The hours passed by in what felt like seconds. Anemoi Citadel approached quickly, and Tedric's heart began to beat painfully in his chest at the thought of seeing Aeden again, especially after everything he had said. Griffin and the rest of the Ten veered away in a different direction when they reached the silver path, leaving Tedric alone with the guards, who led him after the Red King's carriage. They came to a halt before the silver path, and Tedric dismounted, gritting his teeth as one of the guards took stance behind him and the other took Dario's reins, leading the stallion away.

The Red King stepped out of the carriage and looked around with that aggravating faint smile still plastered to his lips. The guard urged Tedric forward, and they followed the Red King and remaining guards up the path, toward the main castle.

Tedric tried his best to take in calming breaths as they approached the arched gates and courtyard beyond. The memories of Clamidas still clung to his heart, and it gave a terrible squeeze as they entered the covered passageways. Servants and nobles milled about, filling the open castle with noise and laughter, but it didn't stop the memories of fighting and the stench of death from flooding into Tedric's mind and nearly paralyzing him.

"Follow me, Drazak," the Red King said through the silence. "Guards, you are dismissed."

Tedric forced his feet to move, and every step was agony as he followed the Red King to the throne room—the very place where he'd killed someone and the floors had been slick with blood.

The doors swung open wide, and Tedric was immediately transported back to the night on Clamidas. The night that Aeden had revealed herself as a monster. The room looked completely repaired, if not perhaps slightly modified since that night. The crystal wall that had crumbled after King Sorren's death had been rebuilt, aside from the fact that there were now two large windows instead of one. Only one throne now sat on the dais, and glowing plants in thick marble pots stood on raised platforms of altering heights behind it.

And then there was Aeden, seated upon the crystal throne as

if it were her home. She gazed down upon the Red King with a smile and nod of her head, but her eyes flashed with a look that promised death as soon as she met Tedric's stare.

"Your Majesty." The Red King inclined his head, and Tedric forced a small bow as well.

"I expect that your journey was uneventful?" Aeden asked, and the Red King nodded.

"Most certainly. The new addition along the border is working quite efficiently."

"Good," Aeden said shortly. "Have your men found their quarters?"

"Yes." The Red King smiled. "And I am off to find my own for a brief rest before you and I discuss further matters."

Aeden inclined her head, and the Red King turned to leave. Tedric started after him, but something stopped him abruptly, as if an invisible wall kept him from going any farther. The Red King only gave him the briefest of looks before he continued walking, and Tedric was once again left alone with Aeden. He turned back and looked up at the queen, at a loss for words. Even through all of his pain and hatred, Tedric thought she looked beautiful.

Deadly, but beautiful.

"Why are you here?" Aeden asked coolly.

"The Red King appointed me as one of his guards for the coronation." Tedric swallowed back his hate before he added, "And I came to see you."

Aeden raised her brow. "I thought you never wanted to see me again unless completely necessary. You made it quite clear that you don't approve of my actions."

You are far stronger than you think you are. Egharis's words echoed through his head, and Tedric took a steadying breath as he spoke the words he would never be able to take back. "I didn't mean what I said that day. I was incredibly hungover and in awful spirits because of it."

Aeden did not respond, and Tedric forced himself to continue. "I was angry and hadn't yet taken the potion against the curse. Aeden, please forgive me." Tedric took a step up toward the dais, and words began to fly from his mouth before he could stop them. "I want to keep seeing you, Aeden. I don't know what's happening between you and the Red King, but I have to trust that it's for the greater good. I can't even begin to imagine what you have to do as queen or the pressure you now face with an entire kingdom on your shoulders. I suppose the commander in me was afraid that something terrible was going to happen if you and the Red King worked together."

Tedric spotted the slight tension in Aeden's shoulders relax as he spoke, and satisfaction flickered in his chest, followed by a healthy dose of self-loathing. He was making this girl trust him again for his own gain.

But it wasn't only for his gain, not truly. It was for the gain and safety of the entire realm.

He continued, "I thought the Red King hurt you with that scar, and it made me angry. I don't want to see you hurt, Aeden. It breaks me to see you in pain."

He wasn't lying about that part. But was that enough to see the rest of Raymara burn?

"Forgive me if I don't believe you entirely," Aeden said, though the noticeable softness in her tone betrayed her. "You said some awful things."

Tedric took the first step up the dais and looked at her with as much conviction as he could muster. "I know I did, and it's plagued me ever since."

Tedric reached the top step, and without another word, he knelt before her with disgust and confusion rising inside him like a raging dragon. He tamped the feeling down, instead focusing on finding whatever remnant of the girl he'd fallen in love with that remained inside the queen before him.

"Aeden, I love you."

The words were out of his mouth before he could stop them, and he quickly bowed his head to the ground so that she would not see the look of distain that crossed over his face. He could not take back those words, not now and not ever. He was digging himself into a grave of thorns and darkness that wouldn't let him leave again.

Aeden's skirts rustled, and then a cold finger was under his chin. Tedric schooled his face before he let Aeden tilt his head up to look at her. A tremor of shock went through him at what he beheld. For it was not triumph or haughtiness that Tedric was greeted with, but tears. Aeden was crying freely as she gazed down upon him, and Tedric found a small corner of himself wanting to wipe her anguish away.

"Do you mean that? Truly?" Her words were no more than a whisper, but Tedric nodded.

"Truly, with my entire heart. But I understand if you—"

Aeden broke him off mid-sentence as her lips came crashing down upon his, hungry and fervent. He lifted his hand to cup her cheek and returned the kiss with his own vigor, using whatever pent-up desire and frustration he had to deepen the kiss even though his mangled heart screamed for him to stop. Her lips tasted of honey and tears as she kissed him, and he let her guide him up to a stand without breaking away. Tedric pressed himself against Aeden's chest, gliding his hands up her back only to find it bare. He attempted to ignore the sudden desire that tore through him at the discovery.

They broke away panting, and Tedric met Aeden's green stare with the most promising look he could muster. Aeden's red lips parted as she took in his face and then the rest of his body.

"I suppose this is part where I tell you that I love you too."

Perhaps in another lifetime, he would have felt like the luckiest man in the realm to hear those words part from her lips, but now, he felt nothing other than burning guilt that threatened to make him sick.

He forced a smile onto his lips anyway and kissed her again when words failed him. For he wasn't sure if he could say any more, if he could let another lie fall from his lips without regretting agreeing to Egharis's proposal. However, a silent part of him didn't regret kissing her, touching her, simply being in her presence, and that terrified him.

Aeden broke away again, and a look of mischief danced across her face as she took his hand and led him toward the large throne behind her.

"What are you doing?" Tedric asked with a sudden surge of nerves.

"You know what I'm doing," Aeden said with a voice of velvet as she spun them around so that Tedric's back was to the throne.

She pressed him down onto the throne before sitting upon his lap, her skirts sweeping across the floor with a light whoosh. Tedric met her hungry stare with what he hoped was one to match, and Aeden brought a hand up to brush a stray strand of hair from his forehead.

"Do you not want to?" she asked shyly, and Tedric tilted his head toward hers.

"I do, but in here? People could walk in."

"So?" Aeden shrugged with a mischievous grin. "It's my castle. I can do as I wish."

Tedric looked down at her body and was met with a painful surge of longing. She was beautiful, and he hated her for it. He let the darkness win and his hand traveled up her bodice and then down again before resting against her waist. Nether damn him, he wanted her, no matter how terrible he knew it was. She was the shade of a tree on a sunny day, the cool whisper of a breeze that kissed the heat of summer away. But she was also a viper dressed like a queen, and he was more than willing to be struck by her venom.

"Though it would be an exhilarating experience to take you on the throne, I think it would be best if we were truly alone."

Aeden's face fell, but her smile quickly returned and she stood. "As you wish."

She held out a well-manicured hand, and Tedric took it, forcing away the sickness and overwhelming desire that rose in his body. He hated that his feet moved all too willingly, that though he was angry, a rush of excitement thrummed in his veins. He wasn't so shallow as to just want her body; that wasn't the only reason he felt so light through the heaviness.

He loved her and was beginning to find that he loved her madness too.

30
LORIAN

"Are you sure this is going to work?"

Lorian strapped his dagger to his belt and looked up at Finriel, who was seated on their bed, watching him with a concern-muddled expression. Lorian straightened and took two long strides toward her, then took her hand and squeezed it gently.

"I'll be just fine."

Finriel's fingers tightened around his before he could pull away. "You are *wanted* in Mitonir, Lorian. It will be a death trap if you fail."

Lorian looked into her swirling caramel-and-orange eyes and winked. The fact that she was so scared for his safety touched a place inside him he wasn't sure he liked. She gave him a reason to complete this task without getting caught, and that made him question his chances.

"You're making me more nervous. I swear I'll be fine. Besides, I've got my dear old brother to watch my back," Lorian replied, and Finriel let his hand go as he turned and reached for a leather jacket similar to Odonir's typical attire.

He could not afford to wear his cloak into the city for fear of being too obvious about his identity. A strip of dark green cloth lay over the arm of the small seat, and Lorian considered it. Odonir had insisted he tied his hair with the cloth, which was customary for all elf scouts who chose to wear their hair long. Lorian wished to be as different from an elf scout as he possibly could, but today was not a day for being picky. Lorian snatched up the cloth and turned to Finriel.

"Would you mind? I'm afraid I don't know how to do anything to my hair other than wash it."

Finriel motioned him over, and Lorian obliged, handing her the green strip before turning and sitting on the floor with his back turned to her. Finriel's fingers ran through his hair, and Lorian winced as she snagged on a knotted curl.

"Careful. You don't want to rip out my prettiest feature," Lorian bit out as the pain continued.

"I need your hair untangled before I can do anything with it," Finriel replied haughtily, then paused. "I'll need to hide your ears somehow."

Lorian reached up to feel the very slight point to his ears, though to someone far away, the slight elven feature was not noticeable. He dropped his hand and leaned into Finriel's knees, taking the opportunity to sink into her warmth. "Too pointed for men but not pointy enough for elves." Lorian sighed. "Do what you must."

Finriel got to work then, and in a few seconds, his hair was tied off with the front ends left out to hide his ears. Lorian stood and turned toward Finriel, lifting his arms out with a smile.

"How do I look?"

Finriel rolled her eyes and stood so that they were mere inches from each other. "Good, unfortunately."

Lorian screwed up his face with confusion. "How are my dashing looks unfortunate? Would you rather I looked like a pig?"

Finriel shook her head and gave him an exasperated look.

"It's unfortunate because I know you'll never try this hard to look nice again."

Lorian's face molded into a grin, and he couldn't help glancing down at her lips. "Just wait until the coronation. You might die from astonishment if how I look now is already making you weak at the knees."

He leaned toward her, aching to break the space between them, but Finriel only brought a hand up to his lips and shook her head. "You don't get to do that until you've returned safely with our supplies *and* all of your body parts intact."

Lorian raised his brow and grinned as she removed her hand and let it fall to her side. "Oh, don't worry. I'll ensure that all of my parts come back to you safe and sound."

"You're terrible." Finriel rolled her eyes, but Lorian thought he saw the hint of a smile on her lips as they both turned toward the bedroom door.

~

"GOOD BOY, OATS," Lorian said as he dismounted Finriel's horse and gave him a pat on the neck.

They had all agreed that it would be safer for Lorian to ride Oats instead of Ed, just in case someone remembered his steed from their pursuit in the city five days prior. Odonir had let Lorian and Oats into a smaller barn behind the main royal stables, glancing behind his shoulder as he closed the back doors behind Oats's tail. Lorian led Oats into a vacant stall and removed his bridle before exiting. Odonir was now waiting by the door, his booted foot tapping against the dirt with either nerves or anticipation, Lorian was not sure.

"The festival is going to start any minute now," Odonir said, glancing toward the sounds of music and cheering beyond.

"Don't worry. I'm ready," Lorian said as he closed the stall door behind him and approached his brother.

"You remember the plan?" Odonir asked, and Lorian nodded.

"You get to the queen and keep an ear out as I sneak in, steal her masks, and leave. Simple."

"You need to be serious about this." Odonir scowled, and Lorian simply smiled.

"That takes all the fun out of it." Lorian clapped his brother on the shoulder. "Well, come on, then. We're going to be late."

Odonir cursed under his breath as he and Lorian stepped out of the barn and into the bright winter day. Frost coated the street in a glittering blanket, and puffs of crystalized breath swirled from their mouths as they made their way down the small slope and toward the side entrance of the castle. They walked in silence until they reached the thick stone wall. Odonir turned to face the street and glanced around, likely to check if they were alone.

"In and immediately to the third floor, remember?" Odonir said, and Lorian sighed.

"Yes, yes. You forget that sneaking into people's homes is my favorite pastime. Now let's go. You'll be late for your post."

Odonir clenched his jaw but gave Lorian one last nod before picking up his pace and leading him to a small wooden door built into the stone wall. Lorian's footsteps were like a ghost's in comparison to Odonir's booted steps that clicked quietly on the polished stone floor. They walked side by side down the corridor. Soft golden light filtered through a small window. The plan was easier than most jobs Lorian had been sent on, but he was still excited about a bit of lawbreaking, even if it would be quite simple.

They would separate around the next corner, Odonir heading to the queen's throne room to escort her outside with the other elf scouts. She would give a lengthy speech about peace and rebirth or whatever royal nonsense she was supposed to say. Lorian was going to head in the exact opposite direction, toward her wardrobe. The thought of having an entire room simply for the purpose of clothing baffled Lorian, but he didn't let the pointless usage of perfectly good space occupy his mind for long. Odonir's breath was shallow, and the muscles in his arms that occasionally brushed against Lorian were taut as they neared their checkpoint.

"Do I sense nerves radiating from you, brother?" Lorian asked. "I would have thought elf scouts like you were trained to control their fear or maybe just had any remotely human emotions beaten out of them."

"You forget, brother"—Odonir growled the word *brother*, making it sound like a verbal slap—"I'm not human."

Lorian recoiled slightly at the venom in his brother's words and was unsure what had caused his sudden mood. "Have I done something wrong?" he asked. "Or have you been nice until now just for Finriel's sake?"

Odonir paused and turned on him. "I am having a hard time knowing that I'm about to help my little brother steal from the queen I have pledged to protect for the last eleven years. Excuse me if I'm a little bit on edge."

Lorian lifted his hands in a calming motion. "I understand. But you aren't helping me, not really. You are helping the queen more by allowing me to do this."

Odonir gave a humph of indignation and started walking again. They remained in silence until they reached the fork in the passageway, one turning right and the other left. Lorian stepped toward the passage to the left and gave Odonir a mocking salute.

"If I get captured, please don't feel obligated to say you know me."

Odonir offered Lorian a half smile and shook his head as he turned to the passage on the right. "Don't worry. I wouldn't dream of ruining your reputation."

Lorian smirked at his brother's brief return of humor, then started down the passage. It was still quite empty at this hour, being the level just above the servants' maze that Odonir had shown them ran below the entire castle. They had considered using that as an entry point for Lorian but decided against it since going through a main door would seem less questionable. Lorian adjusted the sleeves of his leather jacket, not liking the slight noise it made whenever his arms brushed against his sides. It would hinder his invisibility when he hid, but it would have to do.

Sunlight filtered through the slanted windows and spilled onto the tiled floor. Lorian clung to the remaining shadows as he slipped through hallways and doors, using his memory of Odonir's explanation of the castle layout to guide him. Excitement thrummed through his veins with each step, adjustment, and quick dash to hide from the occasional passing servant or noble. They all seemed quite preoccupied with the festival, however, and paid him no mind, even if he was seen.

Minutes passed in this way, and Lorian soon neared the plain arched door Odonir had described to him. Lorian glanced from left to right, ensuring there was no oncoming nobleman or servant to see him. When the coast was clear, he darted across the hall and gripped the wooden door handle.

The door opened silently, and Lorian was assaulted by a barrage of fabrics and bright colors that muddled his brain. The room was almost as large as Odonir's entire house, and nearly every inch was full of clothing hanging from large metal racks. A narrow passageway snaked around the hordes of fabrics, shoes, and hats, and Lorian started down the first one. How in the Nether would he find three masks in this enormous mess of a room? Lorian clenched his jaw and peered over a window ledge laden with hats, finding that the sun was already quite high up in the sky. It was almost time for the queen's speech.

He was running out of time.

Faint cheers and clapping filtered through the thin window, and Lorian half wondered if the Festival of Ashes had changed much since the last time he'd been to the event. A smile danced on his lips at the memories that flowed through his mind. Of weaving in and out of flowing skirts and laughing faces as the citizens of Mitonir and beyond came together for dances and parties. Of stealing fresh sartol and other pastries from stands and then watching the fertility gatherings from his perch on rooftops and stone walls. He'd always been too young to participate in the gatherings, but Lorian had always liked the thought of being able to openly court a woman without the stuffy rules of Farridian culture stopping him.

But there was no time to waste on childhood memories now; he needed to find the suphieras. Lorian narrowed his focus on the plethora of clothing items, his nerves rising a bit, much to his distaste. Perhaps this wasn't the most treacherous job, but certainly the most mentally taxing.

Lorian began his search with haste, sorting through piles, hangers, and overstuffed drawers of fabrics. He moved across the room to a section with glittering jewels and necklaces that any bandit or thief would be willing to be cursed for stealing, but the suphieras were still nowhere to be seen.

A sound from the other side of the door made Lorian's stomach lurch into his throat, and he dove behind a giant wall of hanging dresses before he could think. Adrenaline pumped madly through his veins, and he held his breath as the door opened and a young serving boy with a bundle in his arms walked into the room.

The boy was humming and seemed utterly oblivious to Lorian's presence as he walked to the corner of the room, stopping mere feet from where Lorian stood. He dropped something wrapped in brown paper unceremoniously onto the floor, then pulled a thick card from his pocket and placed it on the package. The boy turned without a second glance and closed the door behind him, his keyless tune following his retreating footsteps.

Lorian exhaled sharply and stepped out from behind the dresses, looking down at what the boy had dropped. This close, he could now discern it was a finely wrapped package. Curiosity tingled within, and Lorian knelt before the box. A simple note written in an elegant scrawl was tucked underneath the blue ribbon holding the lid closed. Lorian lifted the note off the package, and satisfaction warmed him as he read:

To be worn on the fourteenth day of the second waxing winter moon. Warm regards, the Proverian court.

"That was easy," Lorian whispered and promptly lifted the lid from the box.

Ten different masks were stacked within the box, each sculpted into the face of a different animal. Lorian lifted two from the box, not caring which animal they were. They were made of a thin yet hard black material. Lorian unzipped his jacket and tucked them inside, looking down to find only a slight bulge protruding out. Lorian replaced the lid and note, then tied the ribbon once more.

Lorian stood with a satisfied smile, though a new thought entered his mind as his gaze drifted toward the wall of hanging garments. He took two long strides and began rummaging through the sea of dresses, but none caught his eye. Lorian sighed with a small tinge of frustration when he was met with endless folds of glitter and revealing cuts. Moments later, his hand faltered on a stretch of black fabric. Lorian's eyebrows drifted upward, and new excitement pulsed through his veins as he removed the dress from its hook and looked it up and down with an approving nod.

The dress was folded tightly and tucked under his arm in one swift movement, and Lorian slipped out of the room and into the empty hallway. His footsteps were light and sure, and it was nearly impossible to keep the smile from his face at the thought of three successes in a single morning. Lorian avoided and leapt out of people's paths almost casually, and soon, crisp winter air greeted his face as he stepped back out onto the gravel path.

Loud cheers and merry music carried through the air, and Lorian had no trouble moving through the streets unnoticed. The crowd thickened as he reached the street next to the barn, but none of the revelers in their bright colors and thickly lined eyes paid him much attention as he walked past. A jolt of sadness squeezed his heart as he looked to his left and found a group of people engaged in the dance of winter fallings. It had been his mother's favorite dance to watch, and he'd always groaned in annoyance whenever she dragged him to the sidelines to clap along to the beat of the thrumming drums and stomping feet.

Lorian turned his head away from the revelers and quickened his pace toward the end of the crowd, and his shoulder bumped into hard muscle.

"Apologies," Lorian muttered, and the man only grunted and said a word in a language Lorian didn't know.

This made Lorian look up and watch the man walk away. He was able to catch soft black boots, thick leather pants, and black hair that was braided in a thick rope down the man's back before he was swallowed by the crowd.

Lorian frowned and then shrugged, but not before something on the ground caught his eye. He stooped and snatched it up, gaze narrowing in confusion as he inspected the simple black bag in his palm. He tucked it into his jacket pocket before setting off once more and heading into the dimness of the barn where Oats whinnied at his return.

THE MUSIC and loud shouts disappeared almost completely as Lorian walked astride Oats through the forest, the thick silence seeming to eat at the distant noise. Lorian's chest swelled in satisfaction at the thought of their two new suphieras, as well as the black dress now tucked into one of the saddlebags behind him. It had been a successful mission, and Lorian had yet again escaped Mitonir without getting caught.

The memory of the strange man filtered through his mind once more, and Lorian withdrew the small bag from his pocket. He sniffed at it warily to find that it smelled faintly of spices. His lips tilted down, and he opened the bag, only for his frown to grow.

"What in the Nether?"

He reached two fingers into the bag and withdrew what looked like a dried-up cricket. Its hard black shell was covered in red powder, which Lorian could guess was the source of the spice smell. He glanced at the eyes of the cricket and cursed again at the pearly white orbs. He'd never encountered blind crickets in his life, though he had to admit he'd never spent much time thinking about or trying to notice crickets at all. Lorian shrugged, putting the bag back in his pocket. It was a curious find, and he was unsure of what language the man had spoken. Perhaps he was from Naebatis and had traveled down for the Festival of Ashes.

Smoke spilled merrily from the cabin chimney, and Oats bopped his head and quickened his pace at the familiar sight. Lorian's bones were aching from the cold, and he desperately wanted to sit in front of the fire with a warm mug of Odonir's ridiculous tea. Finriel and Nora were two smudges in the distance as they waited by the house. Lorian was still surprised by the leap his heart gave at the sight of the witch.

"I see you're still in one piece," Finriel said as Lorian came to a stop in the clearing and swung off Oats.

Lorian reached for the saddlebag attached to Oats's saddle and withdrew the suphieras, handing them to the witch with confidence. "I told you I would return with my body parts intact," he said, but Finriel ignored him as she inspected the masks.

"These are beautiful," she murmured.

"More creepy than beautiful to me, but suit yourself." Lorian shrugged and began to lead Oats back to the barn.

"I want this one," Finriel said and lifted what looked to be a wolf's face.

Lorian smiled. "Just as long as I left the worst one for Odonir. I hope Queen Arbane gives him a gerbil suphiera."

"You didn't check what they were before taking them?" Finriel asked.

"I had a bit of a time constraint."

She didn't reply as he finished untacking Oats and then grabbed the dress from the saddlebag. He kept it tucked under his arm as he and Finriel walked toward the house with Nora bounding in front of them.

Finriel narrowed her eyes at the bundle. "What is that?"

Lorian moved it away from her with a grin. "Nothing. Just a little surprise for later."

31

TEDRIC

"I missed waking up with you like this," Aeden murmured against Tedric's chest, her breath tickling his skin.

Tedric kept his gaze out the wide window beyond, trying to let the beauty of the forest distract him from the sick feeling in his stomach. He knew it was partially because he hadn't yet taken the Red King's potion, but it was also because of what he had done with Aeden last night. The words he had spoken and his confession of love.

Nothing could be taken back again.

"We've only woken up like this twice before," Tedric replied and brought himself to look down at her faint smile.

They were pressed together under the sheets of her large bed, their legs tangled together as Aeden nestled in closer to the curve of his body. The castle was slightly cold, though Tedric was surprised by the bit of warmth that existed, considering there was no logical source of heat.

"Yes, but I missed it all the same." Aeden brushed a soft kiss against his chest.

"I don't know how often we will be able to do this, with you being a queen and me a guard for the Red King," Tedric said, hating every word that came out of his mouth.

"I'll just have to visit often," Aeden said. "Or you could stay here... with me."

Confusion and something like fear swelled in Tedric's abdomen, and he looked back out the window. Was this some sort of sick plan she had with the Red King to share his duty and his time?

"You don't want to," Aeden said as more of a statement than a question.

He had to act at least a little bit interested instead of repelled by the idea. Perhaps this was his chance to learn something. Perhaps this was part of Aeden's agreement to help the Red King. The thought made Tedric feel even sicker, but he shoved the feeling down as he picked his next words carefully.

"It's not that I don't want to. I just don't think the Red King would be very happy to see me go." Tedric looked back down at her as she made a face.

"The Red King has so many guards and that special force of his. I don't think he would complain all that much. Besides, he knows of our feelings. He's the one who brought up the idea anyway."

There it was. A secret. The faintest sliver of information. But it was something. Tedric schooled his face into one of surprise and sat up.

"Did he really?"

Aeden sat up and shivered as her bare skin was exposed to the cool room, and Tedric quickly pulled the sheet over her. He couldn't suppress his own shiver of discomfort and grabbed the blanket they had kicked to the bottom of the bed during their nighttime activities. Aeden looked at him and then down at the sheet, picking at the fabric.

"He offered it—that you come to live here."

"But why?" Tedric asked. "Not that I don't want to, but my entire life is in Keadora. I thought my services would still be needed there."

Aeden paused and retreated from the bed. Too far. He had pushed too far. Aeden crossed to a small wooden dresser and released the latch to reveal bottles and boxes within. She retracted her hand, now holding a small wooden box, and pulled a silver chain that hung down from the wall near the door. Tedric watched her as she moved, apparently mulling over his words as she did so.

"He didn't say you wouldn't be needed. Not exactly," Aeden said and then turned to him with a smile. "It doesn't matter though, does it? You could come here if you wanted to."

"And be with you," Tedric said as a soft knock sounded on the other side of the door.

Aeden opened it to reveal a tray with two steaming mugs of water on the silver floor. She picked up the tray and crossed the room toward him, the sheet trailing behind her like a flag. Tedric sat up fully now and covered himself waist down with the blanket. Aeden set the tray down on the bed and proceeded to open the small wooden box, revealing a fine shimmering powder. Tedric recognized it as the king's potion, and he hated the lurch of desperation his stomach gave. He waited as Aeden sat on the bed again, his eyes tracing the lines of her body beneath the sheet. The scar on her forearm was stark against her skin, and Tedric bit back the question that had been trying to escape for hours now.

What happened to you?

"Yes," Aeden said finally as she put a healthy pinch of the powder into each mug and handed him one.

Tedric lifted the mug to his lips, forcing only a sip to trickle down his throat, even though his body begged him to take the whole thing in one gulp. Egharis was right; he was slowly becoming addicted to the potion, which was not a good thing. He hated relying on anything other than his perseverance to get by, but it was becoming hard to ignore his need for the Red King's potion. It was a way to ease his suffering, if only enough to make the days go by easier.

He would find a way to live without the potion once this was all over, but right now, he could afford no such thing.

Aeden took a long sip of the potion, and Tedric considered her. He could not refuse her offer so quickly, not when this arrangement could help his cause. He would truly be on the inside and able to discover what it was the Red King wanted, as well as what happened to the Aeden he'd fallen in love with.

"What would I be? Your lover?" Tedric asked, and Aeden screwed up her nose with distaste.

"Nether no. That sounds terrible," she replied, then brought the cup to her lips once more.

Tedric watched in surprise as she drained her cup. His own potion was boiling hot, and even though that odd part of him that yearned for the liquid was asking for more, he did not drink it with such fervency. Aeden returned her mug to the tray and licked a droplet of the drink from her lips.

"What would I be, then?" Tedric asked. "I must have a title if I am to be in your court."

Aeden's lips twitched upward as she took up his free hand in hers and began to play idly with his fingers. "What title would you want to have?"

Tedric shrugged, allowing the sick part of himself to play along. "I don't know. I certainly don't want to be known only as someone who warms your bed."

"You wouldn't just be someone who warms my bed." Aeden's smile drifted downward. "I don't want that."

"You don't?" Tedric lifted his brows.

"I love you, Tedric," Aeden said, and a pang shot through his heart at how genuine her words sounded. "I know you would go mad if you had to be locked up doing nothing but entertaining me for the rest of your life."

Tedric only looked at her, and she continued, "You could be something more important, like the king."

Tedric snorted in disbelief. "The king?"

"Unless you don't want to be," Aeden said quickly. "I just thought you might like that sort of thing."

"Aeden, I'm a warrior, not a politician," Tedric replied with laughter in his voice but quickly sobered as he watched the confidence in her face change to sourness. "But if that's the position you would want for me to have, then I'll do it gladly."

Aeden raised a brow of incredulity, and Tedric raised the cup to his lips to finish off the rest of his potion, if only to give himself a few extra moments to gather his thoughts. Aeden watched him as he set the empty mug on the tray next to hers. He sighed, his mind whirling. Aeden was right; he most definitely would go mad if he agreed to take on the title she was offering him. But he wouldn't be taking on the title, not truly. He hoped this sick game would be over long before it got to that.

"We will find a proper title that suits me," Tedric said finally. "As long as I can be by your side."

The smile returned to Aeden's face, and she took up the tray, then opened the door to drop it outside the room before pulling on the silver chain once more.

"Good," she said with her back still turned to him. "Because I want to announce it at the coronation."

Tedric's world tilted at her words. "What?"

Aeden turned to him and glided back to the bed. "I want my people to know that my father's old rule of forbidding magical races to mingle is no longer valid. Maybe it will jog the elves into changing their rules too."

Tedric opened and closed his mouth, unsure of what to say.

The thought of her announcing him as her plaything in front of thousands of people sounded like the last thing he'd ever want to agree to, but he wasn't sure he could voice those thoughts without sounding too obvious. This wasn't something he would've thought Aeden would want either, not ever. Their relationship had felt equal before, but now it felt like she was a cat and he was a mouse caught in her claws.

"You don't want to do that either, do you?" Aeden said, and Tedric gave her an apologetic smile.

"It's a lot of people to announce that sort of thing to," Tedric said honestly. "I don't know if I want to go from being known as the commander of the Ten to your companion so suddenly. At least not to the entire realm."

"The Red King will never give you back your position," Aeden said with slightly narrowed eyes, and Tedric couldn't stop the sharp taste of bitterness in his mouth at her words, even if the thought of serving the Red King in that capacity again made his blood boil.

"Did he tell you that, or are you guessing?" Tedric asked.

"It's not a guess if it's the obvious truth," Aeden replied with a bit more harshness than Tedric thought necessary. "You fought against him on Clamidas."

"I didn't know who to fight against," Tedric muttered in defense, which was partially the truth.

He remembered that night now, remembered his confusion and pain at Aeden's betrayal, which caused him to be unsure of what was up or down anymore. Even after Aeden murdered her father and after the Red King's praise of Aeden's service to his mysterious cause, Tedric didn't know what to think. There was only the gut feeling and overwhelming anger that made him know he could no longer trust the Red King—or Aeden.

The desire to run from the room and search for his lost companions was suddenly overwhelming. Tedric clenched his fists in his lap, the pain of his fingernails biting into his palms a grounding force. Aeden sighed and reached for his hand, the harsh lines on her face melting away again. Angry red crescents lined his palm, and Tedric let out a pained sigh at the comfort her touch gave him.

Goddesses above, he was a mess.

"I'm sorry," Aeden said softly. "We can talk about it later. There's still time before the coronation."

Tedric mustered a smile he prayed looked grateful and quickly leaned in to kiss her before she could second-guess the expression. She returned the gesture with enthusiasm, and Tedric forced himself to focus only on her touch instead of the dreadful thoughts swirling through his mind.

A soft knock sounded on the door, and Aeden leapt away from Tedric's embrace to race to the door. He watched her in confusion as she opened it and picked up yet another tray, returning to the bed with two fresh steaming mugs of water, now joined by a bowl of fresh berries. Tedric glanced at the box of potion that had been kicked to the end of the bed, a terrible thought crossing through his mind.

In confirmation of his thoughts, Aeden set the tray down and grabbed the box from where it lay.

"Haven't we had enough already?" Tedric asked. "I'm not sure having more than one cup a day is a good idea."

Aeden rolled her eyes at him, which instantly made him think of Finriel's default response whenever Lorian said anything stupid—or anything at all, really.

"It's harmless," she replied casually as she pinched more shimmering powder into the mugs. "Besides, it's better the second time in a day."

Worry gripped Tedric's stomach. This wasn't the Aeden he remembered. Everything was different, from the way she talked to her current actions. The Aeden he knew would not indulge in an addictive substance, nor talk with such flounce in her words. But he hadn't known her for very long before the untimely end to their mission, so maybe he was wrong about his assessment of the fairy.

Aeden had already grabbed her mug and taken a sip, a wild look in her eyes as she watched Tedric reach toward the tray with reluctance. He grabbed a handful of red and black berries instead and popped them into his mouth with a burst of sweet flavor.

"How are these still growing at this time of year? I thought berries only grew in the spring and summer," Tedric said, trying his best to sound casual, though his words came out a bit stiff.

Aeden gave him a half-interested look. "I don't know. I don't ask how the food here is grown. And since when have you been interested in crops?"

Tedric shrugged. "I was just curious."

He watched her with caution when she didn't answer but instead lifted her cup to her lips and drank steadily, tilting her head back to empty the contents of the potion into her mouth without stopping. Alarm bells sounded in Tedric's mind as she set it down and eyed his full mug hungrily. There was something very wrong with her, and Tedric had a feeling it had something to do with the concoction before him.

COLD AIR BIT into Tedric's skin, the winter day warmer than in Keadora, though still distasteful in Tedric's mind. But he needed fresh air, cold be damned. Aeden's strange behavior and his terrible actions called for him to be alone, even if it was only for a few minutes.

The Red King hadn't called on him for some time, and Tedric was beginning to wonder if the only reason he had been brought here was for Aeden's enjoyment. Tedric cringed at the thought and fought away another wave of anger. Perhaps there was a better and easier way to find out the Red King's motives, like a knife to his throat in the middle of the night when the king wasn't expecting it. Tedric shook his head at the thought. The Red King was likely prepared at all times for an attack and guarded to the teeth at every moment. If Tedric could only see his other companions and know that they were all right, perhaps it would make things worth it.

The flash of a gray hat made Tedric sit up straight on the hard stone bench. He scanned the covered walkway, searching through the maids and nobles that were beginning to pour in for Aeden's coronation. And there it was again. Moving against the sea of tall willowy bodies was a gnome.

Tedric sprang to his feet and started after the figure, his pulse pounding in his ears at the possibility he dared not think about too hard. For if it was Krete, he would have to remain as unassuming as possible to not raise alarm. Any obvious movements and his companion would be arrested on the spot.

Fairies, humans, and a few elf nobles moved out of his way as he shoved through the masses and followed the occasional appearance of a vest-clad back and gray hat. It was Krete. It simply had to be. Tedric quickened his pace, slipping past bodies and apologizing when he bumped into the shoulder of a rather tall and stuffy-looking fairy noble. The hat went out of sight for a few moments before it came back into view by one of the arched walkways. Tedric moved into a slow jog and reached a hand out to touch the gnome's shoulder just as they were about to turn around a corner. The gnome swiveled around, and Tedric nearly staggered back with joy as he met a kind face and storm-gray eyes.

"Goddesses be damned. It's so good to see you." Tedric beamed, and Krete clapped him on the arm with a grand smile.

"It's so good to see *you*. We all thought you were dead," Krete replied with the same raised voice that seemed to consume him whenever he was overly excited or nervous.

The mention of their other companions jolted Tedric, and he lowered his voice. "The others, are they all right?"

Krete nodded and glanced around before ushering him toward a small wooden door to the left. The gnome opened the door, and Tedric followed him inside, finding himself in a room much larger than he'd expected. It was furnished lightly, with a simple long couch of silver satin and a large wooden table with six chairs lining either side.

"It's a haven room," Krete explained as Tedric inspected their surroundings. "They are hardly noticeable when you aren't looking, but they are the safest rooms in the entire citadel. They're impervious to fire, floods, or any kind of magic you could think of."

"Can you fight in here?" Tedric asked, and Krete shook his head.

"Causing another person harm in these rooms is impossible, though I'm not sure how exactly. Likely some ancient magic that is now lost to us."

Tedric rounded on Krete, forgetting about the interesting room. "Lorian and Finriel, you said that they're alive?"

Krete nodded again. "Yes, they are both alive and quite well."

Tedric let out a sigh, the tension relaxing from his body.

Krete moved to the couch and sat down. "They were wondering if you were alive. It's the whole reason I came here under such dangerous circumstances."

Tedric's eyes widened. "It is?"

"I have little desire to come here anymore, and it is dangerous for me anyway, with the three of us being wanted and all."

"How did you know I was going to be here?" Tedric asked curiously.

"I didn't," Krete replied with a small snort. "Finriel and Lorian asked if I could send a letter to Aeden in hopes of learning if you were alive. It seems as though I made a good decision in simply coming to speak to her myself."

Tedric smiled at the gnome. His coming here was utterly stupid, but he couldn't help but feel relieved and happy to see his friend. "How long are you staying?" Tedric asked. "The castle is swarming with both Proverian and Keadoran guards, as well as the Ten."

"Oh, not long," Krete replied with a smile that faded slowly. "You speak of the Ten as though you are not a part of them anymore."

Tedric gritted his teeth and shook his head. "I'm not. The Red King thought my services would be better suited to guard Egharis while he creates his beasts."

Krete perked up at this. "He's creating more beasts?"

"An entire army of them." Tedric nodded grimly.

Krete blew out a breath, concern glazing his eyes. "Do you know why he's creating the army and when or whom the Red King wishes to use it against?"

Tedric shook his head. "Egharis can speak of the Red King now, but the curse still takes its toll on him whenever he tries to speak of the intent for his creations."

"That's inconvenient." Krete huffed, and Tedric nodded.

"Very. I've been more frustrated with not knowing what exactly I'm guarding than being stripped of my title."

Krete's expression turned grim, and his voice lowered as he spoke again. "How are you doing with all of this? The curse, Aeden..."

Tedric clenched his fists, a wave of loathing rolling through him at the mention of her name and the unfortunate turn his life had taken. "I'm... living," Tedric started. "But I won't lie and say that everything has been good and dandy either. The curse is manageable, but only if I take a wretched potion from the Red King that I fear is addling my brain somehow. Aeden is addicted to it; I'm certain of that."

Krete's skin took on a sallow pallor as Tedric spoke, and he remained quiet even a few moments after Tedric finished speaking.

"I feel terrible for what that night did to you, both of you," Krete said.

Tedric did not need to ask who Krete meant by *both of you* and ignored the tightness in his chest as the gnome continued.

"I visited Aeden a few weeks ago, and she seemed different. I wasn't sure if it was the effects of the curse or something entirely different, but now that you say she may be both addled and reliant on some strange potion given by the Red King—"

"She's on his side, Krete," Tedric growled.

Krete blanched, and Tedric continued through his silence. "I can see it in her eyes. The Red King has offered her something, and she's hungry for it. She won't tell me what it is, but I think she might over time."

"Are you two speaking again?" Krete asked with wide eyes, and a bark of pained laughter escaped Tedric's lips.

"The Red King has forced me to grow close to her again. I think it's simply another ploy to keep her compliant and happy. If I could forget about her and this entire mess between us, I would." Tedric stopped, a sudden overwhelming need to cry closing around his throat. He coughed, blinking quickly against the burning sensation behind his eyes. He was being pulled in too many directions, and at any moment, he would snap.

Krete was on his feet and crossing the room toward Tedric, and soon, his short arms were clasped around his waist. "I'm so sorry for all of this mess. It's my fault that I didn't tell you of her identity the moment we met you all in the forest."

Tedric tentatively returned Krete's embrace and patted his back before Krete released him and stood back, moisture glistening in his storm-gray eyes.

Tedric shook his head. "It wasn't your secret to tell. Of course it would've been easier knowing the truth, but it was her responsibility to bear."

Krete pressed his lips together and took in a deep breath. He clearly felt guiltier for not telling Tedric and the others than Aeden did, but that was to be expected. Tedric would be surprised if he found out that Aeden had ever thought about anyone else's wellbeing aside from her own in her entire life.

"I should go," Krete said after a moment. "It's best that Aeden doesn't know I was here." Krete withdrew a small stone from his jacket pocket and began to chant and move in a small circle, the floor glowing a familiar orange as it had when he'd teleported them out of Farrador and to the In Between.

"It was good to see you again," Tedric said, a pang lancing through his chest at the realization that he likely wouldn't see Krete again for quite some time, if ever.

Krete looked up from the finished portal and gave Tedric a kind smile. "It was, and we will all meet again very soon."

"What do you mean?" Tedric asked, both in worry of them planning something terribly stupid and excitement of possibly seeing Lorian and Finriel again.

Krete simply winked, and then the smile faded from his lips. "She does love you. She just never got the chance to show it in a healthy way."

And then he was gone, jumping into the portal, which vanished behind him with a faint pop. Tedric stood alone in the haven room, now wishing more than anything that he could stay within its hallowed walls forever.

Cold air bit into Tedric's face as he stepped back into the open. The number of people walking through the courtyard seemed to have doubled since his conversation with Krete. He closed the door and started walking, not really caring where he was going. Someone from behind barked his name, and he spun around to see Sparrow, one of the swordsmen of the Ten, heading in his direction. Sparrow was a sturdy and slightly squat man of around thirty years, with a shock of red hair and dark brown eyes. The harsh lines of his face were drawn as he approached, and Tedric prepared himself to speak with his old comrade.

"The Red King wants to speak to you," Sparrow said in a low voice as he approached, and trepidation crept up Tedric's spine.

Had he been seen with Krete? Had he done something out of character? Tedric could only gesture for Sparrow to show him the way, and Tedric followed him back through the herd of moving bodies toward a tall crystal archway that led into the citadel.

The Red King was waiting by the doorway, his obsidian eyes piercing holes through Tedric's head as they approached. Sparrow bowed before turning back the way he had come, leaving Tedric alone with the Red King and a quiet guard standing a few feet away.

"You wanted to see me?" Tedric asked as he forced his body down into a bow.

"Yes, I wish to speak to you about something important," the Red King said, and Tedric's insides gave a nervous somersault.

Tedric rose to his full height, which was thankfully a few inches taller than the Red King, making him feel less powerless against the ageless ruler.

"I have good reason to believe there could be a few potentially dangerous individuals attending Aeden's coronation."

Tedric's mind went immediately to Krete's promise that they would see each other soon, and he cleared his throat before answering as smoothly as he could. "It's certainly possible, with all non-cursed kingdoms confirming their attendance."

The Red King smiled thinly. "Aeden told you that, didn't she?"

Tedric clenched his jaw, not wanting to confirm the Red King's suspicions. She had told him after their second potion, in a moment of passion that even Tedric had to admit had taken his mind from the awful things he was being forced to do.

"It's no matter," the Red King continued. "But I wanted to ask you if you would be my private watch guard for the night."

Tedric blanched. Private watch guard? What even was that? And since when had the Red King ever asked him if he *wanted* to do something?

"I'm afraid I don't entirely know what my duties would entail."

"You will simply keep an eye on Aeden's whereabouts, as well as gather any useful information you may find. I do want you to be available to dance with and entertain the queen. It is her special night after all."

Tedric's mouth went sour, but he let the Red King go on.

"The realm is in a state of unease ever since Egharis's beasts were let out of their pages. People talk. There are rumors still floating around."

With good reason too, Tedric wanted to spit in reply, but he only inclined his head and picked his next words carefully. "It's not surprising for people to be fearful after a disruption of the long peace. What exactly would you want me to do with any information I find?"

"Tell it to me, of course," the Red King replied with a smile. "I need to make sure our citizens are beginning to feel safe again after such a terrible accident with the beasts and King Sorren's untimely death."

He's lying, Tedric thought. He knew exactly what the Red King wanted. He wanted to make sure people were going quiet again and that no one was guessing he was responsible for the beasts, or questioning Aeden's sudden move up to the throne.

But perhaps this was exactly what Tedric needed and a perfect way for him to keep an eye out for his companions and protect them, should they be foolish enough to sneak in.

Tedric bowed again. "It would be an honor."

The Red King's smile widened, his thin gaze wandering up

and down Tedric's body. "The potion has helped you greatly, warrior. You could see the title of commander returning soon."

With that, the Red King turned on his heel and disappeared through the corridor, his guard quickly shuffling after him. Tedric let out a breath and inwardly cursed the Red King, though he couldn't help the excitement beginning to ebb its way into the black hole of his heart. It seemed as though his acting was paying off.

Perhaps he was growing to like his role as a liar.

32
FINRIEL

Finriel's backside collided with the ground in a puff of dust, and she groaned in pain. Lorian offered a hand, and she took it, letting him haul her to her feet.

"You were close that time."

"Clearly not close enough." Finriel winced.

Lorian had been throwing kicks at her for almost an hour now and had the brilliant idea of having her learn how to take the blow with a force field charm she'd used a few times before. It had worked at first, with the blows only making her stagger back a step or two, but each time was growing progressively worse as the day wore on.

"I just don't understand why it's easy for me to put a force field around others but not myself," Finriel grunted, rubbing gingerly at the spot where Lorian's foot had connected with her stomach when her force field had failed.

Lorian shrugged. "Maybe you should try actually wanting to protect yourself."

Finriel clenched her jaw and took in a deep breath, wrangling in her frustration. She knew he was likely trying to help and saw something in her that she did not see in herself, but it didn't make his comment sting any less.

"Let's try something else," Finriel said. "I haven't practiced Centering since training with Lizabet."

Lorian's smile wavered. "And I'm assuming you want me to be the target?"

The frustration melted away slightly, and Finriel smirked. "I was going to use the tree over there, but I'd be more than happy to comply with your request."

Lorian shot his hands into the air and backed away. "No, no. The tree will do just fine."

Finriel rallied her strength as Lorian moved to the safety of the house, gracefully leaning his back against the stone wall. Finriel took a step toward a tree by the barn and closed her eyes, allowing for the well of power to grow and swell in her belly.

She widened her stance, bending her knees and arcing her hands up and then down to brush against the frozen earth. A familiar burn crept into her muscles after only a few moments, and a small gasp escaped her lips. The warm-up had gotten easier over time in the Witch Isles, but now it felt like she'd never done it before.

"Sorry to say, but I think Odonir could dance better than that." Lorian's voice rang out from behind.

Finriel's concentration sputtered like a blown-out candle, and she gritted her teeth against the burning in her arms and legs. "I'm not dancing." She closed her eyes.

I've done this once. I can do it again. Finriel let out a breath and shook out her arms before getting into position again.

The strange tickling sensation rose through her feet and fingers within seconds, and Finriel's chest swelled with triumph. The sensation continued to spread as Finriel rose up and down, easing her breath into an even rhythm as she moved. Three breaths later, the tickling snapped into place, and the familiar cord of energy flowed from the top of Finriel's skull all the way down to the balls of her feet.

It was time to try Centering.

The world came back sharper when she opened her eyes, and a strange sense of calm washed over her in place of the awe she'd felt in the Witch Isles. She had a mission to do, and she was going to master Centering before it was too late.

"Give me a name," Finriel called out before she realized it.

"Why?" Lorian replied.

"I'm going to name the tree," Finriel said simply, directing all of her focus on the aged oak.

"You are one strange woman." Lorian chuckled. "I like it."

A coil of electricity settled in Finriel's gut at his words, but she shoved it down with a deep breath when the cord of energy faltered.

"Bertha," Lorian said from behind after a moment of silence.

If she weren't concentrating on the energy flowing through her body, she would have scowled and asked why he would pick that name, but there was no time now. She had bigger fish to fry, and there was no time to waste.

"Okay, Bertha," Finriel whispered, focusing on the center of the trunk. "It's nothing personal."

She lifted her hands, turning her palms to the sky. The flames within spit and crackled like a beast prowling inside a cage. But she would not let them consume her. She beckoned the flame forth, and it leapt to her palms readily. A deep breath into her core dampened the flame, if only slightly, and she willed the crackling embers to swirl into a sphere. She grunted against the power, willing the spheres to shrink until they were no bigger than pebbles. She couldn't stop her smile at the small feat, and sparks popped from the flaming spheres as if they were upset to be so contained.

Before she could think more of it, Finriel looked up at Bertha and shot her hands forward, willing the spheres to join and meld into a thin blade. It shot forward, and barely a sound rang through the air as it passed through the tree, leaving a thin black line and the smell of burning wood.

"I won't say I'm impressed, but that was amazing," Lorian said, and Finriel jumped at the nearness of his voice.

She turned to find him standing right next to her, staring at the tree with raised brows and a grin.

Finriel sighed and looked down at her hands. "I still wish Lizabet had taught me more."

"I know," Lorian replied. "But you've clearly learned something, and maybe you can find another teacher soon."

Finriel snorted. "I doubt I'll find a teacher that can deal with my unruly magic. Lizabet hardly wanted to teach me as it was."

"It will be resolved, but for now, you should get some rest."

A sudden pop sounded through the air, and Finriel looked up to find a shimmering portal above her head. She took two quick steps back, heart leaping in her chest as the swirling blue circle opened up in the sky. Krete's body fell gracefully to the ground, and the gnome rolled and jumped to his feet in one swift movement.

"Hello again," Lorian greeted jovially.

"Tedric is alive," Krete announced, panting.

Relief washed through Finriel, and she sighed at the news. She tensed again and took a step forward. "Is he safe?"

Krete nodded tentatively. "Physically, yes, for now."

"How do you know this?" Lorian asked, his tone more serious than usual. "It sounds like you saw him with your own eyes."

Krete's gaze dropped to the ground with what seemed like embarrassment. "I did."

Finriel gaped. "You were foolish enough to go to Keadora?"

"Goddesses no!" Krete looked back up at them. "I went to

Proveria. He was there. I think the Red King brought him as some sort of private guard for the coronation."

"Going to Proveria was equally stupid!" Finriel exclaimed, and Krete gave her a sorry smile.

"I had to go myself. I'm a messenger, remember? I can get in and out of places quickly."

"How do you know he's guarding the king?" Lorian asked, and Krete sighed.

"From what he told me, he is no longer commander of the Ten and was demoted to a guard position for Egharis. Since the storyteller isn't in Proveria right now, my last guess is that the Red King wants Tedric close to keep an eye on him."

"And having him as a private guard is the perfect way to do that," Lorian finished.

"What of Aeden though? Don't they hate each other now?" Finriel asked testily.

Krete's face fell, and a sour taste entered her mouth.

"I guess—" Krete broke off. "I guess the Red King has forced him to be with her again."

"Like..." Lorian trailed off, and Krete gave a single nod.

Finriel grimaced in both disgust and anger, the flames in her core coiling tightly.

"That is disgusting." Lorian cringed. "The poor man. And I'm assuming he's treating it as some sort of mighty duty."

"I don't think so," Krete speculated. "Though I think part of the reason he agreed to do it is that some part of him still cares for her, no matter how small."

Finriel sighed. "So he's being forced to serve the enemy by laying with a traitor."

"At least he's not utterly brainwashed by the Red King again," Lorian offered. "Seeing him fight the Ten was one of the greatest joys I have ever experienced."

"What do we do, then?" Finriel asked. "He has to get out of there."

"We can suggest that he joins us when we see him at the coronation, if he's still there," Krete said.

"He won't want to leave," Lorian reasoned. "I know him. He thinks he's more useful on the inside, and he's right. His information could be useful in the future. He could even find out what the Red King is planning if we're not able to find out during the coronation."

"You should talk to him, Lorian," Krete said quickly. "It seems as though you two share some sort of brotherly bond. He might feel more comfortable talking with you and coming up with some sort of plan."

Lorian nodded. "I think you're right. I might be able to convince his pompous ass that we need him."

"I don't think you need to worry about that part." Krete smiled. "He seems quite set on the fact that he's going to figure out what the Red King and Aeden are planning to do."

"That makes my job easy, then," Lorian said. "I'll just find Tedric and see if he is willing to be involved with our scheme."

"You won't have to find him," Finriel reminded him. "He'll be quite easy to find if he's the king's private guard."

Lorian sighed. "That does make it a little less fun."

Finriel rolled her eyes and focused on Krete. "Are you staying with us now?"

"Yes, I think it's best to be away from Creonid until the coronation." Krete nodded. "I've been a bit too out in the open for a wanted man."

"Excellent." Lorian clapped his hands and smiled. "I'm not sure Odonir has another bed, but Nora would likely allow you to use her as a pillow."

Finriel smirked, knowing just how correct the thief's statement was. The mogwa was sprawled out by the fireplace when they'd stepped outside for training, and Finriel wouldn't be surprised if she hadn't moved when they went back inside.

"I'm not picky." Krete winked. "But I am cold and would love something warm to drink."

Finriel crossed her arms and turned toward the house, inclining her head for her companions to follow. "Come. We can brew up some of Odonir's special tea."

33

TEDRIC

He awoke to pain.

Blinding flame lashed through his insides, and he was lurching to heave over the side of the bed before his eyes had even opened to the day. Mingled sounds of his misery and birdsong filtered through the morning, and minutes later, Tedric finally opened his eyes.

Sunshine pooled onto the silver floors of the lavish room, though the brightness of the day only made a headache creep into his skull. Tedric let out a groan and sat up, untangling his legs from the silk sheets. He scanned the room and frowned, his mind straying to the previous evening spent with Aeden. They had fallen asleep in each other's arms, but now her side of the large bed was cold.

They had agreed to spend the morning together, and a terrible corner of Tedric's heart had actually looked forward to their plans of riding through the forest and having a picnic by the Lake of Mirrors. He'd always been curious about the fabled lake, even as a child, and Aeden had offered to show him the glassy shores with water that reflected one's deepest desires back at the viewer.

It seemed that she'd forgotten about their date.

No matter, Tedric thought with a groan and rolled out of bed, carefully avoiding his own sick as he padded toward a large pine dresser by the window. He shrugged on a dark green tunic and brown buckskin breeches, followed by his favorite worn leather boots. Bile still threatened in his throat, but Tedric shoved it down as he secured his sword belt and splashed cold water on his face from a nearby crystal basin.

He needed the king's potion and a warm meal, no matter the lurch his stomach gave at the thought of the latter.

Tedric was assaulted by bustling bodies and excited conversation as soon as he opened the door, and he stepped out into a sea of fairies preparing for Aeden's coronation in two days' time. A young serving girl stood by the door with a tray in hand, her head bent down as she offered him the steaming mug.

"Thank you," Tedric said, taking the already prepared potion from the tray. "Did you wait all morning for me?"

The serving girl gave him a nervous smile but didn't meet his gaze, and Tedric gave her an apologetic incline of his head. "I'm very sorry for my tardiness. Please don't feel obligated to clean my rooms. They're a mess."

The girl gave him another smile but didn't reply, and Tedric took a swig of the king's potion before joining the throng of servants that bustled around the crystal walls, baskets, flowers, and swaths of fine fabric held in their arms.

A soothing sensation instantly trickled through Tedric's system as the bittersweet potion met his tongue, and he couldn't stop his sigh of relief. It was alarming how easy it had become for him to drink a poison he knew was addictive and how little he now thought of the repercussions that might follow.

He allowed his feet to wander aimlessly, taking in the servants all dressed in simple white cotton and the guards in their fine golden armor. Guilt nestled its way deeper into his heart with every sighting of the fairy guards. How was he allowed to walk freely through the very home of a man he killed? Tedric brought the mug to his lips and swallowed the rest of the potion in one gulp, savoring the scorching trails of pain the hot liquid left in his mouth. It was the least he deserved.

His mind wandered to his companions and the mission as he strolled through the halls, and a strange heavy feeling settled in his heart. It had been good to see Krete, though he missed Lorian and even Finriel greatly. It felt like a lifetime ago that they had trekked through Farrador and beyond, finding the five beasts that had started this whole mess. The nian's calm yellow eyes and measured voice echoed through his memory, and Tedric once again wondered what the Red King had done with his beast, as well as the brownies. Perhaps now that he seemed to be returning into the king's good graces, he could find out where they were being held.

"You can't tell me what to do!"

Aeden's voice made Tedric snap out of his thoughts, and he instantly moved in the direction of her shout. He made sure to stay hidden as the door came into view, though no guards were to be seen. They were likely stationed inside the room, which gave Tedric the perfect opportunity. He straightened and strode to the side of the door, positioning himself by the handle as though he were meant to be there. The mug was still held in his left hand, and he quickly set it by the wall before straightening again.

The Red King's and Aeden's raised voices weren't hard to hear even through the elegant white wood, and Tedric leaned his head back ever so slightly as he listened with growing apprehension.

"You cannot have your page." The Red King's dark voice was heavy with anger. "I've told you this before."

"You are treating me the same way my father did," Aeden spat. "Like I know nothing and am nothing!"

A chuckle rumbled through the room, sending a feeling of dread coiling down Tedric's spine. "You are nothing close to the sort, my dear."

"How can you say that after how you've treated me? After everything I've done for you?" Aeden's voice wavered with emotion. "I gave you everything, and you're giving me nothing! You promised me full control over my kingdom and the right to rule Raymara by your side once you conquered the rest of the realm. I feel like a puppet, not your ally."

"And that is still our agreement," the Red King agreed. "But I will keep the brownies and the nian in safekeeping until they are destroyed."

The world stuttered, and Tedric's hand flung to the door handle for support before the earth surged back into motion. The Red King could do no such thing, could he? Tedric bit back a curse, willing himself to remain silent even though his heart pounded like the loudest of drums.

"You can't do that." Aeden's voice sounded as disbelieving as he felt.

"I'm afraid I can, and I will," the Red King replied. "In fact, I can't move forward with my plans until each one of those five pages is destroyed."

"Why?"

Tedric had to strain in order to hear Aeden's whispered reply, but there was no issue hearing the Red King's next words.

"Because I know of the prophecy, and I fear that it is all too real," he said. "Those beasts' existences could mean the failure of my plans to take over Raymara once and for all, and I cannot let that happen. I already have two of the keys and locks under my control. All I have to do is find the other three and destroy each lock. For what is a key if it has nothing to open?"

"You *bastard*!" Aeden spoke louder this time. "You promised I would get my page and rule by your side!"

"Remember to whom you're speaking, Aeden." The Red King's voice was spitting now. "I am the rightful ruler of all of Raymara, for reasons not even the oldest elder of the Witch Isles could fathom."

Confusion and anger made Tedric's blood boil, and his fingers turned white under the grip he held on the door handle. He knew deep down that this must have been the Red King's plan all along, but still, a small part of him had hoped world domination wasn't on his bucket list.

It all makes sense now, Tedric thought bitterly. The Red King had sent them on a quest to help destroy the very things that would defeat him. With an army of beasts at his disposal and their own beasts destroyed, the Red King would be virtually unstoppable.

"You're a liar." Aeden's accusation rang out, bringing Tedric back to their conversation.

"And you are treading on thin ice, *girl*." The Red King's voice was a blade ready to strike. "Remember, I have your blood. I can break you."

The handle turned, and Tedric burst through the door before he could think twice. Aeden spun around, her green eyes wide and set with fury as she met his stare. The large room seemed to be some sort of parlor, with lavish couches set in a circle around a large diamond table. The customary wide windows welcomed cheerful sunlight into the heavy air. Tedric narrowed in on Aeden, whose hand was clutched around her right forearm—right where the new angry scar marred her smooth skin.

"Of course it's you." The Red King sighed. "This is going to be quite an inconvenience for me."

"Where are the pages?" Tedric demanded, his hand finding its place around the hilt of his sword.

The Red King's obsidian gaze followed Tedric's movements, and he shook his head with a chuckle. "Do you really think your petty little sword will harm me? I thought we established just how weak you are during Clamidas."

Red flashed across Tedric's vision, and he took a step closer. Aeden stood frozen between them, clearly unsure by whom to stand—the king who'd promised her the world or the man who'd given her his heart?

"I didn't cheat my way to success," Tedric growled. "Unlike you, I still have a sliver of honor left."

"Stop! Both of you, just stop," Aeden pleaded, but Tedric didn't look at her.

"What do you want with us?" Tedric demanded, taking another step toward the Red King.

The king's crimson robes rippled as he stepped closer still, his long white hair catching sunlight with each movement. "I desire nothing from you that I cannot already have," the Red King replied with a smile.

"I heard everything," Tedric spat. "I know what you want, and I will do everything in my power to stop you."

The Red King's smile thinned, and Tedric looked into his soulless eyes with nothing more than a shiver. The Red King's hand dipped into the folds of his robes, and Tedric barely had time to draw his sword before the king took a step away.

"Neither of you can remember this."

"No, please don't!" Aeden pleaded, and Tedric glanced back to find her still clutching at her arm. "I swore my allegiance to you. Please, please don't make me forget again."

Tedric frowned in confusion. The Red King was making her forget? He looked down at the king's hand, where a small vial was held between his pale fingers. Nausea rose in Tedric's throat at the dark substance that shimmered slightly within the delicate glass.

It was Aeden's blood.

"What in the Nether?" Tedric whispered, staggering back.

The Red King merely gave him a tired look, shaking his head. "This is what comes of those who decide to stray from my plans. It is a nuisance, and I hate to do it, but it had to be done."

"You used battle magic," Tedric said dully. "You've used it twice and have gotten away with it."

A smile tugged on the Red King's lips, and he gave Tedric a very human shrug. "I am the dawn of a new world. The old one cannot use its tricks on me."

Fury slashed red across Tedric's vision once again, and his hand was on his sword in a flash.

"Tedric, don't!" Aeden yelled but too late.

Stabbing pain erupted in Tedric's skull, and his vision exploded in a haze of white light. He barely registered his own scream as his knees cracked against the silver floors. Memories of Clamidas came rushing back, and his heart gave a terrible squeeze as it lurched into his throat. Aeden's scream echoed in tandem with his own, and the last thing he heard was the queen pleading for mercy before his body fell into sweet oblivion.

34

AEDEN

She awoke to the sounds of pain.

Aeden blinked slowly and watched Tedric lean over the side of the bed, heaving. Her own body cramped with discomfort, and her head felt foggy. It was an oddly familiar feeling, as though a corner of her mind was held in thick mist. She shook her head, trying to clear it away, but the fog persisted. The curse seemed to take a different shape each day, though the cramping of her bones seemed to be her most consistent visitor.

"Goddesses damn me," Tedric grumbled once it seemed that his body could release no more.

"They already have." Aeden sighed.

She sat up as Tedric moved off the bed and toward a crystal washbasin in a corner of the room. Dizziness made her blink again, and the fog seemed to float away. She sighed in relief and stood, then padded over to the large pine dresser that held a fresh set of clothing for both her and Tedric.

Warm hands slid around her bare waist, and electricity rushed across Aeden's skin as Tedric leaned against her back.

"Do you still want to go to the Lake of Mirrors today?"

Aeden nodded with a smile. "The horses and guards should be waiting for us already."

"Wonderful," he murmured against her neck before moving around and grabbing a bundle of clothes from the dresser.

They dressed in silence, the cramping of her bones growing with each passing second. She needed the Red King's potion, and soon. Aeden was assaulted by bustling bodies and excited conversation as soon as she opened the door, and she surveyed the sea of fairies preparing for her coronation in two days' time. A young serving girl stood by the door with a tray in hand, her head bent down as she offered two steaming mugs.

Desperate need nearly blinded Aeden at the sight of the potion, but she forced her trembling fingers to be slow as she grabbed one of the steaming mugs and brought it to her lips.

"Thank you," Tedric said, and the serving girl curtsied.

Scorching trails burned down Aeden's throat as she gulped the potion, and sweet relief eased through her bones. She licked the bittersweet taste from her lips as she set the mug down, and the serving girl looked at Tedric, who still held his mug. The warrior glanced at Aeden before smiling at the girl.

"I'll take this with me. Thank you."

Tedric offered her his free arm, and Aeden took it before they started down the hall. Servants and nobles parted ways for them, bowing and curtsying as Aeden passed by. She smiled, both the potion and the sight of her people making warmth bloom in her heart. This was all she'd ever wanted, and now with Tedric at her side, the world didn't feel so gray. She was simply glad that he cared for her still, let alone could look at her after everything she'd done.

They rounded a corner, and Aeden let the sounds and sights of preparation fill her senses. She would become the true queen of Proveria in two days, and part of her felt that it was far too soon, yet ages away. The Red King had promised her the world, and now she was getting just that.

As they moved through the castle in silence, Aeden let her gaze wander to the crystal walls and arched walkways surrounding them. A door to her right was unguarded, and she frowned as something tickled at the back of her skull.

An image exploded through her mind: that very door bursting open and Tedric stepping through as she screamed at the Red King.

Aeden stopped, blinking quickly.

"What is it?" Tedric asked, looking down at her with a frown.

Aeden looked at the door again, the same tickling sensation caressing her mind. "Have we had a meeting with the Red King in there before?" she asked, nodding toward the door.

Tedric frowned, looking at the door. He shook his head after a moment. "I don't think so. I would remember."

She noted the slight bite to his reply and narrowed her gaze at him. But the tickling sensation only grew, dampening her care over his strange reaction.

"Your Majesty!"

A young female voice sounded from behind, and Aeden turned to find a maid dressed in a white cotton dress moving toward them. She curtsied deeply, and her eyes remained on the ground as she spoke.

"The royal seamstress requires an audience with you."

Aeden blinked at the girl, unable to form words as more images flew through her mind, and the tickling transformed into a faint sting.

"For the coronation," the maid clarified. "The seamstress needs to make some final adjustments to your dress."

Aeden blinked again, shaking her head. The images were fragmented and broken, but still, she felt the rage and panic. Tedric drawing his sword, the Red King holding a vial of blood.

It was a dream, her mind said.

No dream has ever felt so real, another part of her warned.

But how could she have forgotten something so terrible?

"Aeden?" Tedric's low voice cut through her thoughts, and Aeden blinked.

But when she looked at the warrior, the image of him falling to his knees with a scream of agony tore through her mind. She shook her head again, blinking the image away. Tedric watched her in alarm, and she didn't realize his hands were wrapped around her arms, keeping her from falling to the floor. Aeden stepped away quickly, the sudden need to run flooding through her muscles. Instead, she smoothed out an invisible wrinkle in her riding breeches and smiled.

"I'm needed for the fitting," Aeden said, meeting Tedric's stare. "We can go to the Lake of Mirrors another time."

Disappointment flickered across Tedric's eyes, and her heart sank. He bowed, and that strange coldness she'd seen a few times before returned to his face.

"I will leave you to your duties," he said stiffly, turning away before she could get another word in.

She watched him go, and the image of his body falling to the silver floor flashed through her mind again. Cold sweat trickled down her spine, and panic made her heartbeat take off in a sprint.

"Your Majesty?" The servant's voice cut through the air again, and Aeden jumped.

"Yes, yes." Aeden sighed, trying her best to smile. "Please take me to the fitting."

The servant curtsied before motioning toward a side corridor, and Aeden followed numbly. A shiver began deep in Aeden's bones, and she suddenly wanted another cup of the Red King's potion. Perhaps it would help the feeling go away.

"Queen Siltra." A familiar voice slithered from behind, and Aeden turned to find the Red King striding toward her.

A pleasant smile painted his thin lips, and a strange sense of anger surged through her at the sight of him in place of her usual excitement. He was dressed in pale cream-colored robes, and his long beard and hair nearly blended in with the fabric. Aeden curtsied, and she heard the shuffle of her maid following the motion close behind.

"How are you faring today?" the Red King asked, his obsidian-colored eyes narrowing slightly, though the smile remained.

She opened her mouth, the desire to be honest halting halfway on her tongue. "Just fine, thank you," Aeden said, hoping her voice sounded kind enough.

The Red King peered at her, and Aeden suppressed a shiver at the way he seemed to stare straight into her soul.

"Wonderful," he replied eventually, and the look vanished as his smile widened. "I hope you don't mind the change in our meeting plans today. I've some business to attend to regarding Keadora today."

Aeden held back a frown, trying to remember what in the Nether he was talking about. She couldn't remember any plans for them to meet in the day, as she'd wanted to spend the day with Tedric. The feeling of wrongness returned, but something told her to keep her mouth shut.

"It happens to be that I'm needed for a fitting," Aeden replied, and her sweet tone sounded hollow in her ears.

"No harm, then," the Red King said with a nod. "Good day."

She watched him move away and watched as his hand reached into a pocket within his robes. The movement was all too familiar, and Aeden stifled a cry as blinding light scorched across her vision.

And then she remembered.

35
LORIAN

"I hate these clothes."

Lorian wriggled beneath the stiff black fabric in discomfort, and Odonir simply watched him from the corner of his room with amusement.

"You should be glad that I brought you multiple options at all. I settled on one coat, then remembered how indecisive you are," Odonir quipped and walked toward his brother.

Odonir took Lorian's cuffs and began to fold and arrange them in a way that, Lorian had to admit, was far more comfortable.

"How do you know what you're doing?" Lorian asked, and Odonir only gave him a look of annoyance before moving behind him and grabbing something that rattled slightly as it moved.

"All elf scouts are required to learn how to mend their clothes during training, just in case something breaks or tears on a long trip."

"It looks like you know a lot more than just how to mend things," Lorian remarked, though with more respect than goading.

The fabric bunched and adjusted against Lorian's back, and

the waistcoat was beginning to feel more comfortable with each change Odonir made.

"I found that making clothes was far more interesting than I originally thought, and it's much easier on your pocketbook as well."

"I suppose you have more talent than I give you credit for." Lorian sighed, and he felt Odonir's hands pause on his other cuff.

"Yes, well, you haven't been around me for quite some time," Odonir replied and moved to Lorian's other sleeve.

Lorian shrugged. "I don't think that's either of our faults, though you've never seemed to want to see me since I had to leave Mamma."

Something sharp poked into Lorian's skin, and he hissed in pain, looking down to find Odonir placing pins in his coat, making the fabric bunch in strange angles.

"What in the Nether are you doing? I can't go to a ball with a bunch of pins stabbing me."

"I'm going to sew it, you idiot," Odonir grumbled. "Though I wish it would be acceptable coronation attire, just to see you uncomfortable for once in your life."

"I have been uncomfortable a fair number of times. I've just gotten good at hiding it whenever the occasion arises."

Lorian could almost hear Odonir's eyes roll into the back of his head, but his brother said nothing as he finished stabbing pins in various locations of his coat.

"How do you feel about this entire thing?" Lorian asked. "You've been quiet about our plans nearly the whole time."

Odonir paused his work for a moment before continuing. "I am only doing this to help Queen Arbane from getting killed. And eventually, once we know more information, I will tell her everything so that she can protect the kingdom and her people."

Lorian snorted and bit his lip. Odonir was now standing in front of him and looked up to give him a scathing yet questioning look.

"Are you silently mocking me?"

"No." Lorian quickly shook his head. "You just sound like my friend. He put his blind trust in the Red King for most of his life. The king was his beacon of light, the holy grail that could put everything right. Well, now we all know that the Red King is a massive prick and the one responsible for us being here. And my friend is cursed, trapped in a life he doesn't deserve."

Lorian bit out the last words with some effort. The thought of Tedric stuck in the Red King's grips made his blood curdle, and he wanted nothing more than to get him out of that awful situation, no matter what it took. Weight bore down on his chest, and he let out a sigh, gaze dropping to the floor.

"I do not place my trust in Queen Arbane blindly, Lorian."

Odonir's low cautioning voice made Lorian jump slightly. He was slapped by frustration that overwhelmed him every time he thought about the night of Clamidas and how they had failed to help Tedric. Lorian shrugged and cursed as one of the pins poked his back.

"She is a good queen, and rulers are the ones who are meant to save kingdoms, not thieves, scouts, or wanted witches."

"You doubt yourself, brother," Lorian said, and a faint smile returned now. "I think that's the exact group of people who could save our realm. If the inside of Arbane's closet is any indication of who she is as a person, I would assume her an indecisive ruler."

Odonir's eyes flashed, and he ground out, "It's *Queen* Arbane, and she's a better ruler than most we've got now."

"I suppose you might be right about that," Lorian said and opened his arms as Odonir carefully pulled off his waistcoat.

The sound of the front door opening and closing echoed through the house, and Lorian's heart leapt in his chest.

"That would be Krete."

The gnome had teleported to Creonid for one final meeting with King Drohan, as well as to gather his outfit for the coronation. He'd only been gone since sunrise, but still, a sense of unease had remained in Lorian's chest from the moment his small friend had disappeared through the shimmering blue portal.

Odonir nodded and hung the waistcoat, which looked like it was more pins than fabric, and together they walked down the steps to the first floor to find Krete being greeted by a very excited Nora and perhaps a slightly less excited Finriel. They said their hellos and then gathered around the table, Odonir still moving around the kitchen to make his obligatory tea.

"So we're clear on the plan, yes?" Finriel asked, and the men seated around her all nodded.

Lorian waved a hand. "Yes, yes, it's going to be very simple and easy."

Odonir raised his brows. "You truly are an idiot."

Lorian offered him a toothy grin and reached for a slice of cheese from their leftover dinner of stew and an array of finger foods. "It's called confidence, brother. I also have done much worse in my time, so I suppose there's that too."

His words oozed confidence, but Lorian couldn't deny the strange feeling in his stomach, which didn't subside after Krete's arrival. The thought of entering Proveria again was enough to make him feel sick, and the thought of seeing both Aeden and Tedric again didn't ease such feelings. Lorian wanted to see Tedric dearly but feared what he might do at the sight of the new fairy queen. She had been their friend, his friend. At least he'd thought so. Betrayal pressed deeply into his heart, but he pushed it away as easily as he'd done for the past moon.

"We are all wanted, you know." Finriel narrowed her eyes at him. "All except Odonir, of course."

"So what?" Lorian scoffed, forcing his confidence to return. "Krete gets a free pass because he's escorting his sister and King Drohan. You're acting as Odonir's dutiful wife, and I'll be nothing more than a shadow."

Finriel simply stared at him, and Lorian's smile widened through his mouthful of cheese.

"See? I know the plan perfectly."

"We should get some sleep." Odonir sighed, nodding toward Krete. "I arranged a few cushions for you in the study. I hope it will be more comfortable than sleeping on Nora."

Indeed, Krete had slept by the fire with Nora the night before, though Lorian didn't think the gnome had been perturbed in the least.

Krete inclined his head. "Thank you."

"Did King Drohan agree to tomorrow's plan?" Finriel asked, and Krete nodded.

"King Drohan knows of my meetings with you, and we agreed that the safest way for me to enter Proveria is if I portal in directly and meet his court at the citadel. I should stay hidden until I know for certain that I'm granted safe haven."

"That's smart," Lorian said. "We don't need your arrest as the evening's main spectacle."

Finriel snorted. "I'm sure Aeden will make sure that everyone's attention remains on her."

"Which is exactly what we want and why I'm going to be as careful as possible," Krete said, though Lorian noted the slight fall of his friend's expression at the mention of Aeden.

"I'm going to finish Lorian's coat and get some sleep," Odonir said, standing from his chair with his mug in hand. "I have to be at the castle by dawn."

Lorian smiled at his brother. "So you do love me."

Odonir met his gaze and gave him the flicker of a smile. "Only enough to make sure you can do your job tomorrow. Though I am tempted to leave a pin or two in to make things interesting."

Lorian chuckled, and Odonir bade them all a final good night before slipping away.

Finriel sighed, rubbing her eyes with the heels of her palms.

"We should probably all get a good night of rest. Tomorrow's a big day."

"Indeed." Krete stood with a groan. "I will see you two in the morning."

"Good night," Lorian said with a yawn, though tension began coursing through his body at the realization that he and Finriel were now alone.

"Shall we?" Finriel asked, and Lorian simply followed her as they made their way up the stairs and into the room.

He couldn't help but watch the curves of her body as she moved to close the door behind them, heart thundering in his chest. It was still foreign, knowing that he could love her freely and that she cared for him right back. They hadn't done anything other than hold each other, though Lorian knew by the tension in her body each night that they both thought of more.

"I should get ready for bed," Finriel said.

He moved behind her before she could turn, his hand sliding around her waist. Finriel's breath hitched as Lorian pulled her back against his chest, and a satisfying tingle ran through his body. His other hand snaked around her waist, sending sparks of electricity dancing where their bodies touched.

"Or we could stay up a bit longer," Lorian said demurely into her ear, her hair tickling his cheek.

Finriel shivered, and a sudden ball of nerves and excitement formed in his belly at her response. She stilled, moving only her hands so that they brushed against his scarred knuckles. "I don't know what you mean."

Lorian chuckled, hoping he sounded more confident than he felt. In truth, she made him feel like a young man again, completely inept at the game of love. "You know exactly what I mean."

His lips brushed against her neck, as soft as a butterfly's wings. Her hands tightened against his, and he kissed her again, this time where her jawline met her neck.

"Lorian," Finriel breathed.

He stiffened and retracted his mouth from her skin, uncertainty making him freeze. "I didn't mean to make you uncomfortable. I—"

"No."

She tightened her grip on his arms before he could pull away and then spun around so that she was facing him. The surprise on her face was evident, and his hands tightened around her waist as she chose her next words.

"You didn't make me uncomfortable," Finriel started, and relief mingled with his surprise. "I'm just not used to all of this."

A tentative grin played at his lips. "All of what? Me wanting you?"

He smiled at the red flush that immediately rose to her cheeks, though he was startled by his own open proclamation. He knew that he wanted her though, knew it from the moment he'd laid eyes on her for the first time in ten years.

She shook her head. "Not that. I'm not used to being touched or cared for in a romantic way."

Lorian's heart softened, and for once, she looked uncertain instead of the steadfast and stubborn witch she presented to the world. His hand reached up to brush against her cheek, and he smiled. "I've always cared for you, even when you haven't seen me."

Finriel looked to the ground, and Lorian angled her face up to look at him once more. Her eyes were soft, yet a hunger danced behind that softness in a way he'd never seen before.

"Only if you truly want to, Finriel. But you'll find it's much like riding a horse. Uncomfortable and strange at first, but you get used to it over time."

Finriel grimaced. "I don't want to compare this to riding a horse. It'll just make me think of Ed and Oats."

Lorian chuckled and bent down to kiss her softly, her lips a sweet caress against that hard wall around his heart. But he was beginning to find that wall was no longer as strong as before, for the very woman standing before him, leaning into his lips, was slowly chipping away at its sturdy face.

Lorian forced his racing thoughts to turn off as he molded into her touch, exploring her mouth with his as her hands traveled up his chest and found themselves on his jaw and in his hair. His hand went around her waist, the other still on her cheek and now drifting lower toward the back of her neck. She was a new realm completely, and he was already lost in the depths of her waters.

Lorian broke away, panting slightly, his eyes still trained directly at hers. "Are you sure?"

Finriel was now the one to give him a smile and a light slap on the chest. "Stop asking me or else I'll change my mind. Now kiss me, thief."

Lorian did not need to be asked twice, and his lips found hers like a key fitting into a keyhole. Fire welled in his abdomen, and he let out a soft groan as her teeth nibbled on his lower lip. He let the warmth take over as he led her blindly toward the bed and only barely made it as Finriel tripped on the corner of the thick blue rug below.

She let out a small laugh against his lips as he sat her down and leaned over her, letting his mouth travel from her lips to her jaw to her neck. A small noise escaped Finriel's mouth at the sensation, making him blind with desire and that ever-growing warmth.

His hands traveled freely down her body, and Finriel sighed into his touch. After a moment, she reached for him, and they both paused, smiling and simply taking in each other's company. He had never thought in a thousand years that he would be doing this with Finriel, let alone see her again.

"You're beautiful."

The words were out of his mouth before he could stop them, and Lorian inwardly cursed as his cheeks heated in embarrassment at his loose tongue. But Finriel's smile only widened, gratitude evident on her face. He reached out to tuck a strand of hair behind her ear that had come loose from its braid.

"You're not too bad yourself," she murmured.

Lorian didn't bother to reply as he leaned in again, pressing his lips against hers. They moved in harmony as he guided her back against the bed and hovered over her. Her hand met his back, and a sound of surprise rumbled through his throat as she pressed him flush against her. He broke away, and she met his gaze readily. There was a fire in her eyes that he had never seen before, and his heart nearly burst. He was undone by the realization that *that* fire was only for him.

Their lips collided once again, and now it was much easier to explore the planes of each other's bodies and kiss wherever they pleased. Lorian could hardly think as articles of clothing were strewn on the floor, and soon, he was kissing her bare skin in places he'd barely even let himself imagine before. Her touches were assuring and kind, and Lorian found he felt perfectly safe in her arms as he explored her skin and let the weakening walls crumble away from his heart.

36

FINRIEL

F inriel tugged at the sleeves of her dress, nerves crawling down her throat as she stared at the mirror. Lorian had made an excellent choice in the dress he'd stolen from Queen Arbane's extravagant collection, but the finery against her skin felt foreign and almost overwhelming.

The rich black fabric was soft yet sturdy, which made Finriel feel slightly more comfortable. The dress fell in waves around her legs, though Finriel was also grateful it wasn't *truly* a dress but rather a bodice with a long train of fabric that flowed to the floor like a midnight wave surrounding her pant-clad legs. Intricate patterns of glittering black fabric were stitched along the cuffs and bodice of the outfit, which cut daringly down the front, leaving a long slit of bare skin in between her breasts. She knew Lorian had likely picked the outfit for that exact reason, and her stomach flopped at the thought of his reaction. Though the cut was daring, it still covered her shoulders and most of her chest, with a high collar grazing the back of her neck. The gown was truly beautiful, but her mess of a braid and dirt-smeared face put off the look entirely.

Finriel ripped her hair free from its constraints and ran her fingers through it as best as possible, wincing at the knots that snagged on her fingers. Once it was manageable, she secured the front pieces back behind her head, leaving the rest tumbling loosely to her waist. Finriel scrambled to the water basin and gasped at the frigid water she splashed over her face. She reached blindly toward the washcloth hanging over the side and blotted her face dry.

A soft knock on the door made Finriel jump, and she wiped a stray droplet of water from her cheek as she crossed the room and opened the door to find Krete standing on the other side. She smiled at the sight of him. He wore a simple yet excellently made tunic of deep green trimmed with silver at the collar and cuffs. His trousers were of the same material, and his feet were clad in shining black boots.

"No hat today?" Finriel asked, noting his mousy hair free of his usual gray cap.

Krete smiled and gave her a wink. "I'm keeping it in my pocket and putting it on the moment we're out of the citadel."

Finriel smirked and moved to welcome him into the room, sneaking a glance toward the main living area to see if she could peek at Lorian. When she couldn't see him, she turned to find Krete gazing at her with widened eyes.

"What's the matter?" Finriel asked, doing her best not to sound too defensive, which was her automatic response to being nervous.

Krete shook his head. "You look wonderful, is all."

Finriel dropped her gaze and cleared her throat. "Oh, thank you."

"Lorian told me that he was the one who chose your fit for the night, and I must say, he did an excellent job," he said with the ghost of laughter in his voice.

Finriel rolled her eyes and attempted to keep the smile and warmth from blooming on her cheeks. "He did, this time."

Krete stepped forward and offered a small box Finriel hadn't noticed he'd been holding until that moment. "It's my sister's," he explained as Finriel opened the box to find a thin pen of charcoal, rouge, and something else in a small closed container that she didn't recognize. "I thought you might want to put some on."

Finriel looked at the makeup with uncertainty. "I've never worn any before."

"Ah." Krete smiled. "Here, I'll help you."

Finriel frowned but allowed the gnome to lead her to the chair in the corner of the room and sit her down. She arranged the folds of her train carefully so as to not wrinkle it so soon in the evening, and Krete took the box from her hands. He removed the charcoal and motioned for Finriel to close her eyes.

"How do you know how to do this?" Finriel asked as Krete pressed the coal onto the base of her eyelashes, dragging it toward the corner of her eye.

"Brinna forced me to do her makeup when we were younger and especially when King Drohan began taking interest in her. Mott would run away every time she asked him to help, so that left me responsible for the task."

"So you readied Brinna's face every time she made a public appearance?" Finriel asked in surprise at this new nugget of information.

"Not every time, goddesses no." Krete chuckled. "Only when we were younger. Though I found it to be very fun and therapeutic once I got good at it, and now I enjoy practicing whenever she gives me the chance."

Finriel smiled genuinely at his tale and found a new appreciation for the man blooming in her chest. Krete finished his job in silence, and Finriel let her mind wander as his hands patted and drew on her skin.

"All done," Krete said finally. "You can look now."

Finriel blinked a few times to get used to the strange sensation on her skin before she stood and crossed over to the mirror. She almost didn't recognize the woman staring back at her.

Finriel had always believed herself to be beautiful, but this woman was unearthly. A dark thin line framed the tops of Finriel's caramel-and-flame-veined eyes, winging out slightly at the corners to give her a more feline, sultry look. Her lips were tinted a few shades darker than usual, and a faint shimmer highlighted her cheekbones, the tip of her nose, and Cupid's bow.

"Holy shit."

Finriel jumped at the male voice, and she turned to find Lorian standing frozen in the doorway. Her jaw dropped slightly at the man standing before her, and the exact words that had flown from his mouth nearly dropped from her own. He was dressed in a black tunic and waistcoat, the chest lined in gold stitching. His black boots were polished and looked new, but his old dagger was still at his belt. Lorian's hair was combed back becomingly, and a suphiera that depicted a raven's face and beak was held loosely in his hand. His slightly tipped ears were now visible with his combed-back hair, giving him an ethereal edge.

He looked like a prince bathed in darkness.

Finriel almost cringed at her wild yet also tender thoughts toward the thief and cleared her throat. "You had to choose the most provocative thing in that closet, didn't you?" she managed to say, though her shaky voice didn't quite portray the same resigned exasperation she'd wanted.

Lorian blinked a few times before recovering. "It was one of the more modest choices, actually. It seems as though our dear elf queen is quite risqué."

They simply stared at each other for a few moments, clearly both shocked at the sudden change from worn traveler to elegant noble.

"What's that on your eyes?" Lorian asked and took a step closer.

"Krete did it." Finriel motioned toward the gnome, who was standing near the corner of the room, seemingly quite entertained by their interaction.

"An artist too?" Lorian said with raised brows. "You surprise me more and more every day."

Krete smiled. "Well, I had an excellent canvas to work on, so I must say it wasn't all my doing."

"Stop it," Finriel said, her mind going blank at the compliment. "We should check on Odonir and see if he's ready."

Finriel moved to the bed, where her mask of dark metal shaped like a wolf's head lay. The metal was cold to the touch as she picked up the suphiera and turned, finding Lorian's eyes still glued on her.

"I might have to change if you keep staring at me. It could be hard for you to focus on our mission," Finriel said.

Lorian just smirked. "Oh, don't worry. I'll be just fine."

"Good, then you can focus on getting your brother out of his room."

Lorian's grin only widened, and he bowed low. "Yes, my lady."

"REMEMBER, STICK TO THE PLAN," Lorian said under his breath as they entered the enormous crowd of colors and noise at the front entrance.

"Don't worry. I think we're all more worried about you straying off course tonight," Odonir growled through his owl suphiera, his arm that was now linked through Finriel's tensing slightly.

Odonir had thankfully been given an invitation by the queen and was attending as himself. They had used the formal invitation to forge two others, one for Finriel and one for Lorian. They had changed their names on the invitations, and Finriel would be called Fairen Grey for the evening. Lorian had chosen the name Charles Elliot for himself, wanting to sound as "pompous and average as possible," as he'd put it.

The towering spires of the castle loomed before them, piercing into the starry sky above. Odonir's arm was tense under her hand as they walked toward the large gates together in a sea of all races. Her breathing hitched at the sensation of cool air swathing her skin and warm bodies surrounding her, the contrast almost dizzying.

"Are you all right, or am I going to have to carry you inside?" Odonir's low voice was tight but worried, and she managed a glance at him through her suphiera.

"I'm fine," she bit out, though they both knew it was far from the truth.

Finriel had never been one for big crowds, and the current situation was causing that awful buzzing exhaustion to creep up on her again. Odonir shifted her hand closer in the crook of his arm, which allowed her to lean against him.

"Thank you," Finriel murmured, and Odonir only bumped her softly with his hip in reply.

They passed through the silver gates and into the familiar courtyard of ancient trees and lush grass, the crystal fountain in the center gleaming under the moonlight. Finriel blinked against the wave of memories that slashed through her mind, and this time, she truly did lean into Odonir. The blood moon printed itself into her mind once more, and the metallic copper tang of blood coated her nostrils.

"Finriel." Odonir's voice snatched her thoughts away and brought her back to the courtyard.

She was leaning most of her weight on him now and had clearly stumbled by the stinging pain in her right foot.

"I said I'm fine," she hissed. "I just missed a step."

They followed the crowd into a passageway lined with glittering lights, which was thankfully in the opposite direction of the throne room. Finriel nearly stumbled again as they entered the ballroom and the splendor encapsulated them in an unearthly vision.

The room was grander than any Finriel had ever seen, with floor-to-ceiling windows lining the entire right wall which was curved in a half-moon shape. A dais stood at the back of the room, which was the place where, Finriel could only guess, Aeden would be crowned queen. Gleaming tables covered in flutes of bubbling drinks and decadent foods made Finriel's mouth water, but she dragged her attention away once more.

Musicians played in a corner of the room by the windows, the twinkling fairy music floating merrily through the air. An archway that led to a dimly lit hall stood at the left side of the room near the tables of food, and curiosity as to where the hallway led nipped at Finriel.

The nobles and revelers filed in, filling the room with excited chatter and laughter that mingled with the music. She looked around, expecting to find Krete among the sea of people. A faint glimmer of hope flickered at the thought of seeing Tedric, though Finriel wasn't sure if the Red King would allow him to be present tonight or if he would be forced to remain on the side-lines all evening. Finriel took in a deep breath to calm her nerves and glanced at Odonir to find him surveying the room with mild interest.

A hand took Finriel's and pulled her to the side. Flame leapt to her fingers, and she whirled around, ready to strike. But a familiar tall man swathed in black clothing made her pause.

"Lo—Charles," Finriel stuttered, not daring to use the thief's true name.

He inclined his head, then angled it to face his brother, who still had his hand around Finriel's arm. Odonir only gave them a sharp look before backing away.

"I'll look for Queen Arbane and make sure that she is well," he said behind a shoulder as he disappeared into the crowd.

Finriel followed Odonir's movements through the crowd, noticing a tall woman with ebony skin and a crown full of jewels. *So that's queen Arbane*, she thought. She'd never seen the queen in person before and had to admit she hadn't expected the woman to be a radiant beauty.

She hardly had time to watch Odonir bow to the queen before Lorian led her into an alcove behind the food table she hadn't noticed before. Electricity danced through their fingers. Finriel's nerves were already nearly shot from being at the coronation and hoping they'd make it out with their necks still attached, and now the thief was leading her into the darkness, which was *not* part of the plan. The curtained alcove was dim as they walked into it, and both nerves and confusion swam inside Finriel's stomach as they took off their suphieras.

"What—" Finriel was about to speak but was cut short as Lorian's lips crashed into hers.

She hadn't realized how much she'd wanted his touch until now, and she let her arms circle his waist and press their bodies together as she kissed him back. He broke away from her too soon, and she breathed heavily as she looked up at him, his glacial eyes piercing into hers. The emotion behind his gaze made Finriel's knees feel weak, but she forced herself to stay upright and withdraw her arms from his waist, fumbling slightly with the suphiera as it threatened to slip from her unsteady fingers.

"Why did you do that?" Her question came out in a ragged breath, and Lorian brushed back a lock of hair that had fallen into his eyes with a free hand.

"Does a man need a reason for wanting to show affection for his woman?"

Finriel glared at him. "I'd hardly call that affection, more like mindless desire."

Lorian's faint smile disappeared at this, and he pressed himself closer to her. Her breath hitched at his pine-and-lavender scent. "I'm never mindless, especially not with you," he said with an intensity that surprised her and made a different kind of warmth seep into her core. "I could never be mindless about this, Finriel. And I will do nothing but respect my fire queen."

And then he was gone, ducking into the crowd and adjusting the suphiera back over his face. It took everything in Finriel's power not to sink to her knees as the world spun. But she had a job to do now, and it was time to find Odonir.

He was waiting where they'd seen him last, his hand gripped perhaps a bit too tightly on a flute of pink sparkling liquid, the other holding his suphiera. She considered him for a moment from the alcove, taking in the strong lines of his high cheekbones and chiseled jaw. He and Lorian were quite similar, but while Odonir was sharp elven masculinity, Lorian was a dangerous shadow. Both still beautiful, but different.

Finriel wrangled in her nerves and gathered up her courage as she put on the suphiera, adjusting to the weight of the metal against her face before entering the swollen crowd.

"That took you quite a while," Odonir said as she approached, and Finriel leaned into him, hoping the action would make people think they were a couple.

"He just had to tell me one last part of the plan," Finriel said, fumbling for a good excuse for their sudden absence.

Odonir snorted and tipped the drink—likely some sort of strange fairy alcohol Finriel didn't know of—to his lips, swallowing the rest in one large gulp. He set the flute down on the table and put his suphiera on before offering her a hand, which she took silently.

"Your suphiera is crooked, my dear." Odonir sighed. "I'm sure it was just an accident while you and Charles were so busy making plans."

It was all that Finriel could do not to douse Odonir's existence in a wave of fire right there and then. She took in a deep breath and forced the crackling flame down low inside her core, letting it take up a place with that secondary flame only Lorian could access. The sudden rise of her magic made Finriel's head swim, but she forced it down as deep as she could.

"Are you all right?" Odonir asked, and only then did Finriel realize she was leaning heavily on him yet again.

"Sorry. Just got a bit light-headed."

She could have sworn Odonir tilted his head to give her a look of concern, but their attention snapped forward an instant later as a loud bell rang through the room and the music died.

"Aeden," Finriel breathed, her heart galloping in her chest as the crowd began to bow, giving her the ability to see the dais before them and the goddess-like woman standing upon it.

Finriel and Odonir quickly lowered their gazes and bowed with the rest of the crowd before a loud voice rang out over the room.

"You may rise."

Finriel waited a few moments for the other members of the crowd to rise, hoping Aeden hadn't noticed her already. She and Odonir rose, and Finriel glanced through the cracks between people to take in her enemy.

It was as if Aeden had taken a bath in molten gold, but when Finriel looked closer, she was able to see what looked like a dress of golden bird feathers clinging to her bodice and down half her legs, the bottom half of the dress giving way to fabric of the same color. A train of what looked like liquid gold pooled around her. She was the image of royalty, with a golden choker of serpent scales encircling her throat. A mask of golden flowers and vines woven around each other fit over her eyes, which rose into a crown of coiled and rearing snakes above her braided violet hair.

The band began to play a surging waltz, and couples took each other by the hands, commencing the dance. Odonir turned her and snaked a hand around her waist, making Finriel's mind flash to Lorian's hands with a jolt. She fumbled to put one hand on his shoulder and the other in his free hand as they began to drift around the room, and she glanced around to see if she could manage a glimpse of the thief. He was nowhere to be seen.

"That's her?" Odonir asked, bringing Finriel back from her fruitless search for Lorian.

Finriel nodded, a twinge of fiery anger fluttering within her at the mention of Aeden.

"She certainly looks like the kind that would betray her friends," Odonir said, and Finriel glanced up into his dark blue eyes with confusion.

"Do you have experience with the backstabbing type?" Finriel asked, and Odonir shrugged under her hand.

"Not entirely, but it's part of my job to keep guard on the queen, as well as monitor the surrounding areas around Mitonir. I've come to know a great deal of people, especially the royal ones. It's quite easy to spot once you get the hang of it."

Finriel listened silently, mulling over his words. Had they all been too blind to see her true motives? Even Lorian, who had surrounded himself with liars and thieves for most of his life?

Finriel dragged her attention away from the golden queen and back to the crowd around them. Gowns and suphieras blurred together as the partygoers danced to the surging music, the glittering lights, full crowd, and extravagant decoration a far cry from how Finriel had last seen Anemoi Citadel. She scanned the party, feeble hope swelling as she searched for Tedric's tall frame in the crowd. But he was nowhere to be seen, and her heart sank.

"Krete," Odonir whispered, and Finriel jumped, glancing at the nobles milling around the dance floor.

Indeed, there was Krete, standing with king Drohan and queen Brinna, who both looked just as jovial as she'd remembered. Krete's hat-clad head was bowed slightly, and the cat suphiera was a bit large on his face. She let Odonir lead her through a spin, and she glanced at the gnome again. He seemed to notice Finriel and Odonir at the same moment and gave her a nod of his head.

"No one has arrested him yet," Finriel said under her breath.

Odonir's hand tightened around hers. "Don't speak too soon."

Finriel shot him a glare, but she could only see his unimpressed stare and lips set in a grim line. He had a point, and she couldn't deny her nerves about them all getting caught.

The dance ended with a rise and fall of the music, and Finriel broke away from Odonir gratefully. He was quite a good dancer, but she couldn't say the same about herself. She felt awkward and stiff and had wanted the dance to end the moment it began.

Odonir led her to the refreshment table, and she took a flute of drink from his hand. She took a sip and cringed at the floral taste. She was about to spit it back into the glass when a man dressed in silver robes and wearing a dragon suphiera sauntered to the table. He seemed older, and Finriel instantly knew by his thin stature that he was a fairy.

"Lovely evening," he said in greeting, and Finriel dipped her head, elbowing Odonir who was gazing out at the crowd.

She felt him jump, and he turned so that he was standing at her side.

"Indeed," Finriel said, forcing her voice to sound inviting.

The man took a drink and smiled after the first sip. "This stuff is delightful."

"And you are?" Odonir asked the man.

She hadn't thought about asking him that.

"Oh, pardon me," the man chuckled. "I am Reginald Darcy, part of queen Siltra's council."

Trepidation lurched in Finriel's throat, and she nudged Odonir again. Her throat seemed to have closed up, for forming words was nearly impossible at the moment. Nether damn her, she hated crowds.

"I am Odonir Grey, and this is my wife, Fairen."

Finriel inclined her head, and Reginald gave her an intoxicated smile. It appeared that this wasn't his first drink.

"Wonderful to meet you two," Reginald said. "I must say, it's quite a relief to be done with the coronation preparations."

"It must have been difficult," Odonir replied, and the fairy chuckled.

"Was it ever? Though it wasn't due to the queen being overly picky. In fact, it almost seemed like she didn't care about the planning at all."

Finriel frowned at this. Aeden had seemed quite keen on keeping clean and having a good appearance throughout their mission to find the beasts, and it struck her odd that she wouldn't care about something as grand as this.

Reginald drained the rest of his drink and placed the empty glass on the table. "I must be on my way, I'm going to enjoy the party while I can."

"It was lovely to meet you," Odonir said, inclining his head.

Reginald waved at them and disappeared back into the crowd. Finriel let out a sigh of relief, sagging slightly.

"Why did you elbow me in the ribs?" Odonir huffed, rubbing his side.

"It wasn't that hard." Finriel rolled her eyes. "Besides, you were much better at talking to that man than I would have ever been."

"Doesn't mean you had to hurt me," Odonir grumbled.

Finriel narrowed her eyes at the elf, who simply shook his head. He was so dramatic, but perhaps that ran in the family.

"Care for a dance?"

Finriel jumped at the low voice by her ear, and she swiveled around with an insult ready on her lips. But it was only Lorian. Her breath left her again at the sight of him. Even with the suphiera covering the top half of his face, he looked gorgeous, and she clenched her jaw against the shy smile that played against her lips.

He outstretched a pale hand, wiggling his fingertips. Odonir stepped forward stiffly.

"That is not your job tonight, brother."

Lorian angled his head to look at his brother but kept his fingers stretched out toward Finriel. "Allow me a few minutes of enjoyment. It is a party after all," Lorian replied casually.

Finriel took his hand before she could think better of it, and electric shocks sizzled up her arm at the touch of his skin. Odonir groaned audibly from under his suphiera but relented and took a step back.

"Just one dance."

If Lorian's face were visible, Finriel was certain he would have been giving his brother a sarcastic smile. He held her hand lightly in his own as he steered her away from Odonir and toward the group of bodies lining up for the next dance, which was just about to begin. Lorian stepped closer to her, and her breath hitched as his hand grazed her back before settling on her waist.

"Lorian, this wasn't part of the plan," Finriel hissed, though she couldn't deny that her body felt electric with his touch around her waist and hand.

She could just barely see the flash of blue underneath the raven that stared back at her wolf, two dark souls in a sea of glittered light. His hand grazed slightly lower, and he leaned forward to whisper in her ear.

"I asked you to save me a dance, so now I'm cashing it in."

His head stayed near Finriel's ear through the slow dance, and his quick breaths tickled her skin. This was a terrible idea, let alone dangerous. But she couldn't help but feel a rush of excitement at his nearness and at the fact that without their suphieras on, they would surely be caught and thrown into some sort of dungeon. Or worse.

"Lorian, this is stupid," Finriel whispered, and Lorian's chuckle vibrated against her chest.

"Stupid is my middle name these days."

"Really? I thought you were getting smarter." Finriel smiled, and his low laugh made her poor heart sing. "Do you see Aeden?" she asked and angled her head to see Lorian shake his.

"Not anymore. She's probably getting ready for the ceremony by now."

"How many dresses does one fairy need to wear in a night?" Finriel grumbled.

"A lot, assuming all royals share Queen Arbane's dressing decisions," Lorian replied easily, making Finriel tense. "What is it?" he asked.

"My dress," Finriel said. "It's Queen Arbane's. She'll know as soon as she sees me."

Lorian shook his head. "I found out Odonir has a strange talent for sewing, so I had him make a few adjustments before tonight."

"I hope he did a good enough job," Finriel muttered.

"Let's not talk about any of that right now." Lorian brushed his hand up her back. "I want to enjoy this moment with you, just the two of us with a bunch of nobles wearing creepy masks."

Finriel screwed up her nose. "You don't make it sound very romantic."

She pressed against him, feeling his heart pounding against his chest. Was he nervous?

"Sounding romantic has never been one of my strong suits," Lorian said as their feet moved in a steady mirror to the symphony of dance music.

"At least you admit it." Finriel glanced around at the swirling dresses and suits.

No one was paying attention to them. It was as though they were invisible and Lorian and Finriel were truly alone in this enormous room, with the music playing just for them.

"Were you able to speak to anyone of interest?" Lorian asked after a moment, and Finriel shrugged slightly.

"One of Aeden's council members, but he was so drunk I'm not sure if any of it was true."

Lorian chuckled. "What did he say?"

"Just that Aeden seemed less than excited about planning the coronation," Finriel replied, and Lorian tensed slightly.

"Very interesting."

"If you say so," Finriel said. "I just found it odd that she didn't want to be part of something so grand when she wanted to be queen so badly."

"Exactly my thinking," Lorian agreed.

They danced in silence for a few moments, and Finriel tried to drown everything out and simply focus on her body against Lorian's. His muscles were oddly tense even though his movements were so graceful, and she looked up at him, only to find him staring at her.

"I wish I could kiss you," Lorian murmured into Finriel's ear, sending pinpricks down her skin.

She let out a shaky breath, unsure whether she was capable of responding at the moment. He was so close, and the memory of his lips on her neck flashed through her entire body at his words. She wanted to kiss him too—and badly. She scoffed inwardly at herself. *When did I become so soft?* But perhaps being soft was not a sign of weakness, but of incredible strength.

"I know," was all Finriel said, and she swore a growl emanated from Lorian's throat at her words.

They continued in silence for the rest of the dance until the music swelled and gave one last burst before drifting to a close. The dancers separated and clapped, but Finriel did no such thing as Lorian let go of her and stepped back.

"Back to the shadows I go," he said and turned away to disappear within the crowd before Finriel could reply.

Finriel simply stared out into the thinning bodies as people meandered toward refreshment tables and clustered in small groups to gossip. A hand touched her elbow, and Finriel jumped, only to relax when Odonir's owl mask came into view.

"You startled me." Finriel sighed, and Odonir tilted his head.

"Sorry. You just seemed like you were about to light someone on fire."

Finriel shook her head and clasped her clammy hands together. "I need a drink."

37

TEDRIC

Tedric leaned against an archway that faced the large crowd of bodies, his thoughts muddled and confused.

The night was passing in an odd blur of unfamiliar nobles and strange music. People laughed and danced with one another, and Tedric watched them all with distaste. How could they come here in such high spirits while in the company of two liars? Tedric supposed that most participants of the night's festivities had no care for politics tonight, and it was their way of ignoring the heightened tensions, if only for a few hours.

Tedric's suphiera dangled in his fingers, but he felt no need to put it on. He'd been condemned to being on the sidelines throughout the night except for the moment when he would be called to dance with Aeden. He had to admit he was grateful for the order of staying on the outside of things, for he wasn't sure if he could take being in the middle of the bustling crowd.

It would soon be time for Aeden's coronation speech, and Tedric shoved down the nervous jolt his insides made at the thought. The memory of her touch whispered against his skin, and Tedric fought off a shudder. He had made a mistake in coming here, in following Egharis's advice. He wasn't sure how much more his heart could take or how long it would be until his lies would be uncovered.

The large room hushed, bringing Tedric back to the present moment. Everyone was now standing silently before the dais, watching raptly as an old fairy priest wearing thick gray robes hobbled to where the throne sat, an extravagant crown of golden leaves and vines interlaced with stunning jewels held in his delicate hands.

Tedric's heart nearly leapt into his throat, and he cursed as Aeden stepped out to stand next to the priest. She was an image of terrifying golden beauty, and he hated that his heart raced when her eyes scanned the crowd before landing on him. Her mouth quirked upward, and her gaze shot electric shocks through his veins. She was no longer wearing her suphiera, and he had to admit she looked even more beautiful without it. Loathing and lust burned inside of him, and his hands curled into fists as their gazes broke and Aeden went to kneel before the priest.

The priest chanted in Old Faerish, his warbling voice echoing within the walls and seeping into Tedric's bones. He didn't understand the words being spoken, but somehow, his very essence understood the power behind them.

"Do you vow to protect your people and uphold the honor that is expected of you?" The priest spoke in the common tongue now.

"I vow it."

Aeden's voice was sure and strong in her reply, and Tedric took in a rattling breath. He knew she believed her own words and also knew they were far from the truth. He wanted nothing more than to snatch the crown from the priest's hands and search for a better ruler, but he knew he could not. Instead, he only watched, paralyzed as the priest lowered the crown until it rested atop Aeden's head.

The crowd cheered and drank from the flutes of bubbling drink in their hands, but Tedric only stood there and watched.

Aeden rose smoothly to her feet and turned to watch the crowd, smiling faintly at the mix of her citizens and the nobles from differing kingdoms. The cheering hushed once more as Aeden raised her hand.

"It is with humility and honor that I take the throne in place of my late father. It is with sadness that I accept this crown, as I deeply wish my father were still here to rule with the strength and wisdom I still have yet to learn."

The crowd watched with intent, but Tedric's insides recoiled at her lie.

"I will do all I can to both retain and protect the laws in place and relationships with other kingdoms, as well as form new relationships and bonds with those that are slightly frayed, and I say that without judgment. I will also strive to strengthen the borders that are weak and protect the purity of this kingdom with all that I have."

Tedric frowned at this but listened on. Aeden was calm and poised, and the words rolled from her ruby lips with more conviction than Tedric thought possible.

"We have placed guards along the places where strange activity has been noted. The Red King has graciously offered his services and bodies of men until our ranks have been properly restored from the terrible accident on Clamidas. Be sure that this is the dawn of a new freedom and a new world."

The room was silent for a moment before clapping began, ringing dully through Tedric's ears. She had spoken in riddles, but he knew exactly what she'd meant regarding the subject, for he'd seen the army lining Proveria's border only ten days before. Aeden curtsied low and gave a heart-crushing smile to the audience before she turned away and disappeared down into the crowd, likely to receive thanks and socialize with the nobles and whichever rulers had dared come. An icy sweat dripped down Tedric's back, and he loosened another shaky breath from his body, suddenly wanting some of the Red King's awful potion.

A black-clad body shot past, and Tedric's attention whipped toward the man, now gone in a darkened corner of the hall. Heart leaping into his throat, Tedric stepped from the archway and started down toward the corner of the hall.

Aeden was still nowhere in sight, having just finished her strange and slightly alarming coronation speech. Tedric didn't understand half of what she'd said, though he knew she had just given away some sort of morsel of information about her and the Red King's plans.

He shoved those thoughts out of his mind, deciding it would be best to think about it all once he was certain that the man who'd shot past was not who he thought it might be. Tedric went down the hall, only to find it empty. He glanced from side to side, eyes narrowing as one of the long shadows shifted. Tedric broke into a sprint without thinking, and within seconds, his body collided with another. The man was in black, which made it difficult to discern his features. His raven suphiera sat askew on his face, and it only took a single chuckle from the man for Tedric to spring to his feet and stumble back a few steps.

"Lorian," Tedric hissed, the world spinning as he took in the sight of his friend.

Lorian grinned and wiped his pants off. "Good to see that your reflexes are still working."

Tedric wasn't sure if he wanted to curse at his friend or embrace him. Perhaps both. Lorian seemed to decide the latter was a better option and stepped closer, clapping him on the back with a hearty laugh.

"I thought you were dead," Lorian said.

"I almost was." Tedric chuckled. "Sometimes I wonder if it would've been better if that chunk of crystal had gotten me a bit harder."

"That's awfully dark," Lorian reprimanded, though Tedric noted the hint of laughter mingling through his words.

"What in the Nether are you doing here?" Tedric led Lorian

deeper into the hallway, which was lit by candles held in polished silver sconces.

"Finriel, my brother, and I decided that it would be worth—"

"You have a brother?" Tedric exclaimed, cutting off the poor thief before he could finish his reply.

Lorian ripped off his raven suphiera with a groan. The thief looked healthier and perhaps calmer, like a man who was at ease with his life. Perhaps it had to do with whatever happened between him and Finriel in Millris Forest before they'd been captured on Clamidas. Tedric would leave that question for later, however. He needed to know why his friends were here and how Lorian had failed to mention that he had kin.

"I have a half brother." Lorian sighed. "He's the elf scout that saved our asses when you dropped your satchel in the Farridian Forest."

Tedric's eyes widened, looking back on the adrenaline-filled memory and the shared stare between Lorian and the short-haired scout who had flung the satchel back up to them without a word to his comrades.

"So he's helping you now?" Tedric asked.

"He says he's helping Queen Arbane and the future of Farrador, but I honestly think he's just bored with his life and wants a change." Lorian shrugged. "Krete is here too, though he came with the other members of the gnome court as an escort to Queen Brinna."

Tedric nodded. "I pray the Red King and Aeden actually respect the safety law he's been granted for the night."

"He'll be just fine." Lorian grinned. "Anyway, I haven't seen you in over a moon. Have you been well? What's life like now that you're working for the bad people?"

"Don't remind me." Tedric grimaced. "It's not too bad if I'm being honest. It could be worse."

Lorian raised his brow and crossed his arms over his chest. "Krete told me a bit about your little meeting the other day. The things he's told me you've been forced to do don't sound very pleasant—unless you aren't truly being forced."

Anger boiled up in Tedric's stomach like a roiling teapot, but he forced a deep breath and growled, "It's not exactly my desire to be Aeden's plaything, if that's what you're suggesting."

Lorian put his hands up in defense. "I didn't want to assume. I just know something was going on between you two during our mission. That's all."

The anger sputtered out, only to be replaced with an aching lull in his chest that Tedric did not find to be much better at all. "There was." He sighed. "But I'm growing to find she's not the woman she pretended to be on our mission."

"Do you know anything?" Lorian stepped forward eagerly, and Tedric knew immediately what he was asking about.

"Not much more than you do, I think." Tedric shook his head, and Lorian's face fell.

It was frustrating not to know more, and for the past day, he'd felt like something was missing from his mind. It was a silly thought though, as he'd done nothing other than spend those hours with Aeden or alone with his misery.

"She's hard to talk to." Tedric huffed. "And she's been acting strange ever since the Red King started giving us a potion against the curse. It's hard to know if her behavior is true or if it's the Red King's doing."

"Tedric!"

A familiar female voice rang out through the hall, making both Tedric and Lorian freeze. Tedric whirled around to find Aeden gliding toward them like an angry golden beacon, her face contorted into something twisted and hurt.

Something hard crashed into Tedric's back, and he lurched toward the polished floor with a grunt of surprise. He twisted expertly before he hit the ground so that he could see his assailant, only to find Lorian raising his fist. Rounded knuckles collided with Tedric's jaw before he could blink, and his vision exploded into bright light at the sudden pain blooming along his face. Tedric didn't know what to do and could barely think before Lorian's hand raised again.

Without thinking, Tedric raised his forearm to block Lorian's assault before using his other arm to hook and flip the thief over so that Tedric was on top. Lorian's face was twisted into anger, but Tedric could see the glimmer of something else hidden behind his expression.

"What are you doing?" Aeden's high-pitched trill rang out through the hall, and her footsteps neared.

Lorian wriggled as if in an attempt to slip out of Tedric's grip, but instead, his lips came up to Tedric's ear. "You can thank me later for this."

Lorian's free leg collided with Tedric's groin, sending the air whooshing from his lungs and his body crumpling in on itself from the pain. Lorian slipped from underneath him and was gone in two seconds, disappearing back into the crowd.

"What is going on here?" The Red King's low voice echoed through the walls, and Tedric forced air to return into his lungs in painful wheezing gasps.

Tedric looked up to find the Red King standing by a pale and clearly livid Aeden, though she remained silent. The king's suphiera—a plain black mask made of what looked like stone—was held between his long fingers.

"There was an assailant," Tedric wheezed.

"Ah," the Red King said. "It was one of your funny little friends."

Tedric turned onto his hands and knees and coughed, blood from where he had bitten his lip now coating his tongue and spattering onto the floor.

"Don't worry. I'll have the Ten take care of them," the Red King said with a smile. "I must thank you for saving Aeden, however."

"I—" Tedric began, but the Red King cut him off.

"Consider your faults forgotten. You will continue to guard the storyteller until he has fulfilled his duties, then you may return to your position as commander of the Ten."

The world tilted under Tedric's feet, and he glanced at Aeden, who was staring at him with a look he could not quite gauge. Was it anger? Pride? Loathing? Regret?

Tedric quickly bowed, unsure of what else he could do. His jaw still pulsed with the memory of Lorian's punch, and he was slowly beginning to understand just why it was that Lorian had attacked him.

The Red King gave Tedric a thin smile and looked between the two.

"Drazak, please lead the queen back to her chambers. I believe she is much too shaken to continue with the festivities. I will take care of the rest of the evening."

Aeden barely managed a nod toward the Red King before the ancient ruler departed in a flurry of red robes. Tedric reached for Aeden's arm, but she dodged his touch. They walked to her rooms in silence, and Tedric's mind was blank and yet oddly spinning with the pain in his jaw and distress that radiated from the queen at his side. They reached her room, and the door closed behind them with a bang as Aeden whirled on him.

"What in the Nether was that?" she hissed.

"It was Lorian," Tedric replied. "I didn't realize you hated him now too."

Aeden's face twisted, and she took a step toward him. "You know I don't, and you know that's not what I'm talking about."

Tedric clenched his jaw and fists, trying to calm his racing heart by sheer force. "You heard what I said. And I won't take it back either."

Aeden crossed her arms and snapped, "You think that the Red King has poisoned my mind, do you now?"

"I don't know!" Tedric realized he was yelling, and tears made his vision blurry. "I don't know anything about you anymore, Aeden. You were everything I wanted, but now I just don't know."

"What do you not know?" Aeden asked, her voice hushed.

"I don't know if I like what you're doing, and I can't keep playing along with this messed up idea the Red King has for me."

Aeden remained silent, her face a blank mask. Tedric growled and continued. "You're a completely different person than the one I met in Millris Forest all that time ago. That Aeden was kind and caring, and she hated her father because he was cruel. But now it seems you're no different than he was."

"You take that back," Aeden snapped, and Tedric shook his head.

"We both know that our whole relationship has been a lie. I've been lying to you since I slept with you after Clamidas, and you've been lying to me since the day we met."

"Do you not want me anymore?" Aeden asked with a rising voice. "Or are you just jealous of the power I now hold?"

A harsh bark of laughter escaped from Tedric's throat, and he ran a rough hand through his hair, clutching at the ends for a moment before dropping his hands. "By the goddesses, you're insane, Aeden!"

She moved too quickly for him to respond, and her nail slashed across Tedric's arm, angry pain blooming across his skin for the third time within the same night. A curse tore from his mouth, and he stumbled back from Aeden with wide eyes. Her hand was dripping with blood—his blood. Tears streaked down her pale face, and fury lined her gaze.

"I can never forgive you for that," she spat.

A cold haze of numbness swept over Tedric, and he took another step back. Something cracked inside him, and it was suddenly hard to breathe. A line had been crossed, and they both knew it.

"I can never forgive you either," Tedric replied, and he could have sworn that her face fell slightly.

She quickly regained her composure, a cool calmness radiating from her instead of the burning rage. A soft splat broke the silence, and Tedric looked down with a sickening lurch to find a drop of his blood had spilled from her coated finger. He wasn't even sure how she had managed to cut him so deep.

"This is the end, then, isn't it?" Aeden asked, her voice strong and calm.

Tedric knew what she meant. It was the end of them—or whatever broken shards of their love had been left after Clamidas. Tedric swallowed down the pain in his chest that surprised him nearly as much as her slicing his arm open.

"I think it is," he said gruffly.

Aeden gulped and blinked twice. "Very well, then. You can see yourself out. I am no longer in need of your services."

In need of your services.

Tedric thought he might be sick, but he nodded and moved to the door. He didn't know if he wanted to scream, cry, laugh, or perhaps do all of those things at the same time. He lifted his hand to the handle but paused, his heart twisting angrily. Tedric took in a shuddering breath and turned, his eyes burning and heart cracking at the image of her. A golden beacon with his blood staining her skin.

"I did love you, truly."

The words fell from his mouth in a whisper, and the same familiar tug in his heart that he'd felt the day they met pulled terribly against his chest. Aeden heaved a heavy sigh, as if she'd felt it too.

"I will always love you."

Her words were a mirrored whisper that almost undid him completely, but Tedric forced himself to turn away, and the woman who'd once held his heart disappeared behind the closing door.

38

AEDEN

The spell wove through the bottle, and his blood dripped into it from the tip of her finger.

Tears swelled in her eyes, but she wouldn't let them fall. She had done this, but she couldn't let him crumble. The Red King's game was far too dangerous, and she was the one who'd put the realm in this mess.

The path had been blurred for some time, but she now knew the way. A loophole was needed, a way out that only she could know of. Cold acceptance filled her bones at the knowledge of what she'd just lost, but she knew the only way to end it all was to allow the power to consume her—and for the world to burn.

For only if it burned could a new dawn rise from the ashes.

39
FINRIEL

"**R**un!"

Lorian's yell rang through the forest. Finriel pushed herself harder, her breath coming out in silvery plumes as she sprinted through the trees. Lorian was on her heels, followed closely by Odonir. Odonir came up past Lorian and eventually Finriel as well, and she followed him through the winding trees and shimmering meridiem.

The Ten trampled behind them, though their footsteps were light and sure as they made their pursuit after the companions. Finriel's lungs burned in the chill winter air, and her train was cumbersome as she tried to sprint through the long folds.

Soon, the sound of galloping hooves came after them, and Finriel's heart leapt into her throat as Krete came running alongside them atop a furry pony that snorted loudly every time the meridiem changed colors.

"Follow me!" Krete urged the pony faster so that it was running alongside Odonir and then veered to the left.

None of them hesitated, and Finriel quickly turned left to follow the swishing tail of Krete's steed. Moments dragged on for what felt like hours, and still, the Ten persisted. Finriel didn't know where Krete was taking them, but she didn't have half a mind to care at the moment.

Lorian had been caught, though it was hardly a surprise. It wasn't like he'd done the most careful job of keeping hidden after finding Tedric. Frustration rose in Finriel's stomach, and she let out a grunt. She hadn't been able to question anyone, let alone mingle with other nobles and glean any new information. The evening had gone too quickly, and now their lives were at risk for nothing.

"Stop here!"

Krete's voice hissed through the branches, and Finriel listened for the Ten's pursuit, only to find that they had trailed off quite a ways behind. Krete swung off the snorting pony, drew a glowing portal stone from his coat pocket, and got to work.

"Do you think they'll catch us before it's ready?" Finriel panted, looking over her shoulder once more.

"I doubt it," Lorian replied through gulps of air. "Remember how quickly he made the portal when we ran from the minotaur?"

"How did you encounter a minotaur?" Odonir asked, his breath even and not at all as if he had just sprinted for the goddesses knew how long.

Lorian waved a dismissive hand toward his brother. "It was just a traveler headed into Mitonir."

Odonir gasped. "What?"

"It's ready," Krete announced, and Finriel turned to find the swirling portal waiting at Krete's feet.

"What do you mean—"

"No time! Go!" Lorian's yell sliced through his brother's words, and the thief shoved him toward the swirling depths.

Finriel stepped toward the edge of the portal after Odonir fell through it with a curse, and right at that moment, a harsh yell rang through the night. She didn't think twice before she shut her eyes and took a step, falling through the swirling darkness.

Her stomach lurched into her throat, and Finriel kept her eyes shut tightly as she fell through space and time, the portal carrying her to what she hoped would be Odonir's cabin in Farrador. The ground met her much too quickly, and she let out a gasping curse as her backside collided with hard soil blanketed in snow.

Finriel cracked her eyes open to find that she had landed not two meters away from the barn, where Oats was sticking his head out of one of the openings and staring at her curiously.

"That was a terrible experience." Odonir's shaky voice echoed through the clearing, and Finriel narrowed her eyes to find him sitting against a nearby tree.

Finriel grunted in reply and watched the portal swirl and spit, though neither Lorian nor Krete came through. Something wasn't right. Finriel ignored the pain in her bones as she stood and went to stand underneath the portal.

"What is it?" Odonir asked, and Finriel felt the brush of his coat as he came to stand by her side.

"They should have come through by now," Finriel muttered and bit the inside of her cheek.

"Wouldn't the portal disappear if something had gone wrong?" Odonir asked, and Finriel shook her head.

"It'll only stop if Krete brings the stone through to the other side or if the stone runs out of energy."

Odonir clenched his jaw and shrugged. "I suppose we just have to wait for him to come through, then."

Finriel shook her head. "We need to go back."

"And how exactly do you suppose we leap twelve feet into the air to go back through that thing?" Odonir scoffed. "Besides, it would take too long to go back by horse. They'll likely return soon."

Finriel huffed. "I guess you're right."

"Come on. I'll make us some tea, and we can wait inside." Odonir offered a hand to her.

Finriel looked between the portal and his outstretched hand, feeling much more inclined to stay outside and watch the portal until Lorian and Krete came back.

Odonir rolled his eyes. "Come inside. You're no help to any of us if you catch a cold."

Finriel grimaced, but she took Odonir's hand, allowing the elf to lead her into the house. The kitchen was dark yet still quite warm as they stepped inside, and Odonir let go of her hand, moving toward the fire and smoldering coals. Finriel almost leapt forward to stop him.

"Please, let me do it," Finriel said, attempting not to sound too desperate. "You can make the tea and light some candles."

Odonir lifted a quizzical brow but thankfully didn't say anything as he turned back into the kitchen and began to light candles. Finriel let out a shaky breath and moved toward the unlit fireplace, her body humming with anxiety and thoughts of Lorian and Krete's failure to come through the portal.

"Don't you think someone might see the portal just swirling in the air?" Finriel asked, kneeling before the dark dry wood that had been placed in the hearth.

"I doubt it," Odonir replied, and a small flicker of light bloomed from the match in his fingers. "No one ventures this far into the forest, and besides, I'm sure anyone who matters is still in Proveria."

Finriel didn't answer as she rearranged the logs. She quickly looked over her shoulder, and when she found that Odonir's back was turned to her, she faced the logs once more and placed her hands over them, closing her eyes. The fire surged immediately, and Finriel suppressed a gasp as flames erupted from her fingers and lit the logs, relief tingling through her body. She knew her body needed to release more, but right now, a meager fire was as good as she could do.

Finriel reluctantly removed her hands from the inviting warmth and stood, turning to find Odonir working on tea now that the house was sufficiently lit.

"Still nothing?" Finriel asked as she entered the kitchen and moved to the table.

She glanced out the window, finding that the portal was still swirling in place, though no gnomes or rogue thieves were falling out of it. She sighed and looked away, worry anchoring itself in her stomach.

"Here." Odonir held out a steaming mug toward her, and Finriel reached up to take the tea from him with a halfhearted smile.

Peppermint and rose swirled around her tastebuds, and the heat scorched down Finriel's throat as she swallowed, but the pain was almost welcome, if only to tether her to reality instead of the panic that had dropped like lead into her bones.

"You seem to be quite calm about the fact that your brother could have been captured," Finriel said, her words coming out less biting than she had wanted.

Odonir's mouth quirked up. "I am a bit worried, just not worried enough to cry about it."

Finriel huffed and lifted the tea to her lips again. She knew Odonir was right, but it didn't make her any less worried. Perhaps her worry worried her as well, for only a few moons ago, she wanted him to get out of her sights forever.

"You still don't trust him," Odonir said.

Finriel nearly spit out her tea. She spluttered and set the mug down before she could drop it and narrowed her gaze at the elf. "I think you're confusing your own anger with mine, Odonir."

"I'm quite clear on where my relationship with Lorian stands," Odonir replied. "I don't trust him, and that's because I know him. He tries too hard to fix everything under his arrogant cover. He feels too much, Finriel. And that's going to kill him one day."

Finriel inhaled sharply, knowing that given their current circumstances, she couldn't really defend Lorian's pride. He had pushed Odonir through the portal with the stupid thought that he could take care of himself and escape from the Ten on his own. It wasn't that she didn't trust his morals or desires; she didn't trust his inability to ask for help instead of relying only on himself. Finriel snorted. It sounded exactly like her own trust issues.

"Something funny?" Odonir lifted his brows.

"No." Finriel shook her head. "I just think I understand him a bit more than you do."

"Oh? And why is that?"

Finriel shrugged. "I've had to live my entire life alone, fixing my own problems and watching my own back. My mother disappeared when I was a baby, and I don't even know who my father is—or was. There's never been anyone to help me with things, and so I've learned to function completely alone. It was a shock when I was suddenly thrown into a life-or-death mission with four others, and I have to admit, it was hard to get comfortable with the idea that I had to help them too, not just myself."

Odonir remained silent for a few moments after Finriel stopped talking, his eyes set upon the table.

"I've learned to be the same way, for the most part. I still know of duty and working together with the other scouts, but otherwise, I am alone," he said finally. "And perhaps I simply haven't fully forgiven him for everything he did."

"Leaving your mother?" Finriel asked.

Odonir nodded sharply. "We shared the duties of her care, but then one day, he simply disappeared, and I was left with an angry, sick, and sad woman who was dying before my eyes. Nursing her to the grave was no easy thing, and to have believed that he'd abandoned us wasn't something that made the process easier."

Finriel gulped and blinked away tears that threatened to spill over. She understood his pain so deeply and the hurt that kind of betrayal bred.

"I understand that too," Finriel whispered. "I was almost murdered when I was ten, the same day he left your mother.

Lorian watched most of the occurrence before running away, and I didn't see him again for ten years. I thought he had abandoned me to save his own skin, and so I grew to hate him. When I learned that he had been captured trying to find help, then forced into a life of lies and running, it changed everything."

Odonir blinked quickly and took a swig of tea. "I didn't know that. I'm sorry."

"It's not really something I like to talk about freely," Finriel replied but offered him a small smile that faded quickly.

"It seems as though he did more damage on accident than on purpose that day." Odonir chuckled, and Finriel smiled again.

"It seems so."

"He cares about you more than I think you know," Odonir said.

Finriel blinked, a strange current of electricity beginning to creep into her chest at his words.

Odonir smiled. "I know you don't see it, but I think he would do more for you than he'd ever do for me, and I'm not just saying that because he's my little brother. I see the way he looks at you, Finriel. It's real, even if sometimes those memories and pain return for you."

Finriel opened her mouth and promptly closed it after realizing that no words would come out. She knew Odonir was observant above all else, and she could sense the truth in his gaze and tone.

"I—"

"Get out of the way!"

Finriel was on her feet and sprinting out the door as soon as the familiar yell rang through the darkness. Cold air assaulted her bare hands, but she paid the sting no mind as she hurtled toward the two shapes standing shakily to their feet.

"Blast the goddesses, that hurt." Lorian groaned, and Finriel nearly cried out in relief.

"You toadstool, of course it hurts when you land on your back!" Krete's sharp reply rang out.

"Not all of us can land on our—" Lorian cut off with a grunt as Finriel collided with his hard body, nearly sending both of them sprawling to the ground once more.

"Don't *ever* scare me like that again," Finriel hissed, wrapping her arms tightly around his torso and breathing in his pine-and-lavender scent.

His arms wrapped around her, and she closed her eyes at the familiar rumble of his chest against hers as he let out a low chuckle. "I didn't realize you'd miss me that much after such a short time."

Finriel pulled away just enough to glare at him. "I was worried about you, idiot. It's not exactly a calming experience to have you be nearly an hour late from escaping armed warriors."

"Lorian had the brilliant idea of diverting them." Krete huffed. "The stupid plan nearly killed Amaranthe in the process."

Finriel looked down at Krete with a raised brow.

He shook his head. "My pony."

"I'm guessing he's alive though?" Finriel asked.

"Yes, yes. He's likely causing havoc in the Anemoi barns," Lorian replied for Krete, whose scowl was visible even in the near darkness. "What? As you said, he was *nearly* killed, not actually killed."

"You're a reckless fool." Krete stomped off to the cabin, where Odonir was now standing in the open doorway, his mug of tea still held in his hands.

They followed Krete inside and gathered around the table, the chill snowy air still clinging to Finriel's clothes as she settled into her seat.

"What happened?" Odonir asked before Finriel had the chance to open her mouth.

Lorian propped his elbows on the table and said, "We kept running from the Ten. I had Krete get off his pony and strap his suphiera and cloak to him. That way, the Ten would think there was someone still riding him."

"It was a stupid plan," Krete snapped. "Only four of them went after Amaranthe, and the others kept following us."

"We made a large circle and tried to get back to the portal," Lorian continued on, cutting off Krete before his beet-red face exploded.

"That's when the noises started." Krete shivered. "Terrible sounds."

"What kind of sounds?" Finriel asked.

Lorian and Krete exchanged a look before Krete answered.

"We don't know. There were two of them though, and I only saw a flash of something red before we went through the portal."

"But what happened with the Ten?" Odonir asked, now hunched over the table in the same manner as Lorian.

"They disappeared as soon as we started hearing the noises," Lorian replied with a shrug.

"We think they could've been more of Egharis's beasts, but I heard shouting and curses from the Ten before we went through, which makes me think they could have also been something else entirely."

"They had to be Egharis's new beasts. There's no way a creature that sounds like *that* could exist with the peace law," Lorian replied. "But we're safe now anyway. They won't find us either way."

"I hope you're right, for all our sakes." Krete shivered. "It was terrifying."

Finriel glanced between Krete's and Lorian's pale faces and knew that whatever it was, what they'd heard was no laughing matter. Lorian looked up to meet her gaze and smiled softly, and the memory of his lips on hers and his touch on her waist flashed through her body.

Damn her feelings.

"We should get some rest. It's been a long night," Odonir said. "We can discuss everything else in the morning."

Finriel stood with the others and looked down at Krete. "Nora likely hasn't moved from the study. She'll keep you company again tonight."

40

LORIAN

Discomfort coursed through his tired bones as he ran and ran, but he slowed down with each step. The world was dark and scattered, as though he were looking through a shattered mirror. Ragged breathing pulsed behind him, spurring him on, but he was still too slow. He let out a grunt of frustration and looked down at his feet, only to find what was slowing his pace.

It was blood.

Thick currents of it swelled around his legs, bathing the ground in a crimson sea. The taste of coppery metal coated his tongue and filled his nose, threatening to swallow him whole.

Lorian jolted upright, his body shaking and slick with sweat. The bedroom was dark, though a stream of moonlight flowed through the window beside their bed. Lorian closed his eyes and covered his face with his hands before sliding them up to clench his hair in his fists. His scalp stung, but the pain was grounding and helped the image of blood fade.

Finriel was still asleep, her back turned to him. Lorian sighed and shook his head, as if the movement could rattle the dream from his mind. Cold began to seep into his bones, and Lorian looked down at the tunic now plastered against his skin with drying sweat. Lorian swung his legs to the floor, icy pinpricks shooting up the soles of his feet. He plodded to the small dresser, peeling off his tunic and wrinkling his nose at the thick scent of his sweat as it passed over his head.

Better sweat than blood.

Lorian shuddered and flung the tunic to the floor, then yanked a fresh tunic from the dresser and shrugged it on. He turned to face the bed and Finriel. His heart gave a near-painful squeeze, and he watched as her closed eyes twitched and fluttered with a dream. *Hopefully it's a good dream*, Lorian thought.

The stone floor was frigid as Lorian padded to the door and closed it gently behind himself before heading for the kitchen. There was no chance of sleep returning to him now, and he didn't want to disturb Finriel with his tossing and turning. Lorian blinked in surprise to find that a candle still burned on the table, and Odonir was seated in his usual spot with his legs propped upon a corner of the old table.

"Still awake?" Lorian asked as he entered the room, but Odonir did no more than incline his head at Lorian's sudden arrival.

Odonir's dark gaze landed on Lorian as he sat at the opposite end of the table. "I don't think I'll be able to sleep for a long while after tonight."

Lorian wanted to reply, but the dream reared back into his mind, and he closed his mouth. Odonir raised a brow and considered his brother.

"No bullying?"

Lorian gave a weak smile. "I don't have the energy after tonight."

They sat in companionable silence for some time, and Lorian mulled over the night with sluggish exhaustion. It had been wonderful to see Tedric again, if even only for a few minutes. Regret for causing his friend such pain made Lorian wince, but he knew it had been for the best. Tedric's standing was in less danger if it seemed as though he'd been trying to detain Lorian, not help him.

"What did Queen Arbane say about the evening?" Lorian asked, remembering the dark-skinned woman dressed in green and gold finery who'd passed him during the evening. Her cold presence had been enough to make him avoid her at all costs. That, and he had a sneaking suspicion she would have remembered him.

"I wasn't able to ask," Odonir replied. "We're not exactly friends."

"Oh? I thought you were thick as thieves," Lorian replied with a smirk, though the joke made him all the more tired.

Odonir rolled his eyes and sighed, an almost visible heaviness settling over his shoulders. "I didn't believe you, not at first," he said, and Lorian blinked in surprise. "Something felt . . . wrong last night. Like it was all so carefully executed that it wasn't real."

Lorian nodded, knowing just how right his brother was. Aeden's announcement of using the Red King's soldiers to guard the Proverian borders made his blood curdle. She'd been dressed in such finery and surrounded by nobles too stupid to fully realize the meaning behind her actions.

It was all a lie.

"Finriel told me about her meeting with Aeden's council member," Lorian said, and Odonir chuckled.

"She didn't say a word. She elbowed me in the ribs and made me do the talking."

Lorian grinned, shaking his head. "She is a confusing one."

"Just hot-headed with a distaste for crowds," Odonir said. "The council member was so drunk it was hard to get much conversation out of him."

"I blew my cover too soon," Lorian grumbled, annoyance making his cheeks hot. "We would've learned more about what's going on if I hadn't been so excited about seeing Tedric."

"But asking Tedric was our only plan," Odonir reminded him. "It was clear none of us could have walked over to the Red King and asked. I'm nothing more than a scout. He and Aeden would've turned me down if I'd tried speaking to them, and the rest of you are wanted criminals."

Lorian nodded, though it was still difficult for him to accept that as the truth. He wiped a hand down his face and sighed, feeling slightly better. As thoughts of tea and food entered his mind, a strangled scream echoed in the distance. Sweat sprang to Lorian's palms, and he listened again as a strange scratching sound dragged through the night, followed by a terrible ragged breath that sang in tandem with the distant cry.

Odonir straightened, his body rigid as he listened for the strange sound. Odonir's hearing capabilities were far superior to his own, but when the ragged breathing sounded once more, they were both on their feet in an instant.

"What was that?" Odonir whispered, his face drained of color.

Lorian shook his head, and a quick movement by the kitchen window caught his eye. Finriel, Nora, and Krete emerged seconds later, Finriel's expression of confusion a far cry from Krete's mask of alarm.

"What—"

The ragged breathing sounded again, but this time, it was joined by a guttural snarl that sent up the hairs on Lorian's arms. He knew that sound, and he nearly felt sick because of it. It was the same sound that echoed faintly in his mind, the ghost of his pursuer in his dream. His gaze locked onto Krete's, and his stomach dropped at the gnome's look of pure dread. They had heard those sounds moments before jumping through the portal, and only Krete had been able to catch a glimpse of what that sound belonged to before the portal had closed around them.

"It found us." Krete gulped.

"We need to go," Odonir whispered. "Now."

The companions dispersed in a quick and silent march, Lorian quick on Finriel's heels as they entered their room. Nora remained in the kitchen, and her low growls emanated through the stone walls, sending a shiver down Lorian's spine. They moved quickly and silently, throwing on better clothes and their cloaks.

"Did you get a glimpse of whatever this thing is?" Finriel whispered, and Lorian cringed, wishing she hadn't spoken.

He shook his head. "Only Krete."

Lorian felt through his pockets to ensure that his page was still there, and he glanced at Finriel, who quickly withdrew the map and her page, giving them a once over before shoving them back into the pockets of her cloak. They strapped their daggers to their belts and turned to face each other. Finriel's eyes were wide with fear, but her lips were set in a determined line. Lorian took a stride toward her and gave her a swift kiss. He knew that they needed to leave now, but he didn't care. She leaned into his touch and returned the kiss, but then the faint sound of Odonir and Krete descending the stairs broke them apart.

"We'll be okay," Lorian assured her, though his racing heart and thick nerves were yelling at his lie.

A slow scraping sound against the wall outside made them both freeze, and thick breathing accompanied the scraping in horrific harmony.

Finriel gave him a halfhearted nod before they hurried down to the kitchen, where Krete and Odonir stood and Nora paced before the front door with her hackles raised and razor-sharp teeth bared.

"How in the Nether are we going to get out of here without running right into it?" Finriel asked in a whisper.

Odonir stepped forward and extinguished the candle with his forefinger and thumb just as another snarl and gasp of breath floated on the otherwise silent air, followed by something hard slamming against the front door. Nora growled again. Lorian's muscles were tense in both terror and anticipation. Alone, he might've been able to slip out of the house unnoticed, but even so, he wasn't sure. Whatever was out there sounded different than anything he had ever encountered.

"Come with me," Odonir mouthed and gestured for them to follow him with a wave of his hand.

Finriel hissed at Nora, who turned and followed her with hackles still raised and her bristled tail swishing. Lorian took the rear of the line, looking over his shoulder just in time to see the flash of something red and sinewy pass by the kitchen window. Bile rose in his throat as he quickly turned and followed Nora and his companions into Odonir's study. The front door rattled again, this time followed by the sound of splitting wood. Lorian jumped, and Finriel's sharp intake of breath in front of him spurred him on.

The companions stood and watched as Odonir swept toward the large bookshelf, his hand skimming over the old spines in concentration. Lorian closed his eyes with a jump as the door banged again, but this time, the familiar creak of it opening made him feel sick. Krete turned and quickly closed the study door as the scrape of claws and heavy wet breathing moved for them. Finriel's cold hand found his, and Lorian squeezed her fingers as Odonir worked on finding their way out. Lorian wanted nothing more than to encourage his brother to work quicker, but they could not speak, not now. The sound of shattering glass made Finriel jump and tighten her hand painfully against Lorian's, and Odonir let out a shaky breath of terror as strange thumps, grunts, and loud sniffing passed beyond the closed door.

Odonir pulled a red leather-bound book downward as if to tip it out of the shelf, but instead of falling, the book merely tilted, and a faint click sounded within the wall. The bookshelf swung inward to reveal a small room. Odonir ushered them forward, and Lorian led Finriel into the room just as a heavy smack shuddered the study door and a large crack splintered the thick wood.

Krete ran forward, followed by Nora. They passed by Odonir, who then swung the door shut once more, bathing them in darkness. Their collective breaths echoed through the cold darkness in a maddening song as they waited. Lorian didn't know what was after them but could only guess that the Red King's sick mind was to blame. A loud splintering sound made Finriel and Krete jump beside him, and Lorian knew that whatever was after them had just broken the study door down.

Odonir's tall frame brushed past Lorian, and he turned his head to follow his brother's movement, but it was no use in the darkness. The ragged breaths approached and passed by the wall before them, followed by a separate growl from farther back in the study. Lorian stifled a gasp. There were two of them, whatever they were. He wasn't sure that a fake bookcase would be much use against them. Shallow breath filled Lorian's ears, and his heart beat so fast he was afraid it might burst through his chest. Silence filled the room beyond, and fear made the air electric.

A loud bang crashed against the bookcase, sending vibrations through the air. A muffled gasp sounded behind him, but it was soon swallowed by another growl and booming collision against the bookcase. The sound of cracking wood filled the darkness, and a body brushed past Lorian's side. A rustle and then a click, followed by cold air biting into Lorian's side. Another bang rattled the wall, followed by more splintering wood.

"Follow me," Odonir hissed.

Lorian swiveled to find his brother slipping out a small door and into the forest outside. He ushered Finriel and Krete after him, and bits of wood flew against his face as a large hole opened up through the bookshelf wall. Lorian caught only the glimpse of a hollowed-out eye socket and gleaming fangs before he turned and ran out the door and into the winter air.

The moon illuminated the way as Lorian and the others sprinted through the thinning trees. A large stretch of plains was just in sight, followed by the shimmering border wall of Crubia. Lorian's heart gave a feeble jump, but he kept running. Krete was surprisingly fast but still lagging behind. They broke out into the plains, and the sting of tall grasses and light snow whipped against his legs.

A distant cry split through the night, and Lorian cursed under his breath as he turned to look over his shoulder at their pursuers. He nearly staggered and fell on his face at the nightmares following and quickly gaining on them.

One was tan with a sickly green hue to its Plasticine-textured skin, the gaping singular hole where its eye should have been sending Lorian's stomach to the ground. Its sleek long body ran on four legs, the large birdlike feet ending in talons. The second was equally terrifying, if not even more dreadful than the first. Rough red leathery skin was pulled taught over muscled flesh, the beast's body close to that of a wolf, though it was more than twice the size of one. It, too, had four legs that ended in claws, though a long spiked tail thrashed where the tan monster did not have one. The red monster didn't have eyes either, its gruesome face was full of holes, and parts of its gums and razor-sharp fangs protruded from fraying skin. They were both smaller than he had expected, though still large enough to kill any of them, including Nora.

"What do we do?" Krete panted from a few steps behind.

Lorian stopped and turned toward his friend. Krete let out a yelp of surprise as Lorian scooped him up and flung him over his shoulder before taking off at a run once more.

"What in the Nether are you doing?" Krete demanded.

"Saving your ass before they bite it off," Lorian said and pushed his legs faster.

"There's a field of swallowing sand near the Crubian border. I can lead them there," Odonir called through the still air, and Lorian's stomach flopped at the mention of the cursed kingdom.

"I can help you lure them with my magic," Finriel said

between gasps, but Krete swore from his place on Lorian's shoulder.

"That's far too dangerous! You could get lost in the sand with them."

Odonir ignored them all and veered toward an area that lay dangerously close to the Crubian border, and Lorian gritted his teeth. Nora bounded ahead like a gray arrow, hot on Odonir's heels. Finriel threw Lorian a look that was both question and forewarning, but he shook his head.

"Don't even think about it," he growled, but she only met his demand with a worried glint in her eyes.

They were catching up on them, badly. Lorian glanced behind his shoulder to find an open maw only feet from his back, and he forced his gaze forward again and his feet to move faster.

"I'm sorry. I have to," Finriel yelled, and before Lorian could think, a blinding light flashed behind him and a guttural cry pierced through the air.

The scent of burning flesh infiltrated Lorian's nose, and he fought away a gag, only to look over his shoulder again and find a large bubbling wound on the tan creature's shoulder as it veered after Finriel with an unnerving screech. Its hard side collided with Lorian's back, and both he and Krete were sent flying through the air before landing on their stomachs with pained groans.

"Damn the Nether," Lorian spat as he watched Finriel sprint after Odonir, the red beast hot on his heels. The horrific tan creature was now on Finriel's heels, but Lorian could only watch as she sent another ball of fire sailing toward the monster. It let out a yelp of pain as the flame hit it in the face, and sounds only heard in Lorian's nightmares rang through his ears.

He couldn't just lie there and watch this. He had to help. Lorian's muscles tensed, but Krete's small hand clasped around his wrist just as he was about to stand. Lorian looked at his friend, whose pale face was illuminated by the setting moon. A snap of defense was already prepared on Lorian's lips as Krete spoke.

"I suppose we're dying together, then."

Lorian's retort died on his lips, and he merely gave him a sad smile before nodding. They both scrambled to their feet, and Lorian didn't wait for Krete as he pushed himself as fast as he could toward the sea of swallowing sand and his friends.

Odonir let out a yell of fear as he slipped into the swallowing sand, and the shout died on Lorian's lips as he pushed his legs faster. Nora lunged forward and grabbed Odonir by the collar of his jacket, pulling him up. Flame encircled and arced around Finriel as she fought off the tan beast, her face set in a determined stare. A ball of flame glanced against the creature's side as it reared at her, and it fell into the swallowing sand with a pained yelp.

Relief soothed the fear inside Lorian's stomach, and he found Odonir now standing at the edge of the sand. Finriel sprinted to Odonir's side and looked him over for injury just as the red-skinned wolf sprang toward them. Finriel raised her hands, and flames engulfed them once more, but the beast was too fast. Krete let out a yell of warning, and Lorian saw it before either of them did.

The world set into slow motion as the red monster landed a blow against Odonir's chest, red blood spurting from the wound. He stumbled backward, and Finriel lurched after him with a gasp. She flung out her hand, creating a blast of wind so strong it hit Lorian and the red monster, sending it flying into the swallowing sand and Lorian to the ground. A rattling gasp tore through his body, and Lorian struggled to his feet once more. But it was too late. Lorian stumbled after them, but they were already falling, falling, falling.

The shimmering air shivered as Finriel, Nora, and Odonir fell backward and passed through the kingdom border, landing on the gray sands of Crubia.

EPILOGUE

Tedric shivered against the late winter breeze, though his stomach was warm from the poison he'd drank that morning.

One moon had passed since the night everything changed. Since he'd gotten his old life back. It felt strange to be whole again and yet utterly incomplete. Tedric had lost so much and won back everything that he'd missed so greatly. But the cost was great, and the badge of *Commander* stamped before his name felt more like a curse than a blessing.

He was serving a monster, after all.

The stables came into view, and moments later, Tedric swung from the saddle and gave Dario a pat on the neck. Morning watch had been rather uneventful, though a new tension held thick in the air. Bordin and Griffin knew more than Tedric, and he still didn't know the extent of that knowledge. Aeden's madness made sense after Bordin's explanation, but it didn't make the subtle ache in his chest any better. He ran a hand over the scar on his arm, the memory of his blood dripping from Aeden's fingers making him wince.

"Commander Drazak!"

Tedric jumped and turned to find a guard striding toward him, a man with chin-length hair trailing behind him. Dawn light made it difficult to make out the newcomer's features, but the long limbs and confident stride struck Tedric as familiar somehow.

"What is this?" Tedric asked, and the guard gave him a quick bow before speaking.

"A new recruit, Commander. This man says he wishes to serve as a member of the Ten."

Tedric frowned. "We already have ten members. There's no need for another."

The guard gave Tedric an apologetic grimace. "I know, but he was quite insistent and refused to speak to anyone but you."

Alarm made Tedric stiffen, and he looked past the guard to observe the newcomer, whose eyes were still locked on the ground.

"What's your name?" Tedric asked, his voice slicing through the mist and reverberating against the stone stable walls.

The man looked up, and Tedric had to grab onto Dario's mane to keep from stumbling. Ice-blue eyes stared at him, and angular cheekbones and a sharp jaw set in a determined line. Tedric had to fight his smile, though it quickly died at both the serious look on Lorian's face and the fact that his friend was alone.

"The name's Loxley."

Tedric turned to look at the guard, who didn't seem to remember the fact that he had escorted Lorian from the dungeons not even a year ago.

There was a reason Lorian had come, and it couldn't be good. Tedric knew his friend was foolish, but returning to Keadora was a death trap. He needed to figure out what was going on and where Finriel and Krete had gone off to.

"It's all right," Tedric said finally. "I'll take him in."

ACKNOWLEDGMENTS

It's crazy to believe that there are already two books in *The Raymara Chronicles* out in the world. To say that I'm grateful is an understatement.

This book was written in nearly a quarter of the time it took to write book one. It was as though the companions were yelling at me to tell their story instead of me shining a light in the dark, trying to find all the missing pieces. For that, I would like to thank my characters and the realm of Raymara for being my light during even the darkest of times. Finriel, Lorian, Tedric, Krete, and Aeden (along with Nora and Suzunne, of course) have been with me for many years, and to be able to tell their story is an honor. I love this story with all my heart, and I'm so grateful for it.

To my parents, for supporting me through the last couple of years of uncertainty and the release of book one. Even though it's been difficult at times, you four have always believed in me and have continued to support me through this crazy journey. Thank you so much.

Jadon, thank you for appearing in my life when I needed you most, though I didn't even realize it. You're my real-life Lorian, and I'm so grateful that I finally have a real person from which to take inspiration for my lovable thief. You've made the writing process much easier. Thank you for always asking me questions about the story, world, and helping me brainstorm whenever I need it. Thank you for fangirling and talking about my characters with me like they're real people. I love you so much.

And to the readers who have read book one, thank you so much for experiencing this story. Thank you to the readers who have loved and disliked the story; it has helped me grow as a writer immensely, and it has helped this journey feel less lonely. Thank you to those who have shared book one and helped it reach new people. Thank you for simply reading this story. I'm so grateful that people can find a little bit of home in the world of Raymara.

Damonza, thank you so much for once again creating the amazing cover! I couldn't have asked for anything better. I'm so excited for readers to have this beautiful book on their shelves, even if it's only to show off your artwork.

To Enchanted Ink Publishing for being the best team of editors with whom I've ever worked. Your eye for detail and the constructive help I received is unmatched, and I finished reading through edits with excitement and gratitude for how well done and uplifting each comment and change was.

And to those recently discovering Raymara and my silly characters, thank you so much for giving this story a chance. Everyone is welcome in Raymara, forever and always.

PRONUNCIATION GUIDE

Characters and Goddesses

Lorian Grey: LOR-ee-in Grey

Finriel Caligari: FEN-ree-el Ca-lee-GAR-ee

Tedric Drazak: Ted-rick DRAH-zah-ck

Aeden Siltra: Ay-den Sill-trah

Krete: Creet

Egharis: Eg-GAR-iss

Odonir Grey: Oh-don-eer Grey

Agonur: Ah-GO-noor

Alima: Ah-lee-mah

Lizabet Timore: Liz-ah-bet Tee-more

Maescia Balfour: May-shah Ball-four

Sorren: Soh-ren

Naret: Nah-ret

King Drohan: Droh-han

Kittia: Kit-ee-ah

Adustio: Ah-DOO-stee-oh

Anima: Ah-NEE-mah

Tellas: Tell-ah-s

Noctiluca: Noc-tee-loo-cah

Places

Keadora: Key-AH-dora

Proveria: Pro-very-ah

Farrador: Fair-AH-door

Crubia: Crew-BEE-ah

Drolatis: Drow-LAH-tis

Creonid: Crey-OH-nid

Lake Lagdranule: Lag-drah-nool

Naebatis: Nay-bah-tees

Anemoi: Anne-emm-mwah

Mitonir: Mee-THO-neer

Clelac Crags: Clay-lack Crag

Nivalis: Nee-vah-lis

Xeles: Zell-iss

Tiltha: Till-tha

Fortula: Fort-ooh-la

Things/creatures

Mogwa: Mow-gwah

Chimera: Kai-mare-ah

Sythril: See-thrill

Nian: Nee-on

Youl: Yool

Rakshasa: Rack-SHAH-sah

Veloria: Vel-oh-ree-ah

Meridiem: Mer-id-ee-am

Viure: Vee—ooray

Suphiera: Soo-fier-ah

Also by Gabriela Lavarello

The Raymara Chronicles

Book 1: *Of Liars and Thieves*

Other Books

Gone by Morning, a horror short story anthology

ABOUT THE AUTHOR

Gabriela has been writing and telling stories since she was a young girl. Perhaps it was inevitable that she would call grappling with words and making YouTube videos a career—and love every moment.

When not writing or filming, you can find Gabriela reading, cuddling her dog Raven (better known as "Raisin", dubbed by her doggy grandparents), or riding and training horses.

Of Liars and Thieves, the first installment of *The Raymara Chronicles*, is Gabriela's debut fantasy novel, published in September 2021. She has also dabbled in short fiction and has a story published in *Gone by Morning*, a horror short story anthology.

Get in touch through Gabriela's social media to discover more about her work, writing process, and future endeavors.